VIGILANT ANGEL

Michael T. J. Dean

Vigilant Angel
Copyright © 2013 by Michael T. J. Dean.

First Print Edition

All rights reserved.

ISBN-13: 978-1484122112
ISBN-10: 1484122119

www.author-michael-dean.com

http://www.facebook.com/authormichaeldean

Typeset in Adobe Garamond Pro
by
InPrint Communications, Edmonton, AB, Canada

Vigilant Angel is dedicated to my wife, Betty, who first persuaded me to write a short story about a dream and then continually encouraged me while this yarn evolved.

In the telling of this tale I have mentioned several published authors and their works. In no way am I attempting to infringe on their copyright; nor does any such mention imply any endorsement of this novel by those authors. Rather, I mention them out of gratitude for all the enjoyment they have provided me over the years. Mac has a little bit of me in his character—I still have the hardcover edition of C. S. Forester's <u>Mr. Midshipman Hornblower</u> which I read at the age of nine or ten years and instilled a love of the sea in this prairie boy.

I would be remiss not to extend a heartfelt thank you to all the members, present and past, of the Edmonton Novel Critique Group, Writers Guild of Alberta, for allowing a novice writer to join them and for their invaluable contributions and impassioned critiques during our monthly meetings.

By the way, I would love the chance to fly in, even sit in, an Apache should someone offer. Although flying would likely allow me to add to the list of aircraft that have resulted in me... you get the picture, and which is why I write.

Table of Contents

FOREWORD

IN LATE 1804 England has essentially been at war with France since February 1793. The Peace of Amiens, signed on 25 March 1802, was short-lived. Hostilities resumed between England and France on 18 March 1803. On 3 May 1803 France sold Louisiana to the expansionist United States of America. Britain formally declared war against France on 17 May 1803. Anglo-Spanish relations also continued to deteriorate through 1804 while the French began preparations to invade England. On 5 October the English captured four Spanish ships carrying treasure from Montevideo. A Franco-Spanish alliance signed on 9 October resulted in Spain declaring war against England on 14 December.

I have taken the liberty of creating a nearly concurrent capture of ships by both the English and Spanish. It would not have been a tit-for-tat as neither London or Madrid would have been aware of the seizure of the English merchant ships for some time. It could take a month or more for word to reach London or Madrid from the Caribbean.

The English ships, officers and crew are purely a product of my imagination. H.M.S. *Lionheart*, a 36-gun frigate, would have been one of 43 similar ships in the Royal Navy at the time of this story and would have carried approximately 264 officers and men. The schooner H.M.S. *Seppings* is named, somewhat prematurely, in honour of Sir Robert Seppings, naval architect, who added diagonal framing to hulls in 1811 which vastly improved hull strength.

Given the tense relations between Spain and England in late 1804, and word of the Franco-Spanish alliance, it would not be surprising for *Lionheart* to have engaged the Spanish frigates after they opened fire. The real Spanish frigate *Matilda*, 34 guns, was captured in November 1804 and renamed H.M.S. *Hamadryad*. I took the liberty of changing the location and adding the capture of the *Castellon de la Plana*.

The United States leased the Corn Islands (Islas del Maiz) from Nicaragua for 99 years in 1914 to provide a naval base to protect a proposed trans-Nicaraguan canal. A number of Caribbean islands previously came under United States jurisdiction through the Guano Islands Act of August 18, 1856, (Title 48, U.S. Code, sections 1411-19). Although the Corn Islands lease was terminated in 1971 the United States Coast Guard maintains a base there for its anti-drug patrols.

For clarity a ship's name is *italicised* when referring specifically to her, i.e. *Lionheart.* As a Loyal Subject of the Crown, despite also being Canadian, I have used British spellings, i.e. *colour* instead of *color,* etc. as per The Shorter Oxford English Dictionary.

Lastly, some of the book's characters may, at times, refer to their various foes in rather derogatory terms—that's the way things were back then, right or wrong. So please don't blame the storyteller for a character's bigotry or lack of *Political Correctness...*

BOOK ONE

When life was simple

~1~

COMPOUNDING THE PROBLEM

LOOKING BACK at the last few years of his life, Andrew 'Mac' Appleton had to admit they had not been the greatest. *Okay, they sucked.* His dad had died two and a half years ago; seven months later, his mom. Not even a year later, a drunk driver killed his fiancé, Belinda, two weeks before they were to marry.

Following Belinda's death his military flying career nearly tanked when he could not escape the crippling guilt and depression that sapped him of his will to continue. *If I had picked her up as first planned, instead of having her meet me, she would still be alive. What was the point of even bothering? Everyone I love dies.*

That trouble always came in threes was an understatement— more like fours or fives. The adage, "Cheer up, things could be worse," took a perverse twist. It seemed that every time he tried, they were. When he attempted to find solace hanging out in bars and engaging in casual flings—something he had never done—he found no comfort, only a greater sense of loss and loneliness.

Until this past spring's Exercise Eagle Talon Mac was his squadron's best pilot. That ended when he was 'shot down' not once, but twice. Mac saw it as no big deal—it was 'only an exercise'—and stuck to his belief that what he did on his own time was his own business. Even if it only dulled the pain for a few hours.

Unfortunately, his Commanding Officer did not share this view and ordered a mandatory appointment with the Flight Doc who promptly booted Mac over to a psychologist. The psychologist, ready to declare him unfit for duty, backed off when the C.O. decided to give Mac one last chance.

As far as Mac was concerned being attached to an American unit targeting drug runners and stuck in the middle of the Caribbean on a six square mile patch of dirt was only more punishment. Clearly his boss wanted him far from bars, women and Canada. The Corn Island Officers' Mess was not the place to get shit-faced and there were no civilian distractions on the island. At least frigging Kandahar had a Tim's.

1318 local time, Colombia (exact date and location Classified)

TWO MINUTES until they reached the target. Mac could feel the hairs on the back of his neck tingle—a premonition or nerves?

Captain Andrew 'Mac' Appleton squirmed in the Apache's rear seat to ease a cramp in his right hip. No easy task with his one-hundred eighty pound, six-foot-two frame firmly wedged into the narrow seat. He snugged his harness tight, then scanned the gauges.

A moment later the radio crackled, "Hammer, Strike Team Alpha requires immediate air support, taking heavy fire."

Mac's deep blue eyes turned icy. He ignored the terse transmission from the ground assault team. Instead, he reacted instinctively to Weasel's simultaneous dispassionate intercom warning, "SAM, eight o'clock low."

"Fuck," Mac muttered to himself, "this is exactly how I got our asses flamed during training."

Flying four-hundred feet above the steep ravine, Mac popped decoy flares to confuse the incoming surface-to-air missile, then plunged the Apache's nose forty-five degrees down into a hard left turn toward the SAM. He clenched his abdominal muscles to counteract the g-force; his neck muscles strained as he twisted his head toward the threat.

Mac pirouetted the AH-64 Apache attack helicopter ninety degrees within its own length while sliding sideways. The helo's engines and main rotor shuddered under the strain as it dropped like an elevator in free-fall. Harness straps bit into his shoulders; the muscles in the small of his back reacted to the nervous stress and pinched sharply against his kidneys.

The SAM, now pursuing the decoy flares, streaked past, a scant twenty feet above.

Co-pilot Gunner, Frank 'Weasel' Moscone, securely strapped into the Apache's front seat, spotted the missile's launch site. "Come left twenty."

Weasel locked his helmet sight on the target. The 30 mm M230 Gatling gun, lurking benignly beneath the Apache's nose and linked electronically to his helmet-mounted sight, rotated to the left.

Bullets fired from the opposite slope of the ravine thwapped against the Apache. Mac smiled to himself. Small calibre rounds would have as much chance against the Apache's armour as a mosquito attacking a windshield. His only concern was another missile—the drug cartel mercenaries would have heard the Apache long before he was aware of them. Unlike the telltale whomp-whomp of the twin-blade Hueys, the Apache's four-bladed rotor's distinctive growl should have warned them that this wasn't just another Colombian Army Huey.

Weasel peppered the hillside with short cannon bursts the moment Mac pulled level. The Gatling spat out twelve-hundred rounds a minute and produced a vicious recoil. A long burst could stop the Apache in midair. Despite Weasel's caution, the Apache reared its nose in reaction.

"C'mon Weasel," Mac muttered to himself, "get the son-of-a-bitch." He knew that the mercenary would be ready to fire another missile within seconds. His desperate evasive manoeuvre had placed them so close to the ground he wouldn't be able to evade a second missile. He toggled his Multi-Function Display to the weapons' camera video feed.

Weasel's cannon rounds slammed into the ravine's rocky walls to produce a fury of stone shards and shrapnel. Mac saw the launcher ripped from the mercenary's grasp before he collapsed as if his legs had been shattered.

Mac pulled the Apache into a climb, continuing his turn, as Weasel disposed of the remaining mercenaries on the other side of the ravine. Sweat glued Mac's Nomex flying suit to his skin. If it wasn't for the Apache's maneuverability, he and Weasel would be dead. He sucked in a deep breath then muttered, "Intel bozos!" They should have warned them of the SAM threat.

His kidneys felt as if they were clamped in a vise. Mac was sure his left foot was bouncing against the rudder pedal, but when he looked, it was steady. Just adrenaline, he told himself. He took another deep breath, yawed the Apache's nose clockwise and climbed. "Weasel, target our twelve."

They crested the top of the ravine a hundred feet above the treetops. The compound, an erratic rectangle of buildings surrounded by an eight foot high wall, was directly ahead. Mac could see the Rangers were pinned down.

BARELY NINETY SECONDS had passed since their call for help, but to the Rangers in the compound, it seemed a lifetime. A mercenary in a small concrete guardhouse was armed with a grenade launcher. Fortunately for the Rangers, the first round landed well behind them.

For Chuck Kincaid, however, the situation was deteriorating. His Drug Enforcement Agency boss once described a blown mission as 'A right royal FUBAR' as this one seemed destined to become. The low stone wall protecting him was virtually gone. Kincaid knew he would likely be dead in less than a minute. Where the hell was the promised air support?

A second grenade exploded barely twenty-five feet in front of him. Somehow, the meagre cover protected him from the shrapnel. If the mercenary in the guardhouse managed to split the difference between his first and second rounds the fire fight would be over.

Kincaid screamed into the radio, "Get air support in here NOW," while he continued to inch forward.

Three nearly simultaneous explosions rocked the compound.

Kincaid instinctively pressed his face into the dirt, then cursed, spat out a mouthful of grit and glanced over his shoulder. The guardhouse was obliterated; an Apache hovered above the trees two-hundred yards to the east.

Kincaid looked across the compound as another mercenary took aim at him with an AK-47. Kincaid searched desperately for cover, but he was completely exposed.

A hailstorm of Gatling rounds from the Apache sliced through the man before he could fire. Kincaid, shaking from the adrenaline rush, leapt to his feet and held the radio to his mouth. "Hammer, target secure."

Rangers sprinted toward the workshops and began planting explosive charges while the rotor noise of the evac Hueys echoed reassuringly from the ravine's rocky walls as they approached the grassy landing zone outside the compound.

Kincaid watched the Apache maintain its malevolent hover— its chin gun sweeping back and forth across the compound as seven camouflaged figures ran from the buildings.

"Fire in the hole," Kincaid radioed as he sprinted toward the waiting Hueys.

The Apache wheeled around, then disappeared beyond the treetops while explosions echoed off the ravine's banks; neon flashes coloured plumes of dense smoke. The drug lab was no more.

~2~

A DEAD DUCK?

0542 local, 9 November, Islas Del Maiz (Corn Islands) in the western Caribbean Sea

MAC SLEPT FITFULLY—a dream swirled around in his half-conscious mind as he fought to make sense of the wispy images generated somewhere between sleep and consciousness.

This was the dream's third recurrence in the past two weeks. Each time he was in a strange place. He felt completely out of his element—knowing he did not belong—before he awakened in a cold sweat from the fear of being trapped.

The first time he could see nothing—everything was obscured by fog. In the second, the fog lifted slightly—he was surrounded by water.

Now, as his mind struggled to make sense of a wraithlike form that floated surrealistically in the fog, he was standing on something hard. He reached out to part the fog with his fingers, but was surrounded by solid walls within arm's length. He was unable to see his feet, move or discover where he was when the alarm blared its strident 0600 wake up call.

The world had changed since 9-11. In a new spirit of international cooperation, countries agreed to military operations and overflights by foreign forces in the ongoing war against terrorism and the drug trade that supported it. Mac, a captain and helicopter pilot in the Canadian Forces, was part of Operation Vigilant Angel.

Following years of government penny-pinching, the Canadian military was buying Europe's equivalent to the Apache—the Italian designed A-129 Mangusta. He had been posted to the Americans' 101st Air Assault Division, ostensibly to gain combat experience in the AH-64 Apache.

1407 local, 9 November, the western Caribbean, 250 km east of Big Corn Island

LULLED BY A BLEND of rotor blade whir, engine noise and the radio's static hiss, Mac checked the navigation system's waypoint readouts and made a slight course correction three minutes before scheduled radio contact with Sheriff in the C-130 Hercules AWACS.

The corners of his mouth curled into a grin at today's call signs: Sheriff, Posse and Rustler. Perhaps 'Vigilante' would be more appropriate since Operation Vigilant Angel's sole purpose was to wreak death and destruction on drug traffickers. He chuckled at the thought that somewhere in an office someone was paid to think up these mission names. At least there was no longer the need to conceal missions through covert operations to maintain deniability in the event something went wrong.

Mac's Apache was one of several assigned to bolster the United States Coast Guard's base on Corn; the United States Air Force was supplying Forward Air Controllers in a Hercules AWACS aircraft.

Big Corn Island, nestled forty-five miles northeast of Bluefields on Nicaragua's Caribbean coast, was an ideal base for the current operation. America had previously leased the Islas Del

Maiz from Colombia. Although the islands reverted to Colombia years ago, the war against terrorism made them a valuable base for intercepting drug runners.

Big Corn measured nearly six square miles. Hardly "big" by most standards, it nevertheless possessed an airstrip. The Colombian military had quickly removed island residents living near the new base without explanation eight months ago.

The upgraded airstrip, although unsuitable for larger aircraft such as the F-15 Eagle, was perfect for the Harriers, Apaches and Hercs currently assigned to Vigilant Angel. Rumours, always abundant in the military, speculated that U.S. Navy F/A-18E Super Hornets might be based there since they didn't require the longer runways needed by their 'big brothers'. The Hornet's ability to "lug iron"—pilot parlance for bombs—would give the tiny base more punch and mission capability.

Mac continued northwesterly across the Caribbean, southwest of Jamaica. The Apache's speed and size made it a reasonable approximation of a small fixed-wing aircraft. Using the call sign Rustler, he was simulating a drug runner. Sheriff and Posse were supposed to find him. The AWACS was manned by a fresh crew who had just rotated in. Mac, with over two months experience in theatre, and now one of the 'old guys', was assigned to help the newbies learn the ropes. Although the new AWACS crew was experienced, there was a big difference between intercepting a bomber or fighter versus a solitary small, single-engine aircraft hugging the water.

He acquired his nickname 'Mac' in a reference to the 'apple' portion of his surname while celebrating his arrival at his latest unit in some forgotten pilots' bar. His friend Bob Burgess insisted that it was more likely related to Mac's computer preference.

Mac was now part of a joint counter-terrorism campaign operated by the USCG, DEA, CIA and the Pentagon. Following his initial briefing he concluded there were likely other fingers in the alphabet pie of competing interests after Washington directly targeted the drug operations.

Provided he did not pooch this posting, he might be able use his combat experience to train Canadian pilots on the Mangusta— and show his old boss and the shrink that it was his own damn business what he did off-duty.

BOB BURGESS' AMERICAN FATHER worked in western Canada's oil industry. Bob met Mac during high school; they had been best friends ever since. Mac began dreaming of becoming a military pilot when Bob brought home 'Gun Ship' for his Atari ST computer.

While Burgess was obsessed with electronics and computers, Mac preferred mechanical things that he could see do something and often teased Bob that he had a circuit board in place of a brain.

Mac quickly mastered employing Hellfire and FFAR rockets against the numerous targets that populated the electronic gamescape. He learned how to utilise the Apache's murderous 30 mm chain gun to destroy Russian Hind helicopters in the days before political-correctness would have branded him an antisocial computer freak intent on destruction and world domination.

Now, the way Mac figured it, if he hadn't spent all that time glued to a joystick he might have hung out with the wrong crowd and be one of the bad guys in today's little role-playing adventure.

He grinned. *Hell, today was just like Gun Ship, only with better toys. And I get to play with them just about anytime I want.*

Burgess joined the United States Air Force, and Mac the Canadian Air Force, within a few months of each other. Occasionally crossing paths at joint exercises, each time they met it was as though only a few days had passed, rather than the months or years since they had last renewed their friendship and friendly rivalry. Both knew the other was very good at his job, and each one hated to lose.

Burgess, in charge of the new AWACS team, had gone to great pains to keep his arrival at Corn Island secret. Another AWACS crew member operated the radio to prevent Mac from recognising Bob's voice.

MAC WORKED METHODICALLY through his kneepad checklist until the AWACS controller broke the radio's static hiss.

"Rustler, Sheriff. Squawk and state condition."

Mac pressed the transponder button, sending an identifying signal to Sheriff in the AWACS. His response confirmed that they had the right blip on their radar screens and that there were no other aircraft in the exercise area.

"Rustler is go." Mac would not transmit again unless there was an urgent need, but would hear any instructions from Sheriff. In reality a drug-runner wouldn't be able to hear the secure military radio traffic, but today's exercise had to be conducted safely and the controller had to be able to contact Mac if necessary.

His Apache carried two external 230 gallon fuel tanks, giving it a range of almost 900 kilometers after refuelling aboard the USS *Guadalcanal* that morning. It was armed with twelve-hundred 30 mm rounds, four AGM-114M Hellfire laser-guided missiles and nineteen Hydra-70 rockets. This was unusual. Previous training missions, unless a live-fire exercise, only required dummy weapons.

Apaches carried two crew seated in tandem: the pilot in the rear, the CPG in front. Weasel had the day off; today's training mission wouldn't require firing the Apache's weapons.

"Posse, Sheriff. State condition."

"Posse is go," replied the flight lead of the pair of Marine Corps AV-8 Harriers from the *Guadalcanal*.

Mac's task was simple: reach the GPS coordinates before the Harriers could find him. He was five-hundred feet above the water. Sheriff was flying an elongated oval at 20,000 feet, thirty miles south. Posse was positioned sixty miles to the west.

"Rustler, Sheriff. Execute." The controller then ordered Mac to initiate radio silence and monitor Tac One, his own frequency.

"Posse, Sheriff. Go Tac Two." The Harriers would be on their own frequency to prevent Mac overhearing Sheriff's instructions to them.

Mac swung the Apache's nose around and plunged toward the water before levelling off fifty feet above the surface on his new heading of 010 degrees. The sudden change would require the radar operators aboard the Herc to be on their toes to pick him up against the water and guide the Harriers toward their quarry. He was on his own now.

Using Harriers as interceptors was a different twist. Mac knew they weren't ideal for this sort of mission but they were the only jets currently assigned to Vigilant Angel and it was vital that the task force be able to conduct a variety of non-conventional missions. Furthermore, the Harriers could operate from the Guadalcanal or Corn Island and did not require an entire carrier battle group as did carrier-based Hornets.

"As if you'll ever get close enough for an intercept," he had joked with the Harrier pilots during breakfast. It was great feeling his old self—his boss had been right to ship his ass here.

It was a perfect day for the exercise. A slight haze at sea level ensured the Apache would be difficult for the Harriers to pick up visually.

On the other hand, he was going to have to be careful not to run into a civilian boat obscured by the haze. An earlier AWACS radar sweep of the exercise area had shown it clear, but there was always a certain risk, and Apaches weren't designed to swim.

Mac continued on his 010 heading for another ninety seconds, maintaining an easy 125 knots at fifty feet. He considered dropping a little lower to make the radar operators earn their pay, but it wasn't worth the additional risk. He pulled hard left at the ninety second mark, making sure the Apache's nose didn't come up during the turn and cause him to pop up into radar view, then settled on a new heading of 285.

"Posse, Sheriff. Bogey your oh-eight-oh, five-five miles, deck."

Mac, surprised to overhear Sheriff using Tac One to advise the Harriers of his position, briefly wondered if it was a mistake or deliberate.

He cursed under his breath, "Those assholes are screwing with me."

The Harriers, fifty-five miles ahead on his left, would be accelerating and beginning a shallow descent while they closed.

Mac knew he had only scant minutes to execute an escape. He continued at 125 knots while he assessed the situation. *Harriers closing at almost ten miles per minute. Gives me five minutes to shake them, the radar fix, or both.* The only limitation placed on today's exercise was that he could not hover the Apache. After all, he was supposed to be a plane, not a helicopter.

He considered cheating and monitoring Tac Two but that really wouldn't be correct, even if he could justify it as pay-back for that Tac One conversation. Although competitive by nature, he wasn't prone to cheating.

He wondered if AWACS had picked him up when he turned. *Maybe this course, which put him at almost a right-angle to the Herc, had allowed them to 'paint' him with their radar. However the Radar Warning Receiver remained reassuringly silent, which meant that they probably hadn't. Did they get my heat signature? This course should prevent that; the Apache's near-perfect exhaust baffling reduced the chance of heat sensors picking up the engines' exhaust.*

Resignedly, he admitted, it was too late to worry. They had found him. He must do something about it.

The Harriers closed by ten miles while he deliberated. He made a quick visual check left and right. Visibility near the water was two to three miles, safe enough for him to descend to thirty feet. With only a gentle two or three foot swell he didn't have to worry about a wave crest swatting him out of the air. The controls felt solid at fifty feet. He didn't want to hit a sudden downdraft and not have enough altitude to recover.

Mac deliberately pulled the nose up and climbed to seventy-five feet, then counted to three. He knew the AWACS guys would see him.

His Radar Warning Receiver yelped when the AWACS painted him. He smiled with satisfaction. *Hopefully they'll believe that was a lucky hit on the radar.* He continued his 285 course knowing the AWACS would dutifully alert Posse of the bogey thirty-nine miles away, bearing 085 degrees, heading 285 degrees at 125 knots.

Mac dropped to thirty feet and reduced speed to 100 knots during a hard right turn.

The tight turn at this altitude was risky. If he wasn't careful he could catch a rotor tip in the water. Definitely not a wise career move; the only remains of his Apache and himself would be carbon fiber parts scattered across the water amid a fuel slick.

He came around to 085 and punched up his speed to one-fifty.

Mac whispered to himself, "The Harriers are behind me, approaching at an angle." Sometimes it helped to say the words rather than think them. Admittedly, he was in a bad position if they attacked. "A sitting duck," he admitted. They would have no trouble getting a gun or missile lock at this approach angle.

On the other hand, he was as close to the water, now partially obscured by the haze, as he dared. The Harriers would be above him and their own noses would obstruct the pilots' downward view, making their visual search more difficult. Luckily Harriers didn't have onboard radar.

Mac's scoot across the water lessened the Harriers' rate of closure now that he was, more or less, running away from them. *Have I bought a bit of time or just delayed the inevitable? Hopefully not a dead duck.*

He shook off any feeling of impending failure and concentrated on his next move. He wished the Apache wasn't painted camo green. It must look like a big lump of coal against the crystal blue water beneath him.

He didn't hear AWACS inform the Harriers that radar contact was lost. His last known position was thirty-one miles away when his sudden turn and descent to thirty feet broke contact. The AWACS operators were frantically trying to find him.

The Harriers were less than three minutes from his last known position and his slower speed wouldn't take him very far.

THE LEAD HARRIER PILOT could almost taste his quarry. "Posse Two, trail on my eight."

The second Harrier moved from directly behind his leader to one mile to the left and behind. Each could see ahead and Posse

Two could observe the leader's under-nose blind spot, increasing their chances for a visual sighting.

With Posse just over ten miles from Mac's last known position Burgess recalculated possible positions based on the Apache's speed and last known position. He decided Mac's only hope was to run from the Harriers while trying to edge towards the 'airstrip'.

"Posse, Sheriff. Come left one-five, descend to one-five-hundred. Estimate Bogey on your twelve, five miles."

The Harriers completed their turn, reducing speed to 325 knots. Still more than enough rate of closure and it would give them a few more precious seconds to scan the thickening haze below them.

They were in a near perfect intercept position. A gun or missile lock was a matter of only when, not if, as far as they were concerned since they could acquire simultaneous locks. The game would end if either pilot caught Mac in his sights.

The lead Harrier radioed, "Sheriff, Posse Lead. Negative visual. Estimate range three miles, coming left to three-five-oh." He expected Mac was trying for the 'airstrip' and would be slightly ahead on their left.

BURGESS HAD DEVISED A GOOD PLAN, except for one small problem—Mac made another right turn and was flying away from the 'airstrip' when the Harriers began turning. The Harrier pilots, forced to maintain their relative positions while trying to look ahead, missed the smudge in the haze when Mac passed beneath Posse Lead's right side, just as the Harriers completed their turn.

The lead Harrier requested a radar update from AWACS.

"Negative picture, Posse." The curt reply confirmed the AWACS operators did not have the faintest idea where Mac was.

The lead Harrier ordered, "Posse Two, reverse course to left. Lead going right." Each began opposite 180 degree turns to allow them to search completely around their current position and place them on the same course as Mac.

"Posse, Sheriff, do you have visual?" Burgess asked.

"Negative, request return to base."

Burgess swore under his breath and considered ordering the Harriers to circle above the fictitious airstrip, but the mission orders required that they intercept Mac before he reached the airstrip.

"Affirmative Posse. Heading two-two-five. Maintain Angels five, contact *Guadal.*" Burgess released the Harriers to return to the *Guadalcanal*. Mac had outsmarted them.

"So, just how many beers am I going to have to spring for tonight?" Burgess muttered aloud to no one in particular. "Damn it, I should never have let him play with my Atari."

Burgess stared at his radar screen, empty except for the twin blips of the departing Harriers.

APTLY NAMED, Mac concluded as the Harriers passed overhead—about to descend on a helpless quarry. Too bad they were headed in the wrong direction. He slammed down the right hand rudder pedal to execute a hard turn away from them.

Three minutes later, and with no further sign of the Harriers, he turned toward his destination. When his GPS confirmed he was at the "airstrip" Mac pitched the Apache's nose violently upward, knowing his radar blip would appear out of nowhere on the AWACS' radar.

He selected Tac Two to make sure both the Harriers and Burgess could hear him. "Knock, knock, who's here?" *Okay, it wasn't correct radio protocol, but what the hell, I beat Bob.* It was pure luck that the Duty Clerk had commented that morning about the guy in the new AWACS crew who didn't want anyone to know he was on Corn Island. Mac added, "Rustler requests return to base."

"Roger that, Rustler. Maintain level five-zero-zero, course two-four-eight."

Mac knew Burgess was trying to sound matter-of-fact. Mac repeated the instructions back, adding, "Estimate seven-five minutes." A not so subtle hint when he expected a beer, or three, to be served to him in the Corn Island Officers' Mess. It would be a triumphant return. He could hardly wait to tell Burgess that he had known all along that he was on the AWACS.

~3~

THE DEVIL'S WORK

WHEN MAC JOINED the Canadian Forces he hoped to be assigned to a fighter squadron after being selected for pilot training. Instead, he was offered the chance to try his hand in a helicopter. Five minutes into his first flight he fell in love with the intimate feel of the machine and its abilities and would gladly have paid for the privilege of flying.

His other passion, verging on obsession, was ships. Not twenty foot weekend distractions, but wooden ships armed with muzzle-loading guns. He discovered his love for things nautical years ago while reading his dad's copy of C. S. Forester's 'Mr. Midshipman Hornblower'. Perhaps it was the result of growing up on the prairies in the midst of vast emptiness—always wondering what was beyond the limitless horizon—that lured him.

When he and his mother were clearing out the attic after his father died he discovered additional Hornblower volumes. That evening he sat in his father's favourite chair—imagining him still there—and began reading 'Lieutenant Hornblower'. Mac didn't stop until he finished the book in the wee hours.

His mother, his closest relative other than a few cousins he didn't know, died after a brief battle with cancer. Even now he had to fight back the tears when he thought of the finality of that day. The opportunity to join the 101st couldn't have come at a better time since there was nowhere left to call home.

Something in those pages describing the life of a young Royal Navy officer over two-hundred years ago stirred his imagination. He searched out Hornblower books in used book stores when he moved from base to base. Hornblower's exploits were followed by other authors who swept him across the decks of enemy ships and carried him around the world. Dudley Pope's 'Ramage's Diamond' had taken Mac to the Battle of the Saintes, not far from his current posting. In his imagination he joined those fictional heroes on the Jamaica station. He stared at the haze and imagined a British or French frigate about to appear.

Most people thought that thirty-eight year old Mac remained single so he could devote himself to flying. Only his closest friends knew that his fiancé, Belinda, had been killed by a drunk driver. They did not know that he blamed himself for her death.

Since then he had not found, or allowed himself to find, a serious relationship. Instead, he stumbled through a series of drunken weekends and one night stands—many of which he could not remember—which was just fine with him.

He wondered if he was born in the wrong time—two-hundred years later he was chasing bad guys where his fictional heroes once sailed. Part of him wondered if he had been born back then perhaps his life would not be the mess it was now; the devil on his shoulder told him that there was no problem with his lifestyle. The drug lab mission and eluding the Harriers proved he could still fly.

MAC SHOOK HIS HEAD IN DISBELIEF. The horizon ahead was no longer clear. In the span of his brief distraction a large storm had begun brewing directly in his flight path. There had been no mention of adverse weather during the morning mission briefing. By now the AWACS and Harriers would be down. He set his radio to Corn Island's air traffic control frequency and called, "Corn Control, Rustler inbound."

No response. He tried again. Only silence.

Mac checked his kneepad to make sure he had the correct radio frequency. His third attempt elicited a nearly indecipherable, static-filled response. Must be the storm, he thought. He made a visual check of his airspace then climbed to fifteen-hundred feet hoping to get a better signal. He knew he would be breaking the rules by flying above his authorised altitude, but decided he should be safe with no visible traffic and well clear of commercial flight paths. He repeated, "Corn Control, Rustler inbound."

At last a response. Not clear, but at least understandable. Mac responded, "Rustler heading two-four-zero, range one-five-five miles. Request clearance to angels one point five and weather."

"Roger Rustler. Ceiling unlimited, visibility one-five plus miles. Wind one-niner-five at ten. Pressure one-zero-two. Maintain angels one point five, contact approach at three-zero miles."

The news of clear skies puzzled Mac. The weather at the base was the same as the morning, and the same as the forecast. He recalibrated his barometric altimeter to the current pressure reading.

"Control, I have visible storm on flight path, advise."

"Rustler, weather radar negative. Standby."

The storm cloud visibly expanded within a few minutes. Versicoloured and even more menacing in appearance, it dominated the horizon. Mac estimated the cloud top at 35,000 feet, yet the base weather radar did not detect it. The storm spanned at least thirty miles of the horizon. Clearly he was going to have to go around, but in which direction? Without a reference point it was impossible to determine the direction the cloud was moving. If anything, it appeared to be boiling outward in all directions.

Haze, interspersed with patches of thick fog, completely obscured the sea. He would have to rely on the Apache's artificial horizon to maintain level flight. Mac checked the radar altimeter to ensure he didn't accidentally descend if visibility further decreased.

The cloud appeared to be a giant horseshoe. Mac rechecked the instruments. Fuel wasn't an issue, the external tanks gave him a choice of several landing spots. He could always jettison the Hellfire and Hydra missiles to reduce weight and further increase range.

He opted to head south. Going north would take him farther from land in the event he had to set down. Plan A was to scoot around the left edge of the storm, then turn west toward Corn Island. One of the islands along his flight path, Providencia or San Andres, could provide refuge until the storm passed.

Mac nudged the Apache's nose left toward the horseshoe's southern tip where the sky appeared clearest. He tried raising Corn Island again but got only static. Behind him, out of sight on his current heading, the northern end of the horseshoe had expanded to cover the entire northeast quadrant and now resembled a giant hand ready to close around a fly.

Gusts punched the helicopter sideways; lightning filled the sky. With each flash the clouds became glowing iridescent masses. Mac experienced plenty of lightning growing up on the prairies, but this storm was frighteningly different. For the first time in his flying career, a sudden, chilling doubt about his ability to deal with the storm, intruded. Mac was afraid.

Flavescent flashes ripped through the clouds which now appeared to be two storms—one above the other. Swords of lightning slashed from one to the other as if ancient gods were doing battle. Mac's world darkened as fog and cloud closed in. The Apache suddenly seemed a tiny, fragile toy.

Within minutes he could no longer discern the left end of the storm cloud. The clear sky that once mockingly beckoned him toward safety had been consumed by the storm. His battle to control the Apache intensified—his hands and feet in constant motion on the controls. The artificial horizon swung like a pendulum. The altimeter rose and fell as though attached to a roller coaster. His head pounded. He forced himself to take deep breaths to calm himself.

Four simultaneous lightning flashes ripped the air. The first, directly behind him, then three to his right, almost shook the fillings from his teeth. The Apache lurched sideways and plunged downward over three-hundred feet in a stomach-churning drop.

One bolt knocked out the radar altimeter. Attempts to reset it were futile. He was now dependent on the barometric altimeter which required an accurate pressure reading to establish a baseline. The altimeter showed an optimistic 950 feet of altitude—if it could be believed.

Visibility fell to less than a half mile. Perversely, there was still too much ambient light to use the Pilot Night Vision Sensor goggles. Mac strained to see through the windshield as the wipers lost their battle to clear the torrential rain. The GPS placed him fifteen miles from Providencia. "Screw this!" he muttered and turned toward Providencia.

It was definitely the time for discretion. At least he could sit out the storm on the ground. It would be close, there was probably no more than a half hour of daylight remaining. The Apache felt like it was a bucking bronc. Sweat trickled down his legs and soaked his socks.

"They never put THIS in the training," he muttered under his breath when another violent gust flung the Apache up and sideways through nearly two-thirds of a barrel roll before he regained control. Five miles, two, now barely one; he urged the Apache into a climb, not confident of his altitude.

Thoughts tumbled in his mind. *Providencia has mountains, but how tall are the trees? He could see nothing. Where the hell are they? Exactly where am I going to land?*

His left knee begin its characteristic twitch. He continued talking to himself, "Fourteen meter rotor span, plus a safety margin. I need an area big enough to play around a bit. Wind's too strong to descend from a full hover."

He could barely control the Apache when a wall of wind rolled the helo at least thirty degrees. "I've got one shot to get it right. Okay, no sign of trees, at least not yet. GPS shows half a mile. Are those tree tops in the fog? Gawd, they're high...altimeter still shows fourteen-hundred. Is that land below?"

A horrendous explosion rocked the Apache. Half the electrical system faded to dark submission to the lightning strike. The Apache pitched, rolled and yawed like a crazed beast trying to escape from both Mac and the storm's assault. His world turned topsy-turvy. The artificial horizon gyro spun madly while he fought to stabilise the helicopter. Mac didn't know if the Apache was even right way up.

When he regained control, the gyro showed a descending left turn. Mac fought against the turn, trying to come level but he had no altitude to play with; no way to ascertain where he was in the air.

Everything—the sky, the clouds, even the golf ball size rain drops glowed in a bilious yellow-green hue that varied in intensity as though connected to a pulsating power source in a low-budget sci-fi movie.

The rotor tips trailed phosphorescent crimson streaks. Briefly mesmerised by the bizarre phenomenon, Mac became alarmed when the trail extended ahead of the rotor's rotation, not behind. His logical pilot's mind could make no sense of the ghostly phenomenon.

The sky, now continuously rent by lightning flashes, although each bolt lasted but a moment, seemed part of a nightmare from which he could not escape. The term 'sky' was a stretch, it was at least ninety-five percent solid water. He blinked in an attempt to erase the red trails, instead they doubled in length.

The Apache shuddered as if it had been hit by a massive sledgehammer. All visible parts of the its structure took on an eerie yellow-green aura encased within a pulsating halo. Brilliant crimson fire raced across every surface.

Slammed violently into the seat, his hands were torn from the controls; he could not overcome the massive g-forces to reach them. A catapult launch and nine-g turns in the back seat of an F-14 Tomcat had been a merry-go-round ride compared to this. The airspeed indicator was pinned at maximum; the GPS displayed a nonsensical cascade of numbers. Mac fought for breath against an elephant's weight of g-force pressing against his chest. His vision narrowed and darkened—he knew he was blacking out.

A moment before losing consciousness, he glimpsed his high-tech metal and composite fibre Apache apparently disintegrating into transparent crystalline prismatic fragments of crimson and yellow-green floating away into the storm's dark abyss.

THE CORN ISLAND TOWER OPERATOR visually confirmed the puzzling appearance of a large cloud on the horizon, even though weather radar continued to show nothing. He could not regain contact with Mac—his radar blip had vanished.

The ready room horn blared. The crew of the Search and Rescue Seahawk helicopter sprinted across the tarmac while the ground crew removed the engine inlets' protective covers.

The Seahawk's twin turbines' starting whine settled into a steady roar while preflight checks were completed and the engines reached operating temperature. The pilot applied full-power; the main rotor blades clawed at the air to lift the helo up and forward. Dipping its nose slightly, the Seahawk climbed and accelerated eastward.

Weasel and Bob Burgess stood silhouetted in the Officers' Mess doorway, their untouched drinks on the table behind them. They watched silently as the helo clattered into the distance.

There was only one reason to launch the Seahawk. Mac was in trouble.

~4~
AFTERMATH

A WATERY SUN struggled to break through the overcast. Despite the clouds the Apache's cockpit was a steam bath. Mac, soaked in sweat, slumped against his harness as he struggled to regain consciousness. Absolute silence, discounting his throbbing headache and ringing ears, engulfed him. Gone were the lightning bolts and the wind, screaming like all of Satan's demons, that had tried to rip apart his Apache as if it was a piece of tissue paper.

He cautiously opened his left eye and recognised the familiar confines of his helicopter. Despite the clouds blocking the sun he winced from the sudden infusion of light. It felt as if he had been run over by a truck during what he believed would be a ride into oblivion. Pain was a good thing, he told himself. It meant he was alive, largely due to the Apache's cockpit being designed to withstand a twenty-g impact. Obviously the Apache had not disintegrated into transparent prisms of light but he had no recollection of landing. Had he been hallucinating?

His Rolex had stopped at five thirty-three on the ninth. When he tapped its face the second hand resumed its measured step. Daylight meant that he had been here for at least twelve hours, maybe longer. With painful effort he removed his harness and opened the canopy. Damp air, heavy with the scent of trees, dirt and flowers, revived his downtrodden spirits. He took a mouthful of water from the canteen tucked beneath his knees. Flexing his limbs restored circulation to his extremities. General stiffness gradually replaced the stabs of pain.

Mac didn't think he had any serious injuries. Other than the headache knifing through his brain every time he even twitched an eyelash, he seemed to be okay. It wasn't much worse than the aftermath of some of his previous weekends. He awkwardly clambered out of the cockpit, wondering if his legs would support him, then leaned against the fuselage and surveyed his landing spot.

The Apache was nestled in a grass-filled depression on the top of a hill. He was lucky and decided that the hills meant that he was on Providencia since San Andres was flat. The area was surrounded by underbrush and trees, yet he had somehow managed to set down in the only open space. The breeze was barely a whisper; birds chattered noisily all around. Mac slumped against the fuselage, then pressed his back against the warm metal until he could feel the tightness and pain begin to dissipate.

He began a methodical examination of the Apache's exterior. From what he remembered of the storm, the Apache seemed to be in remarkably good condition. The external fuel tanks were still in place, as were the Hellfire and Hydra missile pods, and he was surprised they hadn't been torn off.

He paused for a moment, then made a closer examination of the subtle changes in the Apache's drab paint. A fine black soot coated his fingertips when he brushed the surface—as though it had been scorched. Perhaps he had not imagined flames licking the exterior.

Mac leaned into the cockpit. The radio was still set for Corn Island's frequency. He confirmed the radio's electrical breakers were 'on' but got no response when he attempted to contact the base. Was he out of range or had the radio been fried by the storm?

The final lightning strike must have shut down the engines. Although their switches were still in the "on" position, he couldn't remember hitting the emergency kill. He activated the external marker lights—their reassuring red, white, and green glows meant he still had battery power, so it wasn't all bad news. He continued around the Apache, then returned to the cockpit and turned off the lights.

When he activated the GPS a blank screen stared back at him. That was unusual. There were no trees close enough to interfere with the satellite signal. Worse, the onboard Litton Attitude-Heading Reference System placed him hundreds of miles from his last known position. The AHRS was known to 'drift' if not regularly updated by a GPS reading, but this was more than the usual small error. The discrepancy seemed impossible given that the fuel gauges showed over half full.

He opened the Emergency Location Transmitter access hatch in the tail and manually tripped the ELT. He left it on for fifteen minutes before shutting it down to conserve battery power. He decided to trip it every hour for five minutes. Any aircraft or ship, civilian or military, would pick up the familiar distress squeal.

The cloud dissipated through the morning. Mac guessed he must have awoken around seven or eight. Judging by the sun's position he estimated it was close to noon and reset his watch. His canteen nearly empty, he needed to find water soon. He tucked the flare pistol, smoke and flare canisters into a pocket for when Search and Rescue arrived and headed due west. He hoped he would find something to explain the discrepancy between his estimated position and the AHRS's reading. As he entered the bush, he wondered if there were snakes. "I really hate snakes!" he exclaimed aloud to himself. "Great! I survive the crash only to be killed by a viper or whatever lurks in this godforsaken place."

Trudging downhill, he caught momentary glimpses of the ocean through the trees. He figured that he must be on an island, but without the GPS how would he know which island?

After walking close to three kilometers the underbrush began to thin enough for him to clearly see the ocean through the trees. The edge of the forest gave way to a wide flat beach. An unbroken expanse of water stretched away to the horizon. He supposed it was too much to expect something as simple as a big 'Welcome To...' sign to tell him where he was. If his assumption that this was an island was correct he needed to retry the ELT. Exasperated that he had not found any sign of fresh water, thirsty, hungry and aching, he decided there was no point in aimless wandering.

By the time he returned to the Apache it was late afternoon and at least a day since the storm. *The SAR team should have found me by now—assuming they have some idea where I am. I sure as hell don't.*

Mac checked the ELT before tripping it—night should increase the signal's range. He sipped half his remaining water and ate one of his emergency rations. He rechecked the flare pistol before settling under the Apache for the night. When his rescuers arrived he wanted to be sure they found him.

He slept fitfully, imagining every sound to be either an approaching Seahawk or snake. He rose at dawn and turned off the ELT—resigned to the fact the SAR team should have arrived by now. *Maybe the damn thing wasn't working.* The now nearly empty canteen meant finding water was of immediate importance. He retraced his route to the beach and turned right, following the pristine sand—a fairly uniform strand a hundred feet or so wide. He was tempted to take a swim to clean off the layer of dried sweat caked under his Nomex flight suit. The dirt could wait. Drinking water was the greater priority.

After walking for an hour, Mac rested with his back against a tree trunk. The sound of shouts startled him: he wondered if it was only a trick of the breeze moving through the trees. He stood upright and peered toward the sound. *Yachters ashore for the day would explain the voices. They could tell him where he was and radio for help.*

Mac continued along the beach until a rock outcropping forced him to veer inland into the woods. After seventy-five yards through the trees, his vision restricted by undergrowth, he again heard voices. They seemed to be speaking Spanish, but his limited vocabulary prevented him from understanding what they were saying.

His first inclination was to run toward the voices calling, 'Here I am, you've found me.' However, it also occurred to him that some idiot dressed in a flight suit with barely visible markings, speaking a foreign language and charging out of the woods might have his intentions misunderstood and advanced cautiously. Eventually the underbrush thinned; Mac crouched before continuing forward, careful to avoid making any sound, then dropped to his knees, finally his stomach, to reach the edge of the forest.

A large boat, oars jutting from its sides, lay at the water's edge. Half a dozen shabbily dressed men struggled to manhandle large barrels along the beach toward the boat. Two-hundred feet away, at the start of the trees, were another six men. Although Mac couldn't tell what they were doing, he wondered if they were drug smugglers. *They certainly weren't a family of cruisers. If they were smugglers, what were the barrels for? And what was the farther group doing?*

The boat was perplexing with only oars and no propellor visible. *Something that size should have a motor. Loaded with the barrels and men it would be an absolute pig to row.*

He watched and waited for another ten minutes trying to decide if he should approach. He crept to a thicket twenty-five yards from a small stream where he watched the barrel party complete another trip. It was strange that men would come here for water. *Had the village well or desalination plant broken down? Why, of all things, wood barrels? Plastic would be so much better; they wouldn't leak like sieves, as these were doing.* When his right leg went numb from a rough spot on the ground he cautiously flexed his leg.

He didn't have time to react to the sound of a twig snapping before something slammed into his skull. A cascade of fireworks and pain tore through his head before everything went black.

MAC DRIFTED IN AND OUT of consciousness. Distant vague sounds—gentle creaks, sloshing water, unrecognizable voices—filtered into his brain. The pervasive stench of an untended outhouse stung his nostrils. Darkness, except for a weak sliver of light at the bottom of what he guessed was a door, encased his physical world. The rough wood floor seemed to rise and fall with the rhythmic motion of a baby's cradle. He could not tell if these sensations were reality or just part of a dream. His head throbbed painfully and every muscle ached. Eventually clarity began to replace the fog in his mind.

Although the dark restricted his explorations to what he could feel, hear and smell, he determined the heavy metal band around his right ankle was secured to a rough chain attached to a large ring fastened into well worn floor planks. The stench emanated from a vile wooden bucket for bodily needs sitting in the corner of what he determined by hand measurements to be a five foot by eight foot room.

He had no recollection of how he had arrived here, where he was or how long he had been unconscious. His Rolex, a thirtieth birthday present to himself, was missing. Maybe drug smugglers or terrorists had captured him. Surely they would recognise his flight suit—even with its dull insignia—and realise that he was Canadian. *Are they holding me for ransom?*

Footsteps thudded outside his door. He instinctively recoiled when it burst open, but the confined room offered no escape.

Someone grabbed the front of his flight suit and pulled him forward. A lantern-illuminated face thrust itself toward him. The flickering light revealed an unshaven face surrounding a nearly toothless mouth that reeked of rotting cabbage, garlic, onions and oral decay.

Mac couldn't tell if it was the man, his clothes, or both that smelled like a redolent stew of rancid grease, long unwashed flesh and decomposing offal.

The man uttered something in Spanish, flung Mac against the wall with such force to knock Mac breathless, then hissed something to a second shadowy figure in the doorway before the door closed.

Mac had no idea how much time had passed since Lantern Face's visit when the lock's metallic clink and a sliding sound awakened him from his stupor. He groped in the darkness toward the source of the sound and located a metal plate with something on it and a metal mug holding a liquid that smelled like swamp water. The object on the plate was hard as a rock. He pushed the plate and mug aside in revulsion before collapsing into another fitful sleep.

Again, the sound of footsteps awakened him. This time he didn't recoil when the door opened. Two burly thugs hoisted him to his feet. One held him securely while the other roughly released the chain from his ankle. He wanted to resist but didn't have the strength.

The silent men shoved him through the door into a narrow passageway illuminated only by their dim lantern. Propelled forward, he faltered on wobbly legs struggling to regain circulation. One man maintained a firm grip on the back of his neck, forcing Mac to remain stooped as he stumbled along. They paused after twenty-five feet.

Both guards laughed when Mac tried to stand erect only to bash his head against the low overhead beams. Momentarily stunned, he almost collapsed. One guard caught him under the arms; the other punched him in the stomach, then cuffed him across the face before depositing him, none to gently, on a wooden box.

His escorts stood silently behind him to either side. A solitary lantern suspended from a heavy wood ceiling beam gave little light—and no indication of an escape route.

Mac expected they were about to kill him. When he instinctively turned his head toward a sound from behind one of the guards struck him with his fist. Footsteps creaked across the wood floor before materialising as a no less smelly, short swarthy man. He stood in front of Mac, arms crossed, staring silently without expression for a good minute.

Mac returned the stare with equal blankness. He was puzzled more by the man's clothing—the coarse woven pants had no zipper and his shirt resembled a blouse. Mac struggled not to show the fear rising in his throat.

When Shorty finally spoke it sounded like a question, but Mac couldn't understand him. Instead, he looked blankly at the man, hoping his visitor would understand that the lack of a response was due to a language barrier, not a reluctance to answer.

Shorty repeated himself.

Mac still couldn't understand what he was saying and replied slowly, "An...drew...Ap...ple...ton, Cap...tain..." Before he could give his serial number, Shorty slammed his fist into the side of Mac's head.

Shorty hissed, "Inglese?"

It was the first word Mac understood. He shook has head and responded, "No, Canada."

A sudden commotion from above interrupted Shorty's response. From the direction of the sounds, Mac guessed he was being held in a basement or cellar.

Shorty spoke curtly to the two escorts who hoisted Mac to his feet and propelled him back along the passageway. He was careful to keep his head down as they pushed him into his cell. They didn't bother attaching the leg chain—the sound of a heavy bar dropping into place on the far side of the door told him the door was well secured.

The commotion above continued for several minutes, growing in volume and excitement as men became increasingly agitated.

"Get me the hell out of this stinking sewer," Mac pleaded in a whisper that only the darkness could hear.

Moments later the cell shook from a sharp explosion. A few seconds later he heard a distant thunderclap followed by the sound of splintering wood, a loud metallic clang, then screams of agony.

Thank God! They're coming. Mac sat in silence, trying to suppress the sound of his own rapid breathing so he could hear every sound of the fight. It sounded as if his rescuers were taking it to those bastards holding him. *Another minute or two and I'm free.*

BOOK TWO

Complications

~5~

CONVERGENT CIRCUMSTANCES

L A SEÑORA DEL NOCHE, brig, departed Cumana in the early morning of 6 November 1804 having delivered fresh slaves to the garrison commander. Eased to deep water by the ebb tide, she set a northwesterly course to clear the eastern end of Tortuga before making a westward reach toward Puerto Blanco, in a remote part of the Viceroyalty of New Granada beyond the northwest corner of the Gulf of Venezuela.

For the next two days *La Señora* heeled comfortably from the steady breeze on her port quarter; her crew relaxed with no danger of leeway pushing her toward land. Fifteen miles of serene azure sea, scarcely flecked by white horses, stretched ahead toward a cloud bank hugging the horizon. The roughly five-hundred mile voyage should take only five or six days, maybe less with favourable winds. The men eagerly anticipated the cantinas, barrios, and other amusements awaiting them.

"Just a rainstorm off Curaçao," Captain Julio Herreros confidently declared when the cloud increased. A slight mist hovered over water undulating in a parade of gentle swells as they plodded westward at four or five knots. Despite his pronouncement, the cloud bank continued to grow until it covered an area slightly south of west to nearly due north, although it appeared to be getting no closer—its westward progress nearly identical to theirs. Swatches of yellow and green coloured the darkening mass now illuminated by lightning deep within. The crew grew more anxious by the mile. Several crossed themselves.

Herreros weighed his options. He could steer south-by-west, keep the wind on the beam and clear the southern tip of the storm. That would take them toward the coastline—a potentially deadly lee shore if the wind shifted. To shape course southward would mean slow progress against the wind and gruelling work for an exhausted crew. Worse, they would have to rework their way northward to weather the peninsula. He knew that it was only the promise of pay, and what it would buy when they reached Puerto Blanco, that had prevented the crew from deserting at Cumana.

It was past the hurricane season and the ominous change in weather baffled Herreros. He opted to attempt to turn northwest in an attempt to skirt or outrun the storm.

In the wee hours, however, *La Señora* and her twenty souls were within the bowels of the storm. Hurricane strength winds howled through the rigging like a banshee, tearing the close-reefed sails from their yards. Somehow, the men managed to rig storm sails in near impossible conditions. She nearly rolled onto her beam ends several times when wind gusts threatened to pluck out her sticks. Miraculously no one was swept overboard, although two crew members suffered broken limbs in the violent tossing. When the gale ripped away the storm sails they had no choice but to scud before the wind under bare poles.

Rampaging seas broke over the stern three times. Sea water entered through deck seams that opened and closed from the waves twisting the hull, sluiced below decks to inundate everything, and eventually collected in the bilges. The metronome clank of the pumps, manned by men who had to be relieved every quarter hour, emphasised their peril. Miraculously, the stubborn ship threw off the tons of water surging across her deck and threatening to push her under. Lightning flashed all about—stabbing from one layer of cloud to the next.

An iridescent vitriol green cloud wrapped itself around the brig like death's mantle. The sailors prayed only for their lives, not salvation, already convinced their souls were eternally damned for past transgressions. Masts, rigging and hull glowed in shades of yellow and green. Scarlet ribbons of St. Elmo's Fire raced incessantly across her upper-works.

None of the men on deck saw the flashing anti-collision lights or heard Mac's Apache pass overhead in the twenty-first hour of their ordeal. The brig's terrified crew, had they noticed, likely would have believed a demon was preparing to feast on their corpses.

By the morning of 11 November, *La Señora*, battered and her crew exhausted, sullenly waddled through the declining storm surge twelve miles off Quinta Ruban. Most of her remaining water casks were shattered during the pummelling; those that survived were in such a putrid state that the crew refused to drink from them. Herreros sought refuge in a small cove to replenish the undamaged casks and repair the most urgent damage to canvas and rigging before attempting Puerto Blanco.

CAPTAIN ULYSSES CATHCART, H.M.S. *Lionheart*, had fretfully paced his quarterdeck since false dawn. Despite doubled masthead lookouts searching for hazards lurking in the reef infested waters and a leadsman near the tip of the jib boom constantly calling out the depth, Cathcart was doubly wary. Threading his ship through the perilous maze of narrow channels and hidden reefs surrounding the Brigadoons was no easy task.

Lionheart, 36 guns, assigned to the Jamaica squadron, was patrolling between Jamaica and South America. Her usual consorts, the schooners *Ringle* and *Seppings*, were on detached duty—leaving *Lionheart*, whose size required the comfort of deep water, to ferret out the pirates, smugglers or slavers potentially lurking in the shallow coastal waters.

Cathcart's orders were to seek out French warships and any vessel trading with the French. That said, he had to be careful not to risk unnecessary damage, lose a battle, or not pursue victory with utmost determination. Any failure on his part could result in court-martial and even execution, as befell Admiral Byng some years earlier.

Cathcart wasn't sure if it was a whim or a premonition that made him decide to check Quinta Ruban, the largest island in the Brigadoons. Originally settled in the seventeenth century by Scots, Quinta Ruban was rumoured to have been used by pirates such as Henry Morgan, and continued to used by corsairs and smugglers. Various attempts at settlement had failed for a variety of reasons and, more often than not, previous checks had been fruitless. However, when the masthead lookout spotted a topmast jutting skyward above the foreground trees, Cathcart ordered the larboard guns run out.

The leadsman, straddling the jib boom forty feet in front of the bow, was the first to sight the brig in the small cove. Cathcart ordered the stern anchor released; they would block the entrance to the cove. He expected this to be another routine game of cat-and-mouse. Although Britain and Spain were at an uneasy peace, a boarding party from the launch would search the Spaniard for any signs that they had been trading with the French. When they found none—the Spaniards always being careful to avoid carrying damning documents—apologies would be made for any inconvenience and *Lionheart* would be on her way. However, when the brig opened fire—albeit only a six-pounder pop gun by the sound—any pretense of politeness ended.

Cathcart, momentarily beyond words, reasoned that it was likely an overzealous dolt of a sailor. Surely no captain was fool enough to risk firing upon a frigate. So his initial reaction, to reply with a broadside which would have instantly rendered the brig into kindling, was replaced by a glance into the waist where First Lieutenant Tobias Baverstock was in charge of the guns.

Something in Baverstock's expression calmed Cathcart's initial anger. Baverstock was an excellent officer, the best he had ever commanded, and would soon have his own ship. Toby always seemed to know his Captain's thoughts.

Cathcart paused for a moment longer to consider that gathering intelligence would be impossible if he succumbed to his initial urge. "Mister Baverstock," he called, "a single ball twixt wind and water." If the ball struck below the brig's waterline, there was a danger she would sink and they would lose any prize money, not that the brig appeared to be worth much. A direct hit on the hull should give sufficient warning not to attempt any further foolishness.

Baverstock lifted his hat in acknowledgement, glanced at the Spaniard, then strode to the forward eighteen pounder. Cathcart could not hear what Baverstock said to the gun captain.

After the gun crew placed a ball directly through the offending gun's port Cathcart enthusiastically called out, "An extra tot for those men!" If the brig had the temerity to fire again, he would fire a broadside—no matter Toby's look.

It was not until the launch, carrying a boarding party of two dozen armed sailors and Royal Marines, was halfway across the quarter-mile of water separating the ships that Cathcart saw the Spanish flag fall to the brig's deck. He had instructed Midshipman Barnes, in command of his first boarding party, to tolerate no resistance from the brig.

BARNES SCRAMBLED OVER the brig's rail, a pistol clutched in his left hand, his heart racing in the expectation that the last thing he would see would be a Spanish cutlass blade about to cleave his forehead.

In the few seconds that it took for the red-coated Marines to join him Barnes surveyed the enemy's deck. The ball had shattered a six-pounder's muzzle, overturned the gun and crushed two men. Another three bodies, torn apart by a lethal flurry of iron and wood splinters, lay at grotesque angles amid their own blood and gore. The dispirited crew crouched behind pin rails or guns; some slumped morosely on the deck. Her captain was nowhere in sight.

Barnes ordered the Marines to herd the crew into a tight circle around the mainmast and disarm them while British sailors, armed with cutlasses and pistols, searched the prize to ensure no one was hiding below deck.

La Señora's captain, who had retreated to his personal jakes, was hauled, with no hint of the deference befitting his rank, forward to join his crew.

Barnes, scarcely able to contain his contempt for the man who appeared to have abandoned his men, not to mention a fool for firing on *Lionheart*, recalled his own fear only minutes before. Baverstock's quiet words to him as he entered the launch, "Lead your men by example and they will follow," had given him the courage to face his fear and capture his first ship. *Where is the line separating fear from cowardice?*

Before he could answer his question a sailor rushed up to him. "Sir, there's a locked space below. Mister Allnott's respects, sir, do we have a key." Barnes strode into the captain's cabin, found a ring of keys on a cluttered table and went below.

It was only as Baverstock's head ascended above the brig's railing ten minutes later that Barnes remembered he had neglected to hoist the Union flag to indicate that he had the brig under control.

MAC, TRAPPED IN THE CRAMPED DUNGEON, waited for his rescuers. He was sure that they must have had to blow through something solid from the sound of the bigger explosion.

He continued waiting. Although he heard numerous footsteps—some possibly in the hallway outside his door—nothing happened.

Finally, after anxious minutes, a key scratched in the lock; but, when the door opened, Mac's first thought was that he was about to be killed. It wasn't the expected Seal or Ranger, rather, the man appeared to be another of his disreputable captors. Better a dead hero than a dead duck; Mac decided that it was time to escape. He summoned all his strength and flung himself at the man.

Unfortunately, the man's broad shoulders spanned the doorway and prevented Mac from pushing him through the opening. The man recovered his balance, then shoved Mac aside as if he was a beggar.

A second man thrust a lantern into the cell and snarled over his shoulder. "'Ere zur, do this 'un look loik uh-nudder friggin' Dago t'ewe?"

Mac, not sure of his senses and head still throbbing painfully from the recent knocks, could not decipher the strange accent. His mind seemed ensnared in a net, unable to think clearly.

A third person, a pistol in his right hand, his voice squeaky and face obscured by the lantern's glare, demanded, "Who are you?"

Mac struggled to comprehend why someone would carry an antique gun and slumped against the wall in submission. He could not attach reason to what he was seeing. His brain, still functioning at diminished efficiency, had not formulated a response before Squeaky Voice demanded, "Speak up man. Who are you? Where are you from?"

Mac's confused mind understood only "He wants to know where I was born." This was the first logical question in recent memory, and in a form of English he could understand. His addled brain did remember he was born at Saskatoon General Hospital. So, in a spirit of cooperation, and sensing this was a turning point for the better in his otherwise miserable situation, he stammered, "Sa..Sa..Saskewtoonsaskashawon," not intending to slur the words together, but nevertheless doing so in his fragile state.

Squeaky Voice snapped, "Place him with the rest. He doesn't speak the King's English."

Two men dragged Mac from the cell, then forced him up a steep stairway with a complete lack of ceremony, although with slightly more civility than afforded him by his previous captors.

Mac's eyes, accustomed to the dark, burned from the brilliant daylight. His cramped legs threatened to collapse. His mind reeled from the sights that greeted him. Something was terribly amiss and he knew that he must be dreaming or hallucinating. The rocking motion that he had attributed to nausea from a concussion finally made sense. He was on a ship, not in some squalid prison on land as he had believed—that also explained the sounds of sloshing water. Why would drug smugglers use a sailing ship? He struggled to recall the arrangement of masts and rigging that distinguished each type of ship. From his limited nautical knowledge she appeared to be a small brig. His apprehension increased when he realised that he was surrounded by his captors. He looked for the men who had beaten him but could not recognise them.

Despite eyes still watering heavily from the sunshine he saw another sailing ship nearby. *If I'm not dreaming I really must be hallucinating.* It was English judging by the Union Jack fitfully fluttering from her rear mast. A row of sinister black muzzles protruded from her side. Above each gun was a scarlet red panel with a lion's snarling head outlined in yellow. He blinked, hoping that this illusion would disappear. It did not.

A half-dozen men wearing bright red uniform jackets and armed with muskets surrounded his group. He guessed they were Royal Marines. More men, without uniforms, were positioned on the quarterdeck near what looked like miniature cannons perched on the quarterdeck rail.

As the shocking possibility that he wasn't hallucinating became more certain he closed his eyes to convince himself that in a moment he would awake from a dream. When he reopened them nothing had changed.

A second boat made its way between the two vessels then disappeared beneath the brig's side. Moments later Squeaky Voice saluted when a man wearing a blue coat with tarnished trim appeared at the side rail. Mac wondered if this was the English captain. After a brief conversation the two moved to the stern rail.

Mac had witnessed enough 'dressings down' to know that they had moved away from prying ears. He felt a twinge of guilt about watching and tried not to appear obvious. The younger man stood at attention, obviously uncomfortable. Mac couldn't overhear what the clearly exasperated older man said to Squeaky Voice before the officers turned to face the captives.

Mac, with a sudden clarity of thought, realised that his own clothes set him apart from the other prisoners. His throat constricted around a rapidly growing lump. He had perhaps a minute to concoct a believable story to explain his presence when Squeaky Voice pointed at him, then ordered two sailors to fetch him.

Mac struggled to stifle his growing apprehension, then stepped toward the approaching sailors. If I appear cooperative... The metallic click of a gun being cocked made him pause. He glanced over his shoulder toward the sound as a marine levelled his musket at him. Mac almost exclaimed "Holy f..." when the nearest British sailor reached for his cutlass. His heart raced. He slowly raised his arms and opened his hands to show they were empty. "Relax fellas, I'm not one of them." He tried to sound cheerful, and non-threatening.

The tars appeared surprised—obviously not sure if Mac was one of 'them' or not—and another, slightly cautious, step toward him.

Mac remained motionless until they reached him, then slowly lowered his arms. Convinced he was being witty, Mac quipped, "So guys, what say we do lunch? I'm famished."

Unfortunately, both escorts appeared to lack any sense of humour. They positioned themselves on either side, then each grasped an upper arm with their rock hard hands.

When they reached the quarterdeck the sailors stood behind him. Mac felt that things might not be going as well as he had hoped—the pair of scowling officers, standing four paces in front of him, showed no indication of friendliness. He felt alone and naked.

The older officer, obviously the senior, was six feet tall, well tanned and muscular with a rugged look. The high tropical sun cast a sharp shadow from his hat across his face which accentuated his severe expression and a scar on his left cheek. Squeaky Voice, a scrawny pimple-faced youngster, was no more than fifteen or sixteen years, and about five-seven.

Nervously aware of his wary escorts, Mac saluted and said, "Captain Andrew Appleton at your service." Mac could feel the older officer's unblinking steel-grey eyes cutting through him.

After a momentary pause, the man returned Mac's salute and coldly replied, "Baverstock, First Lieutenant, His Britannic Majesty's frigate *Lionheart*."

LIEUTENANT TOBIAS BAVERSTOCK was taken aback by the prisoner's unusual attire and claim to be a captain. Especially since the stranger had been the first to salute. Baverstock had never experienced such deference from any captain and wondered if the man's use of 'Captain' was an attempt to gain an advantage. Baverstock felt his nape hairs prickle at the thought having arrived aboard *La Señora* in an already somewhat testy temperament. Still smarting from Cathcart's earlier frustration at the time taken to secure the brig, he had been instructed to find out "What that infernal Barnes was about."

Now, after what was becoming an awkward pause and only slightly mollified by the stranger's apparently sincere expression, Baverstock continued, "Allow me to introduce Midshipman Barnes. May I ask what brings you aboard this..." Baverstock paused to survey the deck, then wrinkled his face in disgust and added, "...ship?"

Baverstock's pronunciation of his rank as 'loo' rather than 'lef' surprised Mac who replied, "That's a very long story, sir, and I'm really not sure of the exact circumstances myself." Mac continued to address Baverstock as 'sir'. He chose his words carefully to avoid any hint of his military duties or the events leading up to his current predicament.

Mac added, "I was marooned on this island, captured and knocked unconscious, then held prisoner. I have no idea of where I am or how long I've been here."

"Quinta Ruban and thirteen, November," Baverstock replied, his expression softening somewhat.

"Where?" Mac asked. He had never heard of the place and added, "But what year?" as though joking.

Baverstock, visibly bemused by the question, answered, "The year four. They certainly knocked you about if you need to ask! Eighteen ought four, if that is of more assistance. Perhaps our surgeon should see you?"

"Thanks, but no," Mac hastily replied. From what he knew of nineteenth century medical treatment aboard ships most surgeons simply amputated—they weren't called 'sawbones' for nothing—or bled the patient to dissipate bad humours. Neither seemed particularly appealing.

He recounted a carefully edited version of events, skipping any reference to being a helicopter pilot from two-hundred years in the future—such matters best left unsaid to avoid hopelessly complicating his situation.

Eventually Baverstock seemed satisfied that Mac was not one of the Spanish crew but an unfortunate fellow officer seized by the slavers. His expression became more relaxed.

"Mister Barnes will look to your needs while I report to Captain Cathcart. Perhaps the previous owner's quarters will serve?" Mac thought he could detect the hint of a smile when Baverstock ended the interview.

Barnes led Mac to a low ceilinged cabin, not much cleaner than his previous cell. Daylight struggled its way through grimy gallery windows spanning the width of the stern. The cabin was sparsely furnished with an inelegant table and mismatched chair in front of the gallery windows, and several haphazardly arranged dilapidated arm chairs. On the port side, forward of the windows, was a small desk; the floor was covered by threadbare canvas that had been long ago painted in a checkerboard pattern.

When Barnes stationed an armed sailor outside the cabin door Mac knew he was clearly still a prisoner. Mac made a cursory search of the cabin, noting the absence of any charts, maps, papers or logbooks. They were probably in the sack he saw being placed in the boat when he was being escorted to the quarterdeck. What he really wanted was a long, very hot shower, but he knew that was impossible. He did find a straight razor and a jug filled with water. To describe the liquid as stagnant was optimistic, but his urge to get cleaned up outweighed his squeamishness. A greater obstacle was the sinister blade—he was a safety-razor man. With great trepidation, aided by the calm cove, he managed a rudimentary shave without injuring himself.

He pulled off his flight suit, then used his handkerchief for a rudimentary wash. He wasn't sure if he accomplished anything— the water began and ended the colour of dirt—but its coolness revived him. He was forced to wait in his skivvies until dry due to the lack of a towel, then dressed before asking the sentry to pass word for Barnes.

A knock signalled the midshipman's arrival a few minutes later.

Mac greeted him enthusiastically, "Mr. Barnes, I don't mean to be presumptuous, but I'd be most appreciative of the opportunity to meet with your Captain. I have knowledge of matters that may be of interest to him." He hoped that he had struck the right balance of formality while implying he might possess more information than he had so far divulged.

Barnes replied with a hint of scepticism, "Sir, I will pass your request to the Lieutenant when he returns."

Mac noted that Barnes also pronounced it 'lootenant' and wondered if it was some sort of naval thing.

Barnes continued, "There may be some passable food in the starboard locker yonder should you be hungry."

Mac realised that he was damn hungry, although looting somebody's personal space made him uneasy. He discovered some edible cheese, albeit after scraping off the surface mold, then immersed a piece of stale bread in some reasonably palatable red wine and cut a slice of cheese. He was fortunate not to notice the weevil lurking inside the bread. The food restored him, although the wine quickly reminded him of his skull's fragile state. He soon collapsed asleep on the cot.

BAVERSTOCK RETURNED TO *LA SEÑORA*, accompanied by Third Lieutenant, Edward Moore and sailors to replace those in the boarding party who were to return to *Lionheart*. Moore, with young Barnes his second-in-command, would take her to Jamaica where a prize court would decide her fate.

Ringle, currently in Kingston, would transport the prize crew back to *Lionheart* before the men could be assigned to other ships—always a danger in a navy constantly short of men.

Baverstock knocked on Mac's cabin door. When there was no response he rapped his knuckles against the bulkhead and opened the door.

Mac, groggy and vaguely aware of someone in his doorway, looked up at Baverstock. Asleep in his bunk at Corn Island had been a dream.

Baverstock sounded testy. "I am instructed to escort you to *Lionheart*. Do you desire to collect any personal possessions?"

Unfortunately, Mac was wearing the only items that he currently possessed. When he attempted to stand he felt as if the room shifted under him. He placed a hand against the wall to steady himself and ignored Baverstock's questioning look.

"Lucky for me that you arrived when you did. Were you looking for the... *La Señora de la Noche*, I believe that's her name? Or did you just stumble upon her?"

Baverstock's mood became more congenial. "We check here occasionally. This is the only island with reliable fresh water between the mainland and Jamaica and we have been lucky to pick up a few prizes replenishing theirs."

"I didn't see any sign of people until I was captured."

"Quinta Ruban's only sparsely inhabited" Baverstock replied. "Slavers and cutthroats occasionally visit. Other ships only risk stopping if they are desperate for water. Otherwise, they are better off making for Kingston or Caracas."

Mac, relieved that his questions had not roused any suspicion, knew his secret should be safe for now.

Baverstock stepped back from the doorway. "If you are ready, we should return to *Lionheart* as my duties are rather pressing." He paused to clear his throat, "Not to put too fine a point on it, but your situation is somewhat puzzling."

Mac replied with a chuckle, "No doubt." Despite their brief acquaintance, Mac sensed he might grow to like Baverstock.

On deck Baverstock continued, "I have asked the Captain to allow you to berth in the wardroom. Do I have your word as an officer that you will do nothing to bring my request into question?"

Mac nodded solemnly, "Of course."

Baverstock's expression visibly lightened. "Would you care to join us in the wardroom for the evening meal?"

Mac wondered what it had taken for Baverstock to extend the offer and replied, "Thank you, Lieutenant," making sure to use the 'loo' pronunciation, before continuing in what he hoped was a suitably formal tone, "Your invitation is accepted with my utmost thanks."

Once seated in the boat Mac asked, "Lieutenant, I make it to be about noon by the sun, is that correct?"

"Thirty minutes past, Captain, one bell of the Afternoon Watch just sounded." Baverstock lowered his voice to a near whisper, "Please call me Toby when we are in private."

Mac smiled and said, "My friends call me Mac. That would make it half past noon if I understand your time keeping system? May I ask what time we're eating?" He was on the verge of collapsing from exhaustion, his head was pounding, and he desperately needed sleep.

"The start of the Second Dog, or six o'clock, is our custom."

If the wardroom was typical of mess dinners he had attended a liberal supply of wine would encourage conversation. Mac almost revealed that his military used a twenty-four hour clock, which would make dinner at eighteen-hundred. Fortunately, he caught himself in time—that would have required an awful lot of explaining. He continued. "Nothing would give me greater pleasure. Could someone wake me thirty minutes before if I'm still be asleep? I wouldn't want to be late."

Mac followed Baverstock up the frigate's side and was briefly introduced to the other officers, although the Captain was notably absent. A sailor showed Mac to the third lieutenant's cabin. When Mac expressed concerns about displacing the lieutenant the sailor told him that the third was aboard *La Señora*.

The cabin, scarcely more than a cot in a broom closet sized space, was separated from the wardroom by flimsy wood screens that could be quickly removed before battle. At least the bed was clean and the ship lacked the putrid reek of *La Señora*, although *Lionheart* was definitely ripe with a powerful combination of odours from nearly three-hundred souls confined within her 35 by 150 foot hull.

Still in his flight suit, Mac was dead to the world within moments of laying down.

~6~

THE DINNER GUEST

BAVERSTOCK MADE IT CLEAR that it would behoove the members of the Wardroom to muster a festive meal despite limited resources. It had been ages since they had the chance to entertain anyone other than themselves. Each officer raided his personal stores to supplement the galley's usually lacklustre ship's fare. They even invited the two senior midshipmen, despite their inability to contribute personal stores to the meal—midshipmen barely had the means to feed themselves, let alone others.

An hour before the meal, Second Lieutenant George Sloane, their visitor scarcely twenty feet away, wondered aloud if an army captain held a higher rank than a navy lieutenant—pointing out that Captain Cathcart would be a major or colonel on land. They decided that one probably did but since they were currently aboard a ship, a Royal Navy ship at that, no conclusion was reached before Baverstock joined them.

Baverstock chuckled. "Pray remember, he is our guest and foreign to our customs. Would not seating him at the head of the table, and all that position demands, make him ill at ease? I do not believe he is one for putting on airs."

Toby winked at Woodman, then said, mirthful at his own wit, "I will lessen the burden of rank by abdicating my rightful throne for the evening. You will assume the head of the table. A neutral party, as it were." Seating at the table was rigidly determined by seniority: the most senior officer at the head and the least at the foot. Sometimes it fell to who had received promotion earlier if the ranks were equal—even a one-day difference would affect the seating order.

He continued in a more serious tone, "Mr. Woodman is a gifted conversationalist who will steer us clear of boring our guest." Toby knew, all too well, that naval officers tended to revert to matters of their profession at the expense of topics of more general interest.

MAC DID NOT AWAKE, despite the knock at his door and a plaintive "Sir?"

A more forceful knock and a louder "Sir," followed the first.

Mac groaned. Disoriented, he groped in the darkness for the door latch. He opened the door to a boy clutching an armful of clothes.

"Sir, it's time. First Lieutenant's compliments sir, he trusts that you'll find these suitable. May I bring you some hot water for your basin, sir?"

Mac managed to nod, then arranged the clothes on the cot while the lad fetched hot water. When the boy returned Mac grinned and extended his hand. "Andrew Appleton, my friends call me Mac. I don't believe I know your name."

"W...W...William Page, your servant, sir," the boy stammered, obviously ill at ease.

"Well, William Page, it's a pleasure to meet you," Mac responded with a genuine, broad smile. "Tell me, do you go by William or Bill?"

"Why, sir, Will since you ask."

"Tell me, Will, what brings a youngster aboard this fine ship? You can't be more than ten or eleven years old."

Will puffed himself up with pride, "I'll be twelve next month, sir. Me father served wi' Cap'n Cathcart 'til 'e was killed in th' year one. When me mother took sickly th' Cap'n agreed to make me a ship's boy. Th' Cap'n says he'll consider me for a midshipman's berth if I shows I'm a suitable prospec' for the Navy." Will's eyes widened at the mention of becoming an officer. He was fortunate to have Cathcart as a sponsor; without family influence there would have been little chance of him ever leaving the lower deck.

Mac said apologetically, "I'm afraid you must excuse me. It would be exceedingly bad manners if I was late for my first dinner. Furthermore, I'm famished and wouldn't want to miss out on my fare share." Mac chuckled at his play on words. "Perhaps we'll be able to talk more when time permits. I'd be most interested to hear about *Lionheart* and her exploits. I'm sure there've been many."

Mac finished washing after Will departed. Despite its meagre quantity, the hot water helped lessen some of his aches. *What I wouldn't give for a long, hot shower.* He selected a well-used pair of breeches and oft-mended silk stockings that covered his calves to the breeches' terminus. He added a cotton shirt and a blue jacket of rough, itchy wool that fit reasonably well. The coarse fabrics chafed against skin accustomed to modern materials. Beggars can't be choosers, he mused.

He wished there was a mirror, but was satisfied that he now at least looked a part of the crew. Although being dressed in the manner of the early nineteenth century did emphasise his dilemma. If he told anyone that he was from the future and flew through the air in a helicopter they would think him crazy and lock him in whatever passed for a padded cell aboard *Lionheart*, assuming they didn't simply chuck him overboard. Knowing what he did about sailors' superstitions, who would blame them?

Mac recalled the old TV series 'Star Trek' where the crew had to obey 'The Prime Directive'. If he revealed who he really was, would that give them knowledge of the future that could change the course of history? He resolved to keep his secret, at least for the time being. It was obviously possible to travel back through time—after all, he was aboard an English frigate in 1804—but was there a way to return? He set that question aside for the time being.

He was ravenous by the time quadruple chimes of the ship's bell signalled the evening meal. His last proper meal had been breakfast aboard the *Guadalcanal*. He had no idea of how long ago that was and was increasingly apprehensive about what sort of food would be served. From what he had read, shipboard fare was a monotonous diet of salt beef and dried peas that were boiled until almost edible. After months at sea, and no refrigeration, anything fresh was out of the question. Can I even stomach bread riddled with live weevils? Mac opened his cabin door when he heard the others entering the wardroom.

Toby, earlier reticence gone, greeted him warmly then introduced the others before indicating Mac's place at the table.

The meal started with a palatable soup of onions, barley and the ubiquitous salt beef, diced fine enough to overcome its leathery texture. Toby said that he had extracted the barley from the purser in return for a future favour. When the bread basket, containing nearly rock hard ship's biscuits, made its way around the table Mac couldn't help but notice the others carefully examining their biscuit before sharply rapping it against the edge of the table.

George Sloane glanced up, "Unusually fresh." The others snickered.

Mac, having deferred on a biscuit when first offered, now had to make a choice between the remaining pair. He really wanted to pick up each one and carefully examine it, but that would demonstrate extremely bad manners. Instead, he turned the basket slowly to search the biscuits for telltale weevil burrows. When he glanced up the others were watching and Toby appeared bemused. With a deadpan expression, Mac said, "Just choosing the lesser of two weevils."

Toby roared with laughter and slapped the table. Midshipman Smith sprayed a mouthful of soup across the table, fortunately missing his superiors.

The second course, a fresh fish hooked by one of the midshipmen, arrived on a gleaming silver platter to enthusiastic applause. The highlight, however, was a roast leg of mutton from the ship's last remaining sheep, complemented by a capon.

Smith, having indulged a little too freely in the grape, fell asleep midway through the mutton. His last words, "Oh thank you, sir, a capital wine," had followed the topping of his glass. He now snored fitfully.

A Spotted Dick completed the meal and elicited more favourable comments. Although Mac silently wondered about the rate of cardiovascular disease among those who regularly consumed suet puddings.

The steady supply of wine guaranteed free-flowing conversation throughout the evening. Woodman, as expected, tactfully and sometimes gallantly, intervened whenever the conversation turned too nautical. By the time the port decanter and cheese board completed their second circumnavigation of the table Mac was in absolute heaven—it still felt as if he were in the middle of some monumental dream.

He expressed a keen interest in the navy but could not reveal that it came from reading about it two-hundred years in the future. Instead, he told them that he once considered a naval career but circumstances steered him on another course. His nautical turn of phrase was well-received. In truth he had decided that flying, another taboo matter tonight, was a quicker and more comfortable way to travel.

Mac raised his glass, then waited a moment for the others follow, and said, "To absent friends." He knew that this was the naval way of acknowledging absent shipmates while avoiding mentioning death, another taboo subject. Despite an enthusiastic, "Hear, hear," amid clinks of glasses, Mac felt a twinge of sadness. Strained relations lingered between America and Britain following the American Revolution; in another eight years they would again be at war. What would he do if he was still here?

Mac, intent on fabricating how he had become stranded on Quinta Ruban, made a slip of the tongue when he disclosed that he had been born in Canada. He barely avoided exclaiming,

"Shit!" when he realised his error. Canada was still a British colony and his involvement with the Americans would raise questions.

An awkward silence followed as the others exchanged glances. Sloane looked pleadingly at Toby who turned to Woodman for rescue.

Woodman said, "Meaning no offense, but we thought you were an American."

Mac paused to clear a tennis ball sized lump in his throat. He hoped he wasn't turning beet red and that his voice would not betray his anxiety. Fortunately, his previous slurred mention of Saskatoon seemed forgotten.

He replied, "None taken and a very good question. I'll try to satisfy your inquiry to the best of my ability," then went on to explain that he was a captain in the York Foot—hoping no one could contradict that claim. "My uncle, in Kingston..." He almost said Ontario but caught himself, "Upper Canada, not Jamaica you understand, is a close friend of the Governor. When they discussed the ongoing tensions between England and America and the threat posed to Canada they thought that contact between Canada and the Americans might be beneficial. My name was put forth as a possible liaison. I'd guess that it's safe to say there isn't an abundance of goodwill between the American and British governments."

There were several repressed snickers and throat clearings in response.

Mac continued, "The Governor made discreet enquiries of London, but I heard nothing more for nearly two years until I was quietly appointed Liaison Officer. I'm currently involved in investigating the Spanish situation in the Caribbean as it pertains to both British and American interests following Haiti's revolt and recent independence. I regret my orders prevent me from discussing specifics." The hint of clandestine activities and the required secrecy, mixed with a smidgen of family influence, seemed to satisfy the officers who made no further enquiries.

They completed dinner in relaxed conversation while *Lionheart* and *La Señora* continued westward at a steady five knots.

CATHCART DINED ALONE in his cabin—rank demanded that he remain aloof, isolated even—then paced the quarterdeck's windward side in solitude. Evening was his favourite time of day—the men were at ease, his endless paperwork had been attended to, which gave him time to ponder other matters. Amiable sounds from the dinner below floated up through open hatchways. When he overheard Mac's compliments about *Lionheart* and his toast at the conclusion of the wardroom dinner he decided that perhaps Toby's initial trust in the stranger was correct. Cathcart decided to break the isolation of command and host the officers at the first opportunity.

Post Captain Ulysses Cathcart was old for a frigate captain. If he wished he could have command of a seventy-four gun ship-of-the-line, but in his heart he was a frigate man through and through. So, when he was asked by the Admiral, 'As an immense favour,' to command *Lionheart* and her small squadron—something younger captains would kill for—he had difficulty concealing his glee. Satisfied that the dinner had gone well, Cathcart returned to his cabin.

TOBY BAVERSTOCK AND GEORGE SLOANE were anticipating a turn around the gangways linking the quarter and fore decks when the duty midshipman approached and said to Baverstock, "The Captain's compliments, sir. Would you care to join him in his cabin?"

The midshipman shifted his gaze to Sloane, "The Captain's compliments, sir. Do you oblige this interruption and take the watch?" Despite the interrogative form, both requests were orders.

Sloane replied, "My compliments and duty to the Captain. It would give me pleasure."

Toby struggled not to grin. If he had consumed as much drink as Sloane, the last thing he would want to do was stand watch. Toby tugged his uniform straight and made sure his jacket was free of dinner remains.

Two minutes later Cathcart greeted his trusted subordinate. "Do sit you down, Toby. May I tempt you with a glass of this most capital brandy?"

Toby inwardly questioned the wisdom of more drink knowing that he had the next watch in less than ninety minutes. The absent Third Luff meant that he and Sloane would stand watch and watch—four hours on, four hours off—until the prize crew returned. He put on a brave face, "Why thank you, sir, that is most kind and will do nicely to settle a vast dinner."

"Now, Toby." Cathcart paused to close the overhead skylight to keep their conversation from reaching the attentive ears of Oakes, the helmsman, standing directly above. "What do you make of our visitor?"

Toby explained Mac's secret involvement with the Americans.

Cathcart, who once thought that being at sea would insulate him from distasteful politics, mumbled, "Those damn politicos always have their fingers in the pot!"

Toby nodded agreement, then continued. "He is surprisingly well read in naval affairs and was intrigued by Hamilton's *Surprise* and their exploits cutting out *Hermione*; asked had I ever met Hamilton? His face positively lights up whenever we talk about an action or the handling of the ship. I believe he is genuinely interested in *Lionheart* as an entity, a being as it were. Never has he enquired about our current duties. I suspect that is likely due to the circumspect nature of his mission."

Cathcart swirled the brandy in his glass. He contemplated the amber liquid for a few moments and said, "But I am puzzled by his clothing and manner of speech. Would you not say they are somewhat, if not quite, unusual?"

Toby suppressed a laugh, "Sir, he has spent his entire life in the colonies. I should not wonder that he has picked up some of the mannerisms of those ruffian woodsmen that inhabit the forests. We know the colonials do not share our sense of proper dress. As we learned during the war, many rebel soldiers did not bother with a proper uniform. They seem to have some vague notion that clothing should serve a more utilitarian function. Some seem very casual, even cavalier, in the way they dress unless the occasion is indisputably formal. He told me his uniform is one of only a few designed by that Benjamin Franklin fellow and are being tested by certain officers. You will recall Franklin experimented with lightning. Reportedly a brilliant fellow, but no more so, I am sure, than an Englishman."

Cathcart nodded in agreement as Toby continued, "I find the colonials' accent grates on the ears. At times his manner of speech is difficult to comprehend. Although he speaks quickly and merges words I do not believe we should hold that against him."

Cathcart smiled at Toby's description. "I have a great deal of faith in your judgement of the human spirit, that is to say, what makes a man to behave the way he does. I take it that you do not believe him to be a spy, or perhaps an agent provocateur working to unsettle us in some manner?"

"In all the heavens, no, sir. How could he possibly have foreseen that we would capture those brigands holding him? Having said that, I suspect that he may not have revealed some details of his personal life and would not be the first to seek refuge in foreign waters from a sheriff, outraged father or vengeful husband."

Cathcart chuckled. He knew of several officers, and at least one aboard *Lionheart*, who were in those circumstances and said, "And who are we to judge?"

Toby continued, "If you are asking if I trust him to conduct himself honourably while on board I would stake my career on him."

"And well you might be doing."

Toby was visibly hurt by the comment and Cathcart immediately regretted his warning which sounded more ominous than he intended.

In an effort to make amends, Cathcart offered a slight smile and continued, "I believe I should like to meet your new friend. Perhaps he would care to join us for coffee, say the middle of the forenoon watch if duties permit? I would welcome your presence to provide a second opinion on anything that we may discuss."

Cathcart glanced at Toby's empty glass, then pushed his chair back, "Until morning then."

LIONHEART **GREETED EVERY DAY** with guns loaded and run out to prevent being surprised by an enemy lurking in the predawn gloom. Thirty minutes later, the horizon clear of other ships, *La Señora* dipped her ensign in salute and altered course for Jamaica while *Lionheart* resumed her patrol. *La Señora* carried a lead-weighted canvas pouch containing Cathcart's report on her capture, additional intelligence gathered from the brig's crew, and instructions for *Ringle's* rendezvous with the frigate. It also contained a confidential memorandum to the admiral regarding one Captain Appleton.

Mac slept through the drum rattle of call to quarters at two bells of the morning watch—0430 if he had awakened. The thrum of several hundred feet moving about, not to mention the din of the guns being run out, failed to arouse him; nor did the clamour of the guns being bowsed following the lookout's ritual report, "Deck there, grey goose at a mile. All clear." Even the deck pump's rhythmic clank, accompanied by the grind of holystones as sailors scrubbed the deck to a bone white, did not wake him. Nor did the masthead lookout's, "Sail ho," at seven chimes of the ship's bell.

He finally stirred to a vague consciousness at two strikes on the bell in the Forenoon watch, or 0830. He struggled to overcome the exhaustion clinging to him like a heavy blanket, his eyes adjusting to the feeble light seeping in around his door, and glanced around the tiny cabin. He had not been dreaming. He slipped his legs over the edge of the cot, inadvertently nudging the thin door with his toes while searching for his boots.

A moment later there was a gentle knock on the door. "Will 'ere, sir. May I fetch some hot water for your shave? I won't be a moment."

Mac replied, his voice raspy, "Thank you Will, that would be most appreciated."

"An' I'll fetch you some coffee if'n y'like, sir," the youngster offered enthusiastically.

Will returned a few minutes later with steaming water and a mug of near scalding, thick, dark coffee. Mac blew on the coffee before taking a tentative sip. Stronger in flavour than he expected, the caffeine-laden elixir wound its way through every fog-clogged capillary to awaken the deepest recesses of his brain.

"What's happening this morning?" Mac eventually asked, hoping it was morning. He was wrapped in a blanket, preparing to shave, the hot face cloth stripping away the last vestiges of sleep.

"Well, sir, *Ringle* is comin' up 'and ov'r fist. A most pretty sight an' y' should hurry lest y' miss 'er 'proach."

Mac hurried shaving and nicked himself in his haste. He donned his donated clothes and rushed to the deck, closely followed by Will.

"Where is she?" Mac asked.

"Port, sir." A moment later Will pleaded "Forward, sir!"

Mac had been vainly looking astern.

Ringle was indeed a sight, carrying every sail that would draw while she ran down to *Lionheart* who lay hove-to.

Will energetically pointed to the string of coloured flags dancing from *Ringle's* windward halliard. "Dispatches. She fired a signal gun an' broke out our number at first sighting. Mus' be important."

VERBAL ORDERS FROM THE ADMIRAL—the urgency of the mission did not allow time for written—directed Lieutenant Commander Silas Wilson to find *Lionheart* with all haste and inform him that two English merchant ships had been captured and taken to Puerto Blanco, where they were awaiting escort by a pair of Spanish frigates en route from Caracas.

Wilson knew he must carry every stitch *Ringle* would bear. Not finding *Lionheart* in time, the remainder of his career would be spent in command of a water hoy—if he was lucky.

Minutes before *Ringle* was to ship her anchor, an Admiralty packet stormed into Kingston harbour with urgent dispatches from England. France and Spain had signed an alliance on 9 October—war loomed. Wilson received a hastily written warning in the Admiral's own hand.

Six hours out of Kingston, *Ringle* sighted a ship heading toward Jamaica. Wilson recognised her for what she was: a Spanish brig and ordered *Ringle's* guns run out. He maintained the windward advantage despite the British ensign fluttering above the Spanish flag indicating that the stranger was a prize. He had used that ploy himself.

When the brig replied to *Ringle's* challenge with that day's private signal and the two ships were close enough for their captains to hail each other through speaking trumpets Wilson, the senior officer, ordered the prize's temporary commander, Lieutenant Moore, to cross; but Moore did not have sufficient men to both man a boat and guard the prisoners.

Instead, Moore and Wilson met in *La Señora's* tiny cabin which still reeked from her career as a slaver. They agreed *Ringle* would supply a prize crew to get *La Señora* to Kingston then transport *Lionheart's* people back to the frigate.

Wilson kept the deck while *Ringle* charged through the night under a heavy press of canvas until doubled lookouts spotted sails a few minutes before seven bells of the morning watch. Wilson, almost certain that they belonged to *Lionheart*, maintained the weather-gage in the event he had to run from an enemy. When there was no response to his initial signal, possibly due to a lingering haze, he ordered a signal gun to draw attention to the signal flags fluttering from his rigging.

RINGLE **WAS TWO MILES DISTANT** when Mac stepped onto a deck cluttered with sailors reorganising cordage after the frigate abruptly heaved to. Cathcart was conferring with both lieutenants on the windward side of the quarterdeck.

Mac watched *Ringle* close to one mile, then less than half a mile. With no reduction in sail and her lee scuppers awash, she appeared to be steering directly for *Lionheart's* mainmast and continued unchecked to within seventy-five yards. He subconsciously tightened his grip on the railing, certain he was about to witness the seafaring version of a midair collision.

Ringle abruptly veered to starboard—on an opposite course parallel to *Lionheart*. The lithe schooner's mainsail and mizzen top gaffs dropped like stones and her topsails disappeared in a flash. With the fluid motion of a dancer performing a pirouette, her helm was thrown over while her jib was hauled across to the opposite side. She spun like a top, turning in barely more than her own length, and glided to a stop under backed sails, not more than a long arm's reach from *Lionheart*.

Fighter jocks, Mac thought, doesn't matter what you put them in.

Cathcart, whose voice was said to carry a sea mile in a gale and needed only to speak in a loud whisper to converse with *Ringle's* youthful commander, bellowed, "You'll do well to consider my paint work and spars, sir."

Was the corner of Cathcart's mouth beginning to form a smile when he abruptly turned his face away from Wilson? Despite the stern admonition, Mac suspected that Cathcart was having difficulty keeping a straight face. *Perhaps Cathcart had attempted the same manoeuvre when he was Wilson's age—possibly with a less favourable outcome?*

Wilson, a canvas pouch securely wrapped in oilskins held firmly against his side, disappeared into Cathcart's cabin. An expectant quiet descended over the ship.

Mac worried about meeting Cathcart. Eventually there would be awkward questions about who he was and how he arrived here. He also knew that he would quickly grow restless just sitting around—admittedly, this wasn't quite the all-expenses paid sea cruise he had dreamed of. He needed to be active and involved—even if he felt like hell following the crash landing and time aboard *La Señora*—while he waited for the opportunity to return to his own time.

"Lieutenant Baverstock," Mac said with sombre formality befitting the crowded deck, "may I have a word at your convenience, sir? It's nothing urgent, and I don't want to interrupt your duties."

"Most happy to oblige, Appleton, if you could give me to the turn of the glass. I am afraid coffee with the Captain is delayed until he has dealt with the dispatches." Toby completed his duties and motioned toward the quarterdeck lee rail where they could talk privately. He reverted to casual familiarity, "You have a question, Mac?"

"I feel as if I'm a guest aboard a yacht," Mac answered. "I sleep through most of the morning, then lounge about while waiting to have coffee with the Captain." When he suggested being given some work Toby was visibly surprised. Mac emphasised that he was not at all a sailor and made no claim to being one.

Toby replied, "Your offer is unexpected, and most gracious. We remain short of our full complement, even with the return of the prize crew, and more muscle is always helpful. Would you not find such labours demeaning? After all, you do hold the rank of Captain. Surely captains are not required to do such menial chores?" He added with a broad grin, "Even in the York Foot!"

"That's true," Mac chuckled in response, "but I'd be happy to lend a hand if it would be useful."

Toby excused himself, then returned a few minutes later. "You are assigned to the after-guard for the time being. I hope you will not find this position distasteful, but it requires the least training."

Mac was grateful he hadn't been assigned to clean the heads given his lack of experience. His duties would largely involve hauling the mizzen driver from one side to the other when the ship tacked.

Toby introduced him to the mate in charge of the after-guard, then pulled the man aside. Mac couldn't hear what was said, but Toby was the only one who spoke, and that was briefly.

Mac began the difficult task of learning his duties and the names of the myriad equipment and maze of running rigging aboard a full-rigged ship. He lent a hand with a will and never once asserted any privilege of rank. A ship's boy interrupted, summoning Mac to Cathcart's cabin. Mac tugged his clothes straight as Harold Snoad whispered to one of his mates, "Glad it's 'im not me, mate. Oi'd be in mortal fear of putting a foot wrong in there." Snoad gave a knowing tilt of his head toward the cabin.

Toby, waiting on the upper deck, led the way to Cathcart's lair, protected by the ever present scarlet coated marine guarding the door. The sentry stamped to attention and rapped his musket butt against the deck before bawling, "Firs' Lootenan' an' the gen'l'mun, sah."

Eames, Cathcart's ever suspicious clerk, opened the door and lead them through the narrow pantry dominated by a gun, then into the stern cabin which was similarly cluttered by a pair of the nine foot long behemoths.

Cathcart, seated at his table, barely glanced up. "Be with you in a moment. Do sit you down." He signed a sheet then handed it to Eames who sanded and folded it. Eames then applied a molten wax seal and placed the document in a heavy canvas pouch before handing it to Wilson.

Cathcart looked up, "Please, Toby, do introduce our visitor." The formality of the introductions dispensed with, Cathcart extended his hand to Wilson, who was forced to keep his over six-foot height bowed beneath the deck beams. After wishing Wilson a safe and quick journey Cathcart called Eames to serve coffee. Cathcart motioned for Mac and Toby to sit in the chairs arranged in front of his desk and said, "I trust the coffee is to your taste Captain Appleton?"

Although the coffee was bitter Mac answered, "Delicious, sir." Near boiling, it threatened to scald the skin from his hand through the tin mug. Unsure of where to set the mug down—his chair had no arms—he shuffled the mug from hand to hand. Even resting it on his knee soon caused discomfort.

Cathcart continued, "Captain, I understand that you became marooned on Quinta Ruban before being captured by that band of brigands. You are lucky to have survived their care. I trust that you have recovered."

Mac nodded, "Please, sir, call me Mac when the situation permits. The use of my rank in my present situation seems pretentious." He repeated his concocted story leading up to his liaison position which required a hurried recall of Caribbean history from the bit of online research he had done on Corn Island when he was posted there.

He continued, "I'm sure that you have questions about my presence. I'll try to explain as best I can but keep in mind that I'm merely a captain and a foreigner who is not completely privy to America's objectives. I understand that after the Haitian revolt the Americans believe there may be a potential threat to their recent Louisiana Purchase territory, perhaps involving New Orleans or their other Gulf of Mexico settlements. Corn Island might provide an ideal base from which to monitor and, if necessary, counter such threats."

He took a sip of his coffee which had cooled to slightly less than molten lava. "As for Quinta Ruban, I still don't recall exactly how I came to land there during the storm as it suddenly appeared out of nowhere. I was soon captured by the crew of *La Señora*—the rest of her name escapes me. I believe you know the rest. Do you know why they didn't kill me before your arrival?"

"Well, Captain." Cathcart paused, "Excuse me, Mac. Fortunately they believed you to be an English nobleman because of your strange attire and of sufficient means to generate a ransom."

Mac nodded. He had been expecting questions about his clothing. "As to my dress, it's merely my working uniform, as opposed to a dress uniform. I'm afraid it's in a rather disreputable state after crawling about on the beach and my subsequent confinement in that vile cell. I must clean it at the first opportunity and return my borrowed clothing to the rightful owners."

Cathcart sat silently for a few seconds before responding. "I must say that I am most impressed with your forthrightness. I do not want to be remiss mentioning that I understand you volunteered to work while aboard my barky. A meritorious offer if I do say; there was certainly no expectation of such."

"Thank you, sir," Mac replied. "I've much to learn about life aboard your ship and everyone has been most understanding of my limitations."

Toby, silent throughout the questions, gave an almost imperceptible nod in response to Cathcart's glance. Mac had sensed an unspoken bond between Cathcart and Toby and guessed Toby was more than a subordinate.

Cathcart continued, "While I am most appreciative of your comments there is a matter of some delicacy concerning your presence which we must discuss. I trust that you understand that what I have to say is only to establish a clarity of thought between us, and is in no way meant to be disrespectful. As you know we are at war with France and may be required to fight at any moment. We also may soon be at war with Spain. For the time being England and America are at peace, and I wish that we remain so. Unfortunately, mere sailors and soldiers such as ourselves know not the machinations our politicos have in play.

"My first question to you concerns battle. If we must fight, what do you wish your role to be? Assuming, of course, that such a battle does not directly involve America. Please understand that you are perfectly free to declare yourself a noncombatant if you desire. Strictly speaking you are a British subject, although this is complicated by your involvement with the Americans. To speak plainly, I have some concerns about that arrangement, but Toby assures me that you are trustworthy."

Mac's mind spun. He had not expected that question and paused for a moment. "Sir, I have no desire to partake of Spanish hospitality again and would willingly help defend *Lionheart*. However, I must warn you that my knowledge of naval warfare is woefully inadequate, being limited to reading. Your guns are much larger than anything I've ever fired."

Lord, I'm getting too good at avoiding the truth, Mac thought as he resisted the temptation to say that his Apache could sink her with a single missile without *Lionheart* ever firing a shot. Instead, he allowed that although not familiar with the sea cutlass, boarding pike and other weapons, he was a good shot. "Perhaps a musket or one of your swivels would be more suited to my abilities." This last statement was closer to the truth, although either might prove to be a bit of a challenge as he had never handled a muzzle loader.

Cathcart nodded in silent agreement.

Mac continued. "If we're required to fight against the Americans I request that I be considered a neutral until the battle is resolved."

"Well spoken, sir. A man after my own heart." Cathcart stood, motioning for them to remain seated, and poured three generous bumpers of brandy.

Cathcart lifted his glass, "A toast then. To the damnation of our enemies." The fine crystal sang when their glasses touched. "I sense that we could become good friends, time and circumstance permitting. I would be most pleased if you call me Ulysses when we are in private."

Cathcart shifted his gaze to Toby, "We shall exercise the guns. Pass the word for the carpenter to fashion floating targets." He cast a glance toward Mac, "Also something suitable for muskets. Let us see if our friend's aim is as good as he claims." Cathcart winked at Toby. "Perhaps he might be persuaded to place a small wager on the outcome?"

Mac, currently not in possession of anything with which to wager, was stumped. "Sir, I don't have the means to place even the smallest wager."

Cathcart smiled disarmingly. "Well, sir, you do possess what every jack-tar possesses in the forenoon—the prospect of his evening tot. What say you? A tot for your shot?"

Mac suspected Cathcart had set him up and laughed, "That sounds reasonable and is certainly within my ability to pay. Of course I accept."

Cathcart did not intend to let him off so easily. "Just to keep things interesting the wager will also include your messmates' tots."

Any suspicion vanished. Mac knew he had been set up. "Sir, nicely done. Sunk before I even fire a shot, so to speak." Grinning, he shrugged in resignation before Cathcart dismissed them.

The marine sentry's stamp to attention still echoed in the passageway. "Damn, Toby," Mac exclaimed in a hushed voice. "He set me up like a sitting duck. Never knew what hit me."

Toby slapped him on the back. "Just be thankful this was done in jest. He has done the same to an enemy ship on more than one occasion and with much deadlier consequences. It is to be hoped that you are as good as you claim. Your messmates may not take kindly to losing their rum."

Toby lowered his voice to a near whisper, "By the way, you made quite the impression. I was the only person aboard allowed to call him Ulysses, and that not until the end of our first cruise."

~7~

SHOOTING OFF ONE'S MOUTH

WHEN MAC TOLD his messmates about the wager during the noon meal the men said nothing; eventually George Fairbrother broke the silence. Seemingly unsure of how to address a foreign officer who had volunteered to be a common sailor, Fairbrother stared at the middle of the mess table. "Meanin' no disrespecks, sor, but be ye a good shot?"

Mac, who had memorised their names when first introduced, replied, "Well George, I've never fired one of your muskets but I'm a quick study and a good shot with weapons I know although I'd appreciate a few pointers before I embarrass myself completely." He laughed, "I'm looking forward to receiving my tot as much as the next man. Besides, I wouldn't want to put a hole through our lion's heart and send us all to the bottom." The men laughed at his play on words.

Fairbrother assured him, "Ain't to worry, sor, Frog eighteen poun' balls ain't done it."

Josh Barnstaple said, "Least there ain't no Frog or Dago shootin' back t' upset yer aim. Use the 'ammocks to give yerself a steadier shot. Ain't no harm in that. Our lobsters shoots that way."

Before Mac could get any more advice, the drummer's rattle of 'Hearts of Oak' called them to quarters. By the time he reached the deck the carpenter and his mates were ready to release the great guns' first target—a five foot square construct of empty barrels lashed together and topped by a crudely painted French tricolour fashioned from scrap canvas.

Cathcart strongly believed in the benefits of regularly firing the guns, rather than the dumb show of loading and running out drills. Exercises not only included tests of accuracy but also how quickly a crew could fire, reload, and fire again. Cathcart always acquired an additional supply of powder and shot from personal funds—the Navy Board frowned on the frivolous use of its supplies, even if it ensured that crews were well trained. Cathcart's investment had paid off. His men could hammer an enemy with three accurate broadsides in less than two minutes.

For now, Mac and the after-guard were mere spectators until called upon to change course. Small arms fire would provide the last event of the afternoon's entertainment and was eagerly anticipated. Word of the stakes had flashed through the ship within minutes of Mac informing his messmates.

The target towed safely astern, *Lionheart* tacked under fighting canvas, her main and fore courses brailed up to reduce the chance of a piece of burning wad igniting a sail. The reduced sail also lowered her speed, provided a steady platform for the guns, and gave a clear view forward. The slight swell, combined with the wind, imparted a gentle roll which added a challenge to the gun captains as they sighted their weapon.

The port battery would engage first after Cathcart shaped a course to place *Lionheart* a cable length, two-hundred yards, from the target. Each gun would fire independently until all the guns had fired, or the target was destroyed. The carpenter and his mates were preparing a similar target for the starboard battery when the larboard bow chaser unleashed its ball with a sharp bang.

The sound, carried away forward by the wind, was not as loud as Mac had imagined, although he could feel the deck tremble from the discharge. Tendrils of yellow smoke entwined the jib before dispersing on the breeze. The ball splashed into the water thirty yards short and ten yards to the left of the target. Mac wondered if the gun captain had misjudged the range or fired before the top of the up-roll.

Lionheart, rated as a thirty-six gun frigate by her complement of eighteen pounders, also carried a pair of long barreled nine-pound bow chasers and four twenty-four pound carronades, a pair each on her forecastle and quarterdeck. The carronades, affectionately known as 'smashers' for their ability to pulverise an enemy from short range, would not fire today.

Less than a minute later the first eighteen fired with a roar more like the sound Mac had expected while the deck trembled beneath his feet. The ball produced a plume of water ten yards to the right but at almost perfect distance. Of course, Mac thought, since the target was only five feet across, either shot would have struck home if it had been another ship.

After the second eighteen fired Mac loosened the bandana tied around his head and removed the piece of gun wadding protecting his left ear. "Sir," he said to Toby in a formal tone because they were on deck, "would it be possible for me to observe the guns from a closer distance? I promise to stay out of the way."

Toby replied with equal formality, "I certainly have no objection, Appleton. I will check with the Captain as it is an unusual request. Remain at your station while I do so."

Guns three and four nicked the target, their crews cheering when splinters fluttered in the air.

Toby returned. "The Captain agrees but has voiced concerns about your safety. These brutes have a prodigious recoil and you could easily lose a foot or limb if you are not careful. Come with me, I will introduce you to Art Chambers, captain of the number seven larboard gun known as Great Harry. He is a fine shot and has my money to destroy the target. He will give you a quick lesson concerning our artillery. Pay particular heed to his instructions."

Introductions were under way when guns five and six fired in nearly deafening unison. They leapt back against their restraining tackles like crazed beasts. Mac felt the ship shudder and heel from their recoil. A cloud of bitter smoke filled the ship's waist and tore at Mac's lungs, throat and eyes. He couldn't imagine what a full broadside must be like when these behemoths fired simultaneously. Even a rolling broadside would produce a small earthquake for fifteen seconds or more.

"Here, sir, make sure you stand exactly thus." Chambers shouted as he ensured Mac was safely ensconced before resuming his post behind 'Harry'. Chambers crouched at the gun's breech and squinted along the barrel. Mac leaned forward to watch the target ease into view through the open gun port. He knew that Chambers was gauging the ship's roll for the precise moment to fire. Chambers, in one fluid motion, stepped outside the carriage's recoil and tugged the firing lanyard. Mac saw a spurt of flame when the flint ignited the priming charge. The gun leapt back in a roar of defiance as the solid iron ball, selected by Chambers for its perfect roundness, flew from the muzzle.

Mac peered over the rolled hammocks to watch the ball's flight, much as a golfer follows his shot. A black blob flew unerringly to the precise centre of the target which disintegrated in a cloud of splinters.

The port battery ceased firing amid loud cheering and jibes directed at the idle starboard gun crews. After 'Harry's hit there wasn't enough left of the target for the remaining guns.

Cathcart boomed, "Release the second target. Prepare to wear ship." The deck came alive as sailors ran to their stations. Mac sprinted to his post as the officers and warrants issued a stream of orders in preparation to come about for the starboard battery's turn.

"Mr. Sloane," Cathcart called to the lieutenant in charge of the starboard battery, "pass the word. There's an extra tot for the gun which can best 'Harry'."

Lionheart completed her turn, and Mac again obtained permission to observe close at hand. This time he moved from gun to gun, standing clear of both men and recoil. His ears rang, despite the protective wadding and bandana. The starboard guns achieved several minor hits, but none inflicted fatal damage to the target. After the starboard number seven had fired, there still remained considerably more of their target than of the larboard's. The extra tot went to 'Great Harry', accompanied by cheering and good-natured catcalls from both sides.

Cathcart ordered the small arms target, a lightly weighted sealed cask, released. A scrap of canvas, about two feet square and bearing a crudely painted bull's-eye, adorned a stubby stick on top of the cask. *Lionheart* continued several hundred yards past the target before Cathcart ordered *Lionheart* to wear. Instead of tacking, with the bow of the ship crossing through the wind, wearing kept the wind astern and avoided 'missing stays' should the bow not cross the eye of the wind.

After sharpshooters took up firing positions along the hammocks Mac watched them shoot with intense interest. He called out, "I'll fire last. Any laughter at my poor shooting might throw off their aim." This elicited chuckles from the men.

Mac thought back to his boyhood on the prairies where he had hunted ducks, albeit illegally, with an ancient single shot 22-calibre rifle. He could quite handily take a bird on the wing while his friends struggled for a hit using a shotgun—but that was with his feet planted firmly on unwavering ground. Today would be complicated—he and the target could well be moving in opposite directions. He tested the balance of the heavy musket, only vaguely aware of the sounds of the others firing. When he looked up, the target was aft of the mainmast; sailors intently watched him as he made his final preparations.

Remember to fully cock the hammer, wouldn't want to go off half-cocked! Mac braced the heavy barrel on the rolled hammocks and visualised the musket ball's flight. His mind spun with calculations: the ship's movements, the target's movements, how the wind would affect the accuracy of the half-inch diameter ball.

The officers squinted through their telescopes at the canvas target.

Baamm. The musket kicked against Mac's shoulder. A hole appeared in the target barely a thumb's length to the right of dead centre.

Cathcart uttered in a stage whisper that carried at least half the length of the deck, "Perhaps a lucky shot." He called out, "Appleton, would you care to try your luck from the maintop?"

The challenge—loud enough for the entire Caribbean to hear—left Mac no choice but to accept. "Happy to oblige, sir," Mac stoically replied. "May I request Mr. Barnes' assistance in getting my weapon to the top? Being a landlubber, I wouldn't want such a fine weapon, or myself, to get wet." He had an ulterior motive in his request: he was becoming increasingly apprehensive about the possibility of missing the target and the reaction of his messmates. Cathcart did not seem to fathom the real reason and agreed.

"Mr. Barnes," Mac confided as they climbed the ratlines, "I hope you have some sage words of advice. I fear my enthusiasm may have overtaken my ability."

"Not to worry, sir. Take your time climbing, wouldn't want you to be out of breath once we reach our perch. The Cap'n must come about before you shoot, so there's time to get you settled."

Mac felt his body pressed against the shroud as *Lionheart* heeled while tacking. He paused to catch his breath at the upper end of the lower shrouds while Barnes, almost inverted, chose the sailors' way into the top which required hanging backward from the lower shrouds and swinging outward to grab the upper shrouds. Mac chose the other route through the lubber's hole—a convenient opening for those less skilled in the art of ascending rigging.

Positioned on the small platform, Mac glanced down to the water, a dizzying sixty feet below, and loaded the musket. Mac hoped Barnes attributed his slow progress to being methodical rather than inept.

They waited until the yards were trimmed and the ship settled on her new course. The view was breathtaking—the sea and sky dazzling hues of blue. Azure water, flecked with white caps, was scribed by the wake's perfect semicircle as *Lionheart* completed a flawless turn to bring the target onto her port bow, half a cable ahead.

"Now, sir," Barnes ignored Mac's request to call him by his first name and instructed, "wait for the target to be directly abeam, probably fifty or sixty yards range. Consider that your ball will drop as it flies and we are sixty feet above the target." As the target approached in seeming slow motion, Mac tried to visualise the ball's trajectory, brought the musket to full cock, braced its butt against his shoulder and the upper shroud, aimed, and squeezed the trigger as if he had done it a thousand times before. The hole in the flag from his second shot nearly overlapped that of his first. He laughed aloud and glanced down at the quarterdeck.

Toby lowered his telescope, gestured toward the target, and said something to Cathcart. Mac could not hear what was said, but could see that Cathcart did not reply. Toby waited several seconds, then edged away from Cathcart, who continued to study the target through his telescope. After what seemed an eternal silence, Cathcart called in a voice load enough to shake the rigging. "Well done! I believe your messmates are quite thirsty."

"Thank you, sir." Mac replied. He patted the gun's barrel and shouted back, "I believe she sights a touch to the right." Mac winked to Barnes and whispered, "Now they won't know for sure if I'm really good or just lucky."

Toby would later confide that Cathcart's silence was the first in anyone's memory.

Mac was the hero of the day when the after-guard received their evening tot. Instead of the usual half English pint of rum mixed with a quart of water served twice a day, tonight was a double tot, a full pint of rum, as reward for Mac's prowess with the musket. Unaccustomed to the sheer quantity of alcohol involved, Mac cautiously sipped—despite his caution his head soon swam. Unsure if he was slurring his speech, he turned to John Slade. "John, I'm puzzled by your method of time keeping aboard a ship. Your day seems to be divided into watches but I understand there are seven. This doesn't make sense to me as twenty-four hours cannot be evenly divided by seven."

"Why that's because of the Dogs, you see." John swallowed another mouthful of grog and continued, "The First Watch begins four hours afore midnight. Midnight signals the Middle or Graveyard of four hours, then four hours each for the Morning and Forenoon, followed by four of the Afternoon. Finally we have the First and Second Dogs, which are but two hours each to complete our day and bring us back to the First Watch."

"Ah, that makes sense now," Mac nodded. "What do the bells mean then?"

John continued. "One bell signifies the passing of the first half hour, two bells a full hour, and so on until the next watch. Thus each watch is eight bells in duration. The Dogs being leashed together as they are." John, and several others, laughed heartily at his quip. "Leashed together," John repeated for good measure before concluding, "the ringing of the watch bell is timed by the half-hour glass on the quarterdeck."

A breathless messenger interrupted the impromptu class in naval timekeeping and knuckled has forehead in salute to Mac. "Begging your pardon, sir. The Captain sends his regards and requests you attend his cabin at seven bells." The youngster added, "That would be in about fifteen minutes, sir."

Mac didn't bother to explain that he was now fully versed in naval timekeeping.

~8~

DOUBLE TROUBLE

LIONHEART **SHOULDERED ASIDE** another wave as she settled on her new course of southeast by south following the gun exercises. Cathcart ordered every plain sail she could carry—despite the fine furrow already being carved across the wave flecked azure water. He turned to Toby, "I perceive a half reef on the forecourse and full reef on the fore tops'l will better suit." Cathcart sensed that the forward sails were pushing the forefoot down, thus slowing *Lionheart*, and ordered the two helmsmen manning the double-spoked wheel, "Ease off half a point. Let her run."

Two minutes later the logman enthusiastically reported, "Twelve, sir."

Mac felt the deck's pitching motion lessen—replaced by a steady tremble as if *Lionheart* was excited by her newfound speed. Despite his short time aboard, Mac knew that he was in a difficult position. Although he was becoming accepted by the crew he, nevertheless, felt like an enigma: part guest, part common sailor, part officer. Common seamen were not allowed on the quarterdeck unless on duty in the after-guard, but in a moment he would be on his way to the Captain's cabin.

CATHCART MOTIONED FROM BEHIND the large chart covering his table, "Gentlemen, please find a convenient place. *Ringle* brings news that two Spanish frigates are making their way from Cumana to Puerto Blanco where they will escort the Indiamen to Caracas or Spain. The Admiral requires me to ensure this does not happen. I intend to intercept them before they reach Puerto Blanco and am trusting in the Dons' tradition of sailing easy during the night. Additionally, they have been in Cumana harbour under the fort's guns for some time and will be slowed by weeds."

Cathcart jabbed his forefinger at a pencil mark between Curaçao and South America, " I estimate their maximum progress to be thus and intend to be there before first light."

Mac imagined the officers mentally factoring in the wind, plus *Lionheart's* and the enemy's courses—there was a fine line between offering a second opinion and implying an error in your commander's judgement. Their consensus, that dawn should find them very close indeed to the enemy, was heartily delivered.

Cathcart stated he intended to keep the weather-gage—it was vital not to run too far south during the night. His calculations, based on *Lionheart* making twelve knots until midnight then striking topgallants and topsails at the start of the middle watch, would require only the courses aloft at dawn to reduce the chance of being seen.

Cathcart continued, "We will feed the men at one bell of the morning watch, then clear for action. Local sunrise is a few minutes past five bells. With reasonable visibility we should catch them silhouetted against the eastern sky while darkness in the west will help conceal us." He glanced around the table. When there were no further questions he nodded and said, "Gentlemen, until the morning."

Mac, mind racing, slept fitfully through the middle watch, unable to get accustomed to sleeping in a space twenty-two inches wide—the standard space allotted for a hammock. He was almost grateful for the call, 'All hands, d'ye hear, all hands', at the start of the morning watch. Within seconds the bosun's mates were making their way through the mess deck; any laggards roused by blows from the mates' stubby rope starters. Mac scrambled to the pitch-black deck where someone thrust a line into his hand.

"Clasp on 'ere and 'eave hearty on the order," the unseen voice instructed. Mac marvelled how the topmen could work high above in the ink-black void.

Lionheart, sails loosely furled, wallowed in the slight swell as the first half of the men made their way below for a quick breakfast of burgoo, a thick porridge-like substance of questionable origin, accompanied by steaming mugs of cocoa. They were followed, twenty minutes later, by the remainder which included Mac.

The moment they finished eating Mac joined a line passing all movable items below. The officers' and Cathcart's cabin partitions were dismantled; the cabin contents stowed safely in the holds to make room for working the guns and to reduce splinters. Other sailors rolled hammocks into tight bundles and packed them along the quarter deck, waist and forecastle to provide protection from small arms fire. Five minutes after the fourth bell of the morning watch *Lionheart* was in all respects ready for battle. Her loaded guns lurked behind closed ports while she ghosted along under a single jib and single-reefed main course. Doubled lookouts searched the southeastern horizon, their vigilance heightened by the promise of an extra tot for the first to spot the enemy.

The wind had shifted to south-southwest during the night, still helping *Lionheart* but somewhat foul for the Spanish frigates. *Lionheart* was on the starboard tack when the foretop lookout hailed, "Deck there, topmasts three points off the larboard bow." Although the stranger's hull was below the horizon, her upper masts formed black needles against the faint eastern glimmer. A few minutes later, when the light increased marginally, he called again, "Deck there. Ship rigged, an' Dago by the cut uv 'er sails. 'Nother set o' masts astern uv 'er."

Cathcart ordered more sails set and a new course as close to south as the wind would allow. He called Mac to the windward side of the quarterdeck. "Well, Mr. Appleton. What think you now of your decision to take part in our little fracas?"

"Most interesting, sir. We're positioned exactly as you anticipated."

Cathcart nodded. "We know they are Spanish by their sails. We will soon know if they are frigates."

Mac studied the increasing light in the southeast. From his lower position on the deck he thought that he could make out the mast tops although he could not yet see the sails or hull. How the lookout had spotted the masts earlier was amazing.

"If I may ask, sir, is holding the wind-gage your equivalent to holding the top of a hill in my world? Being more difficult to attack uphill, as it were, than down?"

"Succinctly stated and very astute." Cathcart smiled, then continued, "While it is more difficult for them to come against the wind to attack, being downwind means they can choose to run. However, I believe *Lionheart* is the faster and we would eventually catch them."

"But sir, aren't we at a disadvantage? Our gun ports are nearly in the water from the ship's heel."

Cathcart's expression became more serious. "I intend to quickly close the range to maintain the advantage of surprise and anticipate the Spanish gunners are inefficient after a long stay in harbour. Once we are within range I intend to reduce to fighting sails to provide a steady shooting platform."

Mac nodded and said, "How long until I'm needed, sir?" He almost neglected to add 'sir'—Cathcart was chatting more like a friend than a commanding officer.

"My intention is to attack..." Cathcart's voice trailed off at the lookout's hail.

"Deck there. Two frigates. Near 'un 'pears t' be a twenny-hate an' signallin'. She's tryin' t' fore reach us. Bigger 'un's our size an' trailin' by a mile or more."

Cathcart nodded to the signals midshipman, "Make today's private signal." The smaller frigate did not respond, nor did she display an ensign. He turned toward the bow and bellowed, "Shake out the tops'l reefs and get the main t'gans'l on her," then turned toward the helmsmen, "as close to windward as she will stand."

Within a minute Mac could feel the hull vibrating with new energy as the ship responded to the increased canvas.

Cathcart continued after satisfying himself that the sails were drawing. "So the game is afoot. The nearest is our first target and is trying to cross our bows to trap us. The farther will not signify if we are quick. She will take at least an hour to work her way up and we have the advantage in size over the nearest. That said, a well-handled smaller ship can overcome a larger foe so I intend to increase our odds with alacrity.

"We will open with bar and chain. Because of our course and the position of the enemy, we must sight each gun individually and fire in sequence rather than a single broadside. I intend to go for her masts and rigging so she does not figure in the rest of the day. Presumably she will be trying to do the same to us and we will know soon enough whether my money for extra powder and shot was well spent." As the leading Spanish frigate continued to claw her way to windward Cathcart opened his telescope, "You may return to your station, Mr. Appleton." He had resumed being the Captain.

Mac helped secure large nets suspended vertically above the bulwarks to prevent boarders should the ships come close enough. More nets, slung horizontally above the decks, protected the gun crews from falling debris. High above, topmen attached chain slings to the yards to help support them if rigging was shot away. The larboard gun crews crouched beside their weapons— occasionally someone would peer over the hammocks to glimpse the enemy. The bow chaser would be the first to fire, the curve of the bow allowed it to point farther forward than the eighteen pounders.

Mac wondered if they would have to alter course again and whispered to Ralph Franklin, "When will we open fire?"

"Our chaser might try 'im at ten cables," Franklin offered.

Mac knew that was a sea mile—six-thousand feet.

"Them eighteens don't 'ave that range firing bar an' chain. My guess is the Cap'n'll wait 'til about five cables then change course, jus' t' make sure."

"Won't that give our Spanish friend the chance to fire first?" Mac did not want to sound anxious but the prospect of cast iron balls being fired at him in earnest was not very appealing. If they continued on this course the Spaniard would be able to fire broadsides before their own guns could bear.

"Meb'be, but they're terrible poor shots from wont we've seen afore. Not t' worry, Cap'n knows wont 'e's about." Franklin gave a gap-toothed grin to lend weight to his opinion.

Their speed appeared to be working to advantage. The Spanish frigate's angle off their bow increased as *Lionheart* slanted farther to starboard, clawing her way into the wind. Every foot gained decreased the Spaniard's ability to fire a broadside. Mac watched the battle develop before him in slow motion—*Lionheart* was like a cattle dog working a wayward critter. He admired the Spanish captain's determination to engage *Lionheart* when it would be more prudent to rejoin his lagging consort. It was obvious the enemy frigate did not have the speed or sea room to cut across their bow.

A Spanish ensign blossomed from the stranger's mizzen mast, immediately followed by a sooty smudge that obscured her bow, expanding and thinning as the wind swept it along her hull, followed by a dull thump. A moment later a ball landed well short. This was a clear act of aggression—Cathcart was now free to respond without fear of being chastised, or worse, by the Admiralty since England and Spain were still at peace.

Cathcart said to no one in particular, "For what we are about to receive..." a moment before the bow chaser replied with a sharp bang.

Mac began counting in his head, "Thousand one..." He followed the ball's silhouette against the apricot sky until it landed fifty yards short. At the count of fifty the gun fired again. This time the ball struck the Spaniard's hull near the main mast.

The chaser's gun crew, naked from the waist up, glistened with sweat despite the cool morning as they levered the three-thousand pound gun around with handspikes to adjust their aim. Their third shot punched a hole in the centre of the enemy's forecourse.

Mac heard the sails flapping and looked up as the ship yawed slightly to starboard. Seconds later the first eighteen pounder's thunderclap made the deck tremble.

The next five guns fired at five second intervals. The entire ship shuddered and groaned with each discharge; bitter smoke swirled across the deck, obliterating the gunners' view of the enemy. Mac was glad that he had heeded Toby's earlier advice to plug his ears with gun wadding held in place by a bandana tied around his head. Even with the precautions, the din was painful as the gunners found their target. Bar and chain shot ripped apart the Spaniard's mizzen course; the mizzen's top and topgallant masts swayed then collapsed.

The enemy frigate yawed to starboard just as she fired two guns—the shots fell hopelessly off target. Despite opening fire first, she had fired only three shots, all wide and short of their mark.

'Great Harry' and number eight unleashed their bar and chain shot loads. A fluke swirl of the breeze swept the gun smoke away enough for Mac to see the shots shred the Spaniard's fore topmast staysail halliards and jib stay. The forecourse and inner jib collapsed into the water in a tangle of cordage and cloth around her lee bow. This damage quickly proved catastrophic for the Spanish frigate. Her jib gone, coupled with the earlier damage to the mizzen and the added drag of sails fouled against her lee bow, caused her to sag downwind. Cathcart shouted, "Let fly mains'l tacks and sheets.""What's happening?" Mac asked. The after-guard bosun's mate replied, "Reducin' sail so's we doan go right past th' bugger. Be most unfair fer the lads in the aft-battery t' miss their turn at sport." *Lionheart* suddenly threatened to surge past her wounded enemy—her only drawing sail, the reefed forecourse, gave her barely more than steerage way as she crossed the Spaniard's bow. The remainder of her larboard battery could conduct what amounted to target practice at their leisure while the defenseless Spaniard lay bow-on.

"Masts and rigging!" Cathcart's voice boomed across the deck, dutifully repeated by the lieutenants and midshipmen commanding the batteries. Raking the Spaniard was unnecessary;

her day was done—Cathcart felt no compunction to slaughter fellow sailors when it would have no effect on the outcome. They could jury rig or tow her after dealing with her consort.

Each gun captain waited until he was sure of the target. Instead of passing through only a few pieces of rigging as they flew across the enemy, shots travelled the ship's entire length as it severed vital rigging. Unsupported, the Spaniard's upper foremast gave way with a great cracking sound. The shattered mast tore through the mainmast's stays and snapped that mast below the maintop, leaving her unable to sail.

Cathcart turned his telescope to the larger frigate, then ordered a new course of east by half south and the courses and topsails reset.

Mac knew that it was vital to regain speed to manoeuvre against the second frigate who continued to valiantly claw her way to windward despite the sight of her crippled sister wallowing in the swell.

"Larboard battery, make ready. Wear onto the starboard tack, handsomely now," Cathcart bellowed with a note of urgency.

The enemy, just over half a mile away, was within range; Mac glumly realised that was also true for both him and *Lionheart*.

Officers and petty officers barked out a rapid series of orders. Mac only caught glimpses of the frenetic sail handling aloft as he helped overhaul the driver to force their bow around until the leonine figurehead's fire-red eyes gazed unblinking across the water toward the enemy. *Lionheart* slanted downwind toward the Spaniard, sails trimmed for the wind now coming from slightly aft on her larboard side, her lower gun ports scarcely a foot above the water. "Mr. Baverstock," Cathcart shouted almost jovially, "my regards to the larboard chaser, I think we shall test the range."

Toby lifted his hat in acknowledgement – his voice, already grown hoarse from the gun smoke and yelling orders, would never reach the quarterdeck against the wind.

TOBY STOOD IN THE BOW, face masked with a look of fierce determination, and studied the approaching Spaniard framed by the jib's belly while envisioning the chaser's effective range.

"Aye, near close enough," he said to the gun captain. He swept his hat above his head to let Cathcart know they were ready to fire, then pointed to starboard. They would have to alter course slightly for the gun to bear.

Toby expected the Spanish ship to have the advantage in range. *Lionheart's* wind-canted deck, heeled toward the water, would make it difficult to sufficiently elevate the guns. The chaser might be able to achieve a hit at extreme range, but the ball would have to skip off the water at least once. With a little luck they might strike the enemy in the chain-wales or below her jib-boom, possibly knocking down some standing rigging. One never knew what effect any hit might have on the enemy's concentration. If nothing else, the sound of their own gun would steady the men, and perhaps his own apprehension which was unusually high.

The Spaniard fired first, with no effect. The ball landed well short, then skipped twice before plunging beneath the swell.

Toby waited until Cathcart ordered the helm to come two points to starboard. He felt *Lionheart* slow by a knot or two, and the deck level when the maincourse sheets were slackened. The moment the gun fired Toby felt *Lionheart* resume her original course. An acrid pall of smoke clung like a wreath around her bow. The shot landed thirty yards short and twenty yards ahead of the Spaniard's bow; the gun was reloaded and run out at the count of forty. Again, Toby raised his hat to starboard. This time the ball skipped once, then struck the Spaniard's bow but didn't appear to cause any visible damage.

The second Spanish shot fared no better than the first.

Toby smiled; the Spanish were slow and erratic. Now the chaser bore without having to yaw; it's third shot punched a neat hole through the lower third of the enemy's forecourse. Walter Cooper crowed, "An' without a skip, sir, d'ye see?" It was clear the gun captain had found the range.

A panting messenger saluted Toby. The boy's voice an octave higher in his excitement as he shouted to be heard over the squeal of the gun being run out. "Captain's compliments, sir. Chain and bar. Trim their sails if you please."

Toby grinned despite his intense concentration. His nerves had calmed—the second frigate was clearly no match.

THE SPANISH CONTINUED TO RETURN FIRE and Mac heard two balls strike with dull thumps, but no apparent damage. Most of the enemy's shots landed in the water or flew well overhead while their own guns continued to fire at nearly double the Spanish rate. So far the only injury was to a waister who suffered a dislocated shoulder when rigging damaged in the first encounter crashed to the deck.

Mac estimated the Spaniard to be a third of a mile away. The two ships were closing on nearly opposite courses until Cathcart ordered the helmsmen to alter course to starboard. He glanced forward. Toby was studying the enemy and holding his sword upright above his head.

Toby slashed his sword downward.

Mac instinctively crouched, covered his ears and turned his back to the guns. *Lionheart* shook, groaned and bucked under the recoil of the thundering, rolling broadside that flung an avalanche of iron at the Spanish frigate. When he looked up the Spaniard was still under way, but with multiple holes through every sail. Several sails were reduced to tattered ribbons; some yards slumped at drunken angles. Mac expected the gunners to reload after they fired. Instead the men rushed to the starboard battery, crouching below the sides after they crossed the deck.

Over the discharge of the larboard bow chaser Cathcart ordered the rudder 'hard over' to put *Lionheart* onto the starboard tack.

Mac barely had time to notice the jib sails disappear before he was using every ounce of his strength to help manhandle the driver—speed was of the essence. His lungs burned from the brute exertion required to control the thirty foot high sail against the wind. He was nearly pulled off his feet when the wind caught the driver and flung it to starboard. When he looked again, the Spanish frigate appeared to be the one changing course as *Lionheart* continued pivoting.

Cathcart intended to cross the Spaniard's bow. The enemy frigate appeared to be caught off guard. Her larboard guns were run out in the expectation of exchanging broadsides as the ships passed

Mac, doubled over from exertion, struggled to catch his breath.

Cathcart bellowed, "Starboard battery, run out."

As one, eighteen gun ports slammed open against the hull. The squeal of the guns running out reminded Mac of a thousand fingers on a chalkboard. Seconds later, when they fired simultaneously, *Lionheart* staggered as though hit by an earthquake.

Mac covered his ears too late. His head felt like he was the one who had been fired from a gun. A dense cloud of bitter, sulphurous smoke tore at his lungs and stung his eyes. He wiped tears from his eyes and looked up. The Spanish ship, riddled with jagged holes, had part of her bow smashed in. Inboard, massive oak splinters would have scythed through flesh and bone.

Cathcart's training of the gun crews paid off with the second broadside. The Spaniard's main topgallant and fore topgallant masts collapsed over her lee side and fouled her deck with wreckage. His voice boomed above the shouts and screams, "Starboard tack to pistol range." He intended to engage the Spaniard at close range.

Mac's eyes still watered from the smoke and his ears rang from the din of the guns. His muscles felt as if they were being jabbed by red-hot pokers. The wind's pressure against the sail made the line in his hands as stiff as a log.

Cathcart timed their turn so that *Lionheart* was at the limit of the Spaniard's field of fire. If *Lionheart* failed to complete the manoeuvre she would wallow helpless under the Spanish guns. Cathcart shouted, "Marksmen to the tops! Helm take us down to her. Carronades load canister or grape. Double shot the starboard battery."

Mac knew double-shotting meant the gunners would be aiming for the hull. He guessed Cathcart didn't want to inflict additional damage to the Spaniard's rigging as they already might have to tow the essentially dismasted first frigate. Towing both ships would be impossible. He began his climb to the mizzen top, a musket slung across his back, before realising that a sailor carrying an additional pair of muskets followed him.

"Doan y' worry zur, Lootenan' Baverstock says I'm t'load fer you an' look after yer honour," the man called out.

Mac, gasping heavily, scrambled through the lubber's hole. Each breath tasted of burnt sulphur and his ears rang. He removed his bandana and ear plugs then shouted, even though the sailor was only eighteen inches away, "Mac Appleton, and you are?"

"John Williams, zur. Gunner's mate."

"Pleased to meet you, John." Mac extended his hand. "Mac'll do nicely up here, there's no need for sir. I've never done this before, so I'd appreciate any advice you can give."

Williams did not shake Mac's hand. Instead, he looked at Mac through narrowed eyes that betrayed suspicion before responding in a clipped staccato. "The Cap'n's bringin' us down close so's we c'n board 'er. 'R job's t' knock down any Dago sharpshooters."

Mac was tempted to ask Williams to speak slower—he could barely understand him. As Williams continued Mac caught that the enemy sharpshooters would be aiming at Cathcart and the officers.

Williams reassured Mac's questioning look, "Takes yer time, 'tis more 'portant t' keep up a steady fire than t' fire wild-like. I'll try t' keep yer muskets loaded, but we only 'as three. So time yer shots so's I's time t' reload."

Williams pointed out a Spanish sailor, "There, zur."

Mac gave Williams a wry smile and said, "Remember? Forget the 'sir'."

Williams' expression softened, "D'ye see th' bugger in th' mizzen top? Just loik target practice yes'rday. Takes yer toim an' Bob's yer uncle."

Mac raised the musket and squinted along the barrel. The gun kicked against his shoulder; smoke stung his eyes. The ball deflected off the enemy's topmast shrouds with a *whang* and *whir*. He quickly exchanged the discharged gun.

The enemy sailor, partially protected by the shrouds, threaded his musket between the heavily tarred ropes and aimed at *Lionheart's* quarterdeck. Mac knew that he would have to place his next shot through the narrow space between the ropes to hit the Spanish sharpshooter.

"Pretty as y' please," commented Williams appreciatively when Mac's shot shattered the Spaniard's right shoulder.

"D'ye see their main top?" Williams asked as he passed a fresh musket. "Them buggers 'av' managed t'get a swivel up there. Can you 'it 'em from 'ere? Afore they starts about our lads?"

Mac could see the men struggling to get the swivel into position. In a few seconds they would be ready to fire. He cocked the musket and made sure of his aim but *Lionheart* lurched under the recoil of another broadside just as he squeezed the trigger. His heart rate surged when he missed as the mizzen top, fifty feet above the water, dizzily swung through a thirty foot arc. With horror he saw the Spaniard level the swivel at them. "More precisely, it appears to be us they're after," Mac said as Williams thrust another gun into his hand.

Mac aimed instinctively—there wasn't time to be fancy—and fired. The impact of the half-inch diameter musket ball reduced the man's face to a bloody pulp and flung him back at the precise moment the swivel fired. Mac heard a sighing whoosh above his head. He looked up; the swivel's murderous cluster of grape-sized balls had punched ragged holes in the mizzen tops'l a scant five feet above.

"Sweet Jeez..." Williams stopped in mid-oath to suck in a breath. "I'm glad y'done for him when y' did."

Mac responded with laugh. "Me, too, and most grateful for you pointing him out. In all the excitement I hadn't noticed him."

"'Less they send some more, th' tops 'r' empty. See th' weather side o' their quarterdeck. That's th' side nearest us. There's another swivel there, jus' abaf' th' mizzen chains."

Mac's ears, still ringing from the broadsides, asked, "Abaf? You mean toward her stern?"

"'Zactly."

Mac felled one Spanish sailor. Five seconds later, another—but not before the man discharged a swivel's two pounds of iron marbles into *Lionheart's* waist. Mac grimaced at the sight of three motionless bodies and a bloody swath of wounded sprawled on the deck.

Above the din, Mac somehow heard Cathcart call, "Boarders make ready. Grapplers ready at the bow." When he looked down at the Spanish frigate his stomach churned—blood oozed through ragged holes punched through her hull as though the ship herself was bleeding. Yet her men continued to fight. He could only imagine the unseen carnage within the ship.

Forward, a group of British sailors carried boarding pikes and ropes equipped with three-pronged grapnels to lock the ships together. A second cluster of Lionhearts were busy arming themselves with cutlasses and tomahawks from weapon tubs circling the foot of the mainmast. Scarcely twenty yards separated the two ships. Then ten as the tips of their yardarms touched like a pair of scorpions in a deadly dance.

Lionheart fired a final broadside before grapplers flung their hooks across the rapidly diminishing space between the hulls. The moment they caught against anything on the Spanish ship—cordage or wood—*Lionheart's* men tugged furiously to draw the ships closer, while the Spanish frantically tried to sever the ropes or release the grapnels.

Williams rammed home a wad and said, "Look fer Dagoes trying t' cut our ropes. Knock 'em down, there by th' foremast weather shrouds, d'ye see? Jus' watch out fer our lads when y' aims."

Careful not to outpace Williams' ability to reload the muskets, Mac maintained a rhythmic, steady fire. One man after another fell to the enemy's deck. Mac lost track of time, of how many times he fired, and of how many men he killed or wounded.

English cutlasses, axes and tomahawks sliced through the nets slung from the Spaniard's yards to prevent just such an attack. Feral screams filled the air as English sailors stormed the enemy deck. Mac could see Toby and Barnes leading a group battling to gain control of the Spanish fo'c's'le.

Spaniards able to escape the attack regrouped in their frigate's waist near the mainmast while another party rushed to reinforce the quarterdeck against the relentless English assault. Viewed from above, the battle took on a surreal quality as groups of foreshortened men fought with cutlasses and pikes—it was becoming difficult to tell friend from foe. When Spanish sailors ventured to mount a swivel on their quarterdeck's forward rail Mac shot one Spaniard through the arm just as he was about to fire at the British massed on the fo'c's'le.

Williams whistled softly when the partially spent ball ricocheted from the swivel's barrel and struck a second Spaniard in the thigh

Mac heard Toby call, "Lionhearts! With me!" as he lead the advance against the mainmast cluster.

The Spaniards' only hope was to prevent stop the English from gaining control of the main deck. For that to happen, the men in the waist had to stand their ground. Forced astern, they would be trapped and cut to pieces.

"D'ye see the Spanish officer in the middle of that group?" Williams gestured at the men around the mainmast.

"The one wearing the hat?"

"'Zactly."

Mac aimed and fired in what had become a single, fluid motion. His ball struck the man between the shoulder blades. He slumped to his knees, looked briefly skyward disbelievingly, then collapsed.

"Nicely done, zur. One less ..." Williams hesitated, "No offense, zur."

"None taken." Mac was chilled by the realisation that it could just as easily have been Toby in a Spaniard's sights.

Their officer fallen, the defenders were disorganised. A parcel of Spaniards, facing the relentless British advance, retreated toward the quarterdeck ladders after one of *Lionheart's* swivels ripped a bloody path through others gathered at the mainmast.

The English guns fell silent. Their murderous grape made no distinction between friend and foe on the congested deck.

Lionhearts waded into the defenders, beating them back with in a fury of cutlasses and boarding axes.

Mac tried to block out the sounds of battle: the clang of metal on metal, the sickening *thunk* of blade against bone, and worse, the agonised screams of the wounded. He closed his eyes for a moment and missed seeing Cathcart lead a dozen British sailors across the gap between *Lionheart's* stern and the Spaniard's taffrail.

Spanish defenders moved forward to defend the top of the quarterdeck ladders from Toby's assault, not noticing Cathcart's group. Now trapped, the beleaguered Spaniards still held a slight numerical advantage over the invaders.

Williams spotted Cathcart's party. "The Cap'n and a dozen lads 'ave taken 'er from th' stern."

Toby continued to lead the larger force in the pitched battle in the Spaniard's waist. When he saw Cathcart cross he shouted, "At 'em Lionhearts, the Cap'n's got them from astern."

Toby, a brace of pistols tucked into his belt, a sword in one hand and a pistol in the other, led his men from the fo'c's'le toward the main mast. In a savage maelstrom of razor-edged cutlasses and tomahawks, accentuated by bloodcurdling screams, they hacked through anyone in their path. Toby shot one Spaniard in the chest, then employed his empty gun as a club before tossing it aside and drawing another.

Toby, confronted by three Spaniards, shot one in the chest, clubbed another across the head with his empty pistol, and embedded his sword in the third's gut before he slipped on the bloody deck. He attempted to wrench his sword free from his latest victim but had to release his grip. He tried to scramble to his feet, but again slipped in the slime of blood and gore coating the deck and fell on his back as a Spanish sailor stepped over his shipmate's body.

The Spaniard raised his cutlass above his head, poised for the kill.

Mac could see Toby, his face frozen in horror, struggle to free his last pistol.

~9~

PRISONERS

MAC'S KNEE BEGAN ITS TELLTALE STRESS TWITCH when Toby continued to struggle to free the pistol from his belt. Mac braced the musket against his shoulder and silently cursed the time it took to cock, aim and fire. The primer ignited with a satisfying *phuff* and the gun kicked against his shoulder; an instant later the Spaniard's left forearm disintegrated into a mass of bloody pulp.

The man glanced at his arm as though it was no more than a nick, roared an oath and waggled his cutlass.

"Shit," Mac cursed. He had aimed at the man's chest.

The blink of an eye later, Toby finally freed the pistol from his belt, pressed the muzzle against the Spaniard's belly and fired. The half inch ball travelled upward and exited through the man's back in a fountain of blood and flesh. Toby rolled to his right to avoid the corpse landing on him.

"That did the fucker," Williams commented with grim satisfaction. He added in an almost conversational tone, "Y'uv got two rounds."

"Then I'm only going to shoot to protect our own. You watch Baverstock's group. I'll watch the Captain."

Mac's concern was unfounded. In the next few seconds, the quarterdeck defenders dropped their weapons. A bearded man in the centre of the group shouted to the remaining men in the waist who were continuing to fight. When the bearded man shouted again, the remaining Spaniards dropped their weapons.

Cathcart strode to the quarterdeck rail. His stentorian voice boomed across the waist where some English sailors continued the attack, "Avast. She's ours!" Two tars slashed the Spanish ensign's halliard. The flag fluttered limply to the deck to raucous English cheers.

Mac tensed. A Spanish sailor, armed with a sword, was approaching Cathcart. Mac cocked the musket and took aim; his forefinger tightened against the trigger, but some inner sense told him to wait. The man stopped two paces from Cathcart and laid the sword's hilt across his left arm and facing Cathcart. Cathcart made a bow, accepted the sword, then returned it to the Spaniard.

Mac exhaled. The killing was over.

"I don't think we're needed up 'ere any longer, zur," Williams said, grinning from ear to ear. "I'll take th' empty muskets. Y' keep th' loaded one 'n case it's needed. Jus' b' careful climbin' down, zur. Wouldn't want y't' shoot yerself...or me." Williams, agile as a chimpanzee in the jungle canopy, swung out from the top and slid down the back stay to the deck.

Mac paused at the lubber's hole and glanced at the Spanish frigate. The enemy deck was littered with men and body parts amid pools of blood. A pitiful chorus of moans and screams filled the air. Some of the living made feeble movements with their arms or legs. He began shaking uncontrollably; his legs felt like jelly. He could picture himself falling from the ratlines. He had never witnessed such a human face to battle. War in his Apache was sterile. His enemies were remote, often invisible except as a blip in an electronic display. Sweat running down his back felt like Death's icy fingers—a grim reminder that the Spanish grapeshot had barely missed him and Williams. If it wasn't for dumb luck he could be one of those bodies. Mac told himself that he had done what was necessary to survive, then wiped the sweat from his hands and clasped the shroud. The Spanish lieutenant's face still haunted him and he wondered if any of the wounded would survive with the limited medical treatment available.

By the time he reached the deck, an enthusiastic Williams had spread word of Mac's marksmanship. Mac wrestled his hand free from the crushing grip of another well-wisher and saw two sailors kneeling over a small form on the deck.

It was Will Page, the boy who had brought him hot water. One of the men gently lifted Will onto an open hammock, then placed an eighteen-pounder's ball at the boy's feet. Mac knew that burial at sea was necessary—there was no way to preserve a corpse until burial on land. The sailor deftly sewed the hammock shut with a sailmaker's needle and cord, but Mac was not prepared for the final act of burial preparation when the sailor passed a stitch through Will's nose. No response confirmed he was dead. Mac stumbled to the rail and puked.

His legs still felt like rubber when he presented himself to Midshipman Barnes, the only officer aboard *Lionheart* and less than half his age. The other officers and most of the crew were still aboard the Spanish frigate. "Reporting for duty, sir." Mac said, the bitter taste of bile still in his mouth and afraid he would retch again. "I'm unsure of my current duties as most of our men seem to have abandoned us. I trust this is only a temporary arrangement." The humour was lost on the glassy-eyed and visibly shaking Barnes.

Before Barnes could exercise his newfound authority, Cathcart called from the prize, "Mister Appleton, do you please cross so that we may have a word."

Mac gazed apprehensively at the gap between the two hulls, opening and closing like the maw of some great creature waiting to chew him to a pulp between its oak molars.

Williams, hovering nearby, grasped a line dangling from the Spaniard's mizzen topsail yard then tested it before handing it to Mac. "'Ere you go, zur," nonchalantly adding with the confidence of someone who had done it many times, "climb on the rail an' grab this 'ere. A little 'igher if'n y' please."

Williams clutched the back of Mac's shirt to prevent him from plunging overboard when *Lionheart* took an awkward dip. "There y'be. See how th' gap opens an' closes with th' swell. Push off wi' yer feet when th' gap's widest. Make sure y'have a good grip an' doan slide down th' line. I'll be 'ere to catch ye if'n y' doan make it th' first time."

Mac, who couldn't see Williams' mischievous grin, took a deep breath, paused, then swung through the air. He landed on the Spanish quarterdeck in an untidy heap. He scarcely had time to regain his feet before Cathcart arrived, right hand extended, "Damned fine shooting!" Mac couldn't understand, with everything else going on, how Cathcart could possibly be aware of his marksmanship.

Cathcart pumped Mac's hand in a vice-like grip and refused to let go. "I understand several of our people owe you their lives. Capital, absolutely capital! Mere words simply cannot express your service today. Come with me."

His hand finally freed, Mac flexed his fingers to restore circulation—and check for broken bones—while Cathcart led the way to the captain's cabin. When they arrived at the cabin, two other men were waiting. Mac recognised the older hawk-faced man—slim, erect, and now dressed in a meticulously clean uniform—as the one who had surrendered his sword. The older man purposefully strode across the barren cabin which had been stripped for battle. He was followed by a timid young man, both closely watched by the sentry.

Cathcart seemed deliberately formal as he greeted the older man. Even in defeat, the man showed great composure and presence. Mac sensed that he must be the captain. Cathcart needed intelligence about the English merchant ships and would have to be careful not to antagonise the only source. Cathcart bowed and said, "Captain Ulysses Cathcart, His Britannic Majesty's frigate *Lionheart*, at your service."

The Spanish officer returned Cathcart's bow. The younger man stood deferentially behind the older man's right shoulder. In a stilted accent, and making a point of emphasising his captain's titles, the man said, "Captain Cathcart, it gives me great honour to present His Excellency Don Jose y Araboyne, Captain of His Most Catholic Majesty's frigate *Castellon de la Plana*. I am Midshipman Juan Martinez."

Cathcart nodded then glanced at Mac. "May I present Captain Andrew Appleton of the York Foot?"

Araboyne curtly nodded before Martinez continued, "My Captain has asked that I act as interpreter, although he does understand a little English. He inquires about our other officers?"

Cathcart replied, "Captain, please allow me to commend you and your men for the gallant defence of your ship. You have brought great honour to Spain."

Araboyne visibly suppressed his reaction to Cathcart's compliments before the midshipman began translating. Mac suspected Araboyne had a better grasp of English than he was letting on. After the translation Araboyne bowed.

Cathcart continued, "Captain, I regret to inform you that several of your officers were killed. Our surgeon is presently attending to one we believe is a lieutenant. He is badly injured and unconscious." Mac found it interesting that Cathcart avoided addressing Araboyne as 'Your Excellency'.

Cathcart paused while the midshipman translated, then continued, "Lieutenant Baverstock will take you to your wounded shortly. I can assure you that your men, officers and sailors alike, are receiving our surgeon's best care."

Araboyne spoke slowly, "Most deeply I thank your kindness." He could not hide the emotion in his voice.

Cathcart's tone became more ominous, "I regret we must return to the other frigate. She lies two miles north and has been sorely knocked about. I trust that you understand that duty requires me to either capture or destroy her. I have no wish to inflict further casualties but must do so if she resists." He looked directly into Araboyne's eyes as he spoke and waited for Martinez to finish translating.

Araboyne replied in broken English, his voice choked with emotion, "She is *Matilda*, 28 guns. I do my best. Enough good men have died. Capitan de Gamaras is most proud man. I desire he agree your offer."

"Thank you, Captain. However, I must also ascertain the current situation in Puerto Blanco. Please tell me what you know." Cathcart's tone left no doubt that he felt sympathy for a fellow officer who cared about his men and would no doubt face a court martial over the loss of two ships.

Araboyne remained silent until Cathcart said, "The sooner we're done here, the sooner you can see your men." Mac knew from Cathcart's body language that he did not enjoy saying that. They listened as Araboyne spoke in his broken English, occasionally clarified by the midshipman's translation when he lapsed into Spanish.

Cathcart nodded and said, "I regret there is not much time before we close on *Matilda* so your visit must be brief. I trust you will find your wounded well cared for. If they require anything please let me know and I shall do anything within my power to assist them."

When Cathcart and Mac returned to *Lionheart*, Cathcart immediately retreated to his cabin. Toby, who had been supervising securing the prisoners, came across a few minutes later, leaving Third Lieutenant Edward Moore in command of the prize crew aboard *Castellon*. Moore's orders were to proceed to Jamaica once the carpenters had completed sufficient repairs to allow the voyage.

TOBY SQUINTED TO SEE CATHCART'S FACE against the glare of sunlight reflected from the panoramic sweep of azure water beyond the cabin's stern windows. Although pleased that they had taken *Matilda*, Toby's tone became sombre when he reported, "Sir, the surgeon advises our bill is five dead and another dozen wounded, three of whom he does not expect to survive. Some minor injuries will require changes of duties for a few days. 'Tis a remarkably light toll for two fine frigates."

Cathcart said, "Fortunate, indeed."

Toby cleared his throat and continued, "Forty-three dead aboard *Castellon*. Woodman says there are another seven he does not expect to survive along with two score of wounded." A third of her crew had been killed or wounded. "Sir, *Matilda* has six dead. Damage is confined to her poles and rigging. The men are grafting a spare topmast to what is left of her mainmast; we sent over one of our own as she had nothing suitable aboard. The carpenter reports no serious hull damage and expects her to be ready by the First Dog."

Cathcart almost smiled as he said, "Well Toby, that certainly is good news. I am most grateful that *Matilda* will be underway shortly. I was not looking forward to towing her back to Kingston as we must look in at Puerto Blanco and assess what is happening with the Indiamen. The delay sailing to Kingston and back would have been nigh intolerable. Who do you propose for her?"

Toby wasn't surprised at being asked his preference for an interim commander. Some captains would make their own decision, but Cathcart was unlike others. He believed in giving recognition where it was due; his confidence in his officers made them better. If Cathcart ever found fault he let the offender know, and that was the end of the matter—unless they made the same error again.

"Barnes, sir." Toby was confident Barnes was ready to sit his lieutenant's exam, despite having just turned eighteen. "If we give him a middy and bosun's mate that will leave us with George and myself."

Cathcart nodded, "Make it so and pass word for Mac to join us. Being an army type he may be able to provide some insight for a solution to our next problem."

CATHCART'S SERVANT, who still seemed to regard Mac with suspicion, ushered him into the cabin where Cathcart and Toby were perusing several charts arrayed across the large table. Cathcart looked up and smiled, "Ahh, Mac, do come take a look.

Help yourself to wine if you are so inclined." He gestured to the decanter anchoring the curled corner of a chart. Mac declined—his mouth still tasted of bile and sulphur. The last thing he wanted was to toss his cookies in Cathcart's cabin.

Cathcart's expression became serious as he continued, "Captain Araboyne has provided additional information about the Indiamen at Puerto Blanco. Unfortunately our charts for this region are woefully incomplete. The sailing master is attempting to clarify the Spanish ones we captured."

He jabbed his pencil at Puerto Blanco. "A crescent-moon of rocks stretches across the harbour entrance to form a breakwater. A narrow channel runs between the rocks and a large fort commanding the southern shore." Cathcart glanced out the stern window as the battered *Matilda* swung into view. "Our charts have no soundings and I am loathe to trust Spanish depths. We would have to creep in, casting the lead all the while, which is not practical because of the fort and a second battery guarding the far side of the harbour. Obviously, there is enough depth of water for Indiamen to enter and anchor. The question is, where lays the channel? We will need a west wind to gain the harbour, and east to leave."

He paused to sip his wine. "Apparently the commandant is an unsavoury fellow who abuses his own people terribly. From what Araboyne told me, the Spanish governor in Caracas doesn't have much use for the lot at Puerto Blanco. The man was posted there to get him as far from Caracas as possible despite his family's influence. I believe we have good reason to fear for the safety of the Indiamen's people."

Cathcart continued for another five minutes, eventually pausing to refill his glass while Toby and Mac considered what he had said. Cathcart resumed, almost conversationally, "The bomb ketch *Thunderbolt* was to have joined us yesterday." He glanced at Mac, "Do you know what she is?"

"I believe, sir, a floating mortar battery. Most useful in bombarding shore fortifications but not much use against another ship."

"Exactly. Your knowledge of naval matters continues to amaze me. Especially as you claim to be a non-naval type."

"Well, sir, my knowledge is all gained from reading. I may appear to have a grasp of the matter, but in reality I lack the practical experience or training to put my knowledge to any real use."

"We shall have to see about that." Cathcart winked at Toby and continued. "Do take a look at the chart and tell me what you think of our predicament." Cathcart transferred his glass to his left hand, then pointed with his right index finger. "According to our sources the Indiamen are likely anchored here and here." He waited while they visualised the narrow entrance. "The fort," Cathcart gestured again, "has at least six guns while the battery, over here, reportedly has three. I say at least because the commandant is attempting to add to his defenses and it is not clear how much progress he has made. Six or twelve make little difference as three would be enough to do us in if we tried to force entry.

"If we had *Thunderbolt* it might be a different story. There's a spot, about here, where she could anchor and pound the fort. She would be out of the arc of the fort's guns and out of range of the battery—assuming they have not added another gun to cover her possible anchorage. I would dearly love to ascertain the state of the fort and how the guns are situated." Cathcart drained his glass.

"Sir?" Toby asked, staring intently at the chart. "Could we not send a reconnaissance party under cover of darkness?"

Cathcart nodded tentatively, "I had considered that, but sailors stumbling through underbrush might serve no purpose other than providing the Dons with additional hostages, and the marines would draw immediate attention. No, I think we're going to have to find another way of getting more information."

Mac stared intently, silently, at the charts throughout Cathcart's discourse and gave up trying to decipher the naval annotations on the one covering the entrance to the harbour. The other map, showing the harbour and town, was not much more help with no contour lines, no indication of ground cover, and very few buildings shown.

Mac looked up, "Am I correct that the land rises all about Puerto Blanco as you move inland?" He pointed with his finger, "Your map doesn't give any heights except for this spot. The figure '100' is that in feet or yards?" He almost said meters, but caught himself in time.

"Feet," Toby interjected before Cathcart could answer.

Mac resumed studying the chart. "I understand your concern about sending the men ashore. They're not used to walking on solid land, it's not like the deck of a ship. Without adequate maps the risk of capture would be too great. What about one man? I was thinking of myself. Without going into too much detail, I've had some experience with this sort of thing." He had almost flown over Puerto Blanco outbound from the drug cartel mission. *How long ago was that anyway?*

Cathcart looked up, "Go on." His eyes had the same fiery intensity as when the Spanish frigates were first sighted.

"I'll find a vantage point where I can observe unnoticed." Mac continued, "If I'm put ashore at night, and wait through daylight, I could be picked up the following evening, or possibly the second evening if I was delayed for some reason. What do you think?"

Cathcart's eyes didn't move from Mac's. "If you are discovered the Spanish will regard you as a spy."

Mac responded with a mischievous grin. "I'll simply tell them that I'm a shipwrecked American army officer trying to determine if the town was inhabited by pirates before entering. If you set me ashore at night and wait out of sight of land the Spanish will never know I'm from *Lionheart*. They'll never grasp the real reason for my presence—an American army officer spying for the Royal Navy would be the farthest thing from their mind. Anyway, I'm confident I won't be caught."

Mac relented on his earlier choice of abstinence and poured a half glass of wine while Cathcart mulled over the proposal. Mac knew much would depend on luck—the boat not being spotted by a local fisherman, or worse by a patrol. It would be difficult for Cathcart to explain to the Admiral how this plan came about if it went wrong.

Cathcart furrowed his brow. Finally, he let out his breath with a tremendous sigh. "I am almost taken aback by your plan. It could work, although much will depend on good fortune. Getting you ashore unseen may not be too difficult, although there is always risk. Then there is the matter of your land journey. You know that you are liable to be shot before you have a chance to explain your presence." Cathcart shifted his gaze from Mac, "Well, Toby?"

Toby, immersed in thought, took several seconds to respond. "With no moon until the middle watch, and this light cloud obscuring the stars, I do not believe we could ask for much better in the way of weather. Mac has always understated his abilities— his skill with a musket is testimony to that. He is placing a great deal of trust in us to get him in and out safely. If he believes the plan is sound we should press ahead; I do not perceive any alternative with as much chance of success."

Cathcart's steel-grey eyes narrowed. "Now is the time to express reservations. We would certainly not think any less of you if you were to withdraw your offer."

"Sir, I've every confidence in *Lionheart* and her people. I believe that I can accomplish the mission. I know the risks, but we have the advantage of surprise. Can we be in position by tomorrow night?"

Cathcart looked at Toby, thought for a moment, and said, "Very well." Cathcart bent over the table and pointed. "I suggest we use this little cove about five miles from Puerto Blanco. It is well out of sight of the town and there is no road shown on the chart. We will stand off until nightfall. If you are not at the beach by the third night I will assume you have been captured. Work out suitable signals between beach and ship with Toby. Now, if you will excuse me, I will lay out our course and join you on deck directly."

When they left the cabin, Toby exclaimed, "You continue to amaze me. First at target practice, then your musket work against *Castellon*."

Mac merely nodded and said, "If you'll excuse me, I must clean my working uniform. I'd like to be neat when they shoot me as a spy." He immediately regretted his quip at the sight of Toby's ashen expression and slapped Toby on the back, "Don't worry my friend, I won't let that happen."

~10~

EXPECT THE UNEXPECTED

MAC, WEARING HIS DULL GREEN FLIGHT SUIT, came on deck near the end of the afternoon watch. Toby, overseeing repair of battle-damaged rigging, commented, "I never noticed before, but your uniform lacks buttons. What holds it together?"

"Oh, that," Mac replied as if it was of no consequence, although his mind reeled as he tried to come up with a plausible answer. He was so accustomed to the flightsuit that it never dawned on him that zippers and Velcro might be a curiosity in 1804. "Just another invention of Benjamin Franklin. Surely you've heard of his experiments with lightning and kites?" He desperately hoped Toby hadn't heard too much about Franklin and that his hastily concocted explanation would suffice. He also knew that a Canadian had invented the modern zipper early in the twentieth century.

Toby had a blank, somewhat puzzled look but said nothing.

Mac continued, "Well, he invented this thing called a zipper, named, I think, because of the sound it makes. He died before it could be manufactured; I happen to have one of only a few examples." He moved the zipper up and down a few inches to demonstrate.

"Interesting," Toby replied, "but I do not think they will ever find favour. Buttons are much more sensible."

As night approached Mac gazed anxiously across the water while *Lionheart* continued southward, keeping the land mass of the South America below the horizon—thankfully devoid of sails—until it was swallowed by night.

Cloaked in darkness, *Lionheart* altered course for the coast under courses, topsails and topgallants. She ran without navigation lights and with gun ports closed; even Cathcart's cabin windows were draped with sailcloth to prevent internal lanterns giving away their presence. Speed was of the essence. It was vital to land Mac and be out of sight of land before dawn.

Cathcart checked the Admiralty chart for the third time in the past hour. Although it showed reasonable depths to within one mile of the cove's tiny beach, they would creep farther in to reduce the distance the gig's crew would have to row in the dark. When he returned to the quarterdeck, the gig was tethered alongside and ready to receive her crew and passenger. They would save precious minutes by having it ready and waiting in the water, rather than having to lower it over the side in the dark without benefit of light.

Dead reckoning placed them two miles from land; Collyngs, the leadsman, began his casts from the mizzen chain with the nine pound lead weight. Collyngs still hadn't found bottom when Cathcart estimated they were one mile from shore as *Lionheart* ghosted through the Stygian night on single-reefed topsails. The ship was eerily quiet, with none of the usual conversation and banter among the men. Only the usual creaks and moans from the hull, the sporadic slatting of sails when they caught or lost the breeze, and the rhythmic plop and hiss of Collyngs' lead broke the silence.

Less than three-quarters of a mile from shore, Collyngs announced in a loud whisper, "Sandy bottom, twenty-five." He would have felt the coarse sand embedded in the tallow bottom of the weight when he recovered the lead. After his next cast Collyngs called, "Half twenty-four." The next three casts showed eighteen, fifteen and twelve fathoms—a warning that the bottom was rapidly rising. *Lionheart*, drawing three fathoms, continued to gingerly pick her way toward the beach. When Collyngs called "five" Cathcart ordered the stern anchor released and the sails let slack. *Lionheart* snubbed to a stop against the six-inch diameter anchor cable.

Toby leaned over the quarterdeck's forward rail and said in a low voice, "Gig's crew and Appleton." He added, "Good luck, Appleton," as Mac scrambled down the side. The rigidity of naval hierarchy prevented calling him Mac in the presence of the crew.

Mac safely seated, the gig pushed off, oars dipping silently in the water as *Lionheart* merged into the blackness. He could make out phosphorescent waves, just bright enough to give direction, breaking on the small beach ahead.

The moment the gig touched the sandy bottom the order 'Up oars' brought her to a halt with no more commotion than a gentle scuff of wood against sand. Unless someone was within a few yards their arrival would go unnoticed.

Mac slipped over the gunwale into warm, waist deep water. One of the gig's crew handed him a shuttered signal lantern, a pouch containing flints and a fifteen minute sandglass, a water flask and a small sack filled with ship's biscuits, a wedge of cheese, and pieces of salt beef.

Mac recalled Toby's last instructions, "Three blinks every fifteen minutes if it is safe for us to come in." Several of the boat crew whispered, 'Good luck, zur,' but they were barely audible above the lapping wavelets as he waded ashore.

Mac glanced back when he reached the water's edge, but night had absorbed the gig. He shrugged off a cold shiver—he was alone in the middle of nowhere and two-hundred years in the past. He padded slowly across the beach in a half crouch, the pale sand providing just enough visibility to guide him. Using a large log lying across the upper edge of the beach as a reference, he moved directly inland, exactly twelve paces from the log's centre, before concealing the lantern and flints. The lantern had been taken from *Matilda*. If it was discovered it would not arouse the suspicion a Royal Navy lantern surely would.

Mac retraced his steps, using a leafy branch to obliterate his footsteps, then followed the edge of the sand for a few hundred feet until he found a trail leading into the forest. Faint light from the sliver of moon hampered progress but he eventually located a narrow track leading inland. The trail, barely sufficient for a moderate size animal, forced him to crawl under low hanging branches.

Satisfied that he was safely hidden, he settled to ground for the remainder of the night. He wished he had a pair of night vision goggles as he listened for warning sounds amongst the buzz of insects and the occasional animal call before drifting into an uneasy sleep.

Sunlight crept hesitantly through the forest canopy and stirred Mac from sleep. He listened attentively until reassured that nothing was amiss then rinsed his mouth with a swig of water, reminding himself to conserve his meagre supply. He broke off a piece of biscuit and rapped it against a rock to dislodge any weevils lurking inside, and vowed to never again complain about MRE rations. He gnawed on a piece of salt beef he suspected had previously served in the army as a boot sole and took another mouthful of water in an attempt to dissolve the lump of biscuit and meat, chewed for another minute, then gave up and swallowed. He stretched his arms and legs, then crouched and listened intently for sounds of danger. Cathcart's charts, clear in his mind's eye, showed the road farther inland paralleled the coast. Therefore, if he kept between the coast and the road he should eventually reach Puerto Blanco.

Mac made his way back to the trail he had found in the dark. Sometimes overgrown at chest height, it reinforced his belief that it was seldom used—at least by anything over four feet tall. He kept to the hard-packed centre to prevent leaving boot prints. After perhaps a mile—distance was hard to judge—a stream cascaded over a ten foot high rock face with a delightful laughing sound that reminded him of children playing. He moved past the stream until he no longer heard the water—only the sounds of birds, insects and the occasional monkey.

Satisfied that he was alone, he returned to the waterfall and stripped for an impromptu shower. The cool water rejuvenated him as it surged over his body—it was the first time he had felt clean since his doomed flight. He rubbed himself dry with the flightsuit, dressed and returned to the trail.

The narrow path continued to meander through the trees, sometimes doubling back upon itself when it climbed or descended. Mac estimated he had gone several miles when the trail widened and the overgrowth receded. He moved to the side, concealed himself in the underbrush, and listened for several minutes. There were no sounds other than those of the forest.

Each time the trail changed direction he paused before moving cautiously ahead until he could see around the next twist. Slowed by frequent stops to listen and the need to move silently, his caution heightened when he saw boot prints in the softer ground at the edge of the trail. After another half-mile of slow progress he stopped and held his breath—faint human voices intermingled with a repetitious metallic clink came from ahead. He kept to the side of the path, ready to slip into the underbrush, and slowly crept ahead.

The sounds grew louder. A brief flash of colour, visible through the leaves, became a worker's shirt. Two men were repairing a low stone wall; the metallic echo of hammers striking against stone maintained a steady rhythm. The path widened, almost becoming a trail, where it continued past the men.

Mac wondered how far he was from the town. He backtracked until he could no longer see the men, then ducked into the forest. Satisfied he was out of sight, he began working back to his right. The land rose steadily, giving him hope that he would eventually arrive on one of the hills overlooking the landward side of Puerto Blanco and with a good view of the harbour. Sweat from the exertion and humidity soaked into the neck of his flight suit.

He continued through the undergrowth, alert for human signs, until the forest opened onto a small cultivated field with a crude outbuilding on his left. Mac retreated into the trees and paralleled the edge of the field until it ended. He heard livestock as he used the forest's deep shadows for cover. The distinctive, pungent smell of wood smoke hung in the air—a house must be nearby and that meant people and danger. He moved forward in a low crouch for twenty yards, then dropped to his knees for another ten.

The edge of the forest gave way to what appeared to be the outskirts of a town. Half a dozen shacks huddled along either side of a narrow, rutted dirt road. Children played in the distance; a donkey cart plodded along the road which disappeared into the forest on his left—likely to La Quinta.

He skirted the rear of the houses, then continued with anxious caution for another quarter-mile until the terrain descended toward what he presumed was the harbour. As he crawled flat on his stomach through knee-high grass to the edge of the underbrush he recalled how army rangers prepared for a mission and smeared red clay soil on his face to help conceal it, then inched forward on his belly for the final few yards.

A scatter of houses were fifty feet below his vantage point on the crest of a small bluff. He was at the edge of the town, the oval-shaped harbour a half mile distant. Two large ships were anchored below what appeared to be a stone fortress. He assumed they were the Indiamen. A smaller two-masted ship, perhaps a coastal trader, sat closer to the harbour wall.

Mac pulled a small telescope, a piece of paper and pencil from one of his zippered pockets and began sketching a crude map, carefully noting the ships' relative positions to the fort and town. On the side of the harbour entrance opposite the fort he spotted flashes of colour. Without a more powerful telescope it was impossible to tell if it was the other gun battery Cathcart was concerned about. He noted the location on the map.

As the temperature rose Mac retreated into the meagre shade provided by the brush and took sips of water while he considered his options. He had no way of knowing if the Indiamen's passengers and crew were confined on board or being held in the town, or if soldiers were stationed in the town. He mulled over the problems for several minutes then swirled a final sip around his parched mouth. He would use the tall grass for cover and circle to the rear of the town, his movement concealed by the gentle breeze stirring the dry blades.

Mac crept two-hundred yards before returning to the edge of the hill which had curved almost ninety degrees. The previous inconsequential mud and wood dwellings were replaced by more affluent houses capped with red tile roofs.

A large open area in the middle of the more heavily built up centre of the town was dominated by a two storey building facing across a plaza toward the harbour. As he wondered if it might be the town hall or the commandant's house he tensed and held his breath, certain that he just heard English voices carried on the breeze.

He strained to locate their source until he spotted a group of people inside the walled compound of a large house two-hundred feet to his right. Four more men entered the compound from the house and joined the others. He edged back into the trees and crept through heavy undergrowth toward the house. Moving carefully, afraid of disclosing his presence, he edged toward the brow of the hill then cautiously parted the undergrowth to reveal a compound directly below where a dozen men paced inside the enclosure. The men returned to the house after several minutes when someone shouted in Spanish. A second group emerged a few minutes later.

Mac thought that he could see a heavy door in the rear wall of the compound—from the brush growing against it he guessed it had not been used for some time. He was almost certain that the men were from the Indiamen and wondered if the wall concealed other guards.

The second group returned to the house after ten minutes and were replaced by a third, making forty men in total. Cathcart had said there were probably five or six dozen passengers and crew, which meant some were still unaccounted for. Mac surveyed the town with his telescope, but could not locate anything that looked like a prison.

He estimated it was past noon and the town lapsed into siesta. He dozed until awakened by an English voice in the walled yard.

A man who appeared to be a guard watched as a prisoner went to the end of the yard before disappearing near the wall. The prisoner reappeared a few minutes later and was escorted back to the house.

The cooler late afternoon sun brought the town back to life. The pungent aroma of cooking meat, garlic and onions stirred Mac's appetite. He ate his remaining cheese and salt beef, saving one biscuit for later. He shook the water flask—it was less than half full—and took one sip. The meagre rations did little to satisfy his hunger, or quiet his rumbling stomach.

As the sun neared the horizon Mac withdrew into the trees. There was no point risking discovery while the low sun glared directly onto his hiding spot. Once the sun dipped below the horizon he moved fifty feet to his right where scrawny bushes and tall grass provided a concealed route down the hillside to the stone wall. Halfway down the wall would screen him from the house. The heavy shadow along the wall would provide additional cover.

Mac crept to the corner of the wall where the man had earlier disappeared and immediately knew by the stench that it housed the privy. He began searching the wall for loose stones. After several minutes Mac found what he was looking for—one stone barely secured by failing mortar. Without tools to extract it, he could only wiggle it back and forth in the hope of dislodging it. He wondered if it extended the thickness of the wall which he guessed was at least a foot.

He stopped working the stone when an English voice replied to a question in Spanish as muffled footsteps scrunched across the yard's stone chips. The privy door squeaked on rusty hinges, then closed with a dull thud. He gently moved the loose stone back and forth producing a soft scraping sound.

"Jesus! What the...?" The startled voice in the privy trailed away.

"Are you English?" Mac whispered through the gaps in the mortar.

"Bloody Hell," the voice exclaimed.

"I'm from the frigate *Lionheart*. Feel the wall and tell me if a stone is moving."

"No. Keep moving it. I can hear it, but can not find it."

Mac wiggled the stone a half dozen times more.

"It is no use," the voice in the privy said.

"Do the guards also use this privy?" Mac asked, concerned at the prospect that disturbed stones might alert the Spanish.

"No, but I have to get back before the guard gets suspicious. Wait here. I will send someone else in a few minutes."

After fifteen minutes Mac heard another set of footsteps shuffling slowly, almost casually, across the compound. Again, the door creaked.

"Are you there?" a new voice asked.

"Yes."

"Good. I obtained a piece of broom handle. T'was all I could conceal from the guard. Jonas told me you have found a loose stone out there. Try moving it."

Mac moved the stone again. These efforts, greeted by a faint tapping sound from the opposite side of the wall, confirmed the privy's occupant had found the corresponding spot on the opposite side.

"Must go back, I will send someone when it is safe."

Mac continued to work the stone hoping to dislodge more mortar. After another twenty or thirty minutes he heard someone ambling across the compound.

The new voice whispered, "The fool of a guard let me bring a lantern. George said he marked the spot." There was a brief silence. "Yes, I see it. I stole a small knife. I'll try to scrape away the mortar, but I can't be too long."

Mac continued to wiggle the stone after the voice left. A fourth person entered the privy sometime later.

"Still there?" a thick Scot's accent asked.

"Affirmative."

Thin scraping sounds vibrated through the wall. The voice said, "Good, almost have it loose. Try yours again."

Mac wiggled the stone. It moved toward him with a grating sound before suddenly popping loose. He barely managed to prevent it from crashing to the ground and attracting the guard. Lantern light streamed through the opening.

Mac pressed his face to the opening. "How many of you are there? Are there any more being held elsewhere?"

"So it is true! Thank God! Forty-three of us. More at another house, but I know not how many."

"Do you know where it is?" Mac asked. The second house would complicate things if it was very far.

"Not me, but Elliott does. Must go now."

Mac fell asleep with his head against the opening in the wall until an urgent whisper woke him.

"Hello?" the voice repeated.

"Sorry; I dozed off." Mac rubbed his eyes.

"There are another forty or so officers and passengers at the second house. We hzve drawn a map showing where it is. I will pass it through and hold the lantern to the hole for a minute. You might be able to see the map in the light."

Mac carefully unrolled the map. It showed this house and a second to the left with four other houses between the two. He decided to scout the other house before returning to *Lionheart*.

"I must return to the ship and make plans before we can attempt any rescue. Continue your daily routine. Do nothing to arouse suspicion. Don't worry if it takes a day or two, I promise I'll be back."

The voice behind the wall was emotional at the mention of rescue, "Good luck to you and thanks be from all of us."

"Hang in there." Mac replaced the stone in its hole then carefully refolded the map, placed it in a pocket and ensured the zipper was closed.

A watery moon struggled to break through the clouds and helped Mac find the second house without being noticed. He crept along the rear garden wall and wondered if the guards would be asleep. He stopped when a solitary dog barked in the distance. When there was no further noise he continued until he found a narrow footpath running between the garden walls of the second prison and its neighbour. One side was completely obscured in shadow, the other barely illuminated by the faint moonlight. He kept in the shadow until he was opposite an open window at the rear of the house, then crossed the path.

After several minutes of listening and furtive glimpses over the top of the wall he heard a door open, followed by the clink of glass. Minutes later an argument in Spanish grew in volume until there was the sound of shattering glass amidst a string of oaths.

Mac peeked between the uneven stones forming the top of the wall. He instinctively pulled back when he heard wood breaking, then cautiously peered again. A man staggered to the open window. He appeared drunk and steadied himself against the window frame before disappearing through a doorway. Mac could hear the man careering toward the front of the house and crept along the garden wall, following the sounds, until he neared the front of the house.

When the noise stopped Mac cautiously peered over the wall. There was another window, its shutters partly open, but darkness prevented seeing into the room.

A sharp gasp from inside the room made him retreat below the top of the wall fearing he had been spotted. When there was no further sound he cautiously looked again. Faint light oozed under the room's door perhaps twenty feet from him. He could hear heavy, rapid breathing from someone in the room.

The door burst open. A heavyset, ill-kempt man about five feet nine inches tall, with a candle in one hand, leaned awkwardly against the door frame. The candle's feeble light washed over the room, illuminating someone huddled on a crude bed and tied to the bed by a rope knotted around one ankle.

There was no mistaking the female voice when she screamed, "Ramos, you sonofabitch, I'll kill you," when the obviously drunk intruder staggered into the room.

Mac wished he had a pistol. The window sill, almost at eye level, was five feet from the wall across a narrow side yard. It would impossible for him to enter quickly even if he managed to scale the wall and cross the space unseen. The man, if he was armed, could kill him before he was through the window.

Ramos was at the bed. Mac looked around quickly. The neighbouring house remained dark. There was no indication that her screams had been heard. Ramos cuffed the woman's head and began tearing at her clothes as she fought to escape.

Mac scrambled to the top of the wall.

Somehow, she managed to get to her feet but Ramos flung her to the floor. Then he was on top of her—his left hand pressed against her chest while he fumbled with his pants with his right.

The room plunged into darkness.

Mac tested his grip on the wall and gauged the distance to the window.

The sounds of the struggle were broken by a pig-like squeal. For a moment Mac feared it was the woman. Then he realised that despite the shrillness the tone was too deep. He dropped to the ground when a pale shape paused briefly in the window. He barely had time to realise that she was attempting to escape before she leapt. She landed awkwardly with a muffled "Mumph" when she winded herself.

Mac pulled her to him and whispered, "I'm a friend."

When she continued to struggle with surprising strength he clamped his left hand across her mouth to keep her from screaming. Instead, she tried to bite him. He wondered if he was going to be able to control her without injuring her. When she tried to kick him he was suddenly more concerned that her knee or foot would connect with his crotch.

Mac managed to get behind her and pressed her against the wall. He said, "Stop. We need to get over this wall." He didn't wait for her response, although he felt her relax slightly, and grabbed her by the hips. Somehow he managed to maintain his grip and balance while he lifted her to the top of the wall.

"Hang on and put your feet on my shoulders," he pleaded before scrambling up the wall to join her, breathing rapidly and perched on top of the wall.

He dropped to the pathway but before he could offer assistance she jumped down. He instinctively reached out to steady her but she struggled and he lost his balance. When they fell to the walkway it was all he could do to control her. He pressed her to the ground and clamped his hand over her mouth. They were both winded by the landing and he wheezed, "Keep quiet for both our sakes."

Her resistance lessened as he helped her to her feet, but he kept his hand firmly clamped across her mouth while they moved along the path toward the back of the house. His pleas for calm were to no avail as she continued to twist and try to call out. When they were finally behind the rear garden wall, out of sight of anyone in the street, he pressed her back against the wall. His voice was urgent, "I'm a friend. I won't hurt you. You must be quiet."

Her struggles gradually subsided, although he was not sure if it was from acceptance or exhaustion.

He whispered, "I'm going to let go. Please don't hit me,"and felt her relax ever so slightly. "Can you see me?"

Her face was hidden in the shadow of the wall; he could scarcely make out pale clothing that appeared to be torn around her shoulders and neck. He released his grip on her wrists and reduced the pressure of his weight pinning her against the rough wall. She brought her arms up across her chest.

"When I take my hand from your mouth don't scream. Do you understand?"

She responded with the slightest, quivering, affirmative nod before he released his grip. Her voice trembled, "How do I know you're really a friend?"

"Because I didn't drag you back into the house when you jumped from the window." Her breath was rapid and hot against his neck. "You have to trust me. We don't have much time, someone is bound to have raised the alarm. We have to go a few hundred yards along these walls behind the houses. We'll be out of sight but it could mean our lives if anyone hears us. Will you be quiet?"

She whispered "Yes," after a slight hesitation.

She was out of breath by the time they reached the rear wall of the sailors' compound. He paused while she leaned against the rough stone. He gave her thirty seconds to catch her breath, then said, "There's a hill behind me. The edge of the forest is at the top."

Mac took her hand, "I'll go first so hang on. We must be quick, someone might see your light clothes. When we reach the top we can hide in the underbrush and rest for a few minutes. Ready?" A slight squeeze from her hand confirmed she was.

They reached the top with so sign of an alarm—only a solitary dog barking in the distance. Mac led her into the underbrush until he was sure that they could not be seen. She was doubled over and panting for breath.

"We're safe here for a while," Mac reassured as he sat. "Sit beside me and rest."

She sat a discreet foot away and pulled her hand free of his.

"I'm Andrew Appleton from the English frigate *Lionheart*. Are you hurt? Is that blood on your hand?" He could see a dark stain on her shaking hands.

She looked straight ahead. Her voice trembled, "Mr. Appleton, I am Laura Babbett from Baltimore. I think it is from that pig Ramos. You were at the window when..." Her voice trailed off in a series of low sobs.

"Call me Mac." He avoided talking about the house—there was no point in mentioning what happened unless she did. "We'll rest for five minutes, just enough for you to catch your breath. We have to be as far from here as possible by daylight."

The moonlight brightened as the cloud dissipated. Mac saw her nod in agreement and could see that her blouse was torn, revealing much of her left breast. He said, in what he hoped was a matter-of-fact way, "Your clothes are torn."

Laura looked down and immediately tried to cover herself with her right hand.

Mac pulled a handful of flax-like tall grass from the ground, tore off the dirty root ends and offered the stalks to her. He avoided looking at her again, "Here, perhaps you can tie the worst together and make yourself more comfortable."

Through his peripheral vision, Mac could see Laura's hands quivering as she wove strands of grass through the worst tears in her blouse and bodice.

She murmured, "Thank you," when she finished the last knot.

Mac turned to look at her. Laura was strikingly attractive. Although the makeshift repairs covered much of her breast, the repairs had preserved, if not accentuated, an alluring cleavage. He offered his water flask, hoping she hadn't noticed him stealing another glance, and reminded himself that this was not the time or place for such thoughts.

Laura took several sips then he took two more mouthfuls and handed the flask back to her. "Finish it if you wish. We can refill it at a stream near here. We have to get moving. They must have started a search by now."

~11~

PAYING THE PRICE

THE ENGLISH PRISONERS, confined on the upper floor, shackled together by stout chains, could only listen to the crashes and screams below, forced to imagine what was happening to Laura—and powerless to do anything to stop it.

Then there was only silence.

Unknown to them, the first guard lay on the kitchen floor in a pool of blood, a shattered chair beside him. Laura's attacker, Sergeant Ramos, was also dead. Ramos had never been with a woman he hadn't paid, let alone any woman he found as attractive as Laura. Habitually drunk, his slovenly appearance and obnoxious odour restricted him to only the most syphilitic of whores. Never had he been with someone he knew must be a virgin, and certainly not with anyone who so increased his frenzied excitement by her fierce resistance. Laura had only been saved from his previous advances when the other guards had wrestled him away.

The only reason Ramos was still a sergeant, or even in the army, was because Commandante Luis Ortega had married Ramos' younger sister whose plain looks and pittance of a dowry did not attract many gentleman callers. Her constant nagging was Ramos' protection—in any other command he would have been court-martialed by now or, more likely, imprisoned or executed for his incessant bad behaviour.

Unfortunately, Ortega was another misfit, in essence also imprisoned in Puerto Blanco, whose only qualifications as an officer were family connections.

The Governor in Caracas, reduced to a state of complete exasperation with Ortega, had placed him in charge of the small garrison at Puerto Blanco. In better circumstances, command of a small garrison would be the first step in advancement for a young officer. For Ortega it was the last step on the path to oblivion. Puerto Blanco was the smallest, and most remote, garrison the Governor could find.

The wise commander of such a remote garrison would ensure his men were well fed and comfortable while maintaining good discipline and a pleasant relationship with the town's politicians and influential merchants. There could be many profitable opportunities for a wise man—a merchant might need a few soldiers to guard a 'special cargo' that would conveniently arrive when the Guardacostas were absent. In return, the commander might receive a suitable gratuity for his assistance or perhaps the chance to invest in a future shipment with the potential for a healthy profit should the merchant be especially grateful.

Ortega, however, had managed to alienate the entire town and all his men within a few months. He spent most of his day sulking in the large house which also served as an office, bitter about being rebuffed by the merchants and convinced none of it was his fault. His rancour toward his wife increased with her nagging.

She, equally bitter at being relegated to this dirty little town, harassed Ortega relentlessly in the faint hope it might spur him on to better things. Instead, he only grew more bitter and sullen while indulging in dalliances with local strumpets—often bringing them to the house despite his wife's presence.

Then the Indiamen arrived. Their ransom would be his salvation. That hasty plan was overturned when he received word the Governor was sending two frigates from Caracas. The Governor was no fool; he had received word that Spain might ally herself with France. If that happened war was almost certain. If any ransom or prize money was to be collected it would be his, not Ortega's.

The prospect of losing the ransom and the financial means to escape Puerto Blanco angered Ortega even more. He separated the prisoners into two groups: those he didn't regard as profitable were at the first house; the others, obviously gentlemen and possibly wealthy, were in the second. Then there was the matter of the American woman traveling with her father, an American diplomat of some sort.

Ortega's mind lumped merchants, diplomats and governors together with equal disdain. He contrived special plans for her before the Indiamen departed with the frigates. He threatened to harm Laura to control the men locked in the house. He told them, and Laura's father in particular, that any sign of trouble would mean Laura would personally benefit from his displeasure. Ortega went so far as to crudely grope her in her father's presence to emphasise how ruthless he was prepared to be.

Laura occupied a main floor room in reasonable comfort, if one discounted her constant fear. Ortega wanted to ensure she would be available for his special night. He had taken particular pleasure in telling her that he was saving her for the night before the frigates sailed. If she did not please him he would have her father tortured and killed, perhaps after forcing him to watch her violation. His ultimate triumph would be to bring Laura to his house to further humiliate his wife.

RAMOS, DRUNK AND ENRAGED, knew the frigates were about to arrive. He rationalised that his actions were in defense of his sister's honour. His plan was simple—he would rape the American woman first, depriving Ortega of the pleasure of destroying her virginity. Ramos had convinced himself she was a virgin—why else had she fought off his advances. Ramos didn't pause to consider what form Ortega's wrath might take if he succeeded in carrying out his plan, such was his desire for revenge.

Ramos used his bulk to shatter her door instead of simply unlocking it. Her look of fear as he tore open his breeches in eager anticipation of having her increased his lust. He dragged her on to the floor from the bed despite her struggles which only increased his lust. Ramos forced his knees between hers, tore at her skirt, and prepared to plunge into her.

Instead of the expected pleasure, Ramos felt a sudden searing pain in his groin. He let out a solitary, hideous scream and collapsed to the floor. The candle had gone out, but in the dark he could feel arterial blood spurting from a deep wound in his thigh and from his nearly severed member. He quickly bled to death clutching scraps of Laura's blouse—but not before time to contemplate her impromptu surgery.

The second guard died during the night, his skull crushed by blows from the chair when he had tried to stop the drunken Ramos.

At seven o'clock in the morning two guards ambled along the dirt road to Laura's house. One opened the front door and called, "Ramos." When there was no response, he shouted, "Wake up you drunk." When the guards turned into the hallway they saw the smashed door. Ramos lay in a pool of blood, his right hand frozen in a death grip on his groin.

ORTEGA WAS LIVID WITH RAGE when the news reached him—not at the loss of two men—but at Ramos' attempted betrayal. By the time the search began at eight-thirty it was clear the other prisoners had played no part in the night's events. All, still securely shackled, said they only heard the initial fight in the kitchen, followed by the breaking door and the woman's screams before that last scream.

Laura was not in the house. The searchers assumed she ran out the front door and questioned the neighbours. All denied seeing anything, only admitting they heard screams and presumed the prisoners were being interrogated—again.

Searchers spent two hours going up and down the road; everyone they questioned denied seeing anything. Someone eventually found a faint trail of blood in the narrow alley leading to more blood at the back wall, but the trail went no farther. Since there was no indication that Laura had climbed the hillside behind the wall the corporal in charge of the party reasoned she must have gone back to the street as there was no access to any of the houses through the locked gates. He surmised that she must be injured, not realising it was Ramos' blood dripping from her.

Ortega brooded, alone in his office, until the corporal reported that Laura had likely made for the harbour. Ortega knew her only means of escape was by boat. Perhaps a fool of a fisherman had helped her.

~12~
ESCAPE

MAC'S FEARS about bloodthirsty Spaniards hunting them down were unfounded. Moonlight filtering through the trees dappled ghostly patches on the ground as he cautiously led Laura along the edge of the woods. He was sure that by now someone knew Laura had escaped, but each time he paused to listen there were no signs of a pursuit. The silence, except for the occasional animal call mixed with the sound of their own footsteps, increased his anxiety.

He recognised the farm clearing ahead—a pale wisp of smoke rising from a chimney might meant someone was awake. Mac led the way into the undergrowth; with the increasing light Laura's blouse, white with blackened areas of dried blood, would be seen by anyone in the farmyard.

Mac knew Laura was tiring—he heard her stumbling as she followed. He returned to the trail once safely past the farm, following the path from memory until he heard voices somewhere ahead. He paused and placed a hand gently over her mouth then said in a low voice, "Shush." Her warm breath was sensual on his palm.

The voices drew nearer. Their only escape route was a game trail a half-dozen paces behind them. "Quick," he whispered as he tugged Laura's hand. The trail, nearly overgrown by the undergrowth, forced them to crawl on their knees. Mac knew they didn't have much time to hide.

"I'll push branches aside. Hold them until you're past, then let go gently or they'll hear us."

Although he voices were several dozen yards down the main trail he could see the faint wash of a lantern. Mac pushed Laura into a shallow depression and whispered, "Keep still." The hiding place was barely large to conceal one person.

Laura winced when he inadvertently brushed her breast as he tried to conceal her blouse with dead leaves. *Had he triggered memories of Ramos' attack? If she panicked they would be caught.* Mac whispered, "Sorry, but don't move," then pressed against her as she lay on her side with her back toward the trail. He hoped his flight suit would conceal them.

When the strangers paused within feet of the trail their voices remained steady with no hint of alarm. He felt Laura tense, almost rigid; her breaths short and sharp as he lay motionless against her, acutely conscious of her soft, warm body. As minutes passed he felt her relax and her breathing slow. Finally, the strangers continued along the trail toward Puerto Blanco.

Mac waited several more minutes before he risked brushing the leaves from his face then rolled over to cautiously check the trail. He said in a low voice, "Sit up slowly, then move your legs to get your circulation back."

Laura allowed him to help her sit up, then glanced around as if she sensed danger.

"It's all right," Mac reassured. Her hair was covered in leaves and twigs. "Here, allow me." She did not resist when he carefully removed them.

Incessant bird chatter and the brightening eastern sky signalled dawn's approach. For the first time, he could see Laura's fair complexion. The dim light accentuated the dark pools of her eyes, making her appear alone and frightened.

"Thank you," she said, then leaned forward.

For a moment he thought she was going to kiss him on the cheek, but she hesitated and softly said, "I owe you my life." He could see tears welling in the corners of her eyes. Although she had not talked about her imprisonment, he tried not to imagine what she had been through. He came within a heartbeat of taking her in his arms to comfort her before he realised that Laura reminded him of Belinda. Guilt about not being with Belinda after the accident still gnawed at him—not lessened by the police report which said that she had asked for him before the ambulance arrived. The prospect of comforting Laura felt like he was betraying Belinda. He glanced skyward. Belinda was gone, he told himself.

He said, his voice verging on breaking, "We should get moving. We'll go deeper into the woods in case there's anyone else on the trail." He avoided looking at Laura.

He found a path a hundred yards farther into the woods. The terrain became rougher as the path climbed away from the main trail. Mac took her hand. After almost an hour of steady climbing they sat with their backs against trees growing on opposite sides of the narrow trail while Laura regained her breath. Mac was surprised that Laura had the stamina to make it this far—he estimated that they had been walking for at least six hours.

This was the first time that he had been able to clearly see her and he tried not to appear overt as he stole glances. Laura was probably in her late twenties—slim, and alluringly attractive despite her matted and dirty auburn hair. Much of her skirt, blouse and right arm were covered with dried blood—whoever she had stabbed was probably dead judging by the quantity. Her torn blouse and bodice, barely held together by the grass stalks, did little to cover well-shaped breasts.

"Do I shock you?"

He knew that he had been caught. "I'm sorry. This is the first time I've been able to see you. You're beautiful..." His voice trailed off.

"How long have you been at sea," she asked, emphasising 'long'. She laughed aloud at his silence then, despite trying to keep her voice down, exclaimed, "Come, sir!" She continued in a mocking tone, "My hair is a mess. I'm covered in dried blood. My clothes are near completely ruined. I must smell like a decaying skunk as I haven't bathed in ages. You claim to find me beautiful? At least two years, is it?"

Mac was stunned. His mouth hung open like a frog who had just missed the fly. He fully expected women of that era to be less forthright. He could feel his cheeks burning.

Although her tone sounded conciliatory there was a mischievous twinkle in her eyes, "Now I've truly embarrassed you. Not to worry, you were so busy looking at me you didn't notice me doing likewise." Mac suspected that she was taking delight in his discomfort.

Laura continued, "You, sir, are not anything like I expected a hero to appear. Your face is covered in dirt, your hair is also a mess, and what on earth are you wearing?" She laughed, "You look like you've been sewn into a sack."

Mac was not sure if she was laughing at him, or as a release from the terror of her imprisonment.

"That's a long story," he replied, "and best saved for another time." Although he found Laura's resilience amazing he suspected she was running on adrenaline. The last thing he needed was to have her crash before they reached the beach. "You must be thirsty. I know I am. There should be a stream in three-quarters of a mile or so. It's light enough that we should find it easier going." He stood, extended his hand to help her up, and hoped it would be the same stream he had found earlier. He wasn't sure where they were.

Although the trail continued to climb it remained mostly clear of obstacles. Laura seemed to have recovered her energy and they made good progress—with daylight he no longer needed to hold her hand. Instead, he used both hands to move branches aside while she followed.

The sound of rushing water grew louder as the forest gave way to ferns nurtured by moisture from a clear stream tumbling over a rocky bed. Laura could not wait and kneeled at the stream's edge to scoop handfuls of water to her mouth while Mac filled the flask. He refilled the flask twice before they each drank their fill.

The morning sun filled him with warmth and hope. "This should be the stream I found earlier. We'll follow it down to the trail. From there it's just a short distance to the beach. A boat will pick us up after dark so we'll have to remain hidden until then. Ready?"

Laura nodded and reached for his hand. Her grip was confident yet relaxed, with none of the earlier trembling.

The fifteen foot wide stream narrowed as it descended the hillside toward a narrow cleft a hundred yards ahead. As they came closer the water became more agitated. The sound changed to a soft roar. Mac wondered if this was the waterfall he had found earlier.

When they reached the cleft the fall was much higher, at least forty feet, where it plunged over a rock face. The ground was too steep to descend at the falls and they were forced to work around to their left before eventually finding a narrow path. After slipping and sliding down the precarious slope, grasping branches and protruding roots to slow themselves, they rested below the waterfall at the stream's edge.

Mac looked at Laura. Her eyes had a twinkling fire and she seemed to have added colour in her cheeks, but perhaps it was just the light. He said, "I'm sorry I don't have much to eat—just a single ship's biscuit. I wasn't expecting a guest."

Laura laughed. "Can you climb?"

"Why?"

She pointed upward.

He twisted his head around. The tree above was laden with bananas. He chuckled and did his best to imitate an English butler, "Din..ahhh will be served in two minutes, if Your Ladyship is ready."

Her Ladyship was more than ready—they were both famished and ate in silence until Laura clutched her chest and gasped when a solitary gunshot echoed through the woods to shatter their idyllic picnic.

For an anxious moment Mac thought she had been hit, until he realised it was only surprise at the sound of the gun. He glanced about quickly for the source which sounded as though it came from downstream. The shooter was not in sight as he looked for an escape route knowing they could not climb back to the top of the waterfall.

He grabbed the water flask, flung the remaining bananas into the forest, and took Laura's hand. She stifled a protest when he yanked her to her feet and headed toward large rocks at the base of the waterfall. Satisfied that the rocks were large enough to hide behind and in heavy shadow, he turned to her. She wore the same expression of anger and hurt as Belinda when he messed up. For a moment he wasn't sure how he had offended her.

"Sorry about grabbing you like that," he said, "I was more concerned about our safety. Stay down and we'll be okay." He tried to sound reassuring, but his heart was racing—although it would be nearly impossible for anyone to see them, they were trapped if they were spotted.

After a tense ten minutes, interspersed with several cautious glances around the boulder, Mac saw two men crouched seventy-five yards downstream filling their water flasks. When the men stood he could see their mouths moving but could not hear their conversation. If they were soldiers they didn't appear to be wearing a uniform. He retreated behind the rock when the nearest man gestured toward the rocks with his musket.

"What's the matter?" Laura asked.

"One of them looked this way. He couldn't have heard us over the noise of the water and I don't think he saw me."

He waited ten seconds, then carefully peeked around the rock. He had no choice but to take the risk—there was nowhere for Laura and him to go. The men had not moved; the nearest picked up the carcasses of several large birds before they continued downstream, away from Mac and Laura.

"Whew," he said, "just hunters."

The boulders, while providing cover, did not make a comfortable hiding place. Mac made sure that the men were out of sight, cautiously stood, then scrambled toward a rock outcrop.

"Where are you going?" Laura called anxiously.

"To see if there's somewhere more comfortable to hide. We're stuck here until late afternoon and these rocks will cripple me."

"Don't leave me," she pleaded.

"I won't go far," Mac called as he clambered around the rocks to the base of the waterfall, his curiosity further stirred by a rock ledge which seemed to lead behind the waterfall. He gingerly crept along the ledge made slippery by wet moss and followed it to a small cave behind the cascade. A pool, enclosed within the small grotto, was completely hidden from the outside. Small pebbles and sand formed a beach at the inner end. When he returned Laura's eyes were wide with anxiety.

"Are you all right? You said you wouldn't leave me."

"I'm sorry, but I was only gone for a few minutes."

"It seemed much longer."

"Well," he responded enthusiastically, "come and see what I've found."

Mac held her hand until past the ledge. Laura inhaled deeply, then stood silent—enthralled by the grotto. He said, "We can stay here until it's time to go to the beach." He knew that they could not be seen from outside and they could sleep without him having to keep guard. Besides, the sand would be much more comfortable than the boulders. When he offered to fetch more bananas her eyes darted back and forth.

"I really don't want to be alone," Laura blurted with a note of panic in her voice.

"Don't worry, I'll be quick."

Mac scrambled around the rocks, grabbed the bananas and sprinted back to the grotto. When he reached the entrance, Laura was peering out and looked as if she was on the verge of tears.

"Here we are. Sorry the menu isn't more varied, but it's the cook's day off," he quipped.

She brushed his upper arm with her hand and said, "These will do nicely. Bananas are a favourite of mine." She sighed, "At least today," then stepped away and walked around the pool toward the beach.

"Here," she said, motioning for him to sit beside her. "Tell me, Mac, exactly what brought you to Puerto Blanco? Are you in the habit of rescuing distressed damsels, or am I just very fortunate?"

Mac told her about the news of the Indiamen's capture and *Lionheart's* battle with the Spanish frigates and how he had offered to scout Puerto Blanco. "I waited until everyone would be asleep and was checking out your house when..." his voice trailed off when tears welled in her eyes. "I'm sorry, I didn't mean to cause you further pain." Laura didn't resist when he took her hand.

She brushed aside tears with her other hand and said, "No, please go on."

He looked into her eyes and gently squeezed her hand in reassurance, "Well the rest you know, for here we are. There's a beach not far from here where a boat will meet us tonight. We'll follow this stream back to the main trail and then to the beach."

Mac passed another banana to her before continuing, "We'll start out in late afternoon then hide in the forest behind the beach until dark. I've concealed a signal lantern so the boat will know when it's safe to come in."

Laura cocked her head slightly to one side. "Why do I have the feeling that there is more to your story than you have revealed?" She continued without waiting for his response, "No matter, as I mentioned earlier, I live in Baltimore. My father, Jamieson Babbett, is a diplomat with the Department of State. There are some concerns that Spain may not be able to control her South American possessions following the slave revolt in Port-au-Prince. I suspect Father was meeting with certain influential people to develop American relationships in the event there is a separation."

"But you were on the Indiaman. Wasn't she bound for London?"

"No, we were aboard an American ship. The pirates captured us, then used our ship to trick the English vessels with a false distress signal. Father had concluded his meetings and was on his way to Washington to meet with representatives of your government."

"Not my government." Mac emphasised 'my'. "I neglected to mention that I'm from Upper Canada and attached to an American cavalry regiment." He almost said armored cavalry.

Laura's brow furrowed. "Why are you on an English ship?" Clearly baffled by the incongruity she added, "But then I know so little about military matters."

"Yes, it's unusual, and quite complicated," he replied. "Perhaps we should finish your story first, mine will take more time. When were you captured?"

"Well," she paused to finish the last of her banana before continuing, "we were caught in a storm off Jamaica; the captain called it a flaw. Our masts and sails were damaged; while the crew were making repairs a ship appeared and offered to help. At first the captain was wary and sent our crew to the guns. When the ship identified herself as American he accepted their help.

"It wasn't until they were aboard that he realised they were pirates. They had captured the vessel they were on and forced one of her crew to persuade our captain to let them board. With surprise on their side they captured us quite easily.

"The first English ship arrived and thought we were repairing our sails and masts. The pirates convinced her that we needed additional materials and sent a boat to get them. She was boarded and captured, although with some resistance. I understand several of her crew and one officer were killed. Then we were taken to Puerto Blanco, where you found us. Another English ship was also captured and brought to Puerto Blanco."

Mac remained silent until she had finished. "When did this happen?"

Laura told him the storm was the night of October thirteen and they were captured on the fourteenth. "We arrived in Puerto

Blanco on the sixteenth. What day is it now? I've lost all track of time."

"November twenty-ninth."

She did not reply and gazed across the pool in silence.

~13~

A WILLING SURRENDER

MAC STARED AT THE CAVE'S ENTRANCE where Belinda had appeared to him—just as she had done previously when he was troubled. It was as if she was watching over him. This time she smiled, blew him a kiss, then turned away and dissolved into the waterfall's mist. He swallowed to clear the lump in his throat. Was she bidding me farewell?

Laura stroked her matted hair and said, "I don't know about you, but I'm in dire need of a thorough cleansing." She hesitated for a moment, then added, "I must be a sorry sight. Is this water safe? No leeches or hideous creatures lurking below the surface?"

Mac was still pondering possible meanings to Belinda's appearances—fond memories, guilt, ghosts truly existed, or he was just plain crazy—when he realised Laura had spoken. "Oh, sorry," he said and turned toward her. He vaguely remembered something about leeches and bathing, "It's quite safe. I'll wait outside until you're done."

He began to stand but Laura clutched his hand. "I'd prefer you stay. Please don't think my request improper. I need to be with someone I trust so that I know I'm safe."

The earlier wild-eyed desperation in her eyes was gone. Instead, Mac felt as if she were examining him under a microscope. The prospect did not bother him.

"Thank you," she said as he settled beside her. She brushed her hand against his, then removed her ankle boots before stepping to the edge of the pool to test the water with a hesitant toe. "It's lovely," she exclaimed, glancing over her shoulder and giving the first hint of a smile.

LAURA FACED THE WATER to prevent Mac seeing her hands tremble. She untied the grass strands securing her blouse, slipped it off and dropped it at her feet. She released her skirt's buttons and let it fall to her ankles, then ran a forefinger across her torn bodice and checked the ribbon around her waist that secured a pair of long, frilly legged underwear extending to mid-thigh. She stepped out of the crumpled skirt and kneeled at the water's edge, then immersed the blouse and skirt in the water and began scrubbing.

The sight of dissolved blood triggered a flood of memories of her imprisonment and unleashed a rage that she never knew she possessed. She twisted the cloth into knots, then tighter, imagining her hands around Ortega's neck until tears welled in her eyes. She held the blouse to her face and pretended to sniff it to determine if it was clean. She could not, would not, let Mac see her cry.

She remembered how she had overcome her fear during the last moments in her room: Ramos' weight on her, a vague recollection of the feel of the knife's hilt in her hand, the spray of hot blood when she wildly slashed at him, her cathartic, savage joy at his scream. Then she was at the window. She shivered at the memory of her absolute terror when Mac first grabbed her. *Or had I simply landed on him?* The flood of realisation that the blood in the water was Ramos' dispelled her tears. She swirled a toe to disperse the blood then carefully draped her blouse and skirt over a rock to dry. *The past was done. Well, almost. My father is still a prisoner. If Ortega harms him I will make sure that he suffers a worse fate than Ramos.*

Following her husband's death Laura discovered that he had informed his friends that she was 'a marriage of convenience.' Men, attracted by her looks, seemed to think that a young widow would be an easy conquest. That was one of the reasons she had accompanied her father.

She waded farther into the water. Memories of the first minutes after her escape were suddenly clear—she could recall every detail of Mac's concern. She looked up—light reflected from the water danced across the roof of the cave like fairies—and remembered how he had held her firmly but with an underlying gentleness. His calm voice had quelled the bitter taste of panic in her mouth. She felt her heart pounding at the realisation he was unlike any man she had ever known and glanced over her shoulder. He had not moved.

There is something special about Mac, even if he seems out of place and speaks in a strange manner. Moreover, he appears to be sincere—a trait lacking in many men of my acquaintance. I fully expected him to make advances. Strangely, his offer to leave while I bathed made it possible for me to ask him to stay.

Laura plunged her head beneath the surface. *Is his vacant stare toward the mouth of the cave indifference?* She would not let him see her disappointment. She would be strong and held her breath. A sudden clarity of thought overtook her. *Common sense—that it was impossible to know a man in such a short time—be damned.*

Laura resurfaced, swept wet hair from her face, then turned to face him, "Will you join me? The water's lovely, and there's certainly enough room for both of us. I'm sure you'd find it refreshing."

He did not answer.

So much for being strong, Laura thought as she swam away.

MAC KNEW HE WANTED to be with Laura but told himself this was crazy. He had known her less than a day and she had endured unspeakable terror. Despite their present circumstances he was no white knight—proven by the events leading up to his posting to Corn. He could not, must not, take advantage of her vulnerability.

However, whatever resolve he imagined that he possessed nearly melted under Laura's gaze. He struggled to define what attracted him to her and hoped it was more than simply her physical attributes. At least that was what he told himself when he fleetingly glimpsed the curve of her breast as she bent to wash her blouse. This, in turn, triggered more feelings of guilt—he was thinking like a horny teenager. Her auburn hair glistened in the light, despite the dirt encrusting it. She was obviously intelligent, with a sense of humour in spite of their current circumstances. Quick to make up her mind, she had placed her trust in him within minutes of their meeting.

Laura waded deeper into the pool, wet cloth tantalizingly translucent against her pale skin. He continued watching and thinking about her body until the water reached her shoulders. When she glanced back at him he felt like a moth being drawn to a flame. Then she disappeared under the water, as though she was but a dream. Just like Belinda.

He wasn't sure how much time passed before he realised that she had invited him to join her. He had sat immobilised by doubt. He had avoided "first daters" after his first year at university when he had fallen for a girl only to discover that he was only a fling.

That said, he still wanted to leap up, tear off his clothes and plunge into the water. Unfortunately his legs were quivering so much that he was sure he would fall flat on his face if he tried to stand. He had never been this nervous around other women. *Why does she affect me so?* So, there he sat—mouth open and heart pounding uncontrollably. *Lord, she's attractive.*

He eventually sputtered, "Okay," then mentally kicked himself for such a lame response. He removed his boots and unzipped his flightsuit, leaving them in an untidy heap near the pool's edge. Clad only in his boxers, the water tingled against his body as he waded into the pool.

LAURA PAUSED at Mac's response, shook the water from her hair, and turned to see him enter the pool. He was heavily tanned—unusual for someone new to the tropics. She wondered how he kept his undergarment in place for there was no sign of a drawstring.

While he swam to her with a practiced breast stroke she tried to quiet her imagination. "How, exactly, did a cavalry officer find himself aboard an English ship?"

Mac floated on his back while he rendered a condensed version of the story he had told Cathcart, reasoning that if he was going to lie he should be consistent.

Laura laughed at the mention of *La Señora de la Noche*. "Forgive me," she chuckled at the awkward look on his face, "I wasn't finding humour in your plight, rather in the ship's name." Her eyes sparkled with glee. "Do you know what it means?"

"No." He hesitated, not sure if he wanted to know judging by the expression on her face. "I don't understand much Spanish, beyond si and cerveza." He hoped that might get him off the hook.

"It means 'Lady of the Night'." Laura was nearly beside herself with laughter.

Taken aback, he took a deep breath. "Well, certainly not any lady I'd care to associate with again after my treatment aboard her. Maybe that's why one of *Lionheart's* crew called her a 'right hooker'."

Mac recounted his capture and imprisonment in the stinking cell until *Lionheart* arrived. "Her fool of a captain opened fire. Luckily for me Captain Cathcart didn't unload his entire broadside. If he had, *Señora* would have been reduced to splinters in an instant, and I'd be dead. British sailors found me but I mistook them for more Spaniards and tried to escape. That got me another whack on the head for my trouble."

Laura bobbed closer and caressed the side of his head with one hand. "You certainly seem to have a propensity for finding trouble." Her tone was gently mocking, but her eyes expressed sympathy.

He told her how he and Toby had become friends, and of life aboard a frigate.

Mac grasped Laura's shoulder when her foot slipped. Laura winced at his touch then looked at him questioningly. He could feel the tension in her shoulders lessen as he began gently manipulating the muscles.

Laura said, "That feels exquisite," and turned her back to him.

Mac began massaging her back, the sensation of her soft skin surged through her silky bodice to his very core.

Laura stopped his hand at her shoulder, then turned toward him and placed a hand on his left shoulder.

"Your turn." Her voice was soft, yet left no doubt that this was an order. She began massaging his back. Her hands were supple and surprisingly strong as they deftly worked out the knots in his muscles.

When her fingers sensuously traced a scar line across the small of his back Mac fought the impulse to take her in his arms. Instead, he repeated to himself, "No one-night stands," then said, "let's sit on the sand, the water's getting cold." Cold was not the problem. If anything, things were getting too warm.

Mac spread his flight suit on the sand. Laura sat, her legs tucked under her, and used her skirt as a shawl while Mac continued with the story of the musket contest. They both laughed at how Cathcart had outplayed him.

When he described the battle with the Spanish frigates, but not how the Spanish grapeshot had nearly killed him and Williams, Laura put one hand on his shoulder and said, "That sounds very dangerous. You weren't hurt?"

Mac laughed and said, "So far, so good," before recalling how he had found the other prisoners while avoiding mention of her ordeal and rescue. He squeezed her hand and said, "And here we are."

"That's very interesting, although..." Laura paused, then with a hint of a laugh in her voice said, "Why do I still have the feeling that there's more to this story than you've told me? Please don't misunderstand. I'm grateful that such a remarkable series of coincidences brought you to me at the opportune time." She did not wait for him to reply, "It must be fate." With a wistful expression she added, "Do you believe in fate?"

"I might," he replied. "What brought you here?"

Laura paused, looked into his eyes, and thought for a moment about how he might react. Will he be like the others? There was only one way to find out. "My husband died last year, so I decided to accompany my father." The moment she mentioned her husband's death she saw genuine sadness in Mac's expression.

"I'm so sorry." His voice was choked with emotion as he placed his left hand on top of her right. "Do you want to talk about it?"

No man had ever asked her that—her emotions were never their concern. When his eyes did not waver from hers Laura felt like he was reaching into her heart. She looked at him again—his expression had not changed; he still had the same concerned look. "I realised after his death that it had not been a happy marriage." She could not bring herself to tell him about how she had been betrayed. Impulsively she asked, "Are you married?" She immediately realised by the change in his expression that she had touched an old wound.

Before she could retract the question he replied, "Almost. My fiancé, Belinda, was killed in an accident two weeks before..." Mac could not continue and looked down.

"I, too, am sorry. You obviously loved her very much."

Mac kept his head bowed, "It seems that we both have scars." He looked up, "Mine are from what might have been." He caressed her cheek with his free hand then ran his fingers down her neck and held her shoulder. "I suspect yours are from betrayal."

Laura felt a dam full of emotions burst with those six words. She had waited all her life for a man to understand her. *How can someone I have known less than a day do that?* She could not, would not, let Mac see her cry. She stood without saying a word and walked away.

Mac watched Laura enter the pool then pulled on his flightsuit and headed toward the grotto's entrance. His mind reeled from the certainty he had said something to hurt her. How could he apologise or tell her that he cared?

He stared out the cave's entrance in thought. The problem was that Laura was perplexingly both strong and vulnerable. It was her inner strength and intelligence that had first stirred his interest. He knew she must be emotionally vulnerable from the aftermath of her marriage and imprisonment. Common sense told him to proceed slowly despite the growing feeling that she was 'the one'.

Laura plunged below the surface and swam—the cool water immediately washed away her tears' salty sting. She surfaced briefly to suck in a breath and submerged again. At the far end of the pool she thrust her head above the surface and gagged—she could not both cry and swim under water without getting a mouthful of water. She barely had time to catch a lung full of air before she glimpsed him and retreated beneath the water. *God, he must think me a complete dolt.*

Mac heard Laura cough, as though gagging, but when he turned toward her she was swimming away underwater. He desperately tried to sort through his emotions; angry with himself over the damage he had done to their relationship—if they even had one.

Laura reached the beach end and glanced back Mac continued staring toward the waterfall. By the time she completed three lengths and had stolen several cautious glances, her mind was clear. She called to him but he continued to stare out the cave's entrance as though he had not heard her. Finally, he turned to face her. "Sorry, I was thinking about something else."

"I asked, 'Why are you over there?'"

Mac's suspicion that he was falling in love with Laura had given way to certainty despite the inner logic reminding him it was less than a day since he caught her at the window. Yet it felt as if he had been waiting a lifetime to find her.

Following Belinda's death any new relationship always resulted in Belinda appearing to him. She would give him the same questioning look and each relationship eventually failed—the longest had lasted six weeks. At first he had thought it was just a trick of his mind; but Belinda's appearance in the cave made him almost certain she was a ghost. This was the first time that Belinda or her ghost—a possibility he would have rejected a few weeks ago—hadn't overruled his heart. He muttered to himself that believing in ghosts was silly and stifled a chuckle when he had to admit that he had not believed in time travel either.

Should I tell her how I feel? Do I dare reveal the truth behind my presence? Dappled reflected light danced upon her and he fought the urge to run to her. As he came nearer the water droplets glistened on her skin. He took her in his arms and kissed her. Laura did not resist. Instead, she returned his kiss with passion and pulled him closer.

LAURA RELIVED THE MEMORY of their lovemaking and pressed her cheek against Mac's chest, not sure which was louder: the waterfall or her pounding heart. He gently stroked her hair with one hand while his other idly traced random circles on her back. Under any other circumstance she would not have lain with a man after only one day, yet she had no regret about giving herself to Mac.

With a tingling excitement she realised that she had never felt this way about a man—even her dead husband who, she now realised, had never loved her. The excitement of their first few months had soon evaporated like a morning fog when she realised she had only been attracted to the idea of marriage. The bitter knowledge that he had betrayed their vows within months, if not weeks, of their union had left her distrustful of men. How could Mac be so different? The emptiness in her soul was gone. She felt safe with him, but did he feel the same about her? She pulled away slightly, but kept one calf over his. She needed to see his reaction to what she was about to reveal. "Does it bother you that I have been with another man after my husband died?"

Laura held her breath and thought her heart was about to explode. *What on Earth ever prompted me to ask that? Men of previous acquaintance would consider me a trollop for having lain with someone else, yet would believe it was their right, as a man, to sleep with as many women as they chose without impugning their own character. Why was that?*

Mac's expression did not change. Instead, he pulled her closer and said with the gentleness of a summer breeze, "Of course not." He kept his eyes fixed on hers and continued, "I've also been in other relationships." He brushed stray hairs from her forehead and caressed her cheek, "We can't change the past."

Laura thought she must be dreaming.

He kissed her softly on the top of her left breast, then gently ran his hand along her thigh as he sat up. "I need to check the sun to know what time it is. We should start for the beach an hour before sunset so there's less chance of being seen." He retrieved his undergarment and turned to her. "I'm just going to the mouth of the cave. I'll be right back."

Laura, warm in the afterglow of their lovemaking, watched him disappear through the grotto's entrance. He had made it seem as though she was the only one who mattered. No man had ever aroused her so.

"I was getting cold," Laura said apologetically when he returned—she was sitting in the midst of their makeshift bed, wearing his flight suit. She waited until he was closer and confessed, "I so wanted you near me, even though I knew you were but a short distance away." She pulled the shoulder of the too-large flightsuit to her nose as she stood. "It has your scent. It's as though you're wrapped around me." She snuggled against him, "Could you determine the time?"

"I make it between two and three o'clock, which means we have about two..."

"Good," she interrupted and placed her hands on his shoulders as if to embrace him. Instead, she turned him as she stepped around him, and pushed him backward onto the ground before landing on top of him. She playfully opened the flightsuit's zipper a few inches, "There is time for you to show me how this device works. It seems very useful if one is in a hurry."

"Or not," Mac replied.

He held her fingers on the zipper's clasp and continued downward in a slow, deliberate, slide. Laura's breath quickened and goosebumps rose on her skin when he slipped his other hand under the flight suit and caressed her. Their lips and tongues merged.

There was none of the urgent desire of their first. Only a slow, deliberate passion as Mac aroused her. She drew him to her then let him withdraw as they explored every inch of the other's body. He kissed and caressed her until they both exploded. The roar of her blood and pounding heart drowned out the thunder of the waterfall.

Eventually Mac stood, helped her to her feet, and said with a wink, "A cold bath will do me good."

Laura could still feel his touch, even after swimming several lengths of the pool and realised that she might be in love for the first time in her life. *Can I be both strong and in love?*

After they dressed Mac held her hand to guide her along the narrow ledge past the boulders to the stream bed now deep in shadow, where they cast a final glance toward the grotto.

Laura, unused to displays of affection, was surprised when Mac put his arm around her. True, they were in the middle of nowhere and no one could see them, but the greater surprise was that Mac continued to talk to her as an equal, something that neither her husband or previous lover had ever done—especially after satisfying their own desires.

"Good," Mac exclaimed when they arrived at a smaller waterfall. "Now I'm sure where we are. The main path is just ahead." He knelt to refill their canteen.

Laura reached into the water with one hand and playfully splashed him. "Just keeping you cool so you can concentrate on the job at hand," she said, and then laughed. Mac was the first man who made her feel safe enough to be spontaneous. Perhaps it was because he could laugh at himself.

They followed the trail to the beach where Mac recovered the concealed lantern. The lantern wick sputtered to life with his third strike of the flint, then settled to a satisfying flame before he extinguished it. He led the way to the edge of the underbrush and arranged a piece of driftwood so that they could sit reclined.

The setting sun produced a final flash of green as it dropped below the empty horizon. Mac squeezed her hand, sighed, and said, "A bottle of wine would make this a perfect evening."

Laura, fast asleep with her head against his chest, did not reply.

~14~

KEEPING UP APPEARANCES

RINGLE SIGHTED *LIONHEART* standing well to the west of Puerto Blanco at dawn of the twenty-third. Lieutenant-Commander Wilson crossed over in the jolly boat to report to Cathcart.

"I spoke both *Castellon* and *Matilda* four hours out of Kingston. All is well with them," the young commander said. "The Admiral already knew of the prizes. *Seppings* arrived at Kingston just before we sailed. She is a fine sailer, probably faster than *Ringle* in these winds, and should be hot on our heels with the prize crews."

Wilson spoke non-stop until nearly breathless. He sensed he was about to become part of something special—his share of the prize money if they were successful in recapturing the merchant ships and their cargoes from the Spanish already calculated.

Cathcart nodded in approval and smiled. The timing of *Ringle's* arrival fit his plans perfectly. She would fetch Mac—her shallow draft made her more suitable for inshore work, freeing *Lionheart* to rendezvous with *Seppings* out of sight of land.

Cathcart hastily drafted Wilson's orders, appending a map of the cove and the recognition signals. "Secrecy is of utmost importance, d'ye understand!" Cathcart knew Wilson understood and tried to soften his admonition. "Do you join me for some lunch and bring me up to date on Kingston." Gossip was always better dispensed over a meal and wine, especially when a perennially hungry young lieutenant was involved.

ONE TURN OF THE SANDGLASS after sunset, Mac carefully shifted Laura so as not to wake her, then lit the lantern. He shielded the flame while he adjusted the wick, then closed the glass door and shutters. He began the agreed signal of three short flashes every fifteen minutes timed by turns of the sandglass illuminated by the lamp chimney's faint glow.

He had replayed the day in his mind while Laura slept, confident that his attraction to her was genuine—she was not just a passing moment—even if he was tempted to wake her when she had moved in her sleep. Laura was curled tight against him— the bulge of her left breast alluring in the moonlight, her thigh a comfortable place to rest his free hand. Instead, he worried that she might not feel the same about him—as he had previously discovered to his dismay. He flashed another signal and turned the sand glass.

Laura stirred and murmured, "Tell me more about yourself" She nuzzled her head against his shoulder, showing no sign of regret over their earlier intimacy.

Her request reinforced his increasing discomfort with continuing the charade about his true situation. Eventually he was going to have to disclose the truth—but not now.

As they talked about their lives and families it was uncanny how similar his and Laura's interests, beliefs and values were. When she again mentioned her dead husband's betrayals he stroked the side of her head and said, "Not all men are like that." *Yet, am I being exactly that kind of man by withholding the truth?* He tried to rationalise that not disclosing was less of a sin than an outright lie.

Laura kissed his cheek, "So I keep telling myself," but she said it with a note of resignation—as if she did not believe it really possible.

When he signaled for the eighth time a single flash from seaward replied. He counted off ten seconds in his head, then responded with three flashes. These were immediately answered by a pair of flashes. Mac left the shutter open to guide the boat.

"They're here," he whispered.

"I know," she said. "I was hoping they might take longer."

The faint squeak of an oarlock floated toward them. He whispered in imitation of a movie pirate, "C'm along, m' lovely," then called, "boat ahoy."

"*Ringle*," replied a strange voice.

Mac was surprised by the response, wondering if something was wrong. He had been expecting Toby. The boat materialised out of the darkness, a nebulous silhouette against the phosphorescent waves breaking on the beach. Mac extinguished the lantern.

Someone in the boat ordered, "Up oars," a moment later the boat scuffed softly into the wet sand. An unrecognisable figure jumped from the stern and waded the last few yards to the beach.

"Commander Wilson, sir," the man announced. "Captain Cathcart's apologies, he thought it best if we came for you. Not so long a row back to the ship as we do not draw anywhere near the depth." He paused, "Sorry, sir, we were not expecting another passenger."

Mac replied. "This is Miss Babbett, a passenger on one of the Indiamen. Circumstances required that I provide her a safe escort. I apologise if we've overcrowded your boat."

"Not at all, sir." Wilson bowed, " Miss, if you will give me your hand I shall assist you aboard."

Wilson ensured Laura and Mac were safely seated in the bow before climbing aboard at the stern. He said in a low voice, "Shove off. Oars easy back, take us out ten yards."

Laura huddled tight against Mac and shivered; he was acutely reminded that her torn blouse was barely held together, and what that might mean when they reached *Ringle* and light. When he asked for a spare boat cloak Wilson offered his jacket.

"'Ere you go, zur." A pair of work-rough hands handed the jacket to Mac who found it difficult to fit it around Laura's shoulders in the darkness and awkward confines of the boat. She discretely squeezed his hand when he finished.

The passage to *Ringle* was brief. The boat tapped softly against the schooner's side. "Scuse me, sir' and 'Sorry, ma'am' accompanied the crew's attempts to steady the boat against *Ringle* so Laura could make a graceful exit. All lights aboard the schooner were doused, causing some concern about the best way for her to board. Despite Laura's insistence that she could manage on her own, the entire boat's crew took it upon themselves to be the one to assist—the weight of so many bodies on one side nearly capsizing the craft. Fortunately it was securely tied to *Ringle*.

An exasperated Wilson hissed, "Eyes to the boat, you rabid mob. The next one to move will be flogged." Ignoring naval tradition that required the captain to board first, Wilson offered his hand. "Miss," he said, "if you will permit. Just grab hold here and I will place your foot."

Drawn by the female voice and silhouetted against the stars, an enthusiastic group of volunteers loomed at the rail until they were brusquely ordered back by the bosun who assisted Laura over the side as if she was a feather on the breeze.

"Oh thank you," Laura responded, "I was quite afraid I'd plunge into the sea."

By now Mac knew Laura was toying with the bosun. She was naturally athletic—as he had discovered during their escape—and had scrambled to the main chains despite the dark.

"Welcome aboard Miss Babbett and Captain Appleton." An enthusiastic Wilson welcomed them to his ship, although the dark made it virtually impossible to see anything. He excused himself to get the schooner underway and ordered, "Prepare to weigh anchor. Starboard tack, if you please, as close to the wind as she will bear."

Mac was surprised by Wilson's use of 'please'—perhaps on a small ship there was greater familiarity, or a less rigid command structure.

Someone forward called, "Up and down." Mac knew that meant the ship was moving forward and the strain was off the anchor cable. A moment later the capstan began clicking around on its pawls in response.

"Anchor's aweigh, sir." The call from the bow confirmed that *Ringle* had freed herself from the bottom.

Wilson continued to call out a steady stream of orders as the water began to gurgle along *Ringle's* slender length. "I believe she will carry inner and outer jibs." When the mizzen sail fluttered for a moment he growled, " Watch your luff, damn your eyes. I have no desire to be washed up on some beach. Nor do I want to be in sight of land come dawn," Wilson muttered to no one in particular before turning to his guests.

"Ma'am, Captain Appleton, we should have *Lionheart* in sight at dawn. It will take but a few minutes have my cabin made more presentable for the lady if I may trouble you to remain on deck. Please watch your step, there are a number of hazards waiting to trip you."

The preparations completed, Wilson returned to his guests. "I am afraid space is rather limited and I hope you find the arrangements suitable. Please do watch your step over the coaming." He led the way through the hatch, hastily adding not a moment too soon, "And your head on the beams, sir. Not like a frigate."

The cabin was dimly lit by a pair of candles—the scuttles and small stern windows securely covered by deadlights to prevent giving away *Ringle's* presence. Wilson could see that Laura's clothing was in a state of disrepair. Her skirt was visibly bloodstained and she seemed to be keeping his jacket tightly wrapped around her for reasons more than warmth. "If you will pardon my directness ma'am, perhaps we can find some clean clothes for you. I regret we only have trousers aboard if you do not object."

Laura responded with genuine thanks. "Trousers would be most welcome and much more practical under the circumstances. I always wear them when riding as I prefer a proper saddle. I do thank you for your consideration."

Wilson nodded in acknowledgement, "I would offer you some of my own, but I fear they would be rather large. I will pass word forward, several of our crew are similar in size." He hoped he had avoided any perception that he was trying to ascertain either her size or shape, although curiosity—and eighteen months at sea—almost got the better of him.

Mac sensed Wilson's sudden discomfort, but before he could interrupt Wilson turned towards him. "Have you eaten? I can have some food brought to you. Meager rations unfortunately; our galley is not lit and my own private stores are long since exhausted."

Laura responded, although Wilson was still looking at Mac. "Thank you, Commander, that would be most appreciated. I've had but a few bananas. The exertions of our journey have left me ravenous." Her knowing wink to Mac going unseen by Wilson. "I'm sure Captain Appleton must be in the same state. He gallantly surrendered his last half biscuit after rescuing me."

Wilson passed word for food and said, "Sir, it will be few minutes while we ready the bosun's cabin for you. If I can offer anything to make your stay more comfortable I would be pleased to do so."

"Thank you," Mac responded. "I'm sure the lady will be most comfortable. For myself, a spare hammock forward will more than suffice, there's no need to inconvenience your bosun. I'd like to get some sleep before we meet *Lionheart*. Captain Cathcart will want to know what I discovered and I'm exhausted." He added, "Please call me Mac when the situation permits. Captain sounds so formal in our present situation."

"And Laura would be most welcome," she said.

Wilson, visibly relaxed, said, "I would be honoured if you call me Silas. Please excuse me while I make arrangements for'ard."

The moment Wilson closed the door Laura placed her head against Mac's chest and whispered, "I wish we could be together."

"Me, too," he said, "but for the sake of your honour it's best to maintain a polite distance between us. I'll be thinking of you."

"Yes, we'll have plenty of time later. I'll be thinking of you, too."

A soft knock at the door announced Wilson had returned with her new clothes.

Mac stepped silently back. As the door opened he said, "I'll leave you now Miss Babbett. I trust you'll sleep well. Perhaps we'll see each other in the morning."

"Perhaps," she replied noncommittally.

Wilson led Mac forward, crouching beneath the schooner's low deck beams, then said, "Unfortunately we lack an extra cot so a hammock's been rigged for you, I hope you will find it comfortable."

"I'm sure I will, I've been sleeping in one aboard *Lionheart*."

Wilson had assumed that Mac was berthing in the wardroom with the other officers. He was curious to discover the whole story.

"SIR," A REMOTE VOICE SAID. The hammock rocked while Mac tried to decide if this was part of his dream.

"Sir!"

A more vigorous shaking caused him to utter a muffled "Uhhh."

"Sir, Captain's compliments, *Lionheart* in sight hove to."

"Thank you, what time is it?" Mac rasped.

"Four bells, mornin' watch, sir." The voice sounded relieved at the response.

"Very good, I'm awake now, thank you." Mac rubbed his eyes and considered 'awake' might be optimistic. Two minutes later he was on deck, massaging the top of his head as Wilson looked at him quizzically.

"Deck beams." Mac winced. "Being tall does have its disadvantages from time to time, does it not?"

Wilson laughed. "As I'm occasionally reminded. D'ye see *Lionheart* off our port bow? We should reach her this board." He glanced at the main sail and uttered, "Watch your luff," to the helmsman.

Mac reverted to formality on deck. "Sir, you must know I'm rather ignorant when it comes to things nautical. What exactly does the term 'board' mean?"

Wilson seemed surprised by the question. "It refers to tacking as we sail into the wind. At the moment we're on the port tack, because the wind is coming from our port or larboard side. Each board is merely the time we stay on this tack, before starting a new board on the starboard. Sometimes you might hear the expression 'short boards' which means we're tacking in quick succession. Today we're making long boards, hence more time between each change."

"Ahh," Mac nodded appreciatively, "and luff, sir? I've heard lieutenants referred to as 'First Luff' and such, but I know you don't have any aboard *Ringle*. Are you watching a particular one aboard *Lionheart*?"

Wilson laughed aloud. "Oh heavens no! The luff is the aft edge of the sail. If it starts flapping the helmsman isn't steering true. Watch his eyes." He nodded toward the man, "See how he checks the sail and then looks ahead along our course. Now watch the luff; the moment it starts fluttering move your eyes as quickly as you can to him and then back to the luff. You'll have to be quick though."

Mac watched until the luff of the sail shivered slightly.

"Watch your luff," Wilson growled in mock anger.

Mac quickly glanced at the helmsman who shifted the wheel by one spoke. Mac checked the sail, now rock hard in the breeze with not a sign of the previous flutter. He reasoned it was the same as applying a rudder in the Apache to counteract a crosswind.

Wilson commented in a stage whisper to Mac, "Ripley's the best helmsman I have ever known."

When Ripley smiled Mac suspected he'd deliberately let *Ringle* stray.

Laura, clad in a pair of oversize sailor's dungarees and a plain shirt, stepped through the after hatch and blinked in the bright light. The bedraggled person who had collapsed exhausted in Wilson's cot was gone. Her hair, gathered in a tight bun at the back of her head, glistened in the sunlight. She could have easily passed for a young midshipman—the loose clothes successfully concealing her femininity. She looked about, then smiled at Wilson and said, "Good morning, Captain."

"Good morning, Miss Babbett. A fine morning indeed." Wilson responded cheerfully.

"Good morning, ma'am," Mac echoed with enthusiasm, although wondering if she now regretted yesterday in the grotto.

Wilson pointed across the water to where the frigate lay hove to astern of *Ringle*, sharp and clear in the brilliant morning light. "*Lionheart* lies three miles yonder. Perhaps some coffee? I believe the galley has just produced a fresh pot."

"Thank you, captain." Laura smiled beguilingly, "That would be most welcome." She glanced at two sailors near the galley hatch, behind Wilson's back, who were attempting to elbow each other away from the hatch.

The steaming cup arrived within twenty seconds of her acceptance, carried by the breathless victor, a prime topman who could scamper the height of the mast without effort, yet panted from the exertion of carrying a coffee mug less than thirty feet.

"Oh thank you, I hope I haven't inconvenienced you." Laura said.

The sailor stood stock still, as if his foot had been suddenly nailed to the deck, and stared at Laura until Wilson's glare caused him to hastily depart.

Wilson said, "We should be up to *Lionheart* within the hour. You must be famished. Would you care to take breakfast in my cabin?"

Laura's enthusiastic acceptance was quickly followed by Wilson's orders to the galley. "Not your usual sludge, mind you."

~15~

A BITTER END REVEALED

*L*IONHEART LAY A HALF-CABLE DISTANT off *Ringle's* larboard when the schooner came about on the starboard tack. *Lionheart* was more impressive than Mac recalled—the only time he had seen her from a distance was when his mind was still shrouded in fog from captivity aboard the slaver. Every sail was neatly furled, except for the scraps keeping her hove to. Her black hull, sinister against the azure sea, was broken by a buff band running from bow to stern along the gunports which, open for ventilation, revealed their scarlet interior surface. Sailors swarmed over her shrouds and yards to perform the endless maintenance.

Ringle, her upper gaffs lowered to release the breeze from the sails and her helm thrown over as sailors overhauled the jib sails, performed a flawless pirouette under the watchful eyes of the frigate's officers. She came to a stop under the frigate's sheltering lee where she lowered her gig to transport Wilson and Mac.

A voice from *Lionheart* challenged, "Boat ahoy."

"*Ringle*," replied the gig's coxswain, indicating her commander was aboard.

Mac chuckled to himself at the redundant tradition. Not only could the lookout see Wilson in the boat, but Wilson had been ordered to report.

Wilson ascended first—the senior officer was always last in and first out—to be greeted by twittering bosun's calls and the stomp of the marine side party coming to attention. Mac waited, to ensure he didn't arrive on deck while Wilson was being honoured.

After the formalities had been observed Cathcart shook Mac's hand. "I trust that you are well Mr. Appleton. I understand you rescued a lady."

Toby, standing several feet behind Cathcart, arched his eyebrows.

"Yes, thank you, sir. Miss Babbett was a passenger on one of the Indiamen. Her father, an American diplomat, is being held at Puerto Blanco."

Cathcart nodded, "You must tell me more while we take coffee in my cabin. I have some excellent Jamaican mountain-grown beans which arrived with *Seppings*. They are a gift from the Admiral and cannot have been harvested more than a few days ago."

Mac's mouth had been watering ever since he had smelled them being roasted from the gig.

Cathcart ushered Toby and Mac into the great cabin. Mac squinted against the sunlight reflected off the water through the stern gallery windows and shielded his eyes with a hand. Charts covered the table in preparation for Mac's briefing on the situation ashore—clearly Cathcart despised wasting time if there was business to be conducted. Cathcart began, "I should bring you up-to-date on our current situation before I ask Mac to tell us what, and whom, he found."

Mac thought he detected a wry grin when Cathcart glanced at him.

Cathcart continued, "*Seppings* arrived during the night with our prize crews. She is currently investigating a strange sail we espied at dawn. I doubt the stranger will have seen us, hove to as we are, for we scarcely remarked her topsail. In any event, *Seppings* will run her down without giving away our presence.

"The Admiral is concerned that *Thunderbolt* is overdue, possibly missing. At least *Ringle* and *Seppings* will provide a few more men should we venture ashore at Puerto Blanco. Unfortunately it is *Thunderbolt's* firepower that we sorely need. Mac, be so good as to tell us about your adventures ashore; but first, gentlemen, fill your cups."

Mac took a cautious sip of the near scalding liquid before recounting the events leading to his observations, then carefully unfolded the map he had sketched and placed it on the table. He indicated where the ships were anchored cautioning, "I can't vouch for the scale, but the relative positions are correct."

Cathcart's interest in the third ship was apparent. "Can you describe the smaller vessel? You said two masts?"

Mac, curious as he had considered a small ship a mundane matter, continued, "Forgive me if I use the wrong terminology. She seemed to be missing one mast as there was a large space in the middle of her deck. As though there should be another mast."

"Sir," interjected Toby, "that sounds like *Thunderbolt*."

Cathcart didn't comment and asked, "Did you see any large objects on her deck?"

Mac visualised the ship in his mind, "Yes. Perhaps crates of some sort? I thought they were cargo."

Cathcart's brow furrowed. "Did they appear dark and squat?"

"I believe black, certainly very dark, and fat."

"I am confident that you are correct, Toby." Cathcart glanced up from Mac's map. "She has to be *Thunderbolt*." Cathcart's mood noticeably darkened. "Cracking that fort will be difficult, if not impossible, without her. I gather you also located the prisoners during your travels."

Mac attempted to inject a little good news into the pall that had crept into the cabin. "Yes, they're being held in two houses not far apart from each other." He pointed at the map, "The officers and Mr. Babbett are here in the second house, the seamen in the first." He explained finding the loose stone in the wall and talking with the prisoners. Then, pointing at Cathcart's chart which showed only the briefest outline of the town, he described the remainder of the town and the two-storey house facing the plaza.

Cathcart looked up from the table and appeared to be trying to contain a smile. "And your encounter with Miss Babbett?"

Mac provided a simplified version, playing down the events inside the house and omitting their blossoming relationship, saying it was only a matter of being in the right place at the right time to assist her.

"Yes, most fortunate for Miss Babbett." Cathcart lowered his head, then resumed pondering the chart in silence for another minute. "The fort and battery greatly concern me. We still lack reliable intelligence about how many men are at each emplacement, or if there are more in the town. You say you saw only two guards at the second house? Have they increased the guard? Could Miss Babbett provide more information?"

Mac replied, "I'm sure she would be most willing to help in any way." He was eager to see her again.

THE GIG'S OARSMEN quickened their pace at Midshipman Barnes' urging and travelled to *Ringle* in record time where Barnes breathlessly announced, "Captain's compliments, he trusts that the timing is not inconvenient. Would the lady attend to provide information regarding the Spanish disposition?" In his excitement at conveying this important message, not to mention the opportunity to talk with the passenger whose mere presence had the entire frigate astir, Barnes had mangled Cathcart's request for 'Information about the disposition of Spanish forces at Puerto Blanco.'

Laura wasn't sure what she knew about the Spanish disposition, other than they seemed to have been disposed to kidnapping and raping her. Nevertheless, she agreed. She descended into the gig without missing a step and seated herself at the bow despite Barnes' caution, "Watch your step ma'am."

It only took a few minutes to reach *Lionheart*—most of which time Laura spent glancing over her shoulder. She hoped to catch a glimpse of Mac, but she also wanted to avoid Barnes' stare which resembled that of a puppy waiting for a treat.

When they reached *Lionheart* three sailors, poised in the gig to catch her should she misstep, watched her upward progress with more than passing interest. "Eyes to the boat," Toby growled as he peered over the railing, "or you will be a week without grog."

Laura did not see Mac until she reached the railing. Toby continued to glower at the particular seaman who had nudged his mate while watching her.

Mac stepped to one side, "Lieutenant Baverstock, may I present Miss Laura Babbett of Baltimore, Maryland."

"Thank you for your concern, sir." Laura looked at Toby and conspiratorially tipped her head toward the gig.

Toby motioned aft and said, "If you will follow me, the Captain is awaiting you in his cabin."

Cathcart had donned his best uniform coat despite the tropical heat. Toby, not to be upstaged a second time, made the introductions after Cathcart gracefully bowed then kissed Laura's hand, "Pleased to make your acquaintance, Miss Babbett. I trust you had a comfortable journey aboard *Ringle*."

"Why thank you, sir, she is a wonderful ship and seems very fast. I have asked the other gentlemen to call me Laura when circumstances permit and I hope that you will do the same. I must say *Lionheart* made a splendid sight as we approached. I do hope I have the chance to see more of her."

"Ma'am..." Cathcart paused to correct himself. "I'm sorry... Laura. Nothing would give me greater pleasure."

Mac, forced to bite his tongue to keep a straight face, knew he wasn't the only one she had ensnared with her charm.

Cathcart motioned to the charts on the table. "I asked you to join us in the hope you can provide some enlightenment on the disposition of the Spanish forces and the layout of the town. If we are to have any chance at rescuing the passengers and crew we need all the intelligence we can gather. Would you care for a sherry while we talk?"

Laura smiled graciously at him. "I'd much prefer a brandy if that is not inconvenient."

Mac suspected that Cathcart was caught off guard by her response. A large silver tray sat on the sideboard—laden with brandy and sherry decanters, and four glasses: three brandy, one sherry.

After Cathcart's toast to the damnation of their enemies, Laura explained that she had been to the centre of the town several times, always under guard, during the first few weeks of her imprisonment when she still had money to purchase food and necessities. She had also been taken to Ortega's house, although she did not elaborate.

Laura sketched a rough layout of the town, noting the prominent features and the road leading to the prison houses. She also rendered a sketch of the interior of her house, although she hadn't seen all of it and had to rely on what she heard as people moved around inside.

She had not been in the other house, although she understood from a brief conversation with one of the prisoners that most of the men, perhaps thirty, were confined in the cellar—with another dozen on the upper floors. Small groups were allowed to exercise in the courtyard for ten minutes each morning and afternoon. Individuals were allowed to use the privy until eleven o'clock in the evening when they were chained together for the night.

Laura said she knew nothing about the fort or the battery covering the harbour entrance, but didn't recall seeing many soldiers about the town during her visits which were restricted to the shops on the town square. She also didn't know anything about the smaller vessel anchored closer to the town, although she had heard a rumour that it was English and that the crew were being held on board. Rumour said Ortega didn't want them kept with the other sailors.

She took another sip of brandy. "An excellent brandy, sir. French is it?"

Cathcart nearly choked on his mouthful. The presence of French brandy aboard a British warship during war with France could be difficult to explain. One might claim it was taken from a prize, except they hadn't taken any French prizes of late. The only other source was the smuggler who had supplied this particular bottle.

Toby bent studiously over the map but Mac could see the barely contained grin.

"I apologise, Captain." Laura sounded genuinely concerned. "Did I say something wrong? I have not had such fine brandy since Baltimore. It is very similar to the one my father prefers." Her voice trembled, "Do you think there is any hope of rescuing him?"

Mac knew Cathcart would sail up to an enemy and exchange broadsides at pistol range without hesitation, yet he appeared taken aback by the sight of a beguiling young woman, obviously on the verge of tears. Cathcart almost mumbled, "I certainly intend to try."

"Oh thank you, sir." Laura stepped forward and kissed him on the cheek. "First Captain Appleton rescues me, and now you have given me even more hope." Cathcart blushed while Toby tugged awkwardly at his neck stock.

"Gentlemen and Miss Babbett." Cathcart harrumphed to clear his throat and regain some air of authority. "If you will excuse me, I have ship's business to attend to with my clerk and will need some time to consider our options at Puerto Blanco. Please join me for lunch at two bells of the afternoon watch. In the meantime perhaps Captain Appleton would care to escort Miss Babbett? Unfortunately duty requires Lieutenant Baverstock."

Mac and Toby followed Laura from the cabin. She paused, turning to them after the door closed, and said, "I am sorry you won't be escorting me, Toby. You must know *Lionheart* very well. I am sure I'll have many questions that Captain Appleton will not be able to answer. Perhaps I could prevail upon your knowledge when we meet for lunch?"

Toby agreed and excused himself.

"I hope I made him feel better," Laura confided. "I sense he was disappointed that he would not escort me, but not as disappointed as I would have been if you could not."

"Where would you like to begin?" Mac's pulse quickened at the chance to be with her.

"Show me the mizzen top, where you fired your musket at those terrible Spaniards."

Mac pointed at the platform forty feet up. "It's quite a climb. Are you sure?"

Laura looked up, shielded her eyes from the sun and said, "I'll be fine." She swung nonchalantly onto the lower shrouds and began climbing as though it was the ladder of a playground slide, oblivious to watching sailors and Mac who was ready to catch her should she slip.

By the time they ascended halfway Mac suspected the sailors knew there was something between him and Laura—affirmed when he glanced down and saw one mouth, "Lucky bugger." Mac and Laura, both short of breath from the ascent, paused near the apex of the lower shrouds where he explained how to reach the top or platform. "The easiest is to step around the futtock shrouds, here where they join the shrouds that we're standing on. Then through the lubber's hole against the mast. Experienced sailors use the actual futtocks, but that requires hanging backward from them to attain the outer edge of the top. It's quicker but far more dangerous. Certainly not for the inexperienced or faint-hearted."

Laura intently studied the arrangement of ropes. "Which route do you use?"

"I'm ashamed to say the lubber's hole."

"See you in the top!" Laura exclaimed, then reached for the futtocks and pulled herself onto them.

By the time Mac scrambled through the lubber's hole she had pulled herself onto the top.

A roar rose from the deck. It sounded as if the entire crew had been collectively holding their breath as Laura swung outwards and pulled herself up hand-over-hand.

Mac glanced down. They were a dizzying four storeys above the deck; six from the water.

Toby gazed up, a dumbfounded expression on his face.

"You've had quite the morning," Mac said. "First you leave the poor captain all aback. Now I fear you've captured his crew."

"Show me where the Spanish were during the battle," Laura said between gasps, although she was trying to hide her shortness of breath.

Mac described the position of the Spanish frigate and how John Williams kept the muskets loaded.

Laura swept her hand through the air as though emphasising the size of the Spanish frigate. "If it were not for all those eyes watching us," she said, tipping her head toward the deck, "I would insist that you kiss me, here and now. Since that is not a likely prospect, why are you keeping me up here all day for no good reason? Show me the rest of the ship." She laughed. "I think I will try your lubber's hole for the descent. You should go first, that way I can be sure that you will pause to place my foot safely and give those eyes something to reward their interest."

They continued their tour on deck, outwardly maintaining propriety. Laura expressed keen interest in the guns and took great delight in hearing of Great Harry's role in the battle and expressed concern when she spoke with Art Chambers, Harry's gun captain. "Captain Appleton tells me that if it wasn't for your very fine shooting against *Matilda* that he might well be dead. How do you possibly aim this monstrous beast in such confined quarters?" Laura kneeled to sight along the ten-foot barrel of the three-thousand pound gun. "It must be very difficult to see your target through the port, especially something as small as a mast."

"Oh ma'am, it is not so difficult," Chambers replied matter-of-factly.

Mac knew this was a classic piece of understatement.

"Well, I hope I have the chance to observe you fire them during target practice. It must be very exciting."

Mac, noticing that the nearest sailors had stopped working, interjected, "I'm sorry Miss Babbett, we should continue if we're to complete the tour before your lunch with the Captain."

When they descended into *Lionheart's* bowels Laura asked, "Did I embarrass you by talking about his gunnery?"

"On the contrary, it's true. *Castellon* had to watch helplessly while we defeated *Matilda* within a few minutes. I'm sure their hearts weren't in the fight after that. You certainly made Chambers' day brighter; he's a fine shot with those great brutes."

"As long as you know I wasn't trying to diminish your role." She sounded concerned that she might have offended him.

He smiled, "Not at all, milady. This is the orlop deck, the lowest deck. Below are the holds and bilges. We're below the waterline here, directly beneath us is the powder-magazine where the gunner and his mates make charges for the guns; the powder-monkeys, just boys, carry the charges up to the guns."

"It's like a dungeon down here. Don't they worry in a battle? This must be a dangerous place with all that gunpowder."

Mac could see the concern on her face and said, "I asked the same thing." He added, "But they're below the waterline and safe from enemy guns. The biggest danger is from a spark igniting the powder, and they take elaborate precautions to prevent that. A single lantern is housed in a separate room, protected by thick glass The men wear felt shoes and carry nothing metal on their person. I read that L'Orient did explode at the Battle of the Nile in 1798, but it's certainly not a common thing." He squeezed her hand.

"Well, I don't think I'd enjoy being down here. It's so dark and gloomy, and it reeks. At least that horrid room had a window..."

Memories of his own imprisonment aboard *La Señora* reminded Mac of what she must have been through. The depth of his own despair after Belinda's death flooded back to haunt him as he struggled to fight off bittersweet memories of Belinda. When he looked at Laura it was as if he was being held prisoner by both his past and future.

The pain in her eyes was obvious. He wanted to be the one to make it go away. Trying to sound cheerful he replied, "Neither would I. There's more to see forward where they have the sail and rope lockers. They're always repairing and replacing something, and I've yet to learn all the names." He paused next to the massive coil of anchor cable then wrapped his arms around the end of twelve inch diameter cable and chuckled, "This runs to the anchor at the bow and is, I'm afraid, the bitter end!"

She looked puzzled, "Why do you say that? Is it because of the smell?"

He shook his head. "It's dry as we haven't anchored for some time. The smell's worse when it's wet." Despite efforts to keep a straight face he couldn't help laughing. "No, it refers to the 'bits' that hold the cable to the capstan. If the end slips past them you lose the anchor and the entire cable. That's why you never want to reach the 'bitter end'."

He paused while Laura stepped around him to climb the ladder. When she stumbled on the ladder he instinctively placed one hand on the small of her back to steady her.

"Sir," she whispered, "I trust that you're not attempting to take advantage?" The fleeting smile, and the way she scampered up the last few steps, made him think she had deliberately stumbled.

Clusters of sailors on the deck employed needles and heavy thread to repair sails. Others, coils of rope at their feet, spliced in new sections to replace chafed. A sudden decrease in the pace of work went unnoticed by the petty officers and mates who were equally distracted by Laura's presence.

"This is the forecastle." Mac continued in a formal tone for the benefit of inquisitive ears, "Usually called the 'fo'c's'le'. Forward is the bowsprit and jib sails."

"Can we go out there?" Laura pointed toward the bowsprit extending like a narwhal's tusk from *Lionheart's* bow.

"That's not a good idea," Mac cautioned.

Laura was determined, "Oh, I do not mind some more climbing, unless you are too tired."

"It's not that," he replied, already knowing that Laura was not one to be easily deterred once she had made a decision. The memory of the moment she agreed to trust him, a stranger, at the garden wall was suddenly clear. "You can't see it yet, but just below is the beak. It contains the heads—our open privies—and your presence might be disconcerting to any occupants."

Laura blushed and gasped, "Ohhh..."

It was the first time she had shown any vulnerability. He glanced around to be sure he could not be overheard and whispered, "I think I'm falling in love."

Laura continued to stare toward the horizon for several seconds. "I'd much rather be having a few bananas and a dry biscuit with you than lunch with the captain. Unfortunately, duty calls."

~16~
START WITH A PLAN

AMARINE SENTRY, plus a messenger boy, were stationed at Cathcart's sleeping cabin door while Laura sponge bathed from a basin of hot water. Their purpose was not to confine or guard her as such, but rather to delay her should she decide to go on deck. The boy was to alert the men on deck since a man-of-war's Sunday bathing practice was to place a sail in the sea while in tropical waters—its corners supported by ropes to form a shallow pool for those willing to venture into the ocean. However, since most sailors couldn't swim, a wash-deck pump was also rigged with a hose so sailors could parade through the stream. In either case, the majority of the ship's company would be naked.

Church service followed with Cathcart reading aloud, somewhat quicker than usual, the Articles of War which governed all their lives and gave him powers, albeit only aboard ship, second only to God. The Articles were followed by a short sermon and a single rousing hymn, made more so by Laura's pure, sweet voice ascending above the enthusiastic but mostly off-tune sailors.

Laura returned to her sleeping cabin to freshen before lunch while Cathcart assembled the who's who of shipboard life for his impromptu luncheon: three lieutenants, the surgeon, master, two midshipmen, *Ringle's* Wilson and Mac. *Lionheart's* third midshipman was on deck, although with few duties while the ships lay hove to. *Seppings* had yet to return from chasing down the strange sail.

This was to be Laura's shipboard debut, since she had not yet been formally introduced to the majority of the men standing about the great cabin. Conversation ebbed and flowed amongst two groups divided by rank—Cathcart, the lieutenants and surgeon stood near the stern windows, while lesser mortals gathered near Cathcart's sleeping cabin. Mac attempted to float between the two clusters, engaged in casual conversation about the state of the sea and the prospect of weather, and tried not to be obvious about glancing toward the closed door.

Laura opened her door and beamed, "Captain, gentlemen, I trust I have not kept you waiting."

Cathcart responded, "Miss Babbett, you look positively radiant."

Mac excused himself to join Cathcart's group. Dappled light, reflected by the water through the gallery windows, danced across Laura—just as it had in the grotto. Her hair was pulled back into a bun accentuating her face and smile. She wore a pair of blue trousers and a white shirt with a blue bandana around her neck. Mac had trouble believing this was the same person as in the forest—covered in dirt and despondent.

"May I present..." Cathcart plowed through the strict formality of the introductions, with attention to precedence by rank as he did so. Introductions completed, he stepped toward the table. "Perhaps we should be seated, I understand our meal is ready." Cathcart assisted Laura with her chair, seating her at his right, before taking his place at the head of the table. Naval tradition dictated seating order: Toby sat across from her; Woodman, the surgeon, on her right; Mac was relegated to the far end facing Cathcart.

The meal commenced with what Cathcart called 'a lickerous fish,' followed by a saddle of mutton courtesy of the ship's last sheep. The galley had contrived to produce fresh bread, which was most enthusiastically received since it was soft and not full of maggots as were the usual ship's biscuits. Palatable wines, notably a chilled hock, circumnavigated the table while conversation continued unabated. Cathcart and Toby, in deference to the lady, did their utmost to ensure the conversation did not become too nautical, or coarse, as sometimes happened when sailors and wine mingled.

Cathcart proposed toasts to the King and the damnation of their enemies and said, "Gentlemen, let us discuss plans for retrieving the Indiamen." He hesitated, then added almost as an afterthought, "If the lady will kindly excuse us." The presence of a woman aboard his frigate seemed to disrupt his carefully ordered world of rank, routines and discipline.

Laura nodded appreciatively around the table, "Thank you, Captain and gentlemen, for a thoroughly delightful meal. I can't remember the last time I was in such pleasant company." Before she could push her chair back Woodman stood to assist. Glancing over her shoulder to thank Woodman, she turned back to Cathcart. "Sir, would it be permissible for me to stroll on deck while you conduct business?"

Laura went directly to the galley to personally thank the startled ship's cook and his mate for 'the most excellent meal she had tasted in a long time.' Will Smith, speechless for nearly five minutes after, began telling anyone who came within earshot, "She came here to tell me, in person like..."

When Laura spotted Art Chambers fussing over Great Harry he reminded her of a doting father. "Mr. Chambers," she said, carefully standing so her shadow did not disrupt his ministrations, "in contemplating your marvelous artillery I noticed several guns near the bow that are quite different in appearance." She affectionately patted Harry's breech, much as she would a child's head, as she spoke. "Are they carronades? I've never seen their like."

"Why, yes milady, that they are. Would ye care t'see 'em?"

"Most certainly, if that isn't too much trouble," Laura then dropped her voice to a conspiratorial whisper and said, "but only if you call me Laura."

Chambers' rotund face broke into a gap-toothed grin. "Then ye must call me Art. Me own Laura'll be eighteen this year," he confided as he led the way forward to the starboard carronade squatting on its slide.

"I understand they fire a thirty-two pound ball, but not so far as your other guns?"

"That's correct, ma'am."

Her halfhearted scowl gave way to a smile. "Laura," she urged.

"They're used for close work. We call 'em 'smashers' because of the damage they inflict. Their ball will smash through any ship, 'specially we fire from a raking position. D'ye know what that is?"

"I do not believe I do." She sounded concerned. "It sounds very deadly though."

"A ship rakes another when she sails across th' enemy's bow or stern an' fires through 'er end to end. When we fight, the entire deck's open one end t'other, everthun's struck below."

Laura looked astern, trying to see past the clutter. "Everything? That is hard to imagine. It must take you a very long time."

"Un'er fifteen minutes." Chambers' pride was obvious as he continued, "The cabin walls are but partitions. Furniture is removed; only the guns is left. We don't want anythin' in our way when we're servin' 'em."

"Would I be correct that it is preferable to rake from the back, astern as you call it? Your shots would only have the cabin windows to impede them?" She pictured Mac exposed to that kind of danger when *Lionheart* had battled the Spanish frigates, then remembered he was in the mizzen top.

"'Zactly, Laura, 'zactly. Ye've a remarkable grasp for a...non-sailor."

Laura suspected he had almost said, 'for a woman'.

Chambers couldn't conceal his enthusiasm for the guns. "D'ye see how th' carronade rides on a slide rather 'n a carriage. We c'n aim the carronade with this 'ere traversing lever, much easier th'n usin' 'andspikes t' shift the entire carriage under a great gun. We adjusts the range by turnin' the worm screw, quite different th'n 'Arry. Carronades can be handled by just two men. Would ye care t' see 'Arry again? I think ye'll appreciate the differences having seen th' smasher?"

"Oh most certainly!" Laura exclaimed. "As long as I'm not imposing on you. I fear my ignorance must be trying."

"On the contrary," Chambers replied, "you've a fine grasp of the essentials." He sighed, "More 'n c'n be said for some o' the men aboard."

When she looked at Chambers something in his eyes prompted her to say, "You must miss your wife and daughter."

He paused momentarily, caught off guard, then confided in a near whisper, "I've been 'ome but twice in the past six years. Only seen me Laura p'rhaps a half-dozen times in seventeen years." Chambers looked away.

Laura wondered if she should have asked, but she somehow knew that he wanted to share his loneliness. "My word," Laura exclaimed when they reached Harry. "I see the difference. If I understand correctly, you must shift the gun and carriage using a handspike. That must be very difficult, he looks very heavy?"

"More 'n two 'unnerd stone."

By now, a sizeable number of sailors had contrived to move their chores to a more advantageous position on the deck, while making sure that they appeared busy to avoid a petty officer's wrath.

Laura examined one of the six and one-half inch diameter iron balls stored in a rack against the ship's side. "Are these Harry's balls?"

An anonymous voice in the throng quipped, "'arry's ain't near so big." Harry Tait, larboard watch, was slapped roundly on the back by his mates while others collapsed on the deck in convulsions of laughter.

Laura felt herself blushing and stammered, "I...I...I meant..." before realising it was hopeless. "Please forgive me Art, that was an unfortunate turn of phrase." She desperately wanted to hide. "I must take my leave before I embarrass myself any further."

WOODMAN EXCUSED HIMSELF, leaving Cathcart, the lieutenants Baverstock, Sloane and Moore, Wilson and Mac clustered around the table, deep in discussion about Puerto Blanco.

Cathcart growled, "Clearly it is going to be very difficult to free the passengers and crew since they are not aboard the ships. I must be plain about this, I am not confident of a favourable outcome. All surprise will be lost if we attack the ships first; any attempt to get at them while they sit below the fort will prove dangerous and costly. Even with *Ringle* and *Seppings* we lack sufficient force to simultaneously attack the fort, battery, Indiamen and prison houses. Nor can I see how I can get *Lionheart* into a position to attack the fort without an extreme risk of running aground or being destroyed in the attempt. Our chart of the harbour and entrance is woefully lacking in soundings and I must assume there is some sort of boom across the entrance."

Sloane interjected, "If we don't free the prisoners during the initial attack, the Spaniards could force our withdrawal or surrender by threatening to harm them."

Cathcart nodded in agreement.

Toby caught Cathcart's eye and added, "Not to mention this infernal west wind. We would have no difficulty entering the harbour, but would find it impossible to leave."

Cathcart looked around the table, "Perhaps one of you sees things differently." Everyone remained silent and reexamined the chart, noting Mac's meagre intelligence about the harbour defences and location of the ships at anchor.

Eventually Toby said, "We face several problems which, taken in their entirety, are perplexing. Perhaps a resolution to an individual problem will lead to overall success." There was a murmur of agreement before he continued. "We first cut out *Thunderbolt* then employ her mortars against the fort."

"That still leaves the problem of the Indiamen and prisoners," interjected Sloane.

Toby countered, "We would be able to destroy the fort and battery, then enter the harbour with impunity. Once we controlled the harbour, surely the Spanish would see their situation as hopeless and capitulate."

Sloane pressed his point, "But Toby, does that not still leave the problem of freeing the prisoners, and the possibility of the Spanish harming them before we could reach them."

"Gentlemen." Mac spoke for the first time. "I know I'm a guest, but may I make a suggestion?"

Cathcart glanced up from the chart. "Feel free to speak your mind, Mac."

"Which is more important? The prisoners or the ships?" Mac paused when Sloane looked at him with barely polite disdain. Too late, Mac remembered overhearing earlier conversations about the amount of prize money that capturing the ships would bring. He looked at Sloane and continued, "Please hear me out. I'd suggest the prisoners. Without them the Spanish have three ships without crews and I don't believe that they have the means to man them. There were barely half a dozen small fishing boats in the harbour; certainly not enough sailors to handle even one of the Indiamen."

Several of the officers murmured their agreement and Mac continued. "*Lionheart* could blockade to prevent an escape while *Ringle* or *Seppings* return to Jamaica to request reinforcements. The Spanish might send more warships, but would they be any more successful than the first? Furthermore, how long will it take for them to mount such an expedition? I believe we should free the prisoners first, then deal with the ships." Sloane appeared somewhat mollified.

"An intriguing scenario." Cathcart looked around the table, "Gentlemen, please feel free to comment."

Toby couldn't contain his enthusiasm. "Mac is correct. The prisoners are the key. Most of the prize money would come from the cargo, assuming the Dons have not already taken it. However, in the end they would be merely hulls with no crews."

The others murmured agreement with Toby.

Cathcart looked directly at Mac, "How do you mean to accomplish this?"

Mac suspected Cathcart deliberately avoided offering suggestions. If any plan was going to succeed it had to be accepted by all present, not forced. "Well, sir, I believe we have the resources to free the prisoners. We have the advantage of surprise because I'm positive the Spanish are unaware of our presence. As far as the Spanish know Miss Babbett's still at large. Ortega will fully expect an attempt to recapture the ships."

Cathcart interrupted, "If I understand Miss Babbett, Ortega desperately wants to escape from Puerto Blanco. The prisoners have no value unless they can be exchanged for ransom, and only the officers and Mr. Babbett might command a high price."

Toby added, "If we free the prisoners they can then assist us against the forts and ships."

Enthusiastic discussion followed. Possibilities and potential difficulties were weighed until Cathcart spoke again.

"Gentlemen, I believe that we agree that Mac's plan is our best choice. In fact, it is our only choice. Now we must work out the details." He looked at Mac. "Do you have any idea as to the size of the force required?"

Mac knew Cathcart was testing him to make sure he had thought through all aspects of the plan.

"Deck there," the mainmast lookout called, "sail six points off the larboard bow. Hull down, standing toward us."

"Gentlemen," Cathcart interjected before Mac could begin his answer. "We'll have to continue this discussion later. Silas, I'll need *Ringle*."

Wilson excused himself to return to the schooner. His gig's crew were at the oars by the time he reached the railing. "Shove off," he ordered as he stepped into the gig. "Out oars, smartly now." As he scrambled up *Ringle's* low side Cathcart shouted, "Run her down. If she's a Spaniard make sure she doesn't report our presence."

"All plain sail Mr. Baverstock, if you please." Cathcart ordered, "Keep the wind on our beam and make sure we stay between the sail and Puerto Blanco. If she is making for Puerto Blanco I want to be able to stop her."

MAC SURMISED that Laura had returned to her cabin before the meeting started. When the strange sail ended the discussion of tactics Cathcart granted him permission to tell her about the plan, then went on deck.

When Mac knocked softly on the cabin door Laura opened it, dabbing tears from reddened eyes. "What's the matter?" he asked, leaving the door slightly ajar—shipboard rumours didn't need additional fuel.

"Nothing," she replied, wiping a hand across her cheek and pulling back when he tried to brush away another tear.

"Nothing?" He looked at her sternly. "Please tell me."

Laura looked down, "I feel like such a gowk." Amid sobs, she detailed her gaffe about the cannonballs and Chambers' silence when they parted.

"How did the others react?" Mac could scarcely keep a straight face as he visualised the scene.

"Someone said something about Harry's not being that big and then everybody laughed. I fear that I have also shamed you." She turned her head away as more tears cascaded down her cheeks.

He turned her face toward him. "Sounds to me like the crew weren't terribly offended or embarrassed. You forget you're in the midst of sailors. The only way you can offend them is by trampling on one of their many superstitions. Otherwise, the more risqué the joke, and especially one that makes such good use of a double entendre, the more it's appreciated. You're probably the toast of the lower deck. These things get passed around quickly because they brighten an otherwise ordinary day. Don't give it another thought."

Laura lifted her eyes to meet his, "Are you sure?" She snuffled, then said, "Are you going to free the prisoners? My father?"

Mac looked directly into her eyes, "I wanted to tell you in person."

Laura sat on the edge of the cot and motioned for him to sit beside her. A hint of her impish grin returned. She whispered, "There was no other?"

Mac tapped a finger against the partition to emphasise how little privacy it provided and took her hand. "The thought has crossed my mind, but this isn't the time or the place. We haven't finalised anything beyond *Lionheart* creating a diversion by appearing to attack the fort while we free the prisoners."

Laura's eyes darted back and forth like a cornered animal. She blurted, "You said we. Are you going to be there? Will it be dangerous? What about the guards?"

Mac squeezed her hand. "We'll have the advantage of surprise by landing at night and moving into position before dawn."

Laura, on the verge of sobbing, said, "I do not like the thought of you going back."

"I know, but I'm the only one who knows the trail and the houses. I promise I won't take unnecessary risks, but it's vital that I'm there. If we fail no one knows what Ortega might do." Mac paused when he saw her expression at the prospect of Ortega's vengeance. "I'm sorry, I didn't mean to bring back memories of that place."

Tears welled in her eyes. "Do not apologise, I just thought of Father. He doesn't know that I'm safe." She paused to wipe the tears away, "I do not know if he is safe. What if that pig Ortega..."

Mac put his arm around her shoulder and pulled her to his chest. "I'm sure he's all right. Ortega will keep him safe or lose any chance of ransom. Ortega's greed works to our advantage; it might prevent him from harming your father."

"But what if I lose you both?" She nestled closer. "How could I go on? I love you both."

"I love you, too," he whispered, surprised that the words came so easily. "I know you're concerned about your father and that you feel helpless from being so dependent on others. I want to make sure there's a happy ending."

Laura pressed her forehead against his neck. "I wish we were back at our grotto. Our troubles seemed to disappear there. Can you stay just a few more minutes while I repair myself?" Her hand tightened its grip. "I do not want anyone else to see what a state I'm in. If we go on deck can you be with me? You do not have any duties, do you?"

Mac knew by her eyes how important it was for him to be near. He felt the same, despite the knot in his stomach every time he thought about revealing the truth.

CATHCART SAW MAC AND LAURA emerge from the break of the poop deck, then looked up when the lookout hailed, "Deck there. *Ringle* makin' *Seppins'* number an' 'Ship in Sight'." *Ringle's* sails were but a dull patch on the horizon; *Seppings*, hull down from *Lionheart's* deck, showed only the top third of her courses.

Cathcart turned to Toby. "Mr. Baverstock, make to *Ringle* and repeat to *Seppings*, 'Captain report to flag', then you may heave to. I will be in my cabin." Cathcart glanced back. Mac was pointing out to Laura the signal hoist rising on the halyard. He watched them for a few more seconds, noting how alive Laura seemed when she was with Mac. No doubt about it, he thought as he descended the quarterdeck ladder.

THE MEETING RESUMED once Wilson and Jamieson arrived—the strange sail that *Seppings* chased down was an American brig bound for Philadelphia with coffee. Mac continued, "Well, sir, I see the mission in two parts: first the diversion, second the rescue. We'll give the Spanish what they expect: *Lionheart* and *Ringle* will make a feint against the harbour entrance as much before dawn as visibility allows."

"A big unknown is the condition of the prisoners. The men I saw at the first house seemed to be in good health. Miss Babbett believes those at the second house were being reasonably well treated. There's no way of knowing what we'll find, so we should plan with the assumption there will be problems. There you have it." Mac looked around the table. "I'm no sailor, so I won't be offended if you point out errors."

"Will you be taking an active part ashore?" Sloane asked.

Mac sensed a bit of navy pride, or perhaps resentment, in the question. "Yes, but as a subordinate to whoever the Captain selects to lead the mission."

Cathcart looked up from the chart. "Toby will be in charge and will lead the group going to the first house. Mac's party the officers and Mr. Babbett. Sergeant Grego and the marines will secure the road while Mr. Barnes protects the boats. We will require eighteen men for the road, two groups of six for the houses, plus men to guard the boats. That requires boats with sufficient space to transport the landing parties and to bring the prisoners back." Cathcart shifted his gaze to Wilson. "Silas, how close to the beach were you able to anchor?"

"Perhaps four cables sir, although with more determination and depending on the state of the tide, three might be possible."

Cathcart continued, "Well, three or four make no matter. It will be a long pull for boats to remove everyone from the beach. There could be a hot pursuit if the Spaniards discover the real purpose of our attack."

"Sir," Mac interjected, "could we move swivels ashore to cover the trail leading to the beach?"

The murmur of agreement ended when Cathcart continued. "Excellent. *Ringle* will assist in the attack against the harbour entrance. *Seppings* will have our launch, both barges and our gig along with her own gig."

Cathcart winked to Toby, "Just make sure you return them in the same condition you received them," then turned to Jamieson. "D'ye require additional muskets, balls or powder?"

"No sir, I have a good supply," replied Jamieson.

Cathcart continued, "*Lionheart* and *Ringle* are well known in these waters, so it would be logical for the Spanish to expect to see us in company. If we use *Seppings* against the fort the Spanish might wonder where *Ringle* was. As far as I know they are not aware of *Seppings*. Are there any other questions? Is everyone clear about their role?"

They all nodded agreement. Mac suspected by the looks of concentration they were likely visualising their individual roles—exactly as he was doing.

Cathcart cleared his throat, "I will draft my written orders immediately. Toby, Mac, a word in private with you first." Cathcart continued when they were alone. "There is the matter of Miss Babbett. While I have no intention of putting the ship at risk, I will make a credible attempt at gaining the harbour before the Spanish successfully discourage us, or so they will think. However, a lucky Spanish shot could knock down a mast causing us to run aground. If Miss Babbett were captured I do not wish to contemplate her fate at the hands of Ortega. He sounds like a blackguard. Do either of you object if she accompanies *Seppings*?"

Mac knew Ortega would have no compunction about his treatment of Laura given the opportunity. His anger rose every time he thought about what she had been through. He was glad she would be away from danger.

Cathcart continued, "I shall leave the details for the two of you to work out. Let me know how much time you require to free the prisoners; I have no wish to sit under Spanish guns any longer than necessary. Mac, if I could have a word with you before you meet with Toby."

Cathcart motioned Mac to follow him to the far corner of the cabin—as far from Laura's sleeping cabin as possible—then lowered his voice to a whisper. "I want to thank you for all that you have done. If you were one of my lieutenants I would have no hesitation recommending you for promotion."

Mac tried to hide his surprise and almost fumbled, "Thank you, sir."

"This is really none of my concern, but I sense a certain bond between you and Miss Babbett." Mac didn't have time to reply before Cathcart continued, "No matter," then waved one hand as though shooing a fly, "she is a courageous woman but I believe she will be more reassured near you, rather than aboard *Lionheart*. She must be apprehensive about her father's safety."

Mac, startled by Cathcart's observation, found it interesting that he had not called her Laura. For a moment he wasn't sure how to respond, then decided this was not the time for a glib response. "Sir, may I speak in confidence?"

"Of course."

"I'm hopeful there's something lasting between us, although we haven't known each other for very long." Memories of the grotto flashed through his mind. "Thank you for putting her aboard *Seppings*; not because she will be near me, but for her peace of mind."

Cathcart said, "I wish you both well."

Was that said with just a hint of a fatherly warning? His eyes had narrowed, hadn't they?

"Work out the details with Toby while I prepare my orders. Kindly pass word for my clerk when you leave."

TOBY AND MAC BENT OVER the wardroom table, sheaves of blank paper nearby, and completed lists of the best men for each aspect of the mission. Mac described the abilities required while Toby scratched away with a quill pen, occasionally referring to Jamieson's list. Earlier, Toby had approved Sergeant Grego's choice of marines.

Toby added the last name and looked up. "Sailors have the annoying trait of being graceful aboard ship, scampering about the yards and rigging like monkeys, but becoming abominably clumsy on land. The men I have selected are capable of moving about on land with stealth."

He passed the completed list to Mac and added, "Plus they are levelheaded and particularly adept with knife and small sword. We may find ourselves fighting in close-quarters in the houses. The men at the top of the list are strong, with arms like masts; we will need their strength to break the chains and locks securing the prisoners to ensure that we are in and out quickly. A tuppence trollop will give you longer than I plan to be in the houses. Do you agree with the selection?"

Mac nodded in agreement—Toby knew his men—and said, "Since we're going ashore at night, may I make some suggestions from my army experience?"

"By all means."

Mac felt like he and Toby were peas in a pod—both knowledgeable and accomplished officers who recognised and accepted each other's abilities. He asked, "Would Grego be offended if his marines didn't wear their red jackets? They must be inconspicuous in the forest."

Toby chuckled, "Fortunately he is not the miffy type and I'll put your suggestion to him. I'm sure he'll agree."

"Great." Mac, relieved that tradition could be put aside, continued. "Now, about clothing for the others. Do you have enough dark coloured clothes for everyone? It'll make the men harder to see when we land, especially near the houses."

"An excellent idea. I had never considered that as clothes do not matter at sea."

"One last thing." Mac paused. "I want them to obscure their faces and exposed skin. Between that and the dark clothes they'll be damn-near invisible. Also, while we're at it, we should dull the boats. At least the parts above water."

Toby thought for a moment. "We can use soot from the galley chimney for the faces. Is this something you learned in your army, or from the natives who played havoc with our soldiers during the war?"

Mac knew from Toby's expression that he was joking. "I'm not sure where the idea originated, but it works." He couldn't mention seeing Army Rangers use it.

Toby said, "I will have to think about the boats."

Cathcart's clerk Eames arrived in the wardroom just as Toby and Mac finished their plans. "The Captain's compliments, if Captain Appleton could attend at his earliest convenience."

Cathcart was standing beside a small side table when Mac entered the cabin. "You may find this wine enjoyable." Cathcart replaced the stopper in a crystal decanter with a gentle *ting*. "I have been invited to the wardroom for dinner. You and Miss Babbett are welcome to take supper in my cabin if you prefer. I will not have need of the space and I expect you may wish to inform her of the rescue plans. Pass word for Eames and he will attend to your wishes. I have instructed the marine guard to ensure your privacy until you board *Seppings* at two bells of the first watch. Miss Babbett is taking a turn on the deck."

~17~

DISTRACTION AND EXTRICATION

TWO CHIMES OF *LIONHEART'S* BELL were followed by trills of the bosun's calls and strident shouts, "All hands, d'ye hear. Rouse out there." Somnolent sailors who did not immediately stir were roused by bosun's mates wielding their stubby rope starters.

Laura emerged from Cathcart's cabin a few minutes later. "Good evening, Captain, and good evening Commander Wilson, Commander Moore," she said almost cheerfully before crossing to the lee side of the quarterdeck, and out of the officers' way. She gripped the rail when a chill ran down her spine. The ships, out of sight of land and with lanterns suspended from their rigging to aid loading the boats, appeared almost festive in stark contrast to their intent.

Ringle and *Seppings* waited nearby while *Lionheart's* men were sorted into groups destined for the boats floating alongside. Laura spotted Mac in the waist organising the men who would accompany him to her father's prison. Toby was with the second group, while Sergeant Grego was busy inspecting his marines who seemed out of place without their red coats and stark white cross belts. The landing party, including the boats' crews who would secure the beach, wore drab blue or grey clothing.

Laura tried not to stare as Cathcart paced impatiently back and forth along the windward side of the quarterdeck. Concern for her father grew by the minute and conflicted with her anxiety for Mac. A twinge of guilt ran through her—she was no longer sure who she cared about more.

Cathcart mentally ran through the preparations looking for flaws knowing that luck could still play a major part in determining success. "Mr. Baverstock," he called, "are your preparations complete?"

"Aye, sir. We will commence boarding momentarily." Toby's preparations were not as complete as he would like, but he had perceived Cathcart's growing impatience and would finish once they were aboard *Seppings* and out of sight.

Every sailor in the shore party had been issued a cutlass, the most reliable also had a pistol; the marines were armed with cutlasses and muskets; each boat mounted a swivel gun in the bow. The boat crews descended first, followed by the boarding parties and then the officers: Mac in the packed gig, Laura with Toby in the launch. The boats crossed to *Seppings* without incident and discharged their burden of men and weapons.

Toby and Mac had agreed to divide command duties, even though Mac had no official standing. They worked well together, with no hint of the rivalry, class snobbery or petty jealousy that Toby had so often seen during his career. He would have overall control of the mission. Mac, more experienced on land and having previously been ashore, would assume control during the march from the beach to the town. When they reached the houses, each would have independent command of his own group to free the prisoners and deal with any unforeseen problems.

SEPPINGS, her sails sheeted home in a flash, set course for the cove. The boats, secured to stout painters, trailed astern like baby ducklings following their mother. She was a fine sailer and the breeze, one point off her starboard quarter, allowed Jamieson to set stunsails. The water hissed around *Seppings'* knife-edged cutwater.

"She'll easily make thirteen," Cathcart remarked almost casually to Sloane when *Seppings*, her lights extinguished, disappeared into the gloom leaving only a swirling phosphorescent wake astern. "Oh, to be young again, eh George?"

Before the surprised lieutenant could answer, Cathcart continued, "Mr. Sloane, pray get us into position, if you please."

Topmen scampered up *Lionheart's* rigging; *Ringle* responded to the frigate's activity and fell to leeward well clear of her less nimble senior. *Ringle* would sail eight miles ahead for two hours, then reduce sail to allow *Lionheart* to close. This would allow the schooner to scout ahead and identify any strange sails, either dealing with them herself or requesting *Lionheart's* assistance as the situation required. The breeze, steady out of the west, meant *Lionheart* would have no difficulty carrying a press of sails, including royals and stunsails, to close on any ship coming between her and Puerto Blanco.

Meanwhile, *Seppings*, amid a symphony of ship and water noises and surrounded by darkness, cracked on toward the cove. Jamieson's only concession to the night was to strike the stunsails, reducing her speed to eleven knots—more than adequate to meet their schedule and certainly sufficient to rip her bottom out if they ventured too close to shore. His two best lookouts were posted at the masthead and two more in the bows. The leadsman, in the main chains, awaited the order to cast the twenty-five fathom lead.

The landing parties were in high spirits as Toby and Mac supervised the face blacking below deck. Illuminated by lanterns, the men joked and bantered among themselves as they daubed a mixture of grease and soot on one another.

"One would think they were children at a village fair," Toby observed while applying the final touches of soot to the back of Mac's neck.

Mac surveyed the cluster of men. "Are they usually like this before a battle?"

"Maybe not as much as on this particular evening, but generally they are in good spirits. Myself, I am always nervous, but I try not to show it for fear of causing doubt." Toby laughed, "I can't stand being below any longer, let's go on deck."

"No bottom," the leadsman called after his first cast of the lead.

"Deck there," the foremast lookout hailed. "Breakers, two points to larboard, perhaps two miles distant."

Jamieson considered the report for a moment. He knew that the waves would be breaking on the small point that formed the northwest corner of the cove. From there the cove arced sharply inland for approximately one mile which would put *Seppings* three to four miles out. Perfect, he thought. "A cast of the log if you please."

"By the mark eleven," the logman reported when the last grain of sand in the thirty second glass fell.

"Very well. Single reef in the main and strike the fore if you please." Under reduced sail, the next cast of the log showed eight knots as the making tide helped carry *Seppings* toward the beach.

The lookout called, "Deck there, breakers abeam."

"Lieutenant Baverstock," Jamieson called, "are your men ready?"

"Aye, aye sir."

"By the mark twenty-five." The lead had found bottom.

"Two reefs in the main and a single jib," Jamieson ordered. *Seppings* slowed to less than four knots in the slight swell.

"By the mark twenty-four." The bottom had begun its upward slope to the beach.

"Ready the aft kedge." Jamieson wanted to be sure the kedge anchor was ready to stop their forward progress. It would act as a grappling hook when it dug into the cove's floor and brought *Seppings* to a halt.

"Twenty and pebbles." The lead's sticky tallow end had emerged with several small stones adhering to it.

Seppings, reduced to a jib, crept toward the beach as the water shallowed to fifteen and eventually five fathoms before the kedge softly splashed into the water at Jamieson's command. While the anchor plunged to the bottom the jib halyard was released and the sail loosely stowed on the jib-boom. The kedge's flukes dragged along the bottom for ten yards before biting into the sand and pebble floor, bringing *Seppings* to a gentle stop, the making tide keeping the anchor cable taut.

Laura watched from the quarterdeck as the boat crews boarded, followed by the rescue parties, and finally the officers. She couldn't see Mac's face, but recognised his profile when he briefly paused and turned toward the quarterdeck. She silently mouthed, "Be safe, my love," as he disappeared over the side.

THREE BRIEF FLASHES from the shuttered signal lantern told *Seppings* that the landing was successful. Her crew quickly retrieved the anchor cable until it was 'up and down' as she rode directly above her kedge, ready to pluck it from the cove's bottom. A reefed mizzen nudged her stern around until her bow faced the sea. Jamieson studied their movement and position relative to the indistinct shore. Fearful they might drift into shallow water before he could get steerage way he ordered, "Larboard tack. Short board until she has enough way not to miss stays. Then bring her onto the starboard tack."

Forward momentum plucked the kedge free as jib and courses thrust her forward a hundred yards before Jamieson risked tacking. He gasped for air—he had been holding his breath for most of that distance—then relaxed as *Seppings* settled onto the starboard tack while the crew busied themselves tidying up lines and deck clutter.

Laura remained fixed to one spot on the tiny quarterdeck, pivoting to face the beach while *Seppings* moved to the security of deep water.

"Good evening, ma'am. It seems all went well," Jamieson moved next to her.

"Yes," she replied, trying to sound cheerful. "I was relieved not to hear gunshots." She visualised Mac leading the men toward the town and unknown dangers.

"We will be lighting the galley fire directly if you would you care for coffee. It will help take the night chill away."

"Thank you, but I'm quite tired. If you don't mind, I'll retire."

"Not to worry ma'am, they will be all right," Jamieson reassured as she turned away.

The minuscule bosun's cabin had been set aside for her. Space aboard the schooner was at a premium and she was grateful for the bosun's sacrifice. As she prepared for bed, she wondered what was happening ashore. That, and recurring images of her confinement in the house, disrupted her sleep.

SPACED TEN YARDS APART, the boats scuffed unnoticed onto the sand. The men disembarked and dragged them above the high tide mark, then secured lines from each boat to large pegs driven into the sand. Mac and Toby organised the three groups on the beach, reminding them of the utmost importance of silence before Mac and the marines took the lead along the narrow forest trail.

They halted at the little waterfall, drank from the stream and refilled their canteens. A shuttered lantern, its wick trimmed to a flicker, revealed just past midnight on Toby's pocket watch. They were making good progress—starlight provided a few yards of visibility—but Mac didn't want to push the men and risk exhaustion by the time they reached the town. Nor could they afford to be late.

An occasional muffled oath announced that someone's bare foot had found a protruding rock or root. When the trail widened Mac recognised the spot where he had seen the workers repairing the stone wall. He raised his hand to halt the marines, then moved cautiously forward until he was sure the men weren't sleeping at the job site. He returned to the landing party and instructed them to follow him.

Once they reached the farm he knew they could not move undetected through the brush. Their large party would make too much noise, and their passage would be obvious to anyone who saw the disturbed foliage after daybreak. He would have to chance staying on the travelled path that skirted the edge of the field. Although the farm seemed quiet, with not even a whiff of smoke from the chimney the sailors were excited. Faces blackened, stealing through a forest at night, and now skulking like poachers after 'milord's deer'. Mac hissed for quiet when some of the men tittered like schoolgirls.

Mac edged out of the forest, the marines following in single file, then positioned them at intervals along the trail. Groups of three or four men would advance, pausing at each marine to make sure they hadn't been seen or heard before continuing to the next. This would take longer than moving as one group, but ensured that the entire party wouldn't be caught in the open. Mac accompanied Grego and the remaining marines to the far end of the field.

As the fourth group reached the second marine a door at the farm squeaked. Mac tensed and passed the order for the men to stop in their tracks. He crouched and listened intently for several minutes before standing. "Probably the wind moving a barn door," he said to Grego.

"Everything all right?" Toby whispered when he arrived a minute later.

Mac replied, "I thought I heard a door open and had to make sure we weren't seen. We'll rest everyone five minutes, then continue to the edge of town. Can you tell the time?"

Toby pulled out his pocket watch, tipping it toward the sliver of the rising moon. "I make it just after three," he whispered, squinting in the darkness. "How is our schedule?"

"Right on time," Mac replied. "We should be in position well before dawn." He reminded the men of the importance of silence now that they were near civilization. The marines were under orders to fire only if fired upon. If they came across anyone they were to warn the main group and hide. Bayonet or sword were a last resort—any noise could destroy the chance of rescuing the hostages. It might also force the would-be rescuers into a defensive rearguard action as they retreated, empty handed, to the boats.

MIDSHIPMAN BARNES SHIVERED from the damp night air and pulled his boat cloak tighter as he checked the sentries. Some of the men were snoring so loudly Barnes thought they would be heard in Puerto Blanco.

"All's quiet, sir," Henry Carpenter reported. Carpenter, who had volunteered for the navy rather than face poaching charges in England, was said to have the eyes of a cat and could detect even the slightest movement on a moonless night. Tonight's thin moon likely made his duties seem like child's play.

"Thankee, Henry, be sure to keep your eyes open."

"No problem, zur. An' if that bird twenty yards yonder comes any closer," motioning toward the dark, impenetrable forest, "I'll have breakfast looked after."

STIRRED TO LIFE in the predawn darkness by the middle watch quartermaster, the midshipmen, mates and lieutenant of the watch rose a few minutes before four. On the turn of the half-hour glass the bosuns' pipes trilled 'All hands'.

Lionheart and *Ringle* were five miles west of Puerto Blanco when Cathcart came on deck. The ritual heave of the log showed four knots, with *Ringle* ghosting three cables abeam and slightly astern of the frigate. Smoke from the galley fire, heavy with the scent of breakfast, lingered about the deck like a wraith before drifting away on the light breeze.

The morning meal was oatmeal burgoo and Scottish coffee, a concoction of burned ship's biscuit boiled in water and fortified with a half-tot of rum at Cathcart's order. Half the crew hurriedly ate before relieving the others. Once the men had been fed the interior partitions were struck down to the drummer's hearty rendition of Hearts of Oak.

MAC HALTED THE COLUMN, then led Toby and Grego through the underbrush. They crawled the last hundred feet to the crest of the hill that overlooked the town sprawled below, colourless in the pale moonlight.

Mac pointed toward the second house to the right, "The crews are there, four houses to the left are the officers and Mr. Babbett. We'll take the marines down first so they can find a suitable spot on the road to protect us from reinforcements coming from the town." Scraping sounds in the underbrush heralded the arrival of Grego and the marines. Mac continued, "Well Toby, so far, so good. Although I wonder at times if just mentioning good fortune doesn't end it."

Toby chuckled, "I have thought the same thing. You are right in your assessment of the Spaniards, though. The last thing they will expect is us attempting a rescue. I am sure they think we will try to retake the ships."

Mac nodded. "We'll find out soon enough." He pointed out a dark streak running down the slope to Grego. "We'll make our way along the crest to that line of brush running down the hillside, then go down."

"Right, you lot," Grego growled. "Follow th' Cap'n and make sure you don't go over yer arses down the 'ill. An' not a sound."

Mac led the way in a low crouch, the marines following three paces apart. Huddled against the wall, Mac listened for any sound of alarm, but not even a dog barked. "Well done," he whispered. "There's a path between the walls leading to the road just ahead. Ready?" Murmurs assured him they were. "Follow me," he ordered while trying to control his surging adrenaline.

Despite an occasional whispered curse when a scabbard or musket scuffed against the wall's rough stones they reached the roadway with no sign they were noticed. The houses remained dark; there was no one in sight.

"It's in your hands now, Sergeant. Good luck. We'll see you behind the houses after dawn." Mac turned and disappeared in the wall's shadow.

Toby and the main body of men were waiting for Mac behind the wall of the sailors' prison. Toby whispered, "I make it four thirty. A little more than an hour to sunrise."

"Well, Toby, this is where we part. I'll see you back here. Good luck."

Toby replied, "God's speed to you, my friend."

FORTY-FIVE MINUTES BEFORE SUNRISE, *Lionheart*, with *Ringle* trailing by a half cable, turned toward the harbour entrance, three miles away. The night breeze, still out of the west, lay one point on their larboard quarter. Under courses and topsails, *Lionheart* continued toward the harbour and the sleeping fort. *Ringle* would follow until the last quarter-mile, then dash across the entrance to engage the smaller battery on the far shore. Her puny six-pounders would serve well enough against the lightly protected guns and force the battery to engage her.

Cathcart trusted that *Ringle's* last minute change of course would confuse the Spanish defenders, forcing the battery's gunners to shift their aim and range. With luck, both the fort and battery would have their guns trained on the entrance, anticipating catching the British ships in a crossfire as they tried to force their way in. The sudden move might even allow *Ringle* enough time to fire one or two well-aimed broadsides before the battery could effectively fire. In many battles the first few broadsides determined the outcome.

"Deck there." The foremast lookout's hail broke the tension with scarcely half a mile to go. "Smoke arisin' from the fort."

Had they been seen and the fort lit their furnace to heat shot to red-hot orbs? A heated shot could easily ignite either of the ships. Cathcart compared their speed with the remaining distance. He knew it would take at least fifteen minutes to get the furnace hot and another ten to heat the shot. He planned to be out of range by then.

SEPPINGS **CONTINUED TACKING** back and forth across the cove's entrance. Jamieson was able to discern dark shapes of the boats on the beach as the sky shifted from dark pewter to light bronze flecked with wisps of apricot.

Laura, mind swirling from the anxiety that prevented sleep, stared at the underside of the deck barely three feet above. She lit her candle and placed it in its tin holder on the wall, poured water from a small jug into a basin and splashed her face. The cool water reminded her of the grotto, and of Mac. She tied her hair back and left her solitude for *Seppings'* crowded deck.

RINGLE **STEADFASTLY FOLLOWED** in *Lionheart's* wake as they approached the harbour entrance. Cathcart had decided not to waste time with a conventional flag hoist. A sailor at *Lionheart's* taffrail held both arms upright, then pointed toward the battery. The schooner's helm was immediately thrown over. Her slender fore and aft sails clutched the breeze, now at a near right angle to her course, as the fore tops'l and t'gallant were sheeted home. Heeling and accelerating, she had two cables before her guns would bear.

Unseen from the ships the gunners in the smaller battery, the object of *Ringle's* dash, had just completed aiming and elevating their weapons to trap the British ships in a deadly crossfire. Now, they struggled to re-aim their guns.

Lionheart, her courses brailed, glided under driver, partly reefed topsails and a single jib while the captains of her forward guns crouched behind their beasts, sighting along the barrels, ready to fire at the first opportunity.

The fort opened fire but their shot landed some fifty yards ahead of *Lionheart*, whose guns could not yet reply.

AT THE FIRST SOUND of battle Toby reminded his men to wait for *Lionheart* to fire. Two nearly simultaneous thunderclaps announced *Lionheart* had opened fire. A pair of grappling hooks looped over the house's garden wall, the clink of hooks grasping stone went unheard above the din and the incessant clamour of the town's dogs.

Three men scaled the garden wall as Toby led the remainder in a mad rush along the path to the front of the house. Grego's marines guarding the road thumbed their muskets to full cock. Grego peered down the empty road, satisfied they could deal with any threat.

Toby clenched a pistol in his left hand and his favourite sword in his right. He charged through the front door at the same moment others shattered the rear door. Two sleep-befuddled guards at the rear were quickly dispatched by screaming black-faced sailors. The thunder of the heavy guns rattled the windows, increasing the sailors' bloodlust.

Toby raised the cellar trapdoor, paused to ensure there was no guard, then sheathed his sword. He shifted the scabbard to ensure it did not trip him on the stairs and transferred the pistol to his right hand. A sailor thrust a lantern into his left hand. Toby paused for a moment, took a deep breath, and warily tested the narrow steps. When the lantern's amber light revealed three dozen men shackled to a heavy rope he smiled, not realising that the prisoners could only see white teeth gleaming from his soot-smudged face.

The nearest hostage recoiled. Toby realised his error and shifted the lantern to fully illuminate his face. "Baverstock, First of *Lionheart*, at your service." Toby struggled to sound calm despite his racing heart. "Does anyone fancy a stroll through the countryside and a boat ride? Who is in charge here?"

"Bosun George Carter, *Pool of London*," answered a scratchy voice from somewhere in the midst of the prisoners.

"Well, Carter," Toby said stepping toward the voice, "give us a minute and we will have you out of here. Everyone remain quiet, we do not want the Spaniards to know we are here. Are there only two guards?"

"Aye, sir," answered Carter. "They're relieved at six bells of the morning watch."

"Excellent, we will be long gone by then. Ships are attacking the fort to keep them distracted while we complete our work; a schooner is waiting for us at a cove several a few miles from here. Is there anyone who cannot walk that far? We will make sure you get there. Nobody will be left behind."

"Thank God you came for us," a prisoner exclaimed. "We'll make it."

A hammer started its rhythmic clang against chisel to sever the shackles until all the men were released. Carter stood beside Toby until the last man was freed. "Sir, what about the others? The officers and an American gentleman are being held elsewhere."

Toby nodded, "Others are freeing them as we speak."

"Is the officer who found us a few days ago here?"

"We'll have time for questions later."

MAC DASHED ALONG the narrow pathway, glanced briefly at Laura's window before he turned at the road and continued toward the front door. The burly bosun's mate accompanying him splintered the door with his shoulder. Mac flung himself into the hallway, a pistol in each hand.

A guard had his back to the door when it burst open. The man turned toward the noise and instinctively reached for his sword. Mac's right-hand pistol spewed flame; the lead ball struck the man squarely in the chest and flung him back against another door directly behind him. The bosun hacked the prostrate Spaniard's neck with his cutlass, then dragged the body clear of the door.

Mac opened the next door. A second guard, pistol in hand, turned toward him at the same moment two sailors burst through a second door directly behind the guard. Mac couldn't risk shooting—at this range the ball might pass through the guard and strike one of his own men. Instead, he flung his empty pistol, striking the Spaniard's shoulder and causing the man's gun to discharge harmlessly into the ceiling. One sailor nearly severed the guard's neck with his cutlass, then raised the bloody blade for a second blow.

"Enough," Mac shouted. "He's done for. Find the prisoners."

Mac and the bosun's mate darted from room to room on the main floor as daylight began seeping into the dark interior. Mac shuddered involuntarily at the sight of Ramos' dried blood on the floor of Laura's room.

The next door was locked. Mac nodded to the bosun's mate and stepped aside.

The door splintered under the mate's sixteen stone. Mac leaped into the room, pistol at the ready, to find a man sitting on the floor shackled by his wrists to the wall. An empty pair of shackles were attached to the opposite wall.

"We're from *Lionheart*," Mac said. "We'll have you out of here right away. Are there any other prisoners here?"

The man, who appeared terrified and confused, hesitated before saying, "They took away Cap'n McCulloch, the American and half a dozen others days ago. Irving, *Donnington Castle's* luff, is down the hall. The rest are in the cellar." He nodded toward the dark hallway leaving Mac unclear whether he was indicating the other room, the cellar entrance, or perhaps both.

"Which ship?" Mac asked as one of the sailors prepared to sever the man's shackles.

"Henry Keeler, First Mate, *Pool of London*."

"Pleased to meet you Henry, I'm Mac Appleton."

Mac directed Keeler toward the rear door before continuing along the hallway. Other sailors had found the prisoners in the dank cellar; the steady ring of hammer on chisel signalled the severing of shackles. Mac found Irving at the end of the hallway. By the time he freed Irving and returned to the front hall half a dozen dazed men had gathered. Some rubbed their legs to restore circulation.

Mac said, "The guns you hear are *Lionheart* and the schooner *Ringle* attacking the fort as a diversion. Our real purpose is to get you out of here, but it will mean a bit of a walk. Another ship is waiting at a small cove. If any of you can't walk on your own don't worry, we'll get you there. We're not leaving anyone behind. Does anyone know where McCulloch and Babbett were taken?"

Keeler responded, "Somewhere in the town, but I'm unsure where. D'you know that the rest of our men are in another house?"

"A second group is freeing them now." Mac, deliberately curt, was eager to be away from the town before they were discovered. "Everyone ready?" He didn't wait for an answer before instructing them to go out the door and follow the garden wall to the back.

It was clear to Mac that the march to the cove was going to be slow when Lionhearts had to assist several prisoners in obvious pain. Sounds of the bombardment continually reverberated among the buildings. When they had safely reached the rear wall a bosun mate sounded a warble on his call to recall Toby's group and the marines from the road. The marines safely back, Grego detailed two men to remain at the foot of the path before securing the top of the hill with the remainder.

An eerie silence descended over the town when the heavy guns ceased firing.

BREATHLESS FROM HIS WILD GALLOP to the fort after hearing of the English ships, Ortega watched them sail toward his carefully laid trap. The fort and the battery would cut them to pieces in another few hundred yards, but the schooner suddenly veered toward the far battery, throwing into disarray his plan to cripple, then capture, the ships. With sudden clarity he realised that his guns would have to divide their fire and belatedly ordered the shot furnace lit despite the gunner's protests that it would take too long. Only a thin wisp of smoke exited the furnace chimney when the frigate's first ball hammered into the fort's wall. Through his telescope, Ortega could see the gunners at the far battery frantically trying to reposition their guns to respond to the schooner charging toward them.

The first English salvo struck the fort's heavy stone walls. Although causing little real damage, it did increase the anxiety of the soldiers who had never before come under fire at this remote outpost of Spain's empire anxiety. Distracted, they worked feverishly to reposition their guns to return the frigate's fire. Ortega's plan of perfectly sighted guns destroying impudent Royal Navy ships in their attempt to force the harbour entrance was in a shambles.

The English assault continued for more than twenty minutes, until one of the fort's guns struck the frigate amidships and the frigate suddenly broke off the attack. Ortega, convinced the English had failed in their attempt to free the Indiamen and Thunderbolt, stood at the fort's wall, privately admitting that although the battery was poorly situated the British had been thwarted by the fort. When the British broke off their attack he hissed under his breath, "They run like dogs."

RINGLE **OPENED FIRE,** her smaller guns issuing a sharp crack rather than a roar, after Wilson reduced sail to provide a more level deck. His lee guns quickly found the battery's range, kicking up clouds of dirt as shots struck the earth embankments.

The battery's gunners could not traverse their weapons to hit *Ringle* in her current position. The battery had been designed to cover just the narrow harbour entrance. This was a fatal flaw not lost on Wilson. Wind and current calculations ran through his mind as *Ringle* hissed through the water. When *Lionheart* signalled 'Close Action'—normally reserved for ship-to-ship battles—Wilson knew that Cathcart also realised *Ringle* was in no danger from the ill-sited battery. An aggressive attack would convince the Spaniards, if they were in any doubt, that the British were intent on freeing the ships.

Wilson saw *Lionheart* move perilously closer to the fort and ordered *Ringle* to come about to allow the larboard battery to take up the attack. He was encouraged to see *Ringle's* shots fling shards of rock and iron over the crest of the embankment. The Spanish gunners would be wise to keep their heads down, and that would discourage them from returning fire.

Wilson adjusted his telescope. Something about the dirt embrasure had changed. His guns had collapsed the sides of one of the gun slits and he could clearly see the upper backs and heads of the gun crew as they reloaded. *Ringle* would have to briefly come into the battery's arc of fire to take advantage of the opening. He ordered his aft guns reloaded with grape then waited anxiously— through his telescope he could see the Spanish gun being moved into position.

A pair of simultaneous discharges shook the deck, causing Wilson to momentarily lose sight of the enemy gun. He steadied the telescope in time to see a cloud of dirt and dust from the grapeshot's impact. The enemy gun was skewed toward the harbour and its crew were not visible. Wilson snapped his telescope shut and ordered a course toward *Lionheart*.

THE MAIN FORT maintained an erratic fire while *Lionheart* continued to press toward the harbour entrance. Their first rounds landed off target when well placed balls disrupted the Spanish gunners. *Lionheart's* thirty-two pounder carronades took up the assault causing volcanic showers of rock to fly skyward from the fort's walls. Razor-sharp shards of metal and stone scythed through the air with each impact.

Cathcart had originally planned a fifteen minute attack based on the presumption of effective Spanish resistance. So far not one Spanish ball had struck home, but he knew the Spanish furnace was heating shot and calculated that an additional five minutes of distraction would benefit the rescue party.

Lionheart had reached the extreme edge of the fort's field of fire when a Spanish ball struck forward of the foremast deadeyes with a resounding crash and shower of splinters. Cathcart immediately ordered *Lionheart* out of danger, loosing a final rippling broadside to delay the fort's gunners from firing while she was still vulnerable. After a tense few minutes they were out of range. Cathcart, satisfied that they had achieved their main purpose to distract the Spaniards, had *Lionheart* stand off the harbour mouth—for all appearances licking her wounds.

~18~

A NEAR RUN THING

MAC PAUSED at the crest of the hill. So far the rescue mission had gone without a hitch. He asked Toby to take the men into the forest then crouched behind a bush and waited. After a minute or two Grego's party arrived and led Grego to the rest of the men, then turned to Toby. "I'm not sure what we can do about the officers and Babbett at this time. Not knowing where they're being held makes it foolish to attempt a rescue, although part of me wants to go back. What do you think?"

Toby thought for a moment then said, "We have lost the element of surprise and should withdraw."

Mac glanced in the direction of the town now hidden by the trees. "You're right. We might still surprise them, but this isn't the time. It'll be impossible to sneak around the town in daylight. Let's get everyone back to the ships, then make a decision on further action. A bird in the hand, as it were."

He divided the former hostages into three groups determined by their ability to walk: Mac would take the lead group, Toby the middle, Grego the remaining. Mac placed the most seriously injured in his group—the slowest, they would determine the pace. Grego sent two marines, both experienced hunters, several hundred feet ahead to act as scouts. The remainder of the marines formed a rear guard.

Toby nodded agreement, adding, "I am surprised there is no sign of pursuit."

THERE WAS NO PURSUIT. Civilians living on either side of the makeshift prisons were not prepared to risk Ortega's wrath by bringing him the news of the attack and rescue. They knew it was better to plead ignorance after hiding at the first sign of trouble.

A militia private, who stopped at the sailors' house looking for wine, discovered the dead sentries and empty shackles twenty minutes after the escape. He started toward the town to raise the alarm then changed his mind to check the officers' house which delayed him a further fifteen minutes. He arrived at Ortega's office, only to discover that his comandante was at the fort—a mile away.

Nearly ninety minutes elapsed before Ortega was informed of the escape. He guessed nothing of a landing party and assumed the prisoners had somehow overpowered the guards. Believing there was nowhere for the prisoners to go he ordered increased guards around the harbour and search parties to track them down. He remained at the fort, keeping a watchful eye on the ships now lurking two miles offshore.

WILSON REPORTED ABOARD *LIONHEART* at four bells in the forenoon watch. Cathcart, standing at the top of the quarterdeck steps, invited him to join him for a late breakfast and added, "You must be famished after your tour of the harbour entrance." There was the hint of a wry grin on Cathcart's face. "We can discuss this morning's events over a pot of coffee while our Spanish friends," Cathcart tipped his head toward the fort, "wonder what we are about."

"Coffee would be most welcome, sir," Wilson replied and followed Cathcart to the Great Cabin.

"How expensive was our bill?" Cathcart asked. "You certainly took my signal 'Close Action' to heart. I thought you might be planning to board the battery by running up on the beach." He smiled as his servant offered Wilson a steaming mug.

Wilson sipped cautiously from the mug. "None whatsoever, I'm happy to report. The Spanish contrived to site their guns so they could not bear, although that prevented us from doing much more than scatter earth about them. I doubt we landed any shots inside the embankments. How did *Lionheart* fare, if I may ask?"

Cathcart was ebullient. "Nothing more than a minor splinter wound from a ball just aft of the fore chains moments before I disengaged. More damage to the paint work than anything else. The Spanish were such appallingly poor shots that I extended the attack beyond the original plan. I hope it did not cause you any concern."

Wilson was caught off guard by the confession. "Oh no, sir. On the contrary, the men quite enjoyed the work. Far more rewarding than banging away at a floating cask. I was most satisfied with our gunnery and threw in a couple rounds of grape as a parting gesture. If nothing else we encouraged the Spaniards to keep their heads down. By the way, I remarked your gunners removing sizeable chunks of the fort's stonework. Do you know if you struck any of their guns?"

Cathcart smiled. "I don't think so, although it was hard to see if we caused any real damage. The Dons were so erratic I could not ascertain if all of their guns were firing. I am confident our original desire to distract them was fully met. The masthead lookout did not espy any troop activity indicating pursuit of the landing party. Enough of that, our breakfasts are here." Cathcart's servant had arrived with their tray.

THE RETURN TREK to the beach was inexorably slow; the debilitating effects of captivity forced the former prisoners to take frequent rest stops. The rescuers were sympathetic and didn't try to hurry the pace. Four men in Mac's group, hobbled and in obvious pain, had to be supported by their rescuers.

Mac worried he should have arranged some form of transport for the worst cases, but realised that the narrow forest trail would have made even a small cart difficult to haul. Even the strongest men, in the rear group, were beginning to slow as the afternoon wore on.

When he joined Toby during the next pause Mac said, "Perhaps another mile and half. I hope that we can cover this last bit without further stops as I make it about two hours of daylight remaining. I don't want to be in the forest after dark with this many men. Is all quiet with the marines?" He glanced toward the after-guard hunched along the trail seventy-five feet behind the column.

"No sign of anything," Toby replied. "I am mystified, but grateful, that there has been no pursuit."

THE SPANISH MILITIA paused on the La Quinta road after marching some five or six miles in a fruitless search for the escapees. Sergeant Perez, in charge of the dozen men, knew they had followed a false trail. If he had his way he would have first checked the coastal trail, now at least five miles away through the forest on their left. Commandante Ortega had been most emphatic that the escapees would make for La Quinta, then try to capture a ship to make their escape.

Perez sat at the side of the road, wrestling with his dilemma, while his men rested. If he abandoned the road and cut through the forest to intercept the forest trail but failed to find the prisoners Ortega would ensure he regretted that decision. The smart thing to do was to continue until they reached La Quinta, following orders to the letter. He could not be faulted for following precise orders that left no room for creative interpretation—even if he knew that he was searching the road with no hope of success. If Ortega listened to any of his subordinates he wouldn't continue to make such blunders—the pitiful defence of the harbour had been a prime example of that, Perez thought.

Fifteen minutes later, the men rested, Perez led them into the woods and a track leading toward the coastal trail. Four hours of daylight remained.

"COME ON," Mac urged the nearest men when they reached the small waterfall. "We're almost there, another six cables." He hoped his enthusiasm would revitalise their flagging muscles.

Thirty minutes later, when the marine scouts signaled for them to halt, he heard the murmur of excitement run through the column of men. After a tense five-minute wait while the marines ensured the beach and boats were safe before venturing into the open a marine reported, "Everything's in order, sir. We signaled *Seppings* to stand in."

"Very good," Mac responded. "Have your men join Sergeant Grego."

Mac and Toby sorted the Indiamen into groups—the most seriously injured would be in the first boat. With the wind steady out of the west the boat crews would have their work cut out for them rowing to *Seppings*. Fortunately they would be able to rig sails for the return trip.

Grego's marines formed a skirmish line straddling the trail. Laying in wait, close to sunset and with the sun directly behind them, they were nearly invisible in the deepening shadows from the deep grass and brush.

***SEPPINGS* ENTERED THE COVE** under light sail while Jamieson attempted to exchange pleasantries when Laura appeared through the hatch.

She did not respond and abruptly asked, "Is there any word from shore?"

Jamieson wondered if he had said or done something to upset her. "Not yet, but I can discern our men on the beach." He passed his telescope to Laura despite knowing that they were too far away for her to recognise anyone.

Laura said quietly, "I am sorry, Captain, that was very rude of me. My mind was elsewhere."

"I understand." Jamieson glanced over his shoulder at the low sun. "We will lose the light before we finish boarding." He ordered *Seppings* into the wind; an anchor with a spring would enable their guns to protect the beach.

Laura struggled to sort out the telescope's inverted image when the first boat left the beach. Unable to spot either her father or Mac, she watched with a pounding heart as the gig crept toward *Seppings*—its oars resembled the legs of a giant water beetle crossing a pond. As the gig drew closer she recognised several sailors from the Indiaman.

William Watkins stumbled onto the deck before collapsing from the searing pain of blistered feet and ankles. The willpower that had carried him from the prison to the beach dissolved in the safety of the ship.

Laura knelt beside Forrester, *Seppings'* surgeon's mate, while he examined Watkins.

Forrester stood and said, "Nothing serious, I will deal with him shortly."

She offered, "Please let me help in some way."

Forrester moved to the next man and said without looking back, "This is no work for a woman." She ignored the rejection, elevated Watkins' lower leg and placed a rolled up cloth beneath his calf to relieve the pressure.

Forrester looked at her with a half-scowl, relented, then held out a cloth and said, "Apply this." Laura pressed a salve-moistened cloth against Watkins' open sores. Despite her gentle touch Watkins grimaced and opened his eyes. She leaned forward so he could see her face. "William Watkins, isn't it?" She didn't wait for him to reply and continued, "I recognised you from the *Donnington Castle*. I'm Laura Babbett, my father and I are... were...passengers."

Watkins winced; his lips tightened as he fought the pain and his eyes seemed unable to focus. "So 'tis true, you escaped," he gasped.

Laura nodded and continued to clean the open sores. "This should help ease the pain."

Forrester said with a hint of apology in his voice, "I will bandage him in a minute."

While Forester treated Watkins, Laura checked the other men for injuries. A half-dozen reported sores from the shackles, although less severe than Watkins, while a seventh had a wicked toothache that would likely require extraction.

She accompanied Watkins below deck and began checking on the other injured then gasped at the unmistakable bark of a swivel gun, even though dulled by distance and the ship's hull.

MAC COULD NOT TELL if it was an English or Spanish musket that fired—Grego's position was hidden by the hummocks. Until now, the mission had gone well. The gig was reloading even as the launch discharged men onto *Seppings*; other boats were on their way back to the beach. The remaining escapees could be accommodated by the gig and two barges. The rest of the shore party would take the launch.

Toby sprinted across the beach to Mac and gasped, "Can we hold out for twenty minutes?"

Mac replied, "Depends on how many Spaniards there are. I'll find Grego. Put some men with muskets at the crest of the hummocks. We'll need to protect the marines when they withdraw." Sporadic musket fire continued at the forest's edge.

Mac crouched low as he ran along the trail. Fifteen yards from the marines he called out, "Sergeant Grego, coming in from your rear." He didn't want to be mistaken for a Spaniard in the dusk.

FORRESTER, FINISHED WITH THE LAST of the wounded, casually wiped his hands on his bloody apron. This was the first time that he had treated so many wounded. *Seppings* was too small to rate a proper surgeon and his limited skills were usually employed dealing with sprains or an occasional hernia;

sometimes he administered a dose of mercury to a poxed sailor after a rare shore leave.

He could not bring himself to issue an actual apology to Laura despite being inwardly grateful for her assistance. Instead, he turned to her and said in a conciliatory tone, "Well, that's th' lot. Mostly sores from th' shackles. Poor buggers should be all right in a few days, 'though in th' tropics infection's always a concern. Th' worst case was your fellow. How is he?"

Laura finished refolding an unused bandage. "The wound cleaned nicely. I could not discern any infection before I bandaged it. The salve you gave me seems to have worked." She paused then said, "Would it be amiss for me to appear on deck? I am anxious about what is happening ashore, but I do not want to be in the way."

Forrester stared at a bloodstained deck plank, as though unsure of his response, then replied, "I have t' report t' th' captain. Stay close and I'll let y' know. Sometimes 'e c'n be a mite testy."

She followed Forrester, pausing on the narrow ladder, while Forrester reported to Jamieson. Although Jamieson lowered his voice, she could overhear the conversation.

Jamieson asked, "Was she uncomfortable dealing with the wounds?"

"Not at all" Forrester replied. "She 'as a natural touch an' looked after the worst case most admirably, sir. Even sniffed th' wound for signs of infection without hesitation."

Jamieson nodded. "Please convey my respects and ask Miss Babbett to join me."

Laura backed down two steps so Forrester would not know she had been eavesdropping.

The fifteen feet across *Seppings'* deck seemed a mile when she heard more muskets and a swivel. Another boat had reached *Seppings* and Forrester was busy conducting preliminary exams as the men came aboard. Jamieson said warmly, "Miss Babbett, good evening to you. Forester tells me you were of great service tending to the wounded. I am in your debt."

"Thank you Captain, but the debt is mine. It's the least I could do after all the kindness shown to me. What's happening ashore? Is there a battle?"

He replied, "I would judge by the sporadic fire that there is a skirmish involving perhaps less than a dozen Spaniards. If it was a major force there would be a more intense battle. It is almost dark, so Mac's suggestion of blackened faces and dark clothing will make our men difficult to spot. Unfortunately, the dusk also makes it difficult for me to offer support with our guns as I cannot be sure of where our men or the enemy are."

Laura gave an audible sigh. "Thank you for your candour." Staying strong was much more difficult than she had imagined.

Jamieson lowered his voice, "Not to worry ma'am. They have excellent men with them." He called out, "Mr. Teague, I will trouble you to tend the spring so as we may properly present our broadside to yon beach." He glanced at Laura, "It would be safer for you below."

THE SPANISH PURSUERS paused when one of their number clutched his gut and pitched forward. Blinded by the low sun, they searched for the source of the musket shot. Perez ordered two men into the woods on their right to outflank whoever had fired. Then, secure in his belief that the escapees possessed but a solitary captured musket, he ordered the remainder of his men to advance.

The swivel gun's shower of grape mowed down the leading group of four. Perez threw himself to the ground and cursed. The escapees appeared well armed and organised. Clearly they were not cowering in fear on the beach.

TOBY SENT THREE ADDITIONAL MEN armed with muskets to reinforce Mac and the marines. An anxious sailor informed Mac, "Last two boats on their way, sir. Mr. Baverstock's respects, 'e expects they'll be 'ere in p'r'aps eight minutes. Ten at the most. 'E trusts that yer able to distract the Spaniards until then. The lootenant says 'e 'as men at the 'ummocks to pertects us when we withdraws. The boats' swivels'll be firin' an' 'e most respekfully suggests we keeps our 'eads down an' stays together when we runs fer it."

Mac spoke to the concealed men, "Listen up, the boats will be here in eight or ten minutes. We have to hold the Spaniards until then. No one fires until I order. We don't want to be caught reloading if they decide to rush us, and there's no point shooting at shadows in the dark. A muzzle flash will give away our position, so keep them guessing as long as possible. Aim the swivel at the centre of the trail and keep your eyes open."

Toby completed organising the first group to board when the boats were less than seventy-five yards from the beach. The leading boat scuffed onto the sand, sailors leapt over the bow to push her free as men waded to her through the knee-deep water. The second boat's arrival was punctuated by the swivel's bark from beyond the hummocks.

PEREZ DECIDED HE MUST ATTACK, dismissing concerns that the British were too well armed. He anticipated losing his first group of attackers, but the swivel would only have one chance to fire before the rest of his men reached the British position. He was confident that his men would easily overcome the escapees who seemed to be armed only with one or two muskets and a now useless swivel.

The swivel's blast still echoed in the forest when Perez leapt up and ordered his men to charge. Perez's second group surged out of the forest, squarely into a disciplined musket volley that killed half his men—their bodies obstructing the narrow trail—and wounded many of the remainder.

The gunfire was heard by a second Spanish search party sent by Ortega when he decided the escapees might not be heading for La Quinta. Although on horseback they weren't trained cavalry, just ten men straddling horses more suited for agrarian activities.

At the sound of the swivel, their leader slapped his mount and called for the others to follow.

"BACK TO THE BOATS," Mac shouted. He turned to face the hummocks and called, "We're coming through, cover us," as the sailors and some of the marines scrambled from their hiding places.

The Spaniards fired at shadowy figures running toward the beach; one marine was hit in the thigh, a sailor in the shoulder. Willing hands helped both men toward the beach as English return fire forced the Spaniards to take cover. The moment the men cleared the hummocks the remaining marines fired a final volley before sprinting to join the main party.

The last boat signalled *Seppings* that boarding had begun. Mac looked toward the forest. The sweat running down his back turned ice cold. "Horses!" he called out. "Toby, there's a troop of cavalry coming."

Toby shouted, "Boats there, ready yer swivels. Cavalry in the forest."

Both Toby and Mac knew the carnage cavalry would inflict if they caught them in the midst of loading the boats.

"Ferguson," Toby growled, "signal three long flashes."

A horse whinnied and snorted in excitement. They were close.

"Leave the shutter open on my order. Everyone on the ground."

Three riders charged over the middle hummock. The cutter's crew swung their swivel and fired, taking down the rearmost rider and horse. The surviving pair continued toward the boats in a frenzied mixture of shouted oaths and pounding hooves.

The launch, already pushed free of the beach, was blocked by the cutter and couldn't fire.

The lead rider hacked at a sailor and turned toward Mac. Mac fired his pistol from a range of ten feet as the Spaniard charged, the man's blood dripping from his sabre illuminated by the pistol's flash. The ball struck the rider in the shoulder but failed to knock him from his horse. Mac flung himself aside to escape the hooves, discarded the spent pistol and rolled across the sand.

He crouched on his knees only to hear a second set of hooves behind him and turned toward the threat. His entire field of vision was filled by a rearing horse—its front hooves pawing wildly in the air. The rider aimed his pistol as Mac crouched frozen on the sand, time seemed at a standstill. There was a flash of light and an explosion before Mac was hurled sideways into the sand. Blinded by the flash, deafened by the explosion and unable to breathe from the crushing weight against his chest, he felt his mouth fill with gritty sand. Somewhere in his semiconscious haze, he heard more horses and bloodcurdling yells in Spanish. He knew he was wounded, possibly fatally, and thought of Laura. Would she know how much he cared for her? Then a distant series of rippling explosions followed by a whistling wind and more screams of agony—from beast or man he could not tell. Mac felt himself being rolled onto his back, dimly hearing a voice as he tried to spit the sand from his mouth and throat before he choked.

"Are you all right?"

It sounded like Toby. Something, or someone, grasped him under his armpits and sat him upright. Mac tried to focus on the face but he was still blinded from the flash.

Toby ordered, "Get him into the boat. No point waiting to see if there are any more of those Spanish bastards about."

Mac felt himself being hoisted to his feet, his limp legs dragging through the sand and water as they hauled him to the cutter twenty feet from the beach. By the time they reached the boat he had regained some of his senses and realised that he had not been shot, although his chest was mightily sore every time he took a deep breath. He looked at Toby and said, "The last thing I remember was staring at the barrel of a pistol, then an explosion and flash. I don't know how he could have missed at that range."

"He never fired," Toby winked and gave an evil grin. "It was my pistol you heard. I apologise for discharging it so close to your ear but time was of the essence."

"Then it was you who flung me sideways and not his pistol ball?"

"Yes, when I saw the first rider charge you. I realised that the second was about to do you in, so I knocked you over. You seemed to be frozen to the ground, unable to move. I fired as I landed on you and was lucky to hit him before he could shoot. My pistol was less than a foot from your head. I must have knocked the wind out of your sails; for a moment I thought you had been shot."

"You weren't the only one." Mac clasped Toby's shoulder. "What were those explosions? I was nearly unconscious and thought I heard more horses and then hideous screams. I was sure I'd arrived at the Gates of Hell."

"Merely *Seppings* disposing of some unwanted guests. The remainder of the Spanish cavalry, if that's what they were for they didn't seem very well trained, was at the crest of the hummocks and about to swoop down."

Mac tried to sort the jumbled sequence of the sounds. "But how did *Seppings* know when to fire? Or where for that matter?"

"I'd worked out plans with Jamieson that his guns would be aimed across the top of the hummocks, presuming we'd be at the boats and that her shots would fly over our heads. That's another reason I had to get you onto the sand. We were in a dangerous position if any of her shots were low."

"Was she successful?"

"Magnificently. The Spanish were caught in line abreast on top of the hummocks. I doubt there were any survivors, although I did not bother to check. I had no way of knowing if more were coming in support."

~19~

NO RESOLUTION

LAURA LOST TRACK OF TIME while tending to the wounded below deck; it had helped ease her worries about Mac until she realised the sounds of battle had stopped. Now, with the guns silent, she fought the urge to go up on deck. She knew her presence would be foolish and unwelcome—she would only be in the way of the gun crews.

The eerie silence seemed to last an eternity. Laura clenched her hands, took a deep breath, and completed applying a bandage. On the verge of tears, she fought to maintain her composure and didn't notice the approaching figure hunched beneath the deck beams. She turned and looked up with a start expecting to see Forrester.

"Mr. For..." She stopped in mid-word Instead of Forrester on another inspection, Mac stood watching silently. She almost exclaimed "Mac" but caught herself, "Captain Appleton, I was expecting Mr. Forrester. Are you wounded?" She straightened, fighting back both the urge to embrace him and her tears.

He replied, "I've been better. Nothing food and sleep won't fix. Toby and I have to brief Jamieson. He wonders if you could join us in about three-quarters of an hour?"

She took a hesitant step forward, "Is everything all right? My father..." Her voice quivered. Mac seemed distant; his eyes lacked their usual life. It could only mean bad news about her father.

JAMIESON, busy arranging maps and charts on the table that filled most of his tiny cabin, looked up at the knock. "Gentlemen, do come in. Pray help yourself to a glass of wine or brandy."

Toby and Mac gave a careful summation of the mission as the noise and bustle of getting the schooner underway filtered through the oak deck planks. This discussion would help Toby and Mac remember details before meeting with Cathcart— *Seppings* was ordered to rendezvous with *Lionheart* the moment she recovered the shore party.

When Laura arrived Jamieson rose to greet her, "Miss Babbett, welcome. I'm afraid I can't offer you a sherry, only claret or brandy."

"Claret would be most welcome." Laura glanced noncommittally at Mac, then nodded to Toby.

Jamieson handed her the glass he noticed her trembling hand. "Miss Babbett..."

She interrupted him, "Please call me Laura when we're in private."

"You must be anxious for news of your father. He wasn't with the other prisoners. It seems several men, including your father, are being held at the commandant's house. We only learned this when we freed the others. It was impossible to attempt any rescue by then. Toby and Mac will tell you what we know." Jamieson bowed slightly, "Please excuse me, I'm required on deck."

Laura, visibly shaken by the news, sagged into Jamieson's chair. Although Toby and Mac tried to reassure her, the more they tried, the more worried she became.

No one dared mention their inner fear that Ortega may already have exacted revenge for the rescue of the others.

Jamieson loomed like a thundercloud over the tiny quarterdeck—a quarterdeck in name only, as the schooner possessed only one, meagre continuous deck. His domain abaft the mizzenmast was obstructed by the wheel and binnacle.

Seppings was, generally, an efficient and happy ship with a competent crew who understood their captain and could anticipate his wishes even when expressed only by the merest glance at sail or rigging. The past quarter hour had seen Jamieson issue a string of uncharacteristically curt orders to trim the sails, the latest emphasised with "Attend to your duty, damn your eyes."

He regretted the remark the moment he uttered it. He wanted to return to reach *Lionheart* and know there was a plan for rescuing the remaining prisoners. Laura's distress weighed heavily on his mind. The masthead lookout's hail, "Deck there. Sail ho. *Ringle* fine on the larboard bow," broke some of the tension.

Seppings was making fine progress, the wind perfectly situated in her best point of sail. Her razor-edge cutwater sheared through the four-foot swell, throwing the occasional spray up and outwards. The crew knew their captain well enough to surmise that the guests in his cabin were the source of his ill-temper. The sooner they reached *Lionheart*, the sooner their world would return to its usual cheerful state. So, without further urging from her fretful captain, *Seppings'* timbers issued the sweetest trembling, every sail drawing at maximum efficiency. The helmsman steered a perfect course toward *Ringle*—her shimmering topsails now visible from the deck. The crew exchanged knowing winks and grins when the cast of the log revealed thirteen knots.

By the time Mac and Toby arrived on deck a few minutes later, Jamieson's earlier edginess had dissipated as he paced the windward side. "Gentlemen," he called out almost jovially, "would you care to join me for a few turns? Exercise does wonders for the spirit."

Walking three abreast on the narrow deck was impossible so they formed a loose *vee*—Mac and Toby trailed like ducklings in their mother's wake while Jamieson avoided glances at the rigging or sails which would only further antagonise his crew. As Captain he couldn't make an outright apology for his earlier churlishness, but strolling back and forth in pleasant conversation with his guests was a clear statement to his men that things were back to normal. "I trust the lady is comforted after you explained the situation ashore?"

Toby responded, "She is quite improved, sir. She fully appreciates the importance that any rescue attempt be conducted properly to ensure a successful outcome."

Mac asked, "How long will it take to reach *Lionheart*?"

Before Jamieson could respond the lookout reported *Lionheart* was visible.

Jamieson smiled, "An hour if the wind holds." He glanced upward at the mainmast telltale, rapped his knuckles against the binnacle, then said enthusiastically, "Touch wood! She's a fine sailer in this wind don't you think? A bird in flight the way she skims across this pond."

"I couldn't agree more," Mac stated with obvious enthusiasm. "Would Miss Babbett's presence on deck be appropriate? She's an enthusiastic sailer. I'm sure she'd find this invigorating."

Jamieson appeared flustered, "I must apologise, I should have invited her earlier, rather than leaving her languishing in the cabin."

Mac replied before Toby or Jamieson could speak, "I'll pass along your invitation," then darted below and knocked on the door, "Captain Appleton, ma'am."

"Enter," Laura replied.

He opened the door, held one finger to his lips and pointed to the deck above with his other hand. Before he could close the door she asked in a loud voice, "Is there a problem? I wasn't expecting to see anyone until we reached the other ships." The moment the door closed she held out her arms.

Mac pulled her close, and continued their verbal ruse. "The Captain wonders if you would care to join him on deck." He carefully avoided using me or us. "*Ringle* and *Lionheart* are in sight and *Seppings* is running like a greyhound. He thought you might enjoy the spectacle."

"Thank you, I'd enjoy that." She playfully nibbled his ear then pressed even tighter against him.

LAURA ENTHUSIASTICALLY GREETED JAMIESON, "Why Captain, what a sight *Seppings* must be. I am sure she is the envy of every other ship. This must be the sea-borne equivalent of a full gallop across an open meadow."

Much to Jamieson's surprise, she grabbed his hand and shook it in enthusiastic congratulation. Out of fear that she was about to hug, or worse, kiss him—either of which must be avoided in the name of discipline—he managed to pull his hand free.

Laura continued unabashed. "We must be doing ten or twelve knots. It is a wonder that we stay in the water. She feels as if she is ready to take flight!"

Unaware that Laura had overheard the earlier conversation, Jamieson beamed, "Actually, ma'am, the last cast of the log showed thirteen."

She replied, nodding and smiling appreciatively. "I've always wondered what sailors meant when they cast the log. Do you really throw a piece of wood overboard?"

Jamieson offered to have another cast of the log to help with her understanding.

The nearest of two sailors who had contrived, conveniently, to be poised at the rail asked, in a 'Please mummy' tone, "Sir, may we demonstrate?"

Jamieson scowled at the lapse of discipline, but thought it would show poor form to threaten punishment in Laura's presence. He replied with a twinge of sarcasm, "By all means," coupled with his patented look of disapproval. He turned to Laura, "The end of the log is a wedge shaped piece of wood. Lead weights are attached to the line so that the log chip will float, point up in the water. The line is marked with knots, hence the term, which are counted against the log-glass. We use a thirty second glass and knots spaced a little over fifty feet nine inches apart. The glass is turned when the log enters the water."

Laura nodded in understanding and the log was heaved from just abaft the mizzen chains to ensure the line didn't snag as it streamed out. The second sailor turned the glass the moment the log hit the water. The ship became eerily silent while every man on deck watched both the log-line's progress and the lady.

"Mark!" cried the second sailor when the last grain of sand fell.

"Thirteen and one-half," called the first jubilantly, remembering just in time to add a belated, "sir."

Jamieson beamed, "Well ma'am, there you have it. Better than thirteen knots. You know of course that our sea-mile, a *knotical* mile if I may be so bold, is a greater distance than your land mile. In land terms we are travelling over fifteen miles per hour."

Ringle, now fully hull-up, continued tacking back and forth within a small rectangle of sea, dutifully repeating *Lionheart's* signal 'Report to flag' accompanied by *Seppings'* number.

Jamieson had acknowledged the signal, but their sails partially blocked the signal flags from *Ringle's* view. Every man-jack intently studied that each sail to ensure that it drew perfectly as *Seppings* continued her mad dash. Jamieson divided his attention between the sails and *Ringle*, interspersed with an occasional appreciative glance at the ruler-straight wake.

Jamieson grinned, then laughed aloud. *Ringle* was less than a mile away and had finally lowered her signal. "Toby, Mac—if I might have a word with you," he motioned for them to join him at the windward rail. "As neither of you are currently employed on ship's business, would you care to assist me in a small jest at Jamieson's expense?"

Without waiting for their reply he continued, "I'd like a discreet hoist to be made as we approach. Only *Ringle* must see it. Make her number and 'Tally Ho' just long enough for her to read as we pass."

Toby grinned, "With utmost pleasure," adding in a formal tone, "sir," with a tip of his hat. He looked at Mac, "Come on, we best be quick, I will tell you which flags we need while I prepare a whip for the hoist. Do you know what we are about?"

Mac chuckled. "In land-based terms 'Eat my dust' would be a close translation."

Jamieson ordered a course to pass thirty yards from *Ringle's* bow—perfect for their little prank while Toby and Mac arranged the signal flags on a line running to the mizzen gaff, ensuring the full-bellied sails would conceal the hoist from *Lionheart*. Mac hauled furiously on the line when *Ringle* was a hundred yards away; Jamieson doffed his hat in a sweeping, mocking bow as they surged past.

Wilson, his movements controlled by *Lionheart's* signals, was unable to do anything in response. He had to hold his course, like a puppy on a leash, until otherwise ordered. He could not even hoist a response, witty or otherwise, as it would be seen by *Lionheart*. To make things worse, *Seppings'* crew called out a loud, derisive taunt as they passed.

Mac recognised Jamieson's look—the young commander was a fighter jock at heart. He glanced back at the fast receding *Ringle* and mused that both Wilson and Jamieson were always pushing the limits, so confident in their abilities. Mac knew that this demonstration of speed and finely honed sailing skills might only be a game today, but if *Seppings* was giving chase—or worse, being chased—Jamieson's ability to wring every ounce of speed out of her could be crucial. That mischievous signal was akin to a fighter jock doing an unauthorised, low-altitude, high-speed pass in full afterburner over the control tower while throwing in a barrel roll for good measure. *Nothing changes; a few hundred years apart, and they're still the same!* Mac wondered if it was upbringing, genetics, or just innate spirit?

The thought of flight snapped him back to the reality of his present situation, so far in time and place from where he belonged. How to return to his own time festered in his subconscious—only held in check by the need to free Laura's father. He had arrived here by circumstance. *Would finding his way back require leaving her?*

~20~

BETRAYAL

CATHCART FUMED, "Bloody Hell! He damn near carried away *Ringle's* bowsprit." Viewed from *Lionheart's* deck it appeared that *Seppings* had passed much too close to *Ringle* for his liking. However, he also grudgingly marvelled at *Seppings'* approach. With Jamieson in command it was as though man and ship had a bond.

He mused that perhaps a minor wager involving *Ringle's* and *Seppings'* abilities in equal conditions, if duties permitted, would prove interesting. He momentarily recalled the joy of his first command, the sloop *Vigilant*. Anxious for news of the mission, he clasped his hands behind his back and resumed pacing the quarterdeck.

ONCE ALL THE WOUNDED AND RESCUED were transferred, Jamieson, Laura, Toby and Mac crossed to *Lionheart*. Laura scrambled up the footholds on the steep side as nimbly as an experienced hand—Cathcart, knowing she would not accept it, had not offered the customary bosun's chair.

After arranging for the care and berthing of the rescued men, the officers gathered in Cathcart's cabin. Mac spotted Jamieson nudge Wilson with his elbow when they were momentarily hidden from Cathcart's view by the others. Both seemed to be enjoying their private joke.

"Gentlemen," Cathcart raised his glass. "Confusion to our enemies." Glasses clinked musically in response. Cathcart swallowed a mouthful of claret and raised his glass again. "Congratulations to Toby and Mac for their fine efforts ashore." Despite enthusiastic responses of 'Well done' and 'Hear, hear' everyone knew the mission hadn't been entirely successful.

Cathcart looked around the cabin and set down his glass; an errant drop of wine on the base stained the chart like blood. "The problem remains that without the element of surprise how do we rescue the remaining hostages? I do not want to lose several dozen men, or more, to rescue a handful of hostages. Nor am I willing to leave hostages behind after cutting out the Indiamen. From what I have heard of Ortega I believe they would be most cruelly treated. Gentlemen, your thoughts on this matter. Feel free to pass the decanters."

Toby spoke first. "At worst we might have to sink Thunderbolt and the Indiamen to keep them out of Spanish hands. I do not believe we can land another shore party unopposed; there are only a few suitable places within a reasonable marching distance of the town, and they now know about the cove. They would need only a single rider to watch each spot. Even with our marines, we would have difficulty dealing with organised opposition. At the very least, we would be delayed reaching the town and placing the hostages in a perilous position."

Wilson said, "We need to find a way to surprise them."

A verbal free-for-all of possible surprises ensued until an exasperated Cathcart exclaimed, "Gentlemen! If you please, one at a time."

Jamieson offered, "Why not destroy the batteries and then the town? The Spanish would not dare do anything to the hostages with us on their doorstep."

Mac interjected, "I know I'm a guest. It's probably feasible, but the danger is Ortega's response. From what I've heard and seen of him I wouldn't put it past him to harm the hostages. He can't be trusted. What he planned for Miss Babbett, even if a ransom was paid, is proof of that. Ortega's only interested in what benefits him, and that is what may give us the advantage." He emphasised 'us'. "What if we make him an offer he can't refuse by appealing to his greed?"

Cathcart responded immediately, "That would still leave us the option of an attack but might avoid further bloodshed. What do you propose?"

Mac glanced around the table. Every man had edged forward in his chair. "First, we make contact"

Toby interjected, "You just said that we cannot trust Ortega."

Mac looked at his friend and nodded in agreement. "But we can trust his greed."

Cathcart refilled his glass and passed the decanter. "What do we offer?"

"Sir," Mac responded. "We'll guarantee his freedom, but only after we've destroyed the fort. He'll be able to claim that when we destroyed the fort the town was left defenceless. The promised frigates never arrived, and he felt it his duty to report the English invasion rather than lose all his men in a hopeless cause."

Toby interjected, "He needs only to ensure the fort is poorly manned, or not alert. Our attack must appear overwhelming to anyone in the town so that his subsequent actions are justified. Even he should be able to devise ways to ensure the sentries are asleep or distracted at the appropriate time.

Mac said, "Of course, we must be satisfied the hostages are safe. We'll tell Ortega that we've put men ashore to guard the road. With the harbour blockaded the road is his only escape route."

Toby grinned, "We won't allow him to pass until the hostages are recovered unharmed. In return, he gets his life and whatever he can take with him. He has probably already looted the town. Surely that will appeal to him."

Cathcart, deep in thought, stroked his chin while he considered the proposal. The cabin remained deathly silent, the nearly empty decanters becalmed in the middle of the table. Cathcart's normal practice, when contemplating complex matters, was to pace back and forth across the breadth of his cabin spanning the frigate's stern. The cluster of officers made that impossible and the silence made his deliberations seem tenfold longer than they really were. Some glanced at one another in silence; others gazed blankly at the polished mahogany table.

After what seemed an eternity, Cathcart spoke. "It may well work. I wish we knew more about Ortega. So much of what we are anticipating is based on incomplete knowledge, but I do agree that his most basic motivation is greed." He turned to Toby, "How do you propose we achieve this meeting? I am loathe to put men ashore without being certain of their safety."

"Sir, we could send *Ringle* or *Seppings* under a flag of truce. Ortega might be amenable to coming to a ship—he is in his own harbour. I am sure that he would not want witnesses to his treachery and could come aboard alone to hear our proposal."

"Sir, may I offer *Ringle*?" Wilson offered enthusiastically. "I am familiar with the harbour entrance. Might I also suggest we create a ruse by positioning *Seppings* so that she appears to be relaying signals to other ships out of sight of the shore?"

Cathcart beamed. "An excellent subterfuge. Do we use any signals similar to what the Company ships might use? Ortega may have one of their signal books; if he was able to decipher our signals he might think that himself very clever and be more inclined to believe them."

Toby said, "Sir, I'll speak with their crews. There should be someone knowledgeable of their hoists."

Cathcart looked about his cabin. "We have a plan and best get to work. I will provide written orders for *Ringle* and *Seppings*. Toby and Mac, pray stay for a minute. George can speak with the Indiamen."

The cabin empty, Cathcart confided, "We all know this plan is fraught with danger. I will prepare a letter to Ortega outlining our offer, but we are making bold assumptions about his response. Toby, do you speak with Silas. Friendly, mind you, and make sure he understands that at the first scent of trouble he quits the harbour. I do not want to lose *Ringle* or any men to Ortega's treachery." Cathcart shook Toby's hand then indicated for Mac to remain.

The door closed, Cathcart motioned for Mac to join him at the stern windows. "You know that I have the greatest regard for your opinion, especially in matters concerning the land. I fear I have lost almost all sense of solid ground—especially when it comes to battling the enemy. I think it is best for you to inform Miss Babbett of our plans without alarming her unnecessarily about the dangers. I suspect she will imagine enough difficulties without our encouragement."

Mac did not find Laura on deck as expected—she had paced the deck until anxiety forced her to retreat to her cabin. He ensured the wardroom was empty then tapped softly on her door.

He thought he heard a slight gasp before she replied, "Come in." Lit by the warm glow of a solitary candle, she sat on the edge of her cot, hairbrush paused in mid-stroke. Struck by her beauty, Mac closed the door then lifted her from the bed and kissed her. She wrapped her arms around him and whispered, "I wish we weren't on this ship."

"Me, too." He sat at the head of the bed, her head nestled against his chest, and explained the rescue plan. Although he could feel her heart pounding she listened silently until he finished.

CATHCART, TOO TENSE TO SLEEP, arrived on deck thirty minutes before the call for 'All hands' converted the sleepy, darkened ship into organised bedlam. Toby sounded cheerful. "Good morning, sir. Wind's steady sou'east by south and suitable for *Ringle* to work her way out of the harbour. Once we have daylight, I'll signal her to close, if that meets with your approval. *Seppings* is on station to relay our signals."

Cathcart nodded acknowledgment, although seemingly lost in thought as he stared in the fort's direction. "Sir," Toby said, interrupting his thoughts, "I wonder if we should have Mac aboard *Ringle*? He has an appreciation of what goes on ashore and may be able to ascertain where the prisoners are being held."

Cathcart brightened as though a weight had been lifted from his shoulders. "Certainly, and the two of you can join me for breakfast. It may be your last chance for hot food today."

Forty minutes later, the heady aroma of coffee filled the passageway to Cathcart's cabin. The marine sentry thumped his musket butt on the deck as he came to attention and bawled, "First lootenant 'n' Cap'n Appletawn, sah."

Cathcart's large table was covered by a large sketch of the harbour produced from observations made during the rescue mission. The Indiamen's positions were noted relative to other features such as the mole, quay, fort and the clock tower in the centre of the town. Actual depths within the harbour were unknown but, with the Indiamen safely anchored, *Ringle's* shallow draft shouldn't present a problem.

"Most excellent coffee sir," Toby said, savouring another mouthful. "Is this the new man's work?"

Cathcart replied, "Yes it is. I am so glad to be rid of that bilge water Smith produced. I had some cross words with him the other day and told him 'If the enemy did not kill me his sludge certainly would.' As you know, I do not mince words when angered and gather my comments were heard for'ard. This Horton fellow took it upon himself, apparently against the advice of his mates, to brew a pot in his manner. Rather a brave act, considering my mood at the time. It turns out his father owned a coffee house in Bath until he lost it at the tables. Horton took to the sea to support his destitute mother while his father languished in gaol. He may well have believed that he would be keelhauled if I did not fancy his concoction." Cathcart held his steaming mug under his nose and inhaled. "I rated him cook's assistant on the spot. Toby, have you discussed your request with our guest?"

Toby grinned, "Aye, sir. Says he is most agreeable and looks forward to a leisurely yacht cruise about the harbour to view the sights."

"Does he now?" Cathcart chuckled. "Very good, I have prepared *Ringle's* orders and composed a grandiloquent offer to Ortega, anent his importance as the commandant of the fine town, et cetera, although I nearly choked on the words. I hope an interpreter is available should the cove not read the King's English. I wish you both luck and a safe return. Please impress upon Silas that he is to take no unnecessary chances. I believe I have been quite clear about that in the written orders but he is a bit of a rake hell."

ORTEGA, who spent the night at the fort after the English ships were sighted, stood on top of the wall in the early morning sun and thumbed through the captured signal book, secure in the knowledge the English were using the same flag code as the merchant ships. Any fool could decipher the signals being sent by the frigate.

"Commandante." The sergeant pleaded again, "Your Excellency," as he tried to get Ortega's attention away from the signal book. "The frigate and schooner are altering course for the harbour entrance."

CATHCART TOOK HIS TIME with the approach. Jamieson had played his part in the little ruse perfectly and had urgently spun *Seppings* on her heel when *Lionheart* signalled 'Take station ten miles northwest.' It would require at least three-quarters of an hour to reach her position to relay signals to the mythical offshore squadron.

Lionheart ambled sedately under reefed topsails and a single jib—*Ringle* beside her like a baby whale looking for a meal. Their leisurely pace would make life easier for the gig's crew when they ferried Toby and Mac across the fifty yard gap of gently undulating water.

Despite the calm water Toby had Cathcart's orders securely bound in a waterproof wrapping of oiled sailcloth and ensured the package was safe inside his shirt before standing as the gig brushed against *Ringle*.

He and Mac scrambled aboard after *Ringle* momentarily let fly her sheets, taking the way off and steadying her deck. The side party greeting them comprised only Wilson and the bosun.

"Good morning, Silas." Toby offered Wilson the waterproof pouch and added, "A fine bit of sail handling there," to acknowledge the courtesy.

Wilson's eyes twinkled as he accepted the package. "Least I could do for our guest. No point unnecessarily soaking him. Never know if we may have to swim for it later today. Please come below while I read." He nodded to the bosun. Within seconds the sails were sheeted home and *Ringle* resumed her position slightly astern of the frigate.

They sat in Wilson's cramped cabin while he perused his written orders. "I see the Captain's quite adamant that I not take any unnecessary risk in the harbour—seems quite concerned about my safety."

Toby slapped his thigh and laughed, "In fact he required me to remind you of his concern, but I believe he only mentioned *Ringle*, Mac and myself! I don't recall him mentioning you." He nearly fell out of his chair from laughter.

Wilson harrumphed then tried to scowl—but his eyes gave him away before he could be convincing, "We had better get to it." He rose from his chair to his customary stooped position to avoid the overhead deck beams then led the way to the quarterdeck.

"Mr. Ball," Wilson called to the bosun. "A white flag above our ensign at the fore peak if you please. Ease the sheets, let us give 'em plenty of time to decide we are not a threat." Lowering his voice, he turned to Toby and Mac, "Need to make sure those fools in the fort know that we are acting peaceful. For the moment at least."

Ringle slowed to a brisk walk, headed directly toward the centre of the harbour entrance. The masthead lookout called, "Deck there, boat preparin' to git unnerway from the quay. Looks loik a four-pounder in the bow." His second hail two minutes later had a note of concern in his voice, "Deck there, she's flyin' Spanish colours but no white flag."

Wilson ordered *Ringle* brought into the wind. They were perhaps one-hundred yards beyond the fort's arc of fire. While *Ringle* lay motionless in the water, bobbing up and down in the swell, Wilson muttered, "What the Hell..." under his breath and exchanged glances with Toby and Mac when the boat stopped.

Wilson turned toward Toby and said, "We'll assume for the moment that they don't have a white flag. I'm not going to place us under the fort's guns until I'm satisfied about those buggers' intentions."

"Deck there, fort's hoistin' a white flag."

"About bloody time," Wilson said, then gave a series of orders to bring the bow around. Wilson clenched his jaw—sailing into the fort's field of fire was not his idea of a pleasant morning—as the hull resumed its calming hiss through the water, accompanied by the myriad squeaks, thumps and taps of a ship underway. He glanced astern at *Lionheart*, hove to under backed topsails three-quarters of a mile distant.

The boat resumed closing on *Ringle*, oars glinting as sunlight glanced off the dripping blades. Four men manned the oars, with two more seated in the bow and two in her stern. Wilson, the back of his uniform coat wet from perspiration, held his breath as *Ringle* passed directly beneath the fort. He contemplated their position in the harbour and said, "Another ship's length, then bring her about." He turned to Mac, "Do heights bother you?"

"Not particularly, sir."

Wilson looked at Mac for a second. "Kindly take m' best Dollond aloft and see if there is anything ashore I should worry about."

Mac slung the heavy telescope over his shoulder and climbed to the main top—not a convenient platform as on *Lionheart*, just the flattened cap of the lower mast a few feet above the mainsail's upper gaff. He placed one foot on the mast's cap and the other on the thin rope step of the ratline. He cautiously looped an arm around the standing rigging for safety and to steady the heavy telescope, and wished for a pair of lightweight binoculars. The boat, now almost directly below, backed its oars then began moving across his field of vision in an optical illusion caused by *Ringle's* bow turning into the wind.

Wilson stepped to the rail to inform the Spanish he carried a letter for their commandant. A man, slouching nonchalantly in the boat's stern, stared back blankly. Wilson repeated himself, but there was still no response. In exasperation he held up the oiled sailcloth pouch and waved it above his head, pointing at it with his right hand and shouting "Por commandant," in his limited Spanish. The man seemed to grasp that message and gave a curt order to bring the boat alongside *Ringle.* Wilson tossed the pouch to the Spaniard and said, "I am to await his reply," as the anchor splashed into the water for emphasis.

Mac examined the town from his perch, looking for guards posted outside a building that might indicate where the remaining hostages were being held. The only military presence was around the commandant's quarters and at the fort. A throng, civilians judging by their clothing, had gathered along the harbour wall to observe the British warship riding at anchor in the centre of the harbour.

Wilson paced the quarterdeck for fifteen minutes after the boat reached the quay and a solitary figure headed toward the fort. He then went below and fretted for two hours until the lookout announced a boat was putting off from the quay. When he returned to the deck, Toby and Mac were near the fore chains watching the boat approach. Wilson asked, "Care to hazard a guess as to the reply?"

Toby glanced away from the boat, "Not at this point, sir. Their behaviour has been quite strange. With a ship under a flag-of-truce in my harbour I would have made sure a translator was aboard the boat."

The boat stopped ten feet from *Ringle's* side. A different officer, perhaps a little younger than the first but wearing a better quality uniform, stood in the stern. He said in heavily broken English, "His Excellency Commandante Ortega will provide his reply in due course. You are to leave his harbour now." The boat immediately pushed away.

"Prepare to make sail," Wilson barked before striding to the quarterdeck. A cluster of sailors at the bow began retrieving the small bower anchor from the harbour bottom. The southeasterly breeze pressed against the outer jib to push *Ringle's* bow around as the reefed main and mizzen were sheeted home. "Near the shore as she'll stand," Wilson ordered. The hair on the back of his neck felt as stiff as bristles. He intended to pass as close to the fort as possible while making his exit.

Mac and Toby kept out of the way while the crew trimmed the sails and tidied the deck. A party forward was busy cleaning the anchor cable of harbour muck before storing it below. The fort, its stone walls dark and foreboding, loomed directly above them by the time the boat reached the quay. "What did you see?" Toby asked.

Mac replied, "Nothing much, although that in itself was intriguing. The only guards are at Ortega's office or quarters, which makes me think the prisoners are there. From what I've seen of him he seems to be more interested in his own comfort and convenience than anything else. Keeping the prisoners nearby would certainly fit that theory. What do you think?"

Toby nodded agreement, "That's the most likely explanation, although I suppose we must consider the possibility that the prisoners are elsewhere." He almost said, "or dead."

Ringle continued creeping parallel to the shore, with scarcely twenty-five yards between her and the rocky outcroppings. Mac looked up at the fort towering above, "We'll never know for sure without..." An explosion and a nearly simultaneous fountain of water erupted fifty yards beyond *Ringle*.

"Christ!" Toby blurted.

They were a sitting duck, exposed and unable to elevate their guns enough to make even a pretense of a defense. Luckily, Wilson's decision to stay inshore also meant the fort could not adequately depress the gun.

Wilson bellowed, "Every stitch she can carry. Helm steady on this course, not an inch of leeway, or we will all be guests here."

Toby jumped behind a sailor, grabbed the tail of the topsail lift and thrust the line into Mac's hand. "Grab hold and pull when he says."

"One...two...heave." They repeated until the tremble in the lift told them that the sail was drawing. Toby instinctively checked the topsail, then saw chain shot twisting through the air a few yards above the masthead when the fort fired again. If they lost a mast they would be trapped in the harbour. He glanced seaward. *Lionheart* was making sail, but with *Ringle* between her and the fort she would be unable to fire.

Wilson intently studied the last visible rocks off their port bow then checked the sails for the slightest tremor that would indicate a sail was not drawing to absolute perfection. Ordinarily he would have kept to starboard to give the rocky shore a wide berth, but he dared not risk exposing even the extreme tips of his masts to the Spanish guns. Whether he tore the bottom out of her or they were sunk by the fort the result would be the same.

"Toby," Mac asked, "do you think anyone would mind if I fired one of the swivels?"

"They would probably welcome it, especially if it was for a good cause....like saving our sorry arses. What do you have in mind?"

Mac pointed at the nearest swivel, "Still loaded with grape?"

Toby replied, "I believe so, in the event the Spanish boat tried anything. Unfortunately grape will accomplish nothing against the fort."

Mac winked, "But their flag looks entirely too pretty, don't you think?"

Toby laughed, "Only one way to find out." He turned to catch Wilson's attention and called, "Permission to fire, sir?" Wilson, preoccupied with the deadly rocks, didn't respond.

Toby grasped a length of slow-match smouldering above its water tub next to a six-pounder.

Wilson visibly jumped at the swivel's bark. When he turned, Toby and Mac were staring upward through the plume of acrid smoke. Then Toby slapped Mac on the back.

Wilson followed their gaze. The remains of the Spanish flag hung in forlorn tatters above the fort as *Ringle* slipped past the fang shaped last rock, clearing it by a scant eighteen inches.

~21~

REVELATIONS

CATHCART'S FOUL MOOD, bordering on apoplexy, was apparent. Sailors and officers alike gave him a wide berth and avoided eye contact—no mean feat on the crowded deck. For the past hour his usual studied demeanour while pacing back and forth along the windward side had more resembled Attila's advance across Europe. His anger hadn't dissipated by the time Toby, Mac and Wilson came aboard. Before Cathcart retreated to his cabin, he curtly informed Toby that George Sloane had the watch.

An hour passed before Toby and Mac were summoned to the stern cabin—largely due to Cathcart's mood. Joined by Wilson, they were ushered in by Cathcart's unusually cowed servant, who ventured no farther than the door. Cathcart, face scarlet and neck veins appearing near to bursting, paced the breadth of the cabin, head down, as though examining the checkerboard patterned floor canvas for flaws. "God's Teeth," he fumed without looking up as Wilkes closed the door and retreated into the pantry. "That goddamned-whoreson-windward passage-goat fucker has no honour."

Toby's look of surprise at the outburst spoke volumes. Judging by Toby's reaction, Mac suspected that Cathcart's use of expletives was rare.

Cathcart continued unabated, "He fired upon a flag of truce! If I had the ships I would sail into his fucking harbour and personally run him up to the yardarm. It was a flag of truce, damn his eyes..." He paused and looked up as though realising for the first time that he was not alone, smiled wanly and said, "That was a fine bit of close-sailing Silas, although there are probably safer ways to scrape barnacles from *Ringle's* bottom. I was puzzled for a moment, thought perhaps the fort struck her colours when their flag vanished. Even thought there might have been an eruption of honour among those bastards." He motioned for them to find a place on the transom bench or on one of the chairs.

Toby answered, "Sir, the swivel was still loaded with grape. Mac believed he could hit their ensign. He aimed and I fired. You might say it was a minor fleet action, what with it being *Ringle's* gun, fired by a member of *Lionheart's* crew and aimed by our American guest."

"Except," Wilson vexedly retorted, "you didn't have my permission to fire."

Awkward silence filled the cabin, Cathcart's expression darkened at the mention of his favourite lieutenant overstepping his authority.

Fortunately Wilson could not keep a straight face. "'Tis a good thing you destroyed that damned flag. Otherwise I'd have brought you up on charges for wasting His Majesty's powder and shot." He slumped forward in laughter he said, "Couldn't believe m'eyes when I saw it in tatters. Damn fine shot if I do say!"

Cathcart stifled a laugh and said, "This calls for a toast." Their enemies suitably damned and their glasses empty, Cathcart continued in a more formal tone. "We have a considerable problem as I see no point negotiating since Ortega clearly cannot be trusted. Also, I am unsure how to explain to the Admiral that a neutral took part in an action. Silas, do you make your official report with an abridged version of the events." Cathcart refilled his glass, then shifted his chair toward Mac. "I trust you are not offended?"

"Not all, sir. Shredding their flag was satisfaction enough, despite them just trying to kill me."

Cathcart offered, "Even the smallest dog has a bite, what. Well, gentlemen, any suggestions how we rescue the remaining prisoners?"

Toby had been unconsciously thrumming his fingers on his chair's armrest. "There is no question they are in grave danger, assuming they are even alive. Surprise is completely lost; we will have to rely on sheer force."

"Do we know where they are being held?" Cathcart tipped his glass and examined the amber film coating the bowl.

Mac leaned forward. "They're most likely at Ortega's residence on the town's main square. I couldn't see any sign of military elsewhere. Given Ortega's penchant for doing things for his own convenience, rather than to satisfy any useful strategy or tactic, I believe we'll find them there."

Cathcart nodded in agreement and set down his glass. "As Toby stated, we no longer have any hope of surprise. What I would not give to have *Thunderbolt*. I would reduce that fort to road chippings, then give Ortega a taste of our broadside."

Jamieson interjected, "Sir, could not Ortega kill the prisoners and escape overland while we were busy pounding the fort?"

Cathcart downed his remaining brandy and nodded. "Damn me, I do not relish the thought of attempting a full-scale attack with our limited forces. We will lose many good men, possibly for nothing." He reached for the almost empty decanter, paused self-consciously, then called for Wilkes to refill it and invited everyone to refill their glasses.

The lookout's muffled hail from the masthead filtered through the closed skylight of Cathcart's cabin and ended the discussion. Moments later a nervous midshipman appeared at Cathcart's door. "Second lieutenant's duty, sir. He requests your presence on deck."

Cathcart's foot had scarcely left the quarterdeck stairs before Sloane handed him their biggest, gleaming brass *Bring-'em-near* and glumly pointed toward the fort.

A body, dressed in a merchant officer's blue uniform, hung by the neck on a rope suspended from the fort's seaward parapet.

MAC ISOLATED HIMSELF in the mizzen top for most of an hour, ostensibly observing Puerto Blanco. The reality was it was the only place he could be alone to think. The brutality of the sailor's murder and display of his corpse tore at him.

"Enter," Cathcart replied when the sentry announced Mac's presence.

"Sir, I may have a solution to your problem. However, it's very complicated and I need to ask your permission to talk with Miss Babbett first."

Cathcart glared in silence, then began to snarl, "Since when does a woman..." He stopped himself before completing the sentence.

Mac had not expected that response and was taken aback. "Sir, I know it's a lot to ask. May I speak to you in confidence?"

Cathcart nodded his grudging agreement, his hands remaining clenched on top of his desk. Mac knew he was on thin ice. Cathcart was clearly angry and frustrated with Ortega's behaviour. "Sir, my plan involves considerable danger for Mr. Babbett. You must be aware that I have developed feelings for her so I feel I must talk with her first before going too far with my plan."

"I see," Cathcart replied, unclenching his hands to adjust some papers on his desk. "Very well, I will have the wardroom cleared so you may have some privacy."

Mac wondered if Laura would be so accommodating.

LAURA PACED the length of the lee gangway, unable to ease her mounting anguish which now bordered on terror after overhearing news of the murder. She stared intently at the fort and the little splash of colour of the town each time she reached the fo'c's'le. When the bosuns and petty officers began shouting orders she realised with a grim chill that *Lionheart* was turning away from the fort and her father. She fought back the tears welling in her eyes and pounded her fists against the rail in anger then jumped when Mac called her name—she had not noticed him approaching.

"Miss Babbett," he repeated.

Laura could not face him in this state; nor could they show any affection. Instead, she continued to gaze toward the town and brushed away more tears.

When she did turn, Mac could see the redness in her eyes, and the look of fear—a look he hadn't seen before. He wanted to hold her, to tell her everything would be all right despite his doubts. He said, "I need to talk with you. The Captain has said we may use the wardroom for privacy." He hated having to be so proper.

"Thank you, Captain Appleton." Laura motioned for him to go first.

Mac suspected that she preferred walking behind him so he could not see her distress. He descended the aft hatchway ladder to the lower deck, illuminated by shafts of light from the open gunports, then turned toward the wardroom where a marine sentry stamped to attention and slammed his musket butt against the deck.

"No one 'ere sir, checked it m'self. Cap'un says yer not t' be disturbed." The corporal bowed his head slightly, as though trying to see Laura's face in the dim light.

As the door closed behind them Mac reached out for her hand but she stepped back. "Why are they abandoning him...?" Her voice trailed off; tears and sobs overwhelmed her as she slumped against the cabin wall, clasping her arms across her chest. Stress from her imprisonment, the failed rescue of her father, and the murder at the fort had conquered whatever stoic reserve she had been relying upon. Mac knew he must calm those fears before he said anything else. "The Captain isn't abandoning anyone: not your father, not the other men with him." He moved closer and said, "And I'm not abandoning you."

He reached out to hold her but she sobbed and tried to push him away. He ignored her rebuff, drew her to him and wrapped his arms around her. After several minutes she stopped sobbing, although her body remained rigid against his. He said, "We're making a strategic withdrawal to calm the Spanish. If they believe that we've given up perhaps they won't harm more prisoners. I have a rescue plan but I need to talk with you first."

Laura brushed her cheek on his sleeve to wipe away tears. "With me?" she snuffled after a long silence. "Why do you have to discuss it first with me? Is my father alive?" She stepped back and looked at him with reddened eyes, then took his hand—hers was quivering—and said, "Can we sit in my cabin?"

They sat on her cot—his shoulders against the end wall with her nestled against him. He missed having her close; his fear, that she was pulling away from him, dissipated. That worry had been one of the reasons he had sought the solitude of the mizzen top before speaking to Cathcart. All that remained was the knot in his stomach and a pounding heart. He took a deep breath, cleared his throat and began.

"We believe your father is alive, but Ortega will kill him if we attempt another rescue. To regain the element of surprise the Captain is withdrawing out of sight. We're hoping Ortega will believe he's outfoxed us."

"I still do not understand why you must discuss this with me first?"

"Because there's something about me that I haven't told anyone. Do you remember when we first met?" The prospect of revelation seemed to free him and he believed things were going well, even when he told her he was a Canadian and not an American. That ended when he revealed travelling from two-hundred years in the future.

Laura looked like she had just seen a body arise from the grave. She pushed away from him and darted to the far end of the cot. Fortunately, the confined cabin meant there was nowhere else for her to go. However, the look on her face said everything. He reached for her hand but she pulled hers away. He knew he had little time to calm her—although she at least remained huddled at the foot of the cot and hadn't made for the door.

"I can tell that you don't believe me. I wouldn't either." He sat upright and continued his improbable story.

Laura, her eyes like knives, said nothing. Mac wished she would yell, or argue, or do something to indicate what she was feeling. He began to tell her about being a pilot.

She interrupted him. "Men can't fly!"

Finally, he thought, a response. "Of course they can. The Montgolfiers proved it twenty years ago with their balloon." He edged closer to her and reached for her hand. Although she did not pull back, she also did not give any sign of acceptance.

After a few seconds of awkward silence she vehemently blurted, "I do not believe you. Why are you doing this to me? Get out and leave me alone!"

Mac's head pounded from the anguish of her rejection. It was clear that she felt betrayed. All along he had expected her to accept his story—maybe with difficulty at first, but eventually. He mumbled, "I'm sorry," as he left her cabin.

TOBY, A GLASS?" Cathcart held up the wine decanter.

"Thank you, sir."

"Mac says he has a plan to retrieve the prisoners and asked permission to first discuss it with Miss Babbett."

Toby couldn't hide his look of puzzlement. "Did he provide any details?"

"None."

Toby thought he detected a slight scowl as Cathcart continued, "Except to say certain revelations might change their relationship. Most strange and I resent being the last to know. These colonials certainly lack some common social graces, if I do say."

Toby wanted to know more, but Cathcart didn't give him a chance to ask before continuing, "I instructed him to report to me immediately after he talked with her. I would like you here when we meet. If he is up to any sort of trickery I will have him in irons."

Toby was surprised by the threat. "I am sure his intentions are good. Beautiful young ladies sometimes change our priorities, do they not?"

The sentry called out, "Mr. Appleton, sir."

Mac had arrived at Cathcart's door by a circuitous route forward the length of the lower deck, then aft along the main deck, forward again along the starboard gangway and, finally, aft along the larboard. He needed time to think about Laura's reaction. Then he remembered what Toby had said as they prepared to attack the two Spanish frigates: 'In for a penny, in for a pound.'

Toby's glass shattered on the cabin deck when Mac revealed that he was from two-hundred years in the future. The wine spread like blood across the painted canvas covering. Cathcart's face instantly turned crimson, his right hand moved to his waist as though searching for his sword. Mac was relieved to see he wasn't wearing it.

"I know that what I've just told will likely give you cause to believe that I'm a lunatic. A few weeks ago I'd have felt exactly the same if our roles had been reversed and I was confronted by two gentlemen who claimed they were from the past. I'm sure you have many questions."

They had questions indeed. He knew he must dispel their complete disbelief while he had the chance. Unlike Laura, Cathcart had not thrown him out. Yet. Mac noticed sheets of blank paper on one corner of Cathcart's desk and asked to use one. Cathcart nodded, warily passing a piece to Mac. "Sir, you've undoubtedly heard of the Montgolfiers in France? They've demonstrated that it's possible to leave the ground. To fly."

Cathcart said, "Not like a bird, they merely float in a basket." Toby nodded, although it seemed to be without much enthusiasm.

Mac continued talking while folding the sheet of paper. "Do you think it possible that someday men may find better ways to fly than in a hot air balloon? After all, at one time castles were impregnable, but gunpowder changed that didn't it?" He completed the last fold. "da Vinci drew flying machines three-hundred years ago. It's just that no one has figured out how to build them, but, someday, someone will." He gently launched his paper airplane.

Cathcart harrumphed and Toby gasped as the white dart made a graceful spiral around the cabin before landing on the floor.

When Mac tried to explain helicopters Cathcart remained silent, although his normal colour returned. Mac paused for a moment to allow Cathcart and Toby time to think then said, "Some people believe that there's a reason for everything that happens, that luck doesn't enter into it, and many have written about the possibility of time travel. I never believed in these theories—until now that is. I don't know why I'm here. Perhaps fate brought me although I'm not sure if that. Nevertheless, here I am, and I must make the best of my situation."

Cathcart sat forward in his chair, devoid of expression, and studied him. Toby remained ominously silent. Eventually Cathcart spoke, "I do not know what to make of this. My first inclination is to arrange for your immediate transportation to St. Mary of Bethlehem. Either you are completely deranged or are telling the truth. I cannot conceive of anyone inventing such a tale without it being one or the other. Can you prove your claims?"

"Beyond all doubt, sir. I can demonstrate an example of future technology—right here and now." He extended his arm toward Toby. "Do you agree my uniform is made of cloth as is yours? What would happen if you put your sleeve in a flame?"

"I would never do that. It would catch fire."

Mac asked Toby to light the candle on the desk, then placed his thick Nomex sleeve directly in the flame while Cathcart and Toby leaned forward in their chairs. After several seconds Mac pulled his undamaged sleeve from the flame.

Cathcart's interest was piqued. "Why do you need clothes that will not burn?"

"The fuel for my helicopter is highly flammable. I can't just jump out, or off, as you might do from a ship when I'm hundreds or thousands of feet above the ground."

Cathcart replied, with gloomy scepticism, "Perhaps nothing more than an amusing parlour trick. It does not prove that the rest of your story is true."

"Well," Mac replied with a deliberate pause, "I can show you the helicopter, but it must remain a secret between us. The fewer who know the truth about me the better." He added ominously, "For all of us."

When Cathcart looked at Toby Mac wasn't sure if even Toby believed him—he'd been uncharacteristically silent for many minutes. Toby shifted uneasily in his chair, glanced briefly at the paper airplane on the canvas covered deck, then shifted his gaze between Mac and Cathcart. Mac felt his abdominal muscles knot. His knee began its characteristic twitch. Whatever Toby said in the next few seconds would determine Cathcart's response.

After what seemed an interminable silence Toby said, "Sir, I am inclined to believe him. Perhaps not completely because his claims are far beyond our knowledge. Just think back a few years. If I told you twenty years ago that we would have carronades you would have said that firing such a heavy ball from a frigate was impossible, but the Carron Works proved it could be done.

"Mac's claim to be from the future answers some nagging questions in the back of my mind. We know how good he is with guns." Toby grinned and glanced at Mac. "Yet we had to teach him how to fire and load a musket. It was as though he had only read about them in books. Do you not agree that a serving army officer, any military man, would be intimately acquainted with their operation as part of his normal training and duty?"

Cathcart became less stiff in his chair; his face appeared more relaxed. He said, "I take your point, Toby. Perhaps my doubts are merely from being so overwhelmed. 'Tis though our entire world has suddenly turned upside down."

"Mine, too, sir," interjected Mac. "When I found myself aboard that pirate ship I had no idea where I was. The when was even harder to accept. May I make several proposals, some of which are more like requests?"

"Go ahead." Cathcart threw his hands up in mock despair and looked at Toby. "He should be in our navy. I would assign him to making requests of the Admiralty. They ignore most of mine; perhaps could twist them around his finger as he does me." His eyes narrowed, "But how can one man hope to accomplish what a thirty-six gun frigate and two schooners cannot?"

Cathcart had asked the crucial question; Mac knew he could win him over. "An excellent question, sir. What if I told you that I can give you the firepower of six bomb vessels and probably that of *Victory* thrown in for good measure? Furthermore, I can make such an attack on a moonless night, or at any other time I choose?"

When Cathcart and Toby didn't reply he wondered if they could even imagine such a weapon and said, "I assure you that the Apache isn't imaginary." He waited for a moment and said, "I need to retrieve it from Quinta Ruban using *Seppings*. May Toby accompany me?" The request for Toby clearly baffled Cathcart. Mac continued, "The Apache works best with two crew: one to fly and one to operate the weapons. Toby can decide there about the truth of my claims. If he isn't satisfied he can maroon me there, place me in irons or have me shot as he sees fit." And if the Apache wasn't there? The prospect sent a chill down Mac's spine.

Cathcart eyes narrowed, "If I agree both Toby's and my career could be ruined."

Mac nodded. "I understand completely. For my plan to work we must attack at night. This will mean that *Lionheart* and *Ringle* must not be seen from land in the evening. You should be in position at the harbour entrance ninety minutes before dawn. Ninety minutes would still give near total darkness and would mean sentries are at their drowsiest."

Cathcart and Toby agreed anything other than a contrary wind would serve. If *Lionheart* stood out twenty miles under lower sails only she would be invisible to the shore. Even with a five-knot breeze she'd be able to reach the harbour entrance within five hours. Cathcart glanced at the large barometer hanging from a massive rib timber to verify it had not changed. "Twenty-four to thirty-six hours should be adequate for *Seppings* to reach Quinta Ruban."

Mac said, "If we leave tonight, we'll be there Thursday evening at the latest. I'll need a day to ready the helicopter and give Toby rudimentary training in his new career." He winked at Toby and said, "You're going to love being the CPG, that's short for Co-Pilot Gunner, especially when it comes to firing the weapons. Imagine being able to unleash the equivalent of an entire broadside..." Mac paused, positioned his right hand as if he was holding the Apache's stick, flipped open the imaginary trigger guard with his thumb and squeezed the trigger. "...like that."

"How do you aim?" Toby asked incredulously.

Mac grinned mischievously and said, "Just look at the target and wait a moment for the computer to lock on." He hoped Toby wouldn't ask what a computer was. "We'll leave Quinta Ruban Friday evening, assuming Toby is satisfied with the situation and hasn't left me tied to a tree. The return trip will take about two hours." Mac was caught up at the prospect of flying when Cathcart and Toby simultaneously—and most audibly—sucked in their breath.

"Hours," Cathcart exclaimed incredulously, "but it is more than two-hundred miles. Our most eminent scientific minds have determined that anything beyond sixty miles per hour will most certainly cause the human body to explode."

Mac couldn't contain himself. "Not! I'm living proof of how wrong they are. You wouldn't believe me if I told you how fast humans can travel," he exclaimed laughing. "I'm basing my calculations on an average speed of one-hundred twenty-five miles per hour. That may vary a bit depending upon the wind. Although I'm not dependent upon it for flight, it still has an effect. If I'm flying into a ten mile per hour breeze my forward progress is reduced by that rate, if it's a tail wind my speed will increase accordingly."

"Much the same then as with *Lionheart*?" asked Toby.

"Exactly, except I can fly directly against the wind, whereas you would have to tack back and forth. We'll return to *Lionheart* sometime after dark Friday night to avoid being seen."

Cathcart frowned, "I will not be able to attack the fort until *Seppings* returns—Saturday noon at the earliest."

Mac nodded. "Will dawn on Sunday work?" Mac leaned toward the map in the centre of the table and pointed with his forefinger, "I'll approach from here to avoid being seen from Puerto Blanco, then land here," indicating a point on the coast twenty-five miles east of Puerto Blanco. "Toby will need experience using the weapons, so we'll conduct a mock attack on *Lionheart*."

The colour drained from both Cathcart's and Toby's faces. Mac, a chuckle in his voice, reassured them, "Don't worry, we won't fire, but I'll need you to extinguish all lights."

Cathcart looked at him in disbelief. "Surely that is impossible! How will you find us in complete darkness?"

"We'll be able to find you no matter how dark it is. I'd like you to equip your lookouts with a shuttered lantern. If they detect us before we reach *Lionheart* they're to signal us."

Cathcart fidgeted with a pair of dividers. "How will I know you are there if the lookouts do not see you?"

"Oh believe me you'll know, sir." Mac directed another wink at Toby. Mac knew he could approach at low speed from downwind and not be detected; he also knew how much noise the Apache was capable of making.

"Once we've found you we'll land near the beach and wait for nightfall on Saturday. If *Seppings* is delayed we can attack Sunday night instead. I'm afraid you won't see much of the Apache at night, perhaps you would care to see her Saturday morning?" He knew the universal constant among military personnel was that everyone wants to see your toys, no matter what nation or what era—and it was always wise to invite the boss.

Cathcart was clearly taken aback. "I would be most honoured."

Mac continued, "Sir, our presence will raise questions among the crew. I know many are superstitious and some are sure to think the Apache is some sort of monster. We don't want them so rattled as to harm the mission. On the other hand, will telling them do more harm than good?"

Cathcart set the dividers down. "The fewer who know of this, the better." He glanced at Toby who nodded silently in agreement, then pushed his chair back. "Well, gentlemen, I imagine you have matters requiring your attention. I will signal *Seppings* to close. Is thirty minutes sufficient?"

After leaving the cabin Toby spoke softly so as not to be heard by Cathcart's servant, "I have so many questions..."

Mac interrupted him, "I can well imagine. Do you recall all my questions when I arrived? We'll have plenty of time once we're aboard *Seppings*." He tipped his head toward three men at the base of the hatch ladder and said, "It's probably unwise to talk too much until then. If you'll excuse me I must try to make amends with Laura." It was the first time he had referred to her as Laura with Toby, but Toby didn't react.

Mac saw Laura standing at the windward rail in the waist. She appeared deep in thought but when she noticed him she began to turn away, then paused.

He asked, "Are you all right?"

She ignored his question and continued staring past him toward the pencil line smudge of the coastline; her knuckles white from her grip on the rail.

Despite fears that she wouldn't believe him he said, "No more secrets, it's time you know everything about me."

~22~
THE QUINTA RUBAN CURIOUSITY

THE SOUTHWEST BREEZE propelled *Seppings* wing-and-wing across boisterous swells stretching to the horizon and a pencil mark on the chart. There, if the wind held, Jamieson would alter course for Quinta Ruban. His orders were simple: get Toby and Mac there without delay, avoid other ships, and approach Quinta Ruban from the north. He found the lack of written orders unusual in a service ruled by paper. Once there he would await Toby's order to rendezvous with *Lionheart*, then do so with all possible speed.

He wondered if Toby would divulge the purpose of the mission—but his passengers had secluded themselves in his cabin for over four hours. Although Toby apologised for the inconvenience, explaining that he and Mac needed privacy to plan for Quinta Ruban, Jamieson dearly desired sleep after being on deck for almost seventeen hours.

TOBY WAS FULL OF QUESTIONS which Mac did his best to answer in terms Toby could relate to. Their conversation covered everything from technical questions about the Apache and the mission, to Mac's military career, to what the future held. He tried to be forthcoming about the Apache. After all, Toby would soon see it for himself and the need for secrecy would be moot. When questions touched on other aspects of the military, Mac confined himself to a brief general answer, explaining that there wasn't time. If Toby asked about the future, Mac simply declined to answer.

However, when asked how the Apache stayed in the air, Mac realised he must divulge some secrets. Mac found it difficult to relate his technology to concepts familiar to Toby. *How can I hope to condense two-hundred years into a few minutes?* Eventually, despite initially drawing a blank stare from Toby, he explained how the Apache's engines converted liquid fuel into energy by using the analogy of a steam engine.

Mac sketched the Apache on a sheet of paper and said, "So, you see, the wind is produced by burning a combustible fuel which turns blades on wheels connected to the rotors." He pointed out the main and tail rotors on the sketch. "Think of the Apache as a hummingbird—you've seen how they can move forward, stop and then hover in one place." Although Toby said he understood, the look on his face suggested otherwise. Mac shook his head when Toby asked if they could tell Jamieson about their mission. He may have already revealed too much to Toby; there was no point in compounding the problem.

Toby didn't pursue the matter but suggested that they should at least invite Jamieson to join them for dinner. Toby said, "Perhaps you should make the offer. As a fellow officer I can't be the one to invite him to dine in his own cabin, but I'm sure he'll see the incongruity should the invitation come from you."

The meal had progressed to the third bottle of wine when Jamieson said, "Y' know I'm damned curious about our voyage. Can't for the life of me see how going to that godforsaken Quinta Ruban will help the hostages."

Toby nearly gagged on his wine and Mac, unseen by Jamieson, winked at him. "Now that you mention it," said Mac, "that's precisely why I suggested you host this little soirée."

To explain Cathcart's specific order for *Seppings* to approach from the north, Mac fabricated a secret rendezvous with a ship waiting off Quinta Ruban. He told Jamieson that if all went well Toby would signal at dusk for *Seppings* to return to *Lionheart*—implying that he and Toby would return on the other ship. Toby nodded agreement.

Jamieson, apparently satisfied by Mac's explanation, said, "I see, but the hour is getting late."

SEPPINGS **BEGAN HER MORNING RITUAL**, as did every ship in the Royal Navy, by rousing all hands just before dawn. Cleared for action and guns run out, the black tropic night gave way to the brief, colourless predawn while lookouts searched the disc of water forming their world until they were satisfied that Seppings was alone.

"Good morning, gentlemen," Jamieson greeted his passengers when they appeared on deck. "I trust you slept well."

"Quite soundly," which was a lie, replied Mac.

Toby, who had slept fitfully, muttered, "Like a baby," although his lack of sleep made Jamieson's greeting almost annoyingly cheerful.

Jamieson continued, "Breakfast will be ready shortly; one of the men caught a fine fish that's being cooked as we speak. I hope you will find it palatable." Looking past Toby he exclaimed, "Ahh, here comes the coffee."

Mac and Toby returned to Jamieson's cabin after breakfast. Toby—simultaneously awed, mystified, and simply shocked by Mac's description of the Apache's armament—found it inconceivable that such weapons could exist and was frustrated by Mac's reluctance to answer questions about the future.

It was time to change topics. Time was running out, and Toby needed to understand the Apache's weapons systems. Mac described the 30 mm gun, then the differences between the unguided Hydra 70 and guided Hellfire rockets. Toby appeared increasingly mystified—perhaps to the point of total bafflement.

Mac added, "Think of the Hydras as a development of Congreve's rocket," hoping that mentioning Sir William's development of a naval rocket would help.

Toby replied, "Never heard of them," but made a mental note to search out Congreve the next time he was in England.

Mac cursed silently, recalling Congreve first employed his rockets at the second Battle of Copenhagen in 1805—so much for not revealing the future. "Imagine a vessel as nimble as *Seppings*, but carrying the firepower of your most powerful ship of the line. The Apache's gun fires at the rate of twelve-hundred rounds a minute." Mac reiterated the Hellfire and Hydra-70 rocket's capabilities. So absorbed in his discourse, he didn't notice the colour drain from Toby's face when he said, "A single Hydra can penetrate a ship clear to her magazine."

Toby was past asking questions—Mac was describing a world beyond his wildest imaginings. Instead, he listened as he had done as a boy when his grandfather told grand stories of life at sea.

Mac continued, "Just sight the target through a device on your head that uses a pinpoint of light as the sight. Simply place the light on the target by moving your head and wait for the light to lock onto the target. That's where the gun or rocket will hit, even if it's pitch dark. "The Hellfires will work from five miles under ideal conditions, but I prefer less if there's no risk to me. The weapons are more accurate in closer."

Toby, engrossed in the murderous implications of such devices, realised Mac had stopped talking. Danger and death was something Toby understood only too well, grimly realising he had lost count of friends who had died and of enemies he had killed. Afraid his rising emotions would show, he cleared his throat. "I assume the other side has similar weapons? Would not they be trying to destroy you?"

Mac nodded and said, "Yes, nothing has really changed. We've dispensed with exchanging broadsides at point-blank range and hand-to-hand combat. We prefer to kill each other from a distance." He added sardonically, "Much more civilised, don't you agree?"

Toby was dazed. Everything he knew about warfare was instantly irrelevant. In his own battle experiences he could always see his enemy—perhaps only through a telescope at a range of one mile but always visible. Then there was the mixture of sheer terror, fear, bloodlust—there were so many different feelings—that accompanied a boarding. The sights, sounds, smells of past battles were permanently embedded in his mind. If he understood what Mac had said, the Apache could sink the *Lionheart* with a single missile fired from five miles away—sink her with anonymity in the middle of a pitch black night with no warning. He recalled Cathcart's unfinished prayer each time they engaged in close action: 'Lord, for what we are about to receive...'

"Are you all right?" Mac sounded concerned.

Toby shuddered and took several seconds to respond. "I apologise, but I just had a chilling vision of being on the receiving end of one of your missiles. I am not sure that I like your world. At least in mine I know my enemy. You were saying how safe you are in the Apache."

Mac nodded. "Her designers anticipated that others may not take kindly to her. Much the same as *Lionheart's* designers gave her stout sides, the Apache is armoured well enough to withstand musket or even grape. I suppose a cannonball might be a problem, but when you consider the difficulty of aiming such a weapon we'd be damn-near impossible to hit. Furthermore, we'll be nearly invisible attacking at night." Mac reminded Toby how *Lionheart*, despite being outnumbered, defeated the two Spanish frigates after Cathcart assessed the enemy's strength and positioned *Lionheart* in the most advantageous position for his guns.

Toby nodded as he massaged his throbbing temples and said, "Ah, yes. I take your point. Cochrane did exactly that in *Speedy*, a lowly sloop, against the Spanish frigate *El Gammo*." He paused. "On several occasions we've taken advantage of an enemy's weakness to defeat them. Our ships' sides are stoutly constructed—as you say—but the weakest parts of any ship are the bow and stern. Raking means that we can inflict terrible damage with very little risk to ourselves. Our enemies desire to do the same to us, for we have but two guns that can fire directly astern—hardly an effective deterrent against an enemy intent on attacking."

Mac smiled, then explained how he would inspect the Apache and perform maintenance before she could fly.

"The same as we must do before we begin a voyage," agreed Toby. "Make sure we have supplies, that everything is in good order, no hidden damage from rot that could become a problem."

Mac laughed, "The more things change, the more they stay the same."

The lookout's hail, "Land ho, two points on the starboard bow," interrupted them. Emerging into the dazzling light reflected off the water, they shielded their watery eyes against the glare.

Jamieson greeted them warmly, "Good afternoon, I was about to send for you." He pointed just to the right of *Seppings'* bowsprit, "I believe Quinta Ruban lies there. It is not yet visible but our noon sight will confirm our position. No other sails in sight. We're arriving a little earlier than anticipated. D'you wish to go ashore this evening?"

Toby glanced at Mac who shook his head and replied, "Not much point. We'd have to spend the night on the beach. We may as well wait for first light."

Jamieson spent the night five miles off Quinta Ruban, tacking back and forth, carrying only enough sail to maintain steerage way, rather than risk anchoring in uncertain ground.

Mac, after enduring a fitful sleep, impatiently waited for first light and the crew to begin their morning rituals. The sun up and a powerful telescope slung across his back, he climbed the foremast shrouds to locate the hill where he had concealed the Apache. He swept the telescope slowly back and forth—the island appeared so different from the water. Jamieson called out, gesturing toward the cove where *Lionheart* had captured *La Señora*—it seemed so long ago, in another world and another time. With great relief Mac spotted the hilltop and hoped that the Apache was still concealed.

Seppings crept toward the beach under outer jib and reefed topsail while the leadsman methodically called out the depth. The water progressively shifted from a deep azure to a pale turquoise then took on a brown tinge as it shallowed. Mac could see colourful fish: some formed schools, others swam individually. A large ray glided through *Seppings'* shadow with effortless strokes of its wings.

Seppings came up into the wind. By the time Mac reached the deck the jolly boat was bobbing in the water. Men were busy transferring a swivel gun to the bow and loading some small sacks and several small casks.

Toby stood at the rail, watching the loading and said, "Food and water for ourselves and the boat crew."

Mac tapped the heel of his hand against his forehead. "Duh! Glad someone remembered."

Toby chuckled, "And I thought the army always travelled on its stomach."

~23~

A FLIGHT OF FANCY

TOBY THRUST ASIDE ANOTHER BRANCH and wondered again if they were on the right trail. Shank's Pony was not his favourite method to travel and the trail appeared more overgrown than Mac had described. Perhaps, Toby pondered, it didn't take long for the plants to fill any void in their quest for light. However, the trail continued to climb and the position of the sun indicated they were headed in the right direction. They trudged upward for nearly two hours before the ground began to level and the trees gave way to low brush and tall grass.

Mac paused and placed their food sack on the ground. His shirt soaked with sweat, he wiped his forehead with his sleeve and said, "Time for a break."

The tin water canister was already warm from the sun as Toby removed the bung and filled a small metal mug.

Mac waved away the mug, "You carried it up, you should be the first to enjoy it."

Toby drank then replenished the mug for Mac and said, "How much farther? It is difficult to judge distance on land after so much time at sea."

Mac thought for a moment. "I'm almost sure this is the hill, although the trail seems more overgrown than I remember. We'll know for sure in a few minutes. Ready?"

Toby nodded agreement, ensured the canister's bung was snug and slung the strap over his shoulder. When Mac hesitated at the crest of the rise where chest high grass replaced the brush Toby asked, "Not the right spot?"

Mac laughed. "On the contrary, my unfailing sense of direction has led us to exactly the right spot. My earlier misgivings were obviously misplaced."

Toby, several paces behind, could see only grass ahead and the top of the forest in the distance. He muttered, "You are having sport at my expense!" He immediately regretted his tone. Hot, tired and irritable from the climb, he questioned the sanity of wearing his uniform coat.

"Not at all. I told you that I'd hidden her." Mac chortled. "She's just over the crest."

When they reached the crest Toby gasped, "My God!" The nadir of the Apache's dull, dark-green vertical tail stabbed the sky above the brush.

Mac laughed slightly, "You're probably the first person to see what the future holds. I know how confused I was when I first saw *Lionheart*. I can only imagine what this must be like for you."

Toby moved cautiously forward, as if unsure if the machine was truly benign. What Mac called the main rotor more resembled four long oars extending like wheel spokes from a hub. When he looked back Mac was standing with his arms casually folded across his chest—a look of sublime satisfaction on his face. Mac smiled, "Quite something isn't she! Take a closer look. She won't bite."

Toby still wasn't completely convinced of that and hesitantly edged closer until he could touch the Apache's nose. He tapped a finger against the drab green surface and was surprised by a vaguely metallic sound that was unlike anything he had ever heard. Sunlight reflected off the sloping windows emphasised the dark green fuselage which more resembled a coffin with a glass lid. He moved to the left side and cupped one hand to block the sun's glare and peered inside—the space appeared so confined that he wasn't sure a person would fit. Then he remembered Mac telling him the gunner sat in the front seat which was surrounded by a confusing myriad of devices despite Mac's earlier explanations. An icy stream of sweat trickled down his back. He shivered in spite of his wool coat and exclaimed, "This is but glass. How safe can that be?" The thought of being encased in a glass coffin while being shot at brought him back to why they were here and the dangers facing them.

Mac laughed and reassuringly placing one hand on Toby's shoulder. "This from the man who stands on an exposed deck without the slightest protection while the enemy shoots cannonballs at him. Try a shot with your pistol if it'll make you feel better."

"I do not think that would be a good idea," Toby muttered.

"No worries. It's strong enough to withstand grape."

"Oh, I do not doubt you," Toby reluctantly agreed, "but if the boat crew hears a shot they might venture to find us. We certainly do not want that, do we?"

"Good point," Mac slapped Toby on the back. "Follow me while I do an inspection and I'll give you a guided tour." He needed to make sure that the Apache had suffered no adverse affects during her inactivity.

Mac knelt in front of something he called the "TADS turret" in the Apache's nose. Toby thought it resembled the head of a dragonfly. Despite not understanding Mac's explanation of its electro-optical eyes, he nodded knowingly and peered into the 30 mm gun barrel protruding from under the Apache's nose. "The bore is less than a single grape shot. Yet you say it can sink a ship?"

"Here, let me show you something." Mac opened the ammunition bay to reveal the ammunition belt to explain how the alternating armour piercing, fragmentation and incendiary shells worked. Mac then raised the canopy so Toby could see the array of controls and switches nestled around darkened display screens before examining the port pylon laden with Hellfires and a 230 gallon external fuel tank. The starboard carried Hydras and another fuel tank. With much hand-gesturing he described how the engines, various gears and shafts delivered power to the main and tail rotors.

Toby tried to respond appreciatively, although most of Mac's explanations eluded him. When he enquired about the function of the large tail rotor extending from the vertical fin Mac replied, "To counteract the torque of the main rotor. It prevents the entire helicopter from spinning beneath the main rotor. Think of it as the rudder counterbalancing the force of the jib sails. Without it you couldn't sail."

"Ahh," Toby murmured, relieved he understood something at last. Fortunately, Mac appeared oblivious to his general bafflement.

"Well, Toby, what do you think?"

Toby was caught by surprise—Cathcart's instructions had slipped his mind—but he did know Mac must never know about Cathcart's doubts, or orders if the story of the Apache had not been true. "I am taken aback. In spite of all that you have told me, I had no notion, not even the faintest idea, of what you meant. Even now, standing here and able to touch your machine, I still wonder if I am in the midst of a fantastic dream. You said there is much to do before night fall. Shall I have *Seppings'* boat return so Jamieson can get underway?"

Mac, preoccupied examining something under a small hatch, didn't look up. "Are you sure you can find your way back?"

Toby didn't answer; he was already on his way.

IMMERSED IN THOUGHT since leaving Mac, Toby knew he couldn't adequately describe the Apache to Cathcart by the time he reached *Seppings'* boat—Cathcart must see it for himself. That was the only way to keep Mac's secret safe and there would be no need for further discussion or questions. If word ever got out it was almost certain that no one would believe them but they would likely be regarded as insane, their careers in ruin.

A quarter mile into the return trek, Toby felt the hairs on the back of his neck tingle. He stopped—believing for a moment that he sensed something, or someone, behind him. He turned, one hand instinctively reaching for his pistol.

The path was empty, but through a break in the trees he glimpsed *Seppings* riding at anchor—the blue water beyond her stretching to the horizon. Men were busy getting her ready to sail. The realisation that a mile to seaward *Seppings* represented his whole world made him shudder. A world of wood, canvas and water encased in the routine of duty in His Majesty's Royal Navy. A world controlled by four-hour watches, rank and discipline. A world of routine where nothing ever changed. Inland was the unknown. He felt as though he was standing at the edge of a great abyss, trying not to tumble over the edge. He muttered, "Stap me," and resumed walking.

MAC CHECKED AND RECHECKED the hydraulic and control systems, looking for any sign of problems. Even the slightest damage could be a major catastrophe with no forward base, technicians or parts available.

He found it relaxing to return to a familiar routine, more so since he didn't have to explain each step to Toby. Immediately reprimanding himself for the thought, he was amazed how much Toby had absorbed and adapted to within a few hours. He completed checks of the gearboxes and drive shafts, then opened the fuel system petcocks to ensure water had not contaminated the precious supply. By the time he completed the checks the early afternoon was becoming uncomfortably hot with barely a breeze. No sooner had he wondered when Toby would return than he heard the hail, "Ahoy, the Apache," from beyond the crest.

Toby appeared like a ship's topsails rising above the horizon: his head appearing first, followed by the rest of his body until he was hull-up. He was wearing a pair of diagonal belts supporting a pair of canteens.

Mac smiled, "Good to see you. Everything okay?"

Toby laughed. "A little knackered. Not used to all this walking. Now I know why I avoided the army. I do not know about you, but I am hungry and thirsty."

Mac explained what he had accomplished as they sat gnawing on rock-hard ship's biscuits and the remains of salt beef in the scant shade offered by the Apache's fuselage. "We should find more shade until it cools off. I'm going to make sure the batteries are okay and then grab some sleep."

Toby, still drowsy after dozing for several hours, was startled when Mac opened the Apache's canopy. Mac said, "You're awake, I was just about to poke you with a stick. I'm ready to start the final checks after we clear the dry grass from behind the engine exhausts. I don't want to start a fire." It took them a few minutes of work before Mac was satisfied.

Toby tried to ease his nerves as he climbed into the front seat after Mac had pointed out the foot and hand holds and admonished, "Make sure you don't move any of the switches as you get in." However, Mac seemed calm, which helped lessen his own fears. He took a deep breath, wished his heart would cease its frantic pounding, then squirmed into the seat which felt like a rigid hammock. When Mac leaned across to retrieve the seat belts, he glumly realised they bore an uncanny resemblance to the restraints Woodman used before lopping off a limb.

"I'll give you a hand with the harness." Mac held one part of the five-point belt. "You won't need these until we're flying, but we may as well get them adjusted. They'll keep you in your seat if there are any sudden manoeuvres." He placed the shoulder straps over Toby, then showed him the lap belts before directing him to the crotch belt. After Mac positioned the latch ends, Toby closed and released the latch several times.

Mac offered Toby Weasel's helmet. Despite Mac's reassurances, Toby examined the helmet and its protruding sight and microphone with a great deal of suspicion. He was not altogether comfortable with being strapped into what he still regarded as a coffin.

Mac raised his voice so Toby could hear him through the helmet's sound deadening liner. "Don't worry, you'll be able to hear me better once the intercom system is powered up. This is a microphone so that I can hear you when you speak. This," Mac added, swinging the TADS sight into place and locking it, "is what you'll use to aim the weapons."

"A microphone?" Toby twisted his head toward Mac.

"Sorry, more of our technology that I neglected to explain earlier. It's like a speaking trumpet, so I can hear you, and vice versa, over the sound of the engines. It'll take me a minute or so to get ready and then we'll try it."

Mac climbed into the rear seat, slipped on his helmet and began checking the electrical system. The Apache was equipped with redundant electrical systems protected by circuit breakers so that a malfunction or battle damage could be isolated without affecting the remaining systems. The batteries showed a good charge and he activated the intercom system—if it wasn't working it would be impossible to complete guiding Toby through the weapons systems. Every minute counted, even if it provided only rudimentary training.

Toby was dumbfounded—it sounded as though Mac was inside the helmet—and answered "Yes" when Mac asked if he could hear.

"If you have a problem with the intercom tap the side of your helmet with your right index finger." When Toby did so, then Mac said, "Perfect. Let's see how the rest of her's working. You'll see some lights and other interesting things in a moment." He continued through his kneepad preflight checklist. Normally Weasel would be running through his own list—confirming and cross-checking with him.

Toby was bewildered when Mac asked him to 'Press down on the third switch from the right in the second row, and tell me what the gauge reads.' The switches, labelled in bizarre combinations of letters and numbers, defied translation.

Mac, silent for almost thirty seconds, said, "Time to start the engines."

Toby's pulse quickened.

Mac pressurised the fuel system and began the engine start sequence checks. "Here we go, the noise will increase once they start." A faint whine filtered through Toby's helmet. It grew in volume within a few seconds when first one engine, then the second, came up to ground idle speed.

Mac scanned his instruments, talking to himself as he went through the checklist: 'Fuel pressure...check. Fuel flow rate... check. Exhaust temp...check.'

The main rotor blades began turning—slowly at first, but increasing speed steadily until they were a blur. Toby's instincts warned him against being suspended in the air by oversized oars although, he reluctantly admitted despite his misgivings, they had brought Mac here.

His gasp surprised Mac who asked, "Is there a problem?"

"No, just amazed. I wish I knew what all these lights meant."

"Well, you're about to have the world's quickest instruction in Apache one-oh-one."

Mac ran through the basics of the weapons as he continued his preflight routine. The engines had reached operating temperature and he increased the throttle. I'm increasing the engine speed, so you'll hear more noise. Don't worry, we're not going anywhere yet. I just need to complete some checks." A half-minute later he announced, "Shutting down." As the turbines unspooled their sound decreased from a dull roar through a steadily diminishing whistle, the rotor's thump echoing from the ground. Mac pulled off his helmet and clambered out.

Toby, concentrating on the now ominously dark myriad switches, lights, gauges and displays, jumped when Mac tapped him on the shoulder.

Mac, accustomed to flying with Weasel watched as Toby fumbled with the harness release before removing his helmet. With an amused grin, he said, "Cool, eh? I remember my first time...seems so long ago."

Toby didn't mind Mac knowing he was worried. "I don't know how I'll ever remember everything...I thought training lubbers to set sails was complicated."

Mac leaned into the cockpit. "Once you get used to the Apache it's fairly straight forward. None of that swab out the gun, load a cartridge, ram in a ball, add the wad, lug two tons of scrap metal up a heaving deck, lever the beast around, insert quoins and hope you fire at the right point of the ship's roll, before remembering to stand back so the recoil doesn't kill you. Anyway, we've got time to eat and relax before dark. I always run through the mission in my head before I fly."

Neither ate much.

Despite Mac's reassurances, and notwithstanding the Montgolfiers, Toby's apprehensions about the weapons had been replaced by cold dread at the spectre of flight.

Purple shadows closed in. Mac swung and stretched his arms, then said with what seemed to be the hint of a smirk, "Make sure to relieve yourself before we fly. It'll be two or three hours before your next opportunity. A full bladder or bowel during turbulence or tight turns is unpleasant." He leaned into the rear cockpit to retrieve something and said, "Speaking of tight turns, and unpleasant feelings, you should have one of these."

Toby regarded what appeared to be a small paper bag with a look of bewilderment.

Mac, with a look of wicked amusement, said, "Just as people get seasick on a ship you can get airsick. Unfortunately, we don't have an ocean to spew our guts into."

Toby couldn't remember the last time he'd been seasick.

"Fold the flap over when you're done...and try to get your microphone out of the way before you hurl." Mac grinned as he finished demonstrating.

Toby nodded without enthusiasm.

Mac was enjoying himself too much to notice Toby's growing discomfort. "You may be used to plunging over thirty foot waves, but we'll be climbing or descending hundreds of feet; possibly turning at the same time. I'll show you some tricks to deal with that once we take off. It's far easier to learn once you're in the air."

Mac, wondered if he had taken the bag thing too far and glanced westward. The sun was about to set and the tropical dusk would quickly wane. "Looks like it's show time," he said enthusiastically and motioned toward the cockpit. Toby protested when he attempted to help him into the forward seat. Realising Toby's need for independence Mac said, "Weasel and I have the ground crew to help us. Otherwise we'd end up all tangled. Tell you what, I'll only do what they'd do: hold the shoulder harnesses out of the way and hand you your helmet. Nothing more."

Toby paused for a moment to check where to place his feet and hands before slipping into his seat in one fluid motion.

"Nicely done, looks like you've been doing it for years." Mac positioned the shoulder harnesses while Toby found his lap and crotch belts and fastened them without hesitation. Mac handed Toby his helmet, stepped back, then gave him the thumbs-up.

Toby felt the blood drain from his head. *Why has Mac given me the thumbs-up?* He knew from his classical education that it had been the signal the Romans used to show displeasure with a gladiator. *It means only one thing: death.* He was now positive this mission was a bad idea. He felt a moment of claustrophobic panic when Mac closed the canopy—at least aboard *Lionheart* grog was issued before battle. *Nothing like a pint of rum to steady the nerves.* His helmet earphones hissed reassuringly when Mac flipped on the intercom.

"Okay Toby, can you hear me?"

"Aye."

"We use 'Roger' for 'Yes'," Mac corrected. "If the answer is 'No' we use 'Negative'. Helps avoid misunderstandings, think of it as your flag signals."

"Roger."

"Startup procedure will be a little quicker this time. It'll take me about three minutes to get things going. Ready to run through your checklist?"

"Roger," Toby replied as the turbines settled into their ground idle purr.

Mac checked his map to confirm his course, time, and distance calculations. He would have to fly using dead reckoning, since the GPS system didn't work without satellites. "Nice and snug up there?" he asked.

"Roger."

Mac explained that the engine noise would increase until they reached flight power and there might be lurch when they lifted off the ground. "I'll go straight up about fifty feet; it'll feel as though you're riding on a yardarm as it's hoisted upward."

"I've never had that experience."

"Well, there's always a first time." Mac zeroed the ASN-137 Doppler-Velocity Measuring System. The ASN-137 used a downward-looking radar to measure the Apache's movement over the ground. Unfortunately it tended to drift from an exact positional fix after several hours of operation, especially over water, and required a regular GPS update to maintain accuracy. Mac entered Quinta Ruban's longitude and latitude taken from Jamieson's chart and *Lionheart's* estimated position. He had jotted down two additional fixes either side of Puerto Blanco.

Mac nudged back on the collective to test the rotor's bite in the dusk air. The *whap-whap-whap* of the main rotor changed to a growl as the Apache rose. He swung the nose into the wind and balanced forward thrust against the breeze.

Toby clutched the sides of his seat in panic when the seat pushed against his back and butt. His eyes darted from side to side as the Apache rose. He took a deep breath when he felt the crotch belt tighten, then clutched even harder when the Apache's nose dipped and he saw he was facing the ground from masthead height.

His stomach churned—for a moment, he thought he was going need the bag. Instead, he took a deep breath, tucked his chin down and resolved to persevere. When he looked up again they were already above the cove where *Seppings* had been anchored and Quinta Ruban's coast stretched northward. He marvelled that a two hour hike had been reduced to a minute or two in the air. Darkness quickly engulfed them, a paper-thin slice of light on the western horizon the only remaining vestige of daylight. Stars sparkled above and he was surrounded by the cockpit's fairyland of glowing lights. The Apache had settled into a reassuring constancy of noise.

What happens if the noise stops? He had meant to ask Mac earlier, but it seemed a bit late now.

CATHCART WATCHED THE SUN SET through his cabin's gallery windows with mounting anxiety. *Lionheart* had spent the past twenty-two hours relentlessly plodding back and forth in a small square of ocean northwest of Puerto Blanco, well out of sight of the land and prying eyes. He cursed the infernal waiting, then sought diversion on the quarterdeck. He looked about the spotless Bristol-fashion deck as he ascended the stairs to the quarterdeck. "Mr. Sloane, good evening."

Second Lieutenant George Sloane peered upward at the masthead telltale and replied, "Good evening, sir. Steady breeze from the west. All's well, and *Ringle's* on station."

Cathcart invited him to join him on windward side of the quarterdeck. Lowering his voice, Cathcart said, "We will run in darkness with no lanterns for the next few hours. The lookouts must be particularly vigilant so that we do not run aboard *Ringle*. Wear ship on each turn of the glass, steer only due north or due south. Do you call me if the wind shifts."

"Aye, sir. No lights. Wear every turn of the glass, due south or north only," Sloane responded with a puzzled expression.

Cathcart didn't acknowledge Sloane's concern and continued, "Double the lookouts. I want your best men watching to the north. Give them a lantern. Lit, but securely shuttered at all times. If they see anything unusual—I care not what they think they see—they are to call out and give three brief flashes."

"Sir, if we are expecting another ship how will they find us if we are running dark?"

Cathcart didn't answer. "Do you know if Miss Babbett is about?"

"She was in the waist by the lee rail, sir, but I do not know if she is presently there. Do you wish me to send for her?"

"No, I will find her myself. You have the deck."

Cathcart descended to the gangway and followed the lee rail forward. His presence on deck was unusual and several sailors discretely poked their mates in the ribs to warn of his presence. Laura stood at the rail, gazing to the east.

"Miss Babbett, I trust I am not disturbing you?" He realised that he had startled her.

"Oh, Captain. Not at all."

He glanced around in the quickening darkness. Nearby sailors had discretely melted into the inky void. At not much more than a whisper Cathcart said, "He will be all right, of that I am certain."

Laura continued staring into the blackness and did not answer. There was just enough light for him to see tears glinting on her cheeks. "It is obvious that you love him and I believe he loves you just as much." Cathcart paused, wondering if he had overstepped, but he would have said the same to his daughter. "Forgive me." He continued, "It is really none of my concern, except that I regard Mac as a friend. I cannot form many friendships with those I command—such are the requirements of a naval career. Mac and Toby are the two exceptions. I, too, am worried for their safety."

Laura shifted her weight from foot to foot, then let out a barely audible sob. She took a breath and said, her voice close to breaking, "If what he says is true, then he must either choose to stay with me and give up everything he knows, or try to return to his world. I do not know what I will do if I lose him. Yet how can I ask him to stay? To give up everything for me?"

"I presume that you have told him how you feel. You can only trust that everything will work out for the best."

Laura clenched her hands on the rail in silence for several seconds then turned to face Cathcart. "Thank you for being his friend." She leaned forward and kissed him on the cheek.

Cathcart, who would unhesitatingly attack an enemy while standing exposed on an open deck, oblivious to the cannon and musket balls flying about him, was speechless.

TOBY SCANNED THE PUZZLING MAZE of instruments and screens surrounding him, then felt the Apache quit climbing. Mac had said they would be flying one-thousand feet above the ground at a speed of one-hundred twenty-five knots. Only yesterday he would not have believed it possible. He could just make out the phosphorescence of waves breaking against Quinta Ruban's shore and wondered what the view would be like in daylight. After all, he mused, it must be akin to standing on top of a mountain. Except there was nothing beneath his feet save an impossibly thin layer of metal and something Mac called carbon fibre and Kevlar. Despite the constant rhythm of the engines and rotors, Toby involuntarily clutched the side of his seat until Mac interrupted his apprehensions.

"Can't see much without the moon, and the high haze has obscured most of the stars. Are you ready for me to turn on the night vision and targeting system? Make sure you have the viewing lens positioned over your right eye."

"Roger and affirmative." Toby enjoyed these new responses. So much more efficient, and he did not have to always begin or end with 'Sir'.

"Activating," Mac responded. Until now he had been flying by instruments, relying on the ASN-137 to feed the instruments.

Toby's helmet screen erupted into a green and white glow when the TADS became active.

"Are you getting an image?" Mac asked.

"Affirmative. Green and white—almost ghostly—just as you said it would be."

"Remember to keep your eyes straight ahead while you move your head."

Mac waited while Toby surveyed the surreal world in the helmet display. He could hear the hum of the nose-mounted turret obediently following the movement of Toby's head and asked, "How's that?"

Toby replied, "It seems to be working, although I cannot see much of anything." He was expecting to be able to see more.

"Roger that. Nothing much to see at the moment. You're seeing the targeting portion of the night-vision system, while my view shows more of the world. If there was a target, you'd see it. Where do you think *Seppings* will be? I don't want to waste fuel searching."

"The quickest route would be to sail northwest on the larboard tack which would put *Seppings* about one-hundred miles ahead of us."

"Roger, I'll head one-five-oh for a bit then swing south. We should find him within forty-five minutes. In the meantime I'll run through some other things with you." He repeated the drills until satisfied Toby had mastered the rudiments of the weapon systems. Mac reassured Toby that speed in targeting wouldn't be crucial for the mission as he interspersed his instructions with right and left banks, gentle climbs and descents. Eventually, he made some turns while changing altitude, but avoided pulling more than a half-g until Toby was more accustomed to flying.

Mac, silent for several minutes, said, "If *Seppings* is here we should pick up her image in the TADS. Select a three-oh degree angle of view and let me know when you see something."

Toby was unaware that Mac was also scanning ahead.

Mac decided to say nothing unless Toby missed spotting Seppings, only reminding him that, in effect, they were sitting on top of a thousand foot mast which meant at least thirty miles visibility.

Toby, not entirely sure of what he was looking for and not wanting to embarrass himself by reporting a false sighting, delayed reporting *Seppings* until she was twelve miles dead ahead.

"Good work, I've got her," Mac responded encouragingly.

Toby, pleased that he had found *Seppings*, slapped his right hand against his thigh. Nevertheless, it chilled him that they had found the ship, despite *Seppings* running no lights on a pitch black night, over ten miles away. *As easy as if she was anchored in a harbour.*

"Okay Toby, breaking left. I'll pass three miles downwind to make sure they don't hear us. This turn will be tighter than the earlier ones. Do you remember how to counteract gees?"

"Roger."

Mac turned forty-five degrees in a one-g turn.

"How was that?"

Toby took a couple of deep breaths before answering, "All right, I think. Have not needed the bag. Yet."

Mac grinned silently, continuing straight for a minute before calling, "Breaking right." When they resumed a northwest track he told Toby to widen the TADS' angle of view to maintain contact with *Seppings* now bearing ten o'clock. He came back on the intercom. "Okay, here we go, three-sixty to the left and climbing to fifteen-hundred. You're going to feel the seat pushing against your butt during the turn and climb. Ready?"

Toby acknowledged and made sure he had a solid grip on his seat. Mac put the Apache into a climbing turn; Toby felt himself pressed into his seat, fighting to control his breathing as he contracted his abdominal muscles to counteract the g-forces—all the while struggling to keep *Seppings*, now sixty degrees on their starboard, in the TADS.

"Still have her?" inquired Mac almost conversationally.

"Affirmative, ten degrees off the starboard bow." Toby was pleased that he had converted compass points to degrees, then realised he had managed to mix modern with old by referring to their nose as the bow. He was about to correct himself when Mac replied.

"Roger that. Good job! I've seen rookie CPGs lose a target in broad daylight. Make sure you keep her centred and then magnify the TADS image. Just like using a stronger telescope." Mac paused while Toby reset the magnification.

Toby gasped over the intercom, "I can see the men on her deck."

"Good. She's the enemy and you're going to attack with a rocket, where will you aim?"

"Midships." Toby knew he sounded doubtful and wondered if this was some sort of trap. Without other visual references to guide him he didn't realise that Mac had decelerated, yawing the nose toward *Seppings* while flying sideways to match her pace.

Mac asked, "Why?"

"That's where her magazine is. You said a rocket would penetrate her side before exploding, probably in the magazine."

"Affirmative. Just place your visor sight at the middle of her hull and that's where the rocket will go. By the way, did you notice that we're flying sideways. Our nose is pointed at *Seppings* and we're matching her speed. You're looking straight ahead at a ship and fifty men that we could destroy with one press of your finger."

Toby shuddered at the thought that Jamieson would never even know he had been fired upon.

Mac sensed Toby's dismay. "Don't worry, I've locked the Master Arm switch in 'Safe'." He cheerfully added, "Now let's find *Lionheart*." He swung the nose to the southwest, dipping it as if curtseying to *Seppings* before accelerating to cruising speed in a shallow dive until he levelled out at five-hundred feet.

Toby felt more relaxed, his confidence buoyed after successfully intercepting *Seppings*. The displays remained reassuringly blank, the vibration of the engines and rotor soothing.

Mac rechecked his calculations and said, "We'll reach the coastline in about ten minutes. Keep a sharp eye out for any fishing boats and practice targeting them if you have the opportunity. I'll climb to three-thousand feet to cross the land in case there are any uncharted hills. The radar should warn us, but better safe than sorry." He nudged the Apache into a steady two-hundred feet per minute climb as they approached the coast.

Toby rechecked his display. "I think I am getting the shore now, but cannot see any boats. I think the shore is about six miles ahead."

"Affirmative," Mac replied.

"Do they use this night-vision system on your ships? I would never have to worry about how close I was to a lee-shore."

"Yes, but we have other systems that can see farther." Mac didn't want to get into a discussion about radar, GPS and satellites and instructed Toby to switch to the Forward Looking Infrared system. They were less than three miles from the shore and the FLIR sensor would detect any heat source.

"You may see heat sources from fires if there are any houses in the area."

"Roger. What should I be looking for?"

"You'll know it when you see it."

Mac reset the ASN-137 to the beach's coordinates as they passed over. The ASN, their only navigational aid, had drifted out of position by three miles during their flight over the water. When the land began rising he climbed to five-hundred feet.

When they crossed the summit Toby announced, "I have two spots," his pulse quickening from excitement.

"Bearing and range?" Mac queried.

"Three miles, two points off the starboard bow." Toby corrected himself, "One o'clock," while wondering if Mac was annoyed about his error.

"Roger, got them. Keep them in sight as long as you can and increase your magnification. Hang on, I'm going down to two-hundred. We'll be skimming the tree tops so we might have a bumpy ride. Do you still have the targets?" Mac wanted to see how quickly Toby could acquire a target, or worse couldn't, before it was for real.

"Roger, two miles dead ahead." Toby looked from side to side in the hope of seeing the trees. He had the same feeling of apprehension when *Lionheart* was creeping through shoaling waters with constant casts of the lead. He imagined a sharp limb puncturing the thin metal beneath his feet.

"Up for some fun? We'll pass directly over the left-hand fire."

Mac did not sound annoyed, although the meaning of 'up for' eluded Toby. He could feel his temples pounding. "If you think so. One mile."

Mac held the Apache steady as they hurtled twenty feet above the treetops. The temptation to do a low-altitude high-speed pass was too great to resist. Anyway, he rationalised, it was an opportunity for Toby to practice his targeting skills. Besides, it wasn't as if the men on the ground could report the Apache's presence and jeopardise the mission. He chuckled to himself, and there wasn't a court martial board within two-hundred years of this place.

Toby's heart was racing from adrenaline when he called, "Five cables." The ghostly image of the campfire, Mac called it a heat signature, was growing larger. Sweat trickled down his forehead and stung his eyes. He wiped his eyes with the back of his hand. Sylphlike forms, probably sleeping men, were clustered around the fire. "I think I see six people."

Mac edged closer to the ground as the trees thinned and reduced speed.

Toby planned to call out at a quarter-mile as he centred the Apache's gunsight on three men but he was too engrossed watching the figures around the fires. Two had awakened and were standing when the gun locked on. The others only stirred from their slumber seconds before the Apache thundered over the clearing. Downwash from the rotor extinguished the campfire with a maelstrom of dirt and detritus.

Mac switched on the navigation lights and strobe beacon, usually only employed when in civilian airspace, then popped two antimissile flares before vanishing into the night at two and a half miles per minute. He laughed into the intercom, "That will give them something to talk about." They continued westward while Mac continued to expound on the Apache's capabilities. Ten miles from shore he turned north. "High cloud's still obscuring the stars," he noted conversationally. Tonight and tomorrow will be moonless, making them ideal for the attack on the fort. "Time to find *Lionheart*."

Toby, more concerned with the impending attack against the fort than with finding *Lionheart*, asked, "What happens if the fort sees us?"

Mac chuckled over the intercom, "We're damn near invisible. So for now let's concentrate on finding *Lionheart*. I'll keep the speed down to make it easier for you to acquire the target, just as you would reduce sail to lessen the roll and keep your guns level during battle. We'll approach cautiously and select our target with care. The Apache packs a big punch, but we have limited ammunition and no forward base to rearm us." They continued through the darkness for several more minutes before he announced they were clear of land. He turned northwest and said, "I'm climbing to five-thousand to increase our search range."

The constant pressure on Toby's backside reminded him that they were climbing as he peered through the canopy's side in hope of seeing what the world looked like from such a height, but there was only the ghostly green image of his TADS' sensor.

When Mac said they were just below the clouds Toby could not contain his excitement when gauze feathers flitted past the Apache. He exclaimed, "We just went through some." Peering forward, his face scrunched in concentration, he asked, "Is it like fog on the water?"

"Yes, except if you become disoriented you lose your sense of direction and can't tell which way is up. Deadly if you're close to the ground."

"How can that be?" Toby could not believe that his sense of up and down could be so easily confused.

"What direction are we flying?" Mac asked.

"Straight."

"Affirmative." Mac pulled the nose up into a tight left turn. "Now?"

"Turning to the left," Toby asserted, the pressure of the seat reassuring him.

"Roger." Mac brought the nose level, then commenced a right turn as he dropped the nose to counter the g-force generated by the turn. "And now?"

"Straight again." Toby announced confidently.

Mac laughed then said, "We're in a right hand turn descending at a thousand feet per minute," before pulling the nose up to restore positive-g.

Toby was mystified. "I thought we were level. I couldn't feel anything through the seat, I don't understand."

"I'll tell you more about g-forces another time. If we'd been at eight-hundred or a thousand feet when we went into that diving turn we'd be swimming by now and hoping like hell there were no sharks." Mac chuckled, "Back to work, the fun and games are over!" He climbed back to five-thousand, if the ships were where he expected they should pick them up approximately dead ahead.

"Toby, set the TADS for a three-oh degrees view. We're still at the cloud base which may reduce visibility, but this altitude will help us find them quicker." Mac rechecked his nav information. It was one-hour forty-seven minutes since they departed Quinta Ruban—he knew they must be close. "How long do you think *Lionheart* will stay on one course?"

"She will wear, rather than tack, on turns of the thirty minute glass. It would be too easy to run afoul of *Ringle* if either of them missed stays, especially when they are running without lights. If the wind has stayed the same they will be making four to six miles each tack."

"Roger." Mac checked his knee map and the APNS readout, then jabbed at the map with his index finger. "Everything looks good. Keep your eyes peeled."

Four minutes later Toby excitedly announced, "I have two contacts, dead ahead at about nineteen miles. Smaller one on the left must be *Ringle*."

"Roger. Never assume that you're seeing what you expect. Keep your eyes and mind open."

"Roger, sorry."

Mac knew Toby had nothing to be sorry for and said, "No worries, you're learning a tough job quickly. If I stay at this altitude the lookouts will never see us. Let's give them a sporting chance. I'll drop below two-hundred when we're twelve miles out."

The significance of the range wasn't lost on Toby. On a near pitch black night they had found the ships, running dark, at nineteen miles. A crack lookout, on a clear day, could not match that. Then he recalled Mac saying the Hellfires had a range of eight miles.

A few minutes later Mac said he was going to descend in a left hand spiral. "I'll do three complete turns so you might lose contact during the descent. Ready?" Mac didn't want to close on *Lionheart* until they had descended.

Toby barely had time to acknowledge before his seat dropped from beneath him and the harness bit into his hips and shoulders.

Mac, grinned to himself as the compass spun and the altimeter unwound. It was better for Toby to get used to the gyrations before the actual mission. They plummeted sixteen-hundred feet in the first spiral. The twin blips of the ships reappeared momentarily to confirm a full turn. He tightened the turn for the second rotation.

Toby fought the urge to vomit while he fumbled under the front of his seat to confirm the bag was there. He fought his rising nausea as a smaller shape swam across his display. Then a second larger target appeared. Heeding Mac's earlier instructions, he swallowed twice to equalise the pressure in his ears and tightened his abdominal muscles.

Mac, sounded strangely distant. "You okay up there?"

Toby gritted his teeth. "I'm still trying to decide. Almost needed your little bag."

Mac reduced the rate of descent for the final rotation, then pulled the nose up as they approached two-hundred feet.

After the Apache levelled Toby sounded a little more chipper. "I am sure half my organs are in new places. Dead ahead, seven miles."

Mac laughed, "Better to find out now if you can take it rather than over the fort when it really matters." He had the ships on his display. "Roger that. I'm taking us between them. I'll approach at two-hundred feet, then drop to fifty at one mile out. Let me know when we're at two miles. Make sure they're steering straight, we won't be more than deck height above the water and I don't want to run into them." There was little danger of that—he could see them clearly on both the TADS and his PNVS. Nevertheless, he chuckled aloud, "That would make for a bad day at the office."

THE CLOUD DISPERSED enough that *Lionheart's* lookouts could just discern *Ringle's* outline against the horizon when her sails blocked stars. *Lionheart*, five minutes into her latest northward leg, had a pair of fresh lookouts peering anxiously astern.

"Still don't know what we's lookin' fer, Bill," whispered Sam Cooper, careful not to be overheard by an officer.

"Ship, I guesses. What else'd be out 'ere?" asked the exasperated Bill Prentice.

"I dunno, but the Cap'n's bin summat strange ever since th' afternoon watch."

Their first inkling that anything was amiss was a menacing growling sound, a sound they had never heard before, coming from somewhere astern off their larboard quarter.

Cathcart heard it too. For a moment he thought it might be a line squall and considered calling all hands. Quickly deciding it must be Mac and Toby, he peered into the inky blackness in the direction of the sound which rose in pitch and volume as it moved from astern and past their quarter until it was almost abeam. It transformed from a growl to a roar before adding a whistle to its chorus as it swept past. Cathcart held one hand against the sky. He could barely make out his own hand, let alone see anything else. The noise reverberated through the rigging then faded away forward, partially muffled by the sails and carried away by the wind.

"Sir," Prentice finally spoke. "I dunno what that was," emphasising 'that' before adding, "Couldn' see anythin' an' I doan think it was in the water."

"Prentice, is it?" Cathcart was sure he recognised the voice, even if he couldn't see the face.

"Aye, sir," replied the surprised Prentice, "'an Sam Cooper, too."

"You are right lads, it was not on the water." Cathcart replied matter-of-factly before turning away. He hadn't taken two steps before the forward lookout called out.

"Sounds like it's comin' back, two points on the starboard bow. Can't see fu..." He corrected himself, "nuthin."

Cathcart dashed to the lee rail, trying to see past the lower edge of the forecourse.

"HAVING FUN?" Mac asked as he slammed the Apache into a hard-right turn after slicing between *Lionheart* and *Ringle*. He eased the cyclic and turned until they faced *Lionheart's* starboard bow.

Toby, preoccupied with trying regain control of his stomach, didn't reply.

"I just wore ship in not much more than our own length," explained Mac. "You should have her at one o'clock."

"Affirmative. What is next?" In spite of his stomach Toby was enjoying himself.

"Look east, are there stars just above the horizon?"

Lifting his night goggles, Toby squinted. "Roger."

"This time we'll fly down her lee side until we're amidships. Say two-hundred yards off and then turn to face her in a hover. Do you think they'll be able to spot us?"

"Can you make it a hundred?"

"Roger, one-hundred yards it is. I'll approach in whisper mode."

Mac held their speed to eighty knots for the southward run, then decelerated to reduce noise as he turned to face *Lionheart's* lee side. Their sound would be dispersed by the wind and masked by the frigate's own noises. He gently plied the controls until they were slipping sideways at ten knots, parallel to *Lionheart* and slightly above her quarterdeck.

Toby increased his view magnification and said, "I can see individual figures, also the larboard guns and their carriages."

Mac said, "Target the helm, count one...two...three." After a pause he added, "Now select a new target. Count to three." Then he said, "And again."

CATHCART MOVED HIS RIGHT HAND across his face again, almost certain that something was intermittently blocking the faint, hazy stars near the horizon. There it was again—stars were disappearing and reappearing.

"Cooper, Prentice," he urgently called. "Tell me what you see."

Two pairs of bare feet padded across the planking.

Cooper squinted into the gloom, "Where away, sir?"

"Directly abeam, half a point or less forward, watch the stars." Cathcart's voice had an urgent tone.

"Sommat's there, sir. Blockin' the stars and then movin'. Same speed an' course as us but I don't see no sails."

"Flash the lantern," Cathcart snapped.

WHEN MAC ASKED how many targets Toby sounded both elated and sad. "Five; two at the helm, probably George on the windward side, a group of four in the after-guard, a marine at the top of the quarterdeck ladder, and three at the railing."

"Excellent," Mac replied, "you know that counting to three for each target was the equivalent of firing three twelve-pounders loaded with grape? We just gave the quarterdeck the equivalent of a broadside of grape."

"Sweet Jesus!" Toby gasped at the realization that he could have single-handedly killed everyone on the quarterdeck including his friend George Sloane and Cathcart. *Lionheart* would be out of control with no one at the helm and her wheel likely shot away.

The shuttered signal lantern flared three times in his PNVS.

~24~

HELL HATH NO FURY

TOPSAILS BACKED, *Lionheart* crouched five cable lengths from the beach. Aboard the launch, Cathcart squinted eastward against the bright morning sun trying to see the shore obscured in heavy shadows.

"Two men, sir, signalling. Two points on the larboard bow." Thompson announced from the bow, one hand casually resting on the barrel of the primed and loaded and swivel gun.

The launch's bow ground softly into the sand and two sailors leapt over the bow to hold her until the rest of the crew could drag her onto the beach. Cathcart, unable to wait, jumped into the knee deep water.

"Good morning, sir." Toby saluted as Cathcart waded ashore.

Cathcart called to the launch, "Mr. Barnes, rest the crew and wait for my return. Gentlemen, lead on. We shall talk on the way. Is it far?"

"No, sir," replied Mac. "Perhaps two-hundred fifty yards."

Safely out of earshot of the boat's crew, Cathcart spoke. "Belay the 'sir'. Last night was quite impressive. No one saw you before you... I know sailed isn't the correct term."

"Flew," interjected Mac.

"Thank you...flew past last night. However we did see you on your second approach. Will the Spanish be able to do the same?"

Toby tried to stifle a laugh, but not before Cathcart noticed. "Mac deliberately placed us where we'd be spotted. Unfortunately for *Lionheart*, our simulated attack had already killed everyone on the quarterdeck before your lantern signal." He went on to describe, in detail, the placement of every man on the quarterdeck during the attack and recounted the mock targeting and firing. "Mac tells me that each burst would have been the equivalent of three twelve-pounders of grape sweeping the quarterdeck."

Cathcart's face turned white at the prospect. "I had convinced myself that because we could not see you we were safe. Are you saying that you destroyed the helm?"

Mac replied, "The first target is always the command structure. With no command there's no fight," recalling the opening phases of Desert Storm and how "Stormin' Norman's" destruction of the Iraqi command capability had been the first priority.

"Other men would replace the ones you killed." Cathcart was trying to salvage something from what appeared to be the loss, albeit imaginary, of his beloved ship.

Mac said, "Everybody on the quarterdeck would have been dead and the wheel shot away."

Toby interrupted, "We could have sunk you minutes earlier with a missile." It troubled him deeply that he could have destroyed her with none of his shipmates, friends or Captain any the wiser.

"Here we are." Mac tried to inflect some joy into his voice to counter the sombre turn in the conversation. The Apache posed in the centre of a circle of knee-high grass twice the diameter of the helicopter's length. "I regret that I can't offer you a demonstration flight as I only have enough fuel for tonight. Please, sit in the front seat. Toby will explain the weapons while I activate the displays."

Cathcart said nothing. Instead, he crouched to peer at the laser receiver in the nose of a Hellfire missile. "You mean to say this device can see where it is going?"

Toby explained how he could fire several missiles, directing each to a different target. He could also redirect a missile to a different target after it had been fired.

"This from miles away in the dark?" Cathcart, visibly disturbed by the Apache's capabilities, continued to stare at the Hellfire.

"At least five miles," Toby said.

"And we would not have known a thing?"

"No, sir," Toby replied grimly.

Mac wondered if Toby was having second thoughts about the mission. Certainly his body language suggested he might be.

An awkward silence descended until Cathcart spoke. "We must meet with the officers the moment *Seppings* arrives to explain what will be expected of them tonight."

Mac knew that Cathcart had made his decision. He was placing his trust, his career, perhaps even his life in their hands and wondered what the others would think when they were told about the strange sound in the dark.

Cathcart straightened and said, "My apologies for being a poor guest. Please continue."

IF THE LAUNCH'S CREW EXPECTED to find answers to the night's phenomenon after Cathcart's visit to the shore their anticipation quickly turned to brooding silence when they were required to wait on the beach while he went inland. Nor did Cathcart, Toby and Mac discuss the reason for Cathcart's excursion during the return to *Lionheart*.

However, that unseen lower-deck bond managed to communicate the boat crew's disappointment to the frigate. Perhaps it was the way they rowed—by the time Cathcart came aboard a sullen silence had descended over the ship. Men were doing their duty, but nothing more. There was no sense of joy or cheerfulness.

Rumours had already filled *Lionheart*. Nearly all involved the supernatural—from voodoo gods, to lost sailors and ships, to sirens luring the ships. One Irishman insisted the sound had been a banshee's wail warning them of imminent death.

Once aboard *Lionheart*, Mac knew something was bothering Toby. Although he would rather see Laura he asked, "Do you want to talk?"

Toby nodded and lead the way to the deserted wardroom where he pulled out a chair and sat at the table, his face ashen and expressionless.

Mac ensured they were alone and asked, "Are you going to be okay tonight?"

"It is not tonight that is the problem. It is the entire nature of your warfare. Please do not think that I am blaming or accusing you personally when I say 'your'. I mean that only in the sense that it is not what I am accustomed to. We can always see our enemy; but last night, when we found you, the impact of your weapons dawned on me. We could have destroyed both ships before either knew we were there. In your world I could sink a ship, killing every man aboard, without ever seeing them. Does my anguish appall you?"

Mac knew exactly what Toby meant, but for a different reason, and confided, "Absolutely not. The first time I'd seen someone killed was when we engaged the Spanish frigate. The anonymous images in the Apache's sights had always insulated me. However, in the end it still comes back to them or us. We try to take comfort by attributing our actions to lofty ideals such as our country, or freedom, or the rights of man. You're seeing only half the picture. It's true that I can kill without seeing my enemy, but in my world my enemies have the same capability to kill me. I suppose you could say things are fair. If anything about killing another person can be called fair."

Toby sighed. "The realisation that I could' have killed every man on the quarterdeck overwhelmed me. Such power in the hands of one man..."

Mac had once asked himself the same questions. "Perhaps the secret is to use that power wisely—in a just cause and only when absolutely necessary."

Toby pushed back his chair and extended his hand. "You do not have to concern yourself about me tonight."

Mac stood to follow Toby to the deck but was surprised to notice Laura's cabin door slightly ajar—he thought she was on deck. He told Toby he would come up in a minute, but before he could knock Laura opened the door.

After telling him that she had seen them talking but didn't want to interrupt she asked, "Is everything all right?"

He reassured her it was, before closing the door.

Laura put her head against his shoulder and whispered, "I was on deck last night."

Mac sat beside her on the cot and recounted the flight—omitting details of the weapons exercise after seeing its earlier effect on Toby. "I'd hoped you'd get to see her but I thought it best to confine my attention to business."

"I would have enjoyed seeing her. Why do you men always use the feminine form?"

Before he could answer, the lookout hailed that *Seppings'* boat was approaching. Cathcart would want the officers in his cabin.

"GENTLEMEN, PLEASE BE SEATED." Cathcart, unusually abrupt, was clearly not in the mood for socialising. He checked to ensure the overhead skylight was battened so they could not be overheard and continued, "Most of you are aware of last night's events." He recounted the eerie, unidentified sound that approached from astern then swept past and noted, "It took but a few seconds to pass before disappearing off the bow. When it returned off our starboard bow the lookouts were unable to espy it. As you know, there was no moon and high clouds obscured the stars, except for a break in the clouds on the eastern horizon where I saw something blocking some of the stars..."

Jamieson interrupted. "A ship?"

Cathcart appeared to tense then continued, "Not like you are expecting because I could see stars below it." He caught both

Toby and Mac stifling grins and grimly said, "What you are about to hear must stay in this room. If it gets out it will spell the end to all, and I mean all, of our careers. We made a prearranged signal with the lantern before the phenomenon disappeared." He paused when deathly silence filled the cabin then resumed, "You all know Captain Appleton. While it is true that he is an army captain there is more to his presence than first meets the eye. He will explain the rest."

The tension in the room was palpable. A pin, if not a feather, could have been heard dropping to the floor when Mac divulged the source of the unidentified sound and the circumstances surrounding his presence. Toby provided a precise account of the number and location of men on *Lionheart's* quarterdeck during the simulated attack. He emphasised how both *Lionheart* and *Ringle* could have been sunk from several miles away before either ship was aware of the Apache.

Toby looked at the shocked expressions and remembered when Mac first told him about the Apache. Both he and Cathcart had thought Mac must be mad. He paused to look at Mac, "I have a strong feeling that Captain Cathcart, not to put words in his mouth, considered placing him under lock and key, such were the outrageous claims he made. I can assure you that they are all true, in fact Mac has probably understated things."

Cathcart appeared to relax and said, "Gentlemen, we have much to discuss. Mac and Toby will outline their role in the mission and then I will tell you about our roles."

MAC AND TOBY LEAPT over the bow of *Lionheart's* cutter the moment it snubbed against the beach. They waded through thigh deep water to shore where Toby glanced seaward—the cutter was thirty yards out and *Lionheart* was preparing to make sail to rejoin *Ringle* and *Seppings* for the assault. His stomach tightened. There was no turning back.

Mac led the way to the helicopter and completed a visual examination before sitting down with Toby in the shade of the fuselage to work through the details of the operation. They would attack the fort first and then the smaller battery to allow Lionheart and the schooners safe access to the harbour. If possible, they would sever the shore anchors of the harbour's protective boom—a one foot diameter anchor cable taken from one of the Indiamen. Mac warned that they couldn't spend much time looking for the boom—Lionheart might have to sever it on her own. The moment they neutralised the fort and battery they would turn their attention to the road from the fort to the town, looking for additional defenders.

After Toby repeated the procedures for aiming and firing the missiles, Mac said, "We'll use Hydras against the guns. I'm hoping we can locate the magazine entrance and stick a Hellfire into the passageway to collapse the access. We should be able to deal with the fort in three or four minutes, then we'll take out the battery."

Toby, surprised by the small amount of time Mac thought it would take to defeat the fort, knew a pair of frigates would be hard pressed to accomplish that in several hours. He considered saying so but Mac only paused for a moment before continuing.

"We'll do a sweep of the road and take out any targets with the gun. Once we reach the town we'll start with Ortega's headquarters and improvise from there. I've no idea what we might encounter at that point."

Toby had numerous questions about the operation of the weapons systems, in particular how rapidly he could select a new target. It was late afternoon before he ran out of questions.

Mac reminded him to take time aiming, "A few seconds gained in haste is wasted if you miss," then completed his external examination of the Apache just before sunset.

After they turned in Toby scarcely slept and constantly checked his watch which was barely readable in the faint starlight. Finally, when it reached three a.m., he nudged Mac who reminded him that this was the last chance to answer calls of nature. By the time he returned Mac was in the pilot's seat.

Toby didn't mention that he had just been violently ill, or that he hadn't been sick before battle since he was a midshipman. He double-checked his harness to make sure he was well secured then slipped on his helmet. After positioning the TADS sight he announced, "All set up front."

"Roger." Mac ran through the final checklist items, then closed the canopy as the Apache's twin General Electric turbines stirred to life.

"Show-time!" Mac announced cheerfully. After rising straight up fifty feet, he pitched the nose down, accelerating as he turned hard to port. "A perfect night," he remarked. "No moon and high cloud obscuring the stars."

Although Toby thought he was ready for the slight lurch at liftoff he had to fight the bitter taste of bile in his throat.

Mac flew a semicircular course inland, skimming the treetops to reduce the area of their sound footprint. He wasn't worried about being detected—there was no danger to the Apache—but he didn't want to alert the fort before *Lionheart* was in position. At 4:28, after climbing to three-thousand feet five miles east of Puerto Blanco, Mac began to descend under reduced power to keep the Apache's noise to a minimum. A little over a mile from the fort, flying at fifty knots, he held the Apache steady while Toby selected the first target.

Toby's voice had a nervous edge. "I can see three guns, all unmanned. Hydra locked." When he squeezed the trigger the missile's flare momentarily overpowered his night vision goggles.

Mac held them in a hover nine-hundred feet above the ridge as the first Hydra streaked toward the fort while Toby selected the next target.

PUERTO BLANCO WAS ASLEEP—although the few visible lights helped guide *Lionheart* to within a mile of the fort. *Ringle* and *Seppings* trailed her by one-hundred yards on either quarter as they followed her well shielded stern lantern.

Cathcart anxiously noted the time on his pocket watch. Illuminated by the binnacle's faint light, it showed four twenty-five. The attack was supposed to begin at four-thirty, yet he could detect no sign of Mac and Toby. He paced five lengths of the quarterdeck, wondering if they had run into trouble, then stepped over to the binnacle to recheck the time. The last grains of sand falling through the thirty minute glass confirmed four thirty.

Was there a momentary flash of light in the sky to the left of the fort and above the low ridge? He blinked his eyes. It was no illusion—there was a second flash "Mr. Sloane," he called with barely masked excitement, "d'you see? Three points off the starboard bow."

Sloane peered leeward toward a third flash as the first pinpoint of light separated into two, both growing larger as they neared the fort.

EXPLOSIONS REVERBERATED from the fort's stone walls. Panicked men, awakened by the earthquake din, stumbled from bed to the trill of officers' whistles and the call of a lone bugle. By the time the gunners reached their posts the guns were already upended. Sergeant Gonzalez surveyed the shambles as English shots slammed into the wall.

Gonzalez ran to the wall. He could only see the frigate and two schooners. There must be an unseen bomb vessel, but where? Two ships could never cause such damage. The frigate continued to close. In another minute she could fire her full broadside against the fort.

Gonzalez screamed, "The field piece," to the men milling behind him. He gestured toward the stable housing an ancient nine-pounder mounted on a gun carriage. Long neglected, Ortega had ordered the gun to be refurbished after the previous attack. The work had been completed yesterday afternoon and the gun was to be hauled to the town later this morning. Half a dozen soldiers struggled to manoeuvre it into firing position as others brought round shot, wadding and cartridges from the magazine.

"I COULD ONLY SEE THREE GUNS." The excitement of battle raced through Toby's body and he was having trouble breathing.

"Affirmative, three good hits. Take a deep breath Toby, we've got lots of time."

"Really?"

"Roger that, looks like you got all three. Nice shooting." Mac added with a chuckle, "For a rookie."

"What's a rookie?"

"Tell you later. We've still got work to do." Mac eased the Apache's nose down and advanced toward the fort, searching for the magazine's entrance. Screened by the fort's stone walls, the TADS could not detect the men struggling to move the gun to the wall.

"STARBOARD BATTERY, fire as you bear." Cathcart shouted when the first rockets exploded. A quirk of the wind carried the motor sound of the following rockets toward the frigate. Cathcart saw and heard their impact. A resounding cheer erupted in the ship.

A bright flash and loud crack from the fort announced a ball arcing toward *Lionheart*. The shot ripped through *Lionheart's* small cutter before fragmenting against a larboard gun—killing three men and wounding four more with flying splinters from the wrecked cutter.

"Bloody hell!" Cathcart fumed. "They said they would destroy the fort's guns."

TOBY SNARLED, "Another gun, nine o'clock," when its flash flared in his goggles.

"Got it." Mac swung the Apache's nose around in a hard turn. "Call the shot. Where do you want us?"

"Get behind the fort so I can see them better. They will need time to reload."

The nine-pounder's crew was having trouble reloading after the recoil scattered the temporary blocking supporting the limbers. Forced to double wad the gun to prevent the ball from falling out of the downward pointing muzzle, they had placed the carriage against the stone wall and raised its rear with wood blocking to depress the gun enough to fire at the English frigate. One group swabbed out and reloaded the weapon as others hastily reassembled the blocking. The frigate's unrelenting fire pounding the fort's wall slowed their work.

Mac accelerated and climbed.

"Ease your helm," Toby said. "I can see part of the gun and some men, three o'clock."

Mac smiled. Toby still sounded like a lieutenant on a quarterdeck—but he had adapted quickly to this airborne man-of-war.

"Roger." Mac brought the Apache into a hover.

"Got you...you buggers," Toby muttered. "Hydra locked." He released a pair of Hydras at three-hundred yards range.

The rockets' telltale streaks of white-hot light culminated in explosions that echoed across the harbour. Toby couldn't tell if the gun had fired—the exploding rockets momentarily overpowered his goggles. When his PNVS cleared he said, "I can see a few men, they appear to be trying to help their wounded."

When Mac asked if he could locate the magazine Toby said he couldn't. Mac sideslipped the Apache, keeping the nose pointed at the fort, while Toby searched for the entrance. Mac caught the muzzle flash of the far battery flare in his peripheral vision and turned his head. The shot, which landed eighty yards short of *Lionheart*, appeared as a phosphorescent orb in his goggles. He knew the battery was armed with nine-pounders at the most, perhaps only sixes. Left unhindered they could cause serious damage to any of the ships—especially if they began firing heated shot. He wrenched the Apache's nose around and said, "Breaking off. The battery is firing, we'll finish this later."

Toby, neither expecting nor prepared for the violent manoeuvre, felt his gorge rise in protest when the Apache lurched sideways then climbed and accelerated.

Mac levelled out at nine-hundred feet, with *Lionheart* almost directly below, and said that they were safely above a ball's arc.

When Toby could not locate the battery he prompted, "Twelve o'clock low, two guns." Mac's infrared display indicated that the right hand gun was cooler. Most likely it had fired first and would be the first to reload. He nudged the Apache's nose down.

Toby struggled to overcome his queasy stomach and concentrated on the gun. "I'm going for the starboard first. Locked." A momentary flash illuminated the Apache as two Hydras streaked away. He switched his aim to the second gun and unleashed another pair of Hydras—their exhausts producing two brilliant orbs of light before culminating in spectacular explosions. The battery's earth walls, designed to deflect shots from a ship firing from water level, provided no protection from the aerial assault. In the moments before the rockets struck Toby had found what he was looking for. "Mac, behind and a bit to the right of the starboard gun, maybe twenty yards. Do you see a small stone building?"

"Roger."

"I am confident that is the powder room. Hydra or Hellfire?"

Having already expended twelve of their nineteen Hydras, Mac responded, "Switch to Hellfires and make sure you select a single missile."

Toby took several seconds to make the change. Mac was about to say something when Toby responded, "Affirmative, single missile selected. Targeting the middle of the building." He paused for a moment then said, "Hellfire launched."

"Roger. Keep the TADS locked on the building. Breaking left...now." Mac pitched the Apache's nose down and accelerated to avoid being hit by airborne stone fragments.

The Hellfire fell twenty feet before its motor reached full thrust then accelerated past the speed of sound. A fraction of a second before it struck, Toby lost the target in the TADS sight. It made no difference—the Hellfire didn't have time to alter its trajectory. Rainbow hued flames illuminated the hillside as debris spewed from the magazine.

Toby twisted in his seat to catch a glimpse of the fireworks show illuminating the interior of the Apache's cockpit. He only had time to utter, "Son of a..." before he was fighting the dive-induced nausea.

Mac grinned when Toby, perhaps growing somewhat used to the Apache's sudden movements, said, "It appears that there is a boat in the water, ten o'clock. How do we know if it is ours?" Toby was doing better than he had expected; it would be interesting to see him and Weasel go head to head on the range.

"We'll take a closer look. If they shoot, we'll engage."

Seconds later Toby called, "Man in the stern waving like a madman. Must be *Lionheart's* boat looking for the cable." He knew the boat's crew would be afraid they might be mistaken for a Spanish guard boat. He turned his attention to the narrow road leading from the town to the fort. "Can you put us above the road?"

Mac banked and climbed, then reversed his turn to intersect the road seven-hundred feet below. "Toby, eleven o'clock, against the hillside behind the fort. Do you see anything?"

Toby couldn't see what Mac was referring to.

Mac persisted, "Do you see the wreckage of the nearest gun?"

Toby squinted from concentration then confirmed he did.

"Ten o'clock from the gun. Look for a rectangular patch on the hillside showing less heat than the background. It's very faint."

Toby searched for almost fifteen seconds. "Perhaps I am not sure what to look for."

"Roger, standby." Mac took over the weapons system. One of the Apache's advantages was that the weapons could be controlled and fired from either seat, although it was more efficient for the CPG to look after them and leave the pilot free to drive. Mac designated the target with his TADS/PNVS and placed the red laser dot in the centre of the cooler rectangle. "Okay, check where I've designated."

Toby's excitement was obvious when he exclaimed, "Roger. I see it now. A doorway?"

"Affirmative, switching TADS back to you. See if you can find it again."

Toby had no difficulty. "Single Hellfire?" he asked while double-checking that he had selected a single missile.

"Roger, but stand by. I'm taking us back a bit, we may cause a bit of a bang." Mac retreated a quarter mile and climbed five-hundred feet higher.

THE EXPLOSIONS AT THE FORT were the first indication in Puerto Blanco that anything was amiss. Ortega fumbled in the dark with his breeches until his wife lit a candle. He rushed into the large central plaza, his unbuttoned shirt flapping as he ran, and mistook the sharp report of the field piece as English artillery. Why was the fort not firing? Thirty seconds later more explosions echoed off the hills and buildings. A short silence was followed by what sounded like the battery on the far side of the harbour firing. All these sounds were mixed with another he couldn't identify— ever-present in the background, fading and strengthening like the wind—and several screaming, whistling roars that ceased at the moment of an explosion.

He decided the British ships were trying to force their way into the harbour and assumed the strange sounds were caused by a bomb vessel. By the time he reached the harbour wall the fort had fallen silent. Frozen in the flash of the last explosion, the English frigate appeared to be caught against the cable blocking the harbour entrance.

"Carlos," he screamed, "get your fucking ass out here."

Carlos appeared at the far edge of the square just as a much louder explosion and a volcanic fireball followed several sharp explosions at the battery across the harbour.

Ortega spun around. The frigate, illuminated by the fireball's light, was past the silent fort and setting sail. He rubbed his eyes. An angular black shape in the sky had merged into the blackness as the flames subsided. A trick of the light, he told himself.

Partially clothed soldiers stumbled into the square—only a few carried weapons—and Ortega snorted in disgust. How could the governor expect him to protect Spain's empire with these drunken fools?

Carlos and two corporals frantically tried to organise the soldiers. Carlos struck at least half a dozen with the flat of his sword before sending them to collect their weapons or get dressed; the other corporals liberally applied their cane whips to the unready.

CATHCART RECOGNISED THE SOUND of the Apache accelerating across the starless sky before catching glimpses of it in the rocket motors' ignition flashes. The helicopter, momentarily illuminated by the flash, disappeared against the sky as twin streaks of fire raced toward the distant battery. Within moments two brilliant flashes of light blossomed from the battery and explosions echoed across the water.

He shouted, "Starboard tack, lively. Fore and main tops'ls. Outer jib. Then shake out the driver."

The cutter crew were rowing like madmen to avoid being over run by the frigate making for the opening in the cable.

Cathcart anxiously checked the pennant to confirm the westerly breeze hadn't diminished. He saw the momentary flash of another missile being launched. This time the exhaust flame followed a curving course before straightening. Another fireball shot skyward on long fingers of brilliant hues.

The Apache, visible in the near daylight brilliance of the explosions, dove toward the water like a feeding gannet until level with *Lionheart's* quarterdeck. By then it was moving so quickly that it was out-racing the debris splashing into the water in a maze of spumes.

The cutter was almost at the harbour wall when *Lionheart* dropped her anchor and the launch, loaded with heavily armed marines and sailors, cast off from the frigate.

ORTEGA GLIMPSED another flash of light in the corner of his eye and looked toward the source. A brilliant pinpoint of light streaked through the night sky toward the fort at unbelievable speed before an explosion hurled him to the ground. Knocked breathless, he thought he saw an angular shape in the sky illuminated by the explosion's flames but told himself that it must be another trick of the light before he remembered that the English cutter was making for the harbour wall directly in front of the square. He scrambled to his feet, then ordered his soldiers to form two lines and sweep the water with musket fire. Another half-dozen men, mounted on horseback, were positioned to prevent the English entering the town from the road leading to the fort.

LIONHEART **RODE** at a single bow anchor with a spring running aft to the mizzen chains to keep her broadside facing the town while *Ringle* and *Seppings* made their way toward the anchored *Thunderbolt* and Indiamen. Cathcart could still hear the Apache but had been unable to see it after the fires at the fort subsided. The cutter's stern lantern showed her progress toward the harbour wall remained steady and straight. He knew they must be nearly there, although, in the dark it was hard to judge distance. It had been eerily quiet for over two minutes.

SCARCELY A SECOND after Mac broke away in a diving turn, the Hellfire ripped through the entrance door to the fort's underground magazine. The door, facing the town, provided protection against a ship trying to force its way into the harbour; as an added precaution, the passageway made a right angle turn twenty feet from the entrance. The missile's dual warheads embedded into the stone wall at the turn of the passage before exploding. Mac continued to parallel the harbour wall at thirty knots while Toby scanned the waterfront.

Toby said, "I can see two groups of men near the wall, perhaps twenty yards to either side of where the cutter intends to land." He knew the cutter crew would be cut to pieces in a crossfire and added, "There's another group on horseback at the far edge of the town, under some trees." He glanced over his left shoulder and said, "A second boat has left *Lionheart*."

"What do you want to do?" Mac, confident in Toby's abilities, decided to let him make the decision.

Toby rechecked the cutter's position. They were less than fifty yards from danger. "Attack the men waiting for the cutter, the horsemen are too far away."

Mac interrupted Toby's preoccupation with the cutter and said, "Four o'clock, coming out of the big house, a group of men." He jerked the nose to starboard and settled into a hover. "I make a dozen men in the group."

Toby said anxiously, "I can't tell if they're armed."

Mac replied, "Neither can I, and it'll take them time to get into position. We'll deal with the men at the harbour wall first. Fire short bursts with the gun, moving from front to back. Make sure the cutter isn't in your line of fire."

"Roger, standby." Toby selected the gun then inhaled a deep breath to steady himself. He flipped the trigger guard up with his thumb. "Ready."

Mac rotated the Apache until the nearest group of soldiers were dead ahead, then began to move forward while the Apache bucked from the gun's recoil. Every third round was a luminous tracer that produced a parade of fireflies streaming toward the ground.

Short bursts, Toby reminded himself. The nearest group of men, huddled behind a ramshackle barricade of crates and barrels, were clearly visible in his PNVS. Although providing reasonable protection from the cutter attacking from seaward, the crates proved totally ineffective against the Apache's maelstrom. His first burst killed two and wounded two others. When the surviving pair ran toward the second group fifty yards away he aimed a few yards ahead of the leading figure, felling both with another volley. The second group abandoned their position and ran toward a building. Toby glanced to his left. The cutter had stopped but he couldn't tell if they had come under fire.

"Standby," Mac stated matter-of-factly. "I'm going to reposition."

Toby felt the Apache go into a tight climbing turn but his queasiness was gone. "I think I got the nearest group," he grunted, fighting for breath as the g-force pressed him into the seat. When he looked again, the cutter was against the harbour stairs.

Mac said, "Let's give the cutter some help and create a bit of distraction for our Spanish friends." Mac popped five flares from the launcher mounted in the Apache's tail. Normally used to confuse the heat seeker of an incoming missile, the string of flares burned white hot as they floated down, flooding the square in light. The remaining defenders, temporarily dazzled by the flares, huddled under the eaves of a warehouse.

Toby could see Barnes shield his eyes from the flares then pause at the foot of the stone steps until his men were out of the cutter. He scaled the steps two at a time before stopping at the top of the narrow stairway to peer warily over the edge of the wall. The Spaniards at the warehouse hadn't moved. They were trapped in a dead-end alleyway.

Meanwhile, the launch discharged its load of marines armed with muskets and another two dozen sailors carrying cutlasses and pikes. The cutter's men, armed only with cutlasses, were reluctant to cross the open square. Instead they took cover behind the abandoned Spanish position and waited for the marines.

"Toby, a few rounds above their heads might persuade them to surrender." Mac didn't feel the compunction to kill if they were willing to surrender.

Toby aimed ten yards behind the Spaniards and fired a short burst as the marines began advancing line abreast across the square. Within moments the skirmish was over. The remaining Spaniards, arms held above their heads, were surrounded by British marines and sailors.

A HALF-DOZEN LANTERNS scattered around the periphery of the square cast a pallid yellow light over Ortega's hostages who had been brought into the square bound hand and foot with ropes and chains. The guards were under orders to shoot anyone who did anything more than blink.

Ortega turned to check his soldiers waiting to ambush the
boat. The eastern sky was lightening and he wondered why neither
the fort or battery had fired for some time. As he retreated toward
the main square he acknowledged that although the English had
overcome his men at the harbour wall, he still held the hostages.

The growl in the sky briefly subsided, but re-intensified
somewhere farther over the town. Illuminated by the last of the
strange lights in the sky, Ortega saw the English marines advancing
along the harbour front. He sprinted across the square toward the
hostages, enraged that the guards had allowed the hostages to spread
out. In a near hysterical rant he ordered the hostages regrouped.

The sound in the sky drew closer as he pondered the curious
pinpoint of red light dancing on a guard's chest. Ortega looked
for the source of the sound as the nearest guard screamed a curse,
discarded his musket and ran.

Ortega grabbed the musket, brought it to full cock and fired at
the centre of the black shape in the sky. He flung the spent weapon to
the ground and retrieved a second musket from the pavement.

MAC PIVOTED the Apache through a one-hundred twenty
degree arc while Toby watched his TADS/PNVS displays for any
hint of trouble. Four Spaniards, running across the square as if
their lives depended on it, brought a smile to his face.

Something struck the flat, angular armoured glass windscreen
with a *splat*; he instinctively turned his head toward the sound. He
saw the distinctive musket flash, the heat of its discharge flaring
bright in his goggles a fraction of a moment before a second shot
thwacked harmlessly against the Apache's protective armour. He
exclaimed, "Someone is shooting at us with a musket."

Mac replied calmly, "Don't worry about muskets. Keep an
eye on the horsemen."

THE RIDERS, urged on by Ortega's obscenities, whipped their
mounts to a canter and advanced toward the marines and sailors
in the exposed centre of the square.

The sound in the sky increased to a roar and Ortega could make out a sinister black shape. It swept past, barely above their heads, flinging a fury of debris from the windstorm it generated. Terrified horses reared, threw their riders onto the paving stones, then bolted. A series of rapid explosions, like a hundred muskets firing over the span of a few seconds, erupted from the devil in the sky. In the blink of an eye the horsemen were dead. Ortega drew a pistol from his belt, cocked it, pressed the muzzle against Thomas Babbett's head and forced the American to his feet.

"SIR," Sloane turned toward Cathcart who was standing by the starboard quarterdeck rail. "Signal from the shore, three flashes. The town is taken." Minutes before, the boarding parties had signalled that they had boarded the merchant ships and *Thunderbolt* without incident. Pleased, Cathcart called for his gig.

Barnes wore an unexpected somber expression when he greeted Cathcart at the harbour steps. "Sir, we have a problem. Ortega has the hostages in the main square. He is holding a pistol to the American's head and claims that he will kill him if we do not immediately withdraw. I apologise for not informing you earlier, but we had no signal for that eventuality."

Cathcart, his joy dispelled, growled, "Lead on, Mr. Barnes." By the time they reached the square the sun was just below the horizon. Cathcart realised that he had not heard the Apache for several minutes. Ortega, his left arm wrapped tightly around Babbett's neck, held a pistol against the American's temple. The other hostages, bound hand and foot, were huddled in a semicircle in front of Ortega while the marines, armed with muskets mounting bayonets, watched uneasily from ten yards away while sailors fanned out to search buildings surrounding the square.

Cathcart tensed at the sight of movement at the eastern edge of the square but relaxed when Toby emerged from a narrow alleyway leading to the square. Cathcart spotted a woman descending the front steps of a large house behind Ortega. For a moment he considered ordering her to stop, but thought better of it. He did not know what Ortega might do.

He returned his attention to Ortega, an unremarkable man of medium height with a pox-marked face and sallow complexion. Cathcart wondered if he had survived one of the many diseases that killed Europeans spending extended time ashore in the tropics. Ortega's eyes darted back and forth wildly; his face glistened with perspiration despite the cool dawn air. Cathcart's greatest worry was the nervous tremor in Ortega's gun hand.

The woman continued toward Ortega. Cathcart felt sure that she was Ortega's wife and weighed the possibility of asking her to convince Ortega to surrender when she stopped slightly to the right and a yard behind Ortega. "Husband," she called out, but Ortega ignored her.

Cathcart cautiously touched the brim of his hat and made a leg, being careful not to take his eyes from Ortega as he bowed. "Good morning, ma'am. Captain Ulysses Cathcart of His Majesty's frigate *Lionheart*, at your service."

The woman responded with a dainty curtsy.

Ortega, in a heavy accent, spat out, "Silence, English pig." He jammed his pistol against Babbett's temple with enough force to make Babbett wince.

Cathcart stiffened. He considered drawing his pistol, reasonably certain he could kill Ortega at this range, but would it be before Ortega killed Babbett? Cathcart clenched his hands until his nails bit into the palms. Mustering all the self-control he could he replied, "Sir, I am prepared to offer you safe passage if you end this foolishness immediately. You are surrounded and have no means of escape." Cathcart shifted his eyes to the woman, he nodded slightly and said, "I assume I have the pleasure of addressing Mrs. Ortega? Naturally, your safety would also be guaranteed."

"Husband, listen to him," she said in near-perfect English.

Ortega's face had turned bright red and he was breathing rapidly, almost to the point of panting. Streams of sweat ran down his face, streaking his collar; his eyes darted about as though seeking an escape route. He snarled, "Leave now and take your lackeys with you before I kill him." He wrenched Babbett's head around by his hair to emphasise the threat.

Cathcart barely avoided laughing at the absurdity of the situation. If Ortega killed Babbett *Lionheart's* men would hack him into fish bait before he had a chance to draw his other pistol. Ortega was truly mad. He fixed his eyes on Ortega's, looking for the sign of fear as a duelist might when deciding the decisive moment.

Ortega spat out, "Now!"

The woman began awkwardly fidgeting with her shawl. In the split second that it took Cathcart to realise what was happening, she pulled out a small pistol and fired from a foot behind Ortega's head. The ball exited Ortega's forehead in a shower of gore, his eyes frozen in surprise before he pitched forward, landing face first on the cobblestones.

She looked at Cathcart for a moment, then at Ortega's body, and said, with no more emotion than if merely discussing a social engagement, "I accept your offer of safe passage. Regretfully, my husband will be unable to accompany me." She made a polite curtsy, one hand still clutching the pistol.

~25~

GONE AWRY

WHEN WORD THAT THE ENGLISH had freed the ships and hostages reached La Quinta a detachment of soldiers was sent to restore order in Puerto Blanco. Initially the town was happy to see them—soldiers would provide protection from banditos now that there was no further threat from the English. Only one soldier from the garrison had survived his wounds, the tropical climate and lack of a doctor had already claimed the others.

Three days after the detachment arrived, Puerto Blanco's citizens were shocked to see the wounded man dragged from his bed, placed against a wall and executed by firing squad. Within minutes the reason for the execution had spread throughout the town: he had been found guilty of cowardice and heresy by claiming that a giant bird, spitting tongues of fire that lit up the night sky, had single-handedly destroyed the fort, battery and garrison while the British ships sailed unopposed into the harbour.

After witnessing his fate, the citizens decided that it was in their collective best interest to deny such a preposterous story, blaming the outcome solely on Ortega's incompetence.

A SERIES OF FIERCE TROPICAL STORMS swept through the southern and eastern Caribbean in the weeks preceding Christmas of 1804. *Lionheart*, due for a major refit in England, spent a week at Kingston while the Indiamen prepared for the homeward voyage. Acting as escort would mean a slower passage than on their own, but the thought of being home in England in time for spring made the duty less painful—it would be the first time the men had seen their families in four years.

Laura and her father travelled aboard *Lionheart* to Kingston where Babbett bought a supply of food and personal necessities to make his voyage more comfortable. Word had been sent to Washington by way of the mail packet that he was safe.

Laura told her father she was going to wait in Kingston for Mac. When Toby had given her Mac's note following the battle he told her that Mac was going to dispose of the Apache at sea so that no one would find her. *Ringle* would bring him to Kingston.

The last Laura had seen of *Ringle* was before the storm off Puerto Blanco. When they lost sight of *Ringle* Cathcart had searched for a full day before deciding that she had been lost in the storm. Laura, however, clung to her belief that Mac was safe despite what others thought. News that *Ringle* had been sighted two days ago, on course for Jamaica, reaffirmed that belief. She reassured her father that she would be safe alone in Kingston until *Ringle* arrived when she bade him goodbye as he boarded the *Annie Jeanne*.

Ringle limped into Kingston harbour just before noon the next day. Although a few locals casually observed her arrival one young woman appeared to have a particular interest in the battered schooner as it cleared the mole. Laura spoke to the harbour master, requesting that he advise Captain Appleton where she was staying, then returned to her rooms at The Ship, favoured by more affluent naval officers who appreciated the innkeeper's attention to quiet and discretion.

In a moment of guilty pleasure at reuniting with Mac, she had bought some near scandalous undergarments made of the finest silk along with a stunning bottle-green gown with an alluring décolletage. Partially dressed, she stood in front of the mirror and imagined Mac, then extracted his note, safely cocooned within a silk handkerchief in a bureau drawer. She reread it then pressed it to against her chest. She stood there for several minutes recalling how she had once vowed to never again let any man be so important to her happiness—but that was before Mac. She composed herself and donned the gown, then checked her hair one more time. She jumped at the knock on her door.

"Ma'am," the inn's owner announced, "a gentlemen caller wishes to see you and is waiting in the lounge. Says he is from *Ringle*. Shall I send him away?" The man had thought the unkempt visitor might not be welcome and was surprised when Laura instructed him to send the gentleman up.

A few minutes later there was another knock. Laura, resplendent in her new gown, stood in the middle of the room, the brilliant Jamaican sun spilling all about her. "Come in," she called, quivering from giddy excitement.

It was not Mac, but rather a fatigued Wilson who opened the door, sombre in his tatty seagoing uniform with his hat tucked under one arm. He stood at the doorway frozen in place and stammered, "I am so sorry..." but couldn't continue.

Laura collapsed into an armchair, her back to the window, legs pulled tight against the chair and arms clasped around her chest while she desperately fought to control her emotions.

Wilson moved hesitantly to the middle of the room. The brilliant light streaming through the window behind her concealed her face yet allowed her to watch as he recounted the events as if he was reporting to a superior officer. "We could see him about to set his machine on the water. There was a great flash of lightning, then he was gone in less than a blink of the eye. I do not comprehend how such a thing could happen. We searched for him but the storm..." Wilson paused, cleared his nose into his handkerchief, and continued. "We lost our main mast and most of the fore and were blown so far off course I did not know where we were. By the time we jury-rigged a mast *Lionheart* had sailed for Kingston."

Brokenhearted and inconsolable, Laura returned to Boston three days later.

In early February 1805 <u>The Times of London</u> reported that H.M.S. *Lionheart*, 36 guns, Captain Ulysses Cathcart, had arrived at Gravesend accompanied by the *Pool of London*, reportedly carrying a cargo worth in excess of a half million pounds. Unfortunately a second ship, *Donnington Castle*, was lost with all hands in a storm off Bermuda.

A month earlier, the Annie Jeanne had been reported overdue, then eventually presumed lost at sea. Initially it was believed that Laura was travelling with her father, but the report on the loss of the Annie Jeanne did not mention her. Subsequently, an American shipping agent in Jamaica erroneously reported that Laura had booked passage for Baltimore aboard the American packet Camden. However, in mid-January, news reached Baltimore that the wreckage of a ship, believed to be the Camden, had washed ashore on Cape Hatteras. No one realised that Laura was aboard a different ship.

BOOK THREE
From bad to worse

~26~

CONFRONTING THE PAST

MAC THOUGHT HE HEARD A VOICE ASK "Sir?" but there were so many reverberating in his head that he wasn't sure if this one was coming from within or without.

"Sir," it repeated in a soothing, slow, southern drawl, "Can you hear me?" It spoke without the harshness of the others lurking inside his skull. Mac tried to respond but couldn't. It seemed his brain wasn't connected to his mouth. In the time it took for his lips to form the words he had forgotten what he wanted to say. The voice spoke again, but not to him. "He's unresponsive. Get the neck and back braces on him."

Mac felt himself being gently inched upward. Somewhere in the background he thought he could hear the clatter of an idling helicopter. He felt something being strapped around his head and neck.

"Okay. Let's get him onto the stretcher." The voice was a little more clear. "Immobilise his arms and legs once he's on the stretcher. On three."

He felt like he was floating, then realised he was being lifted. When he tried to move his hands and feet he couldn't. Quiet blackness returned, ending the pain.

RECENT TERRORIST ATTACKS in Los Angeles and Boston— by homegrown groups to make matters worse— dominated the news and had thrown America into a state of panic. A brief wire service story, "Army pilot missing," was relegated to the back of the classified ad sections in the few papers that bothered to run it. The story read, "Captain Andrew Appleton, a Canadian Forces exchange helicopter pilot, is reported missing during a routine training exercise in the western Caribbean. His AH-64 Apache is believed to have been forced down during bad weather." There was little news value in the fate of a foreign national.

A military spokesperson explained that continued poor weather in the search area made the search difficult. Naval and air operations would be intensified within the next twenty-four hours once the weather improved. She concluded, "There was every reason to believe Captain Appleton would be found alive as the Apache was equipped with survival gear."

Four days later a follow-up story, 'Missing pilot safe', received even less interest from the media.

MAC FORCED ONE EYE OPEN. The pain had lessened, and the voices had mostly ceased. He was in a room decorated in soothing pastels and filled with medical equipment. When he attempted to raise his hands he couldn't. He twisted his head and saw that both wrists were secured to his bed by cloth straps. An intravenous line was taped to his left hand.

"Good afternoon, Captain."

Mac turned his head toward the voice. He managed to croak, "Where...?" to the nurse checking his IV before succumbing to the exertion.

"Brooke Army Medical Center. You were brought here three days ago after your crash. Don't worry, you're doing well, although you may not feel that way right now. Just relax, you're in good hands."

It was strange that he knew Brooke was at Fort Sam Houston in Texas because he didn't remember any crash, nor had he any recollection of being brought to Texas. Each time he awoke from fitful sleep he felt trapped between two worlds. In his dreams he repeatedly saw faces, including a woman who seemed familiar but whom he couldn't place. The only constant was the hospital room.

The next time he awoke a clock in the hallway read six-eighteen but he didn't know if that was morning or evening, or even what day. However, for the first time, he was aware of sounds and activity: a cart trundling down the hallway, fragments of conversations, and people—most appearing to be medical staff—passing his doorway.

A few minutes later a man pushing a cart looked in and exclaimed, "Oh, you're awake! I'll let the doctors know." Within seconds, he was surrounded by an older male doctor accompanied by a younger male and female. He assumed they were interns or residents by their short white coats—a second woman might be a nurse.

The older man said, "Good morning, Captain Appleton. I'm Dr. Woodman."

The name was hauntingly familiar, but the face was not. Confused, Mac searched his memory and missed Woodman's introduction of the others, but didn't ask him to repeat.

Woodman continued, "You've had a rough time. How are you feeling this morning?"

"I'm not sure," Mac replied. This was the first time he had been able to put a coherent sentence together and move his arms and legs. He was encouraged that the restraints had been removed. Two IV poles, supporting five bags, were positioned next to his bed.

Woodman smiled, "We'll take a quick look, then perhaps you'd like to try a little breakfast. Not too much, some dry toast and a bit of tea to start."

Mac nodded weakly, then closed his eyes. While the doctors examined him he tried to recall how he arrived here. Everything remained a blank, but Woodman encouragingly suggested he was suffering from temporary amnesia caused by a concussion. After the doctors left, he forced himself to eat half a piece of toast and a take few sips of tepid tea before lapsing into sleep.

Unknown hours later he awoke to the sound of voices outside his door. Two uniformed army officers were waiting in the corridor. An older, taller man led the way into his room and said, "Good afternoon, Captain. I'm Major Wilkins and this is Captain Breznewski. If you're up to it we'd like to talk to you about your crash."

"I crashed?"

"Yes, Captain. Eight days ago on Providencia. What do you remember about the events leading up to the crash?"

Mac was reasonably sure that saying anything could mean trouble as he still had no clear recollection of what had happened. The faces in his dreams continued to haunt him; besides the woman, there were now two men, one older, who also seemed familiar but couldn't be placed. He also had a sense of being surrounded by water and fog. Most perplexing, however, was his clear recollection of the less recent past, including the mission against the Colombian drug lab. So he replied, "Not much, wasn't it some sort of training mission?"

Breznewski hadn't taken his eyes off Mac since entering the room. "Do you routinely fire live weapons on training missions?"

Mac returned his stare with a neutral expression. He didn't know why he would have fired, but other images had been appearing in his mind's eye: water—lots of water, explosions, a large stone wall, and buildings. Fearful of where the question might lead, he replied, "I have no recollection of firing." The interview continued for another thirty minutes until Woodman ordered a halt for medical reasons.

Mac steadily improved over the next two days until he was up and walking, albeit unsteadily; his appetite recovered to the point that he visited the cafeteria between meals. Although the cafeteria food had the same blandness, the scenery was better and one nurse in particular smiled at him every time she saw him. The dreams were decreasing and he was beginning to remember more. At least he hoped he was remembering. With his recollections so disjointed he felt like he was trying to put together a jigsaw puzzle—but being given only one piece at a time.

Wilkins and Breznewski returned in the middle of the third morning, accompanied by two civilians. Mac almost laughed when Misters Johnson and Abels were introduced—no first names, and putting them in jeans didn't change the fact they were spooks. They obviously didn't get out of the office much, judging by their sallow complexions, paper-pushers he decided, who likely didn't know a damn thing about the real world.

Johnson and Abels said nothing during the half-hour interview which repeatedly concerned the Apache's weapons. Despite his silence, Mac took an immediate dislike to Abels. He decided that his narrow face, with an overbite that exposed his teeth, made him look like a ferret.

As the men were leaving Mac caught fragments of a discussion between Abels and Dr. Woodman about when he would be able to leave the hospital for further interviews at another location on the sprawling base. Woodman appeared reluctant to allow Mac to leave the hospital for any reason, despite Abels saying it was necessary for 'security reasons'.

That afternoon, as a psychiatrist interviewed him, Mac began recalling a fragmented jumble of people, places and events. He regarded psychiatrists as less trustworthy than spooks and didn't reveal the new memories. Following the shrink, he was taken for another CT Scan and MRI. One aspect of his returning memory puzzled him more than the others. He was beginning to recall a storm—perhaps two—and sailing ships.

The following morning he was intercepted in the cafeteria by an orderly pushing a wheelchair and accompanied by two military cops. Mac thought the senior MP had the expression of a constipated mule when he informed him that he was being taken to a debriefing.

His guards said nothing during the ten minute drive to an office building. During the interview Wilkins and Breznewski sat silent for the most part, but not the ferret-faced Abels. Variations of 'What do you remember about the training mission?' and 'When, where, and why did you fire your weapons?' continued for over two hours. Some questions were couched in references to the Rules of Engagement. As far as Mac was concerned, all were intended to trap him. He wondered if he was being setup as a scapegoat. Clearly shit had hit the fan somewhere and he wondered if he had mistakenly fired on friendlies.

Following the umpteenth denial that he had fired any weapon, ferret-face smirked and asked, "Then how do you explain this?" He turned on a TV with a dramatic flourish of the remote control.

Mac stiffened when the video began. His own voice, and another voice with an English accent, was interlaced with video of Hydra 70s streaking towards a target. Mac was surprised that he recognised the missiles, but not the event.

"This video was recovered from your Apache, Captain Appleton," ferret-face spat out. "Do you continue to deny you fired?"

"Sir," he responded, stifling the dread, "I have no recollection."

"Then it's going to be long day. I want answers." Abels could not disguise his disgust with Mac's continued denial, venomously spitting the words, "And who was your CPG?" His expression turned to one of triumph.

Mac stared at the screen and said nothing. The last time he had seen Weasel was on Corn Island. He had no idea who the other voice belonged to.

Ferret-face paused the video, superimposing an enlarged freeze-frame of the target taken milliseconds before the Hydra struck. The grainy, squat shape of a muzzle loading cannon filled the screen. Mac felt like he had been kicked in the stomach. Strangely, the weapon didn't seem out of place.

Wilkins interrupted, "I think Captain Appleton has been through enough today. I'm placing him under house arrest." He looked at Mac, "You're not to leave the hospital without an escort and you are not to talk with anyone outside this room about these events. Do you understand?"

MAC WAS BROUGHT BACK to the base the next morning, Wilkins accompanying him in the staff car instead of an ambulance. Mac had discovered more pieces of the puzzle overnight. Rather than reassuring him, they only served to increase the mystery. He had a clear memory of the first storm, but everything after that remained a jumble.

Although Wilkins was talkative during the drive, he avoided asking anything about the mission. Instead he asked Mac about his personal life and interests. They returned to the same debriefing room where ferret-face and the other spook were waiting. Wilkins said Breznewski was reviewing documents elsewhere. By the time they were seated Mac had recalled one frightening detail: the first storm had carried him back in time. That explained the cannon in the video, although he still couldn't remember what had led up to launching the missiles. He wondered why Abels hadn't commented on the incongruity.

Abels didn't bother to greet Mac. Instead, he immediately projected the cannon image from the day before. Mac saw Wilkins scowl. Ferret-face leaned across the table. "I want answers."

Wilkins' fingers visibly tightened their grip on his pen. "You're addressing an officer, Mister Abels. This isn't Gitmo." Mac caught Wilkins' not-so-subtle emphasis of 'Mister' and the reference to Gitmo—Guantanamo Bay—increased Mac's distrust of Abels.

Mac stifled a laugh. Ferret-face and his buddy weren't military. Clearly there was no love lost between Wilkins and them. Wilkins might even be an ally.

Ferret-face straightened, "Why did you fire, and who was with you in the Apache?" He deliberately paused before adding, "Captain."

Mac delayed answering and fixed his gaze on Abels' face while silently counting to ten, as though he was thinking. "May I ask your security clearance, sir?"

Abels, caught off guard by the question, hesitated before replying with an air of superiority, "Bravo."

Mac nodded and asked, "And your associate's?"

Ferret-face's air of superiority faded with his reply. "Aurora." He had a lousy poker face. His hesitation and nervous twitch confirmed what Mac already suspected.

Mac swivelled his chair toward Wilkins, deliberately turning his back to Abels, "Sir, if you're not already aware, I'm 'Ultra'. Unfortunately, I'm unable to provide any further information in their presence." Mac rolled his chair back as though he was preparing to leave.

Wilkins looked at Abels. "I'm sorry Mr. Abels, but you must leave. If the company wishes to send someone with the appropriate clearance they are welcome to join us."

Ferret-face, who appeared near to exploding, shoved his chair away from the table. Mac thought he detected a hint of 'gotcha' in Wilkins' expression. Once they were alone Wilkins said, "You haven't asked about my clearance."

Mac smiled. "No reason to, sir. I want to know what happened as much as you do." Somehow, he trusted Wilkins.

The debriefing continued through the afternoon. Although Mac recalled more details the memories remained frustratingly disconnected. Near the end of the session, Wilkins returned to the video recording. "Take another look at the video. We haven't been able to determine where you were."

"Puerto Blanco," Mac blurted. He hadn't known until that moment, but his mouth seemed to be working of its own accord.

Wilkins appeared surprised. "Are you sure?"

Mac nodded. "Puerto Blanco, for sure."

When Wilkins stood and began pacing the length of the room, hands clenched behind his back and head down, every detail suddenly became clear to Mac. It felt as though he had been trapped on a mountaintop enveloped by cloud until the cloud evaporated to expose the entire world in sudden brilliance. His strongest memory was that of Laura. The shadowy image of her at the window when she escaped, at the waterfall, clutching his flightsuit in the grotto, tending to the wounded—all flooded back.

Mac realised that Wilkins, who had been pacing for some time, had spoken. "We repositioned two satellites and photographed every inch of coastline for seven-hundred klicks. There's no structure remotely like the one you attacked and our ground assets confirm no attack occurred."

The knot in Mac's stomach felt the size of a football. "That's because it happened two-hundred years ago."

~27~

A LONG AND WINDING ROAD

IN THE MONTHS FOLLOWING his rescue Mac brooded about Laura. With utter frustration he had discovered nothing beyond her birth record and that she wasn't mentioned in any of the documents he found relating to the death of her father. He assumed that she returned to Baltimore, but perhaps she had gone elsewhere or married. It was as though she had vanished and without some clue he had no idea of where to even begin searching.

He had repeatedly relived the tumultuous weeks following his revelations to Wilkins which resulted in his removal from the hospital in the wee hours to an anonymous bungalow in a nondescript neighbourhood of San Antonio. He caught only a fleeting glimpse of the house through the heavily tinted windows of the transport van. The house appeared to be in the midst of a renovation—the charade supported by recorded construction sounds piped to the neighbourhood through speakers positioned behind plywood covered windows. Visitors usually wore nondescript tradesmen's clothes; those wearing suits always carried bundles of papers or briefcases. Wilkins was ever-present. Notably absent, however, were spooks.

One afternoon, a windowless van backed up next to the disposal bin that blocked the public's view of the house from the street. He was hustled into the van, then taken to an empty warehouse where he was transferred to a private ambulance and zipped into a body-bag before the ambulance arrived at the hospital where he was wheeled on a gurney to a secure examination room where the doctor pronounced him fit. Mac shuddered at the recollection of the sound of the zipper and the rubberised disinfectant smell of the bag.

The days at the house had blurred into one. With no clocks, radio or TV, and with the windows covered, he couldn't tell if it was night or day. His only clue had been the meals—if bacon and eggs meant it was morning. Eventually he decided the house faced south because the plywood covered living room window became warm to the touch after 'breakfast'.

One day, a late middle-aged man arrived at the house. Although Wilkins didn't introduce him, Mac could still see the man's steel-cold eyes. Wilkins, after assuring Mac that the man could be trusted, sat silently as Mac retold the events.

"Well, son, that's quite a story," was all the man said when Mac finished.

He remembered nodding and expecting the man to add 'but' because it certainly sounded like one was coming. Instead he replied, "Yes, sir. Hard to believe, isn't it?"

The man said that the onboard video had kept Mac out of a padded cell—apparently some people still believed he was simply crazy. Mac waited for the other shoe to drop, but the man said that Wilkins had vouched for him and asked that the trust be returned. For some reason Mac did, despite misgivings and what felt like a pair of hands twisting his stomach into knots.

The stranger's words were still clear in his mind: "We can't have word about this getting out. No one can explain how this happened and a team is trying and replicate the events. If they're able to, the implications are mind-numbing."

The man continued, "You're ordered not to speak of these events unless directly asked by Major Wilkins. The official story is that you were forced down by the storm and your weapons fired due to an electrical surge. Too many people have seen, or heard about your 'malfunction' to ignore it. Our technical people are developing a plausible 'fix' for the Apache that will take a few weeks to implement...long enough for this to die down. Because of that, all Apaches are grounded pending an inspection. They'll not be flown in adverse weather until we've announced a solution. Are we clear?"

Mac remembered answering, "Yes, sir," despite wondering what they had planned for him while the subterfuge took place. He eventually received permission to take his accumulated leave once deemed medically fit for return to duty. At least Woodman had reassured him that he was well on the way to a full recovery, but cautioned that he might occasionally suffer headaches and memory gaps. Time passed slowly waiting for Woodman's final approval. He was moved again, this time to somewhere outside the city but the interrogations had ended and Wilkins' visits were a welcome distraction. Wilkins apologised for the move and the relentless questioning. Then Wilkins revealed what Mac already suspected: the military were keeping him—and his time-travel— to themselves. Mac continued to have difficulty making sense of what he had been through. According to Wilkins he had only been missing for three days. Yet, his adventures in the past had seemed longer. During all the interviews, debriefings, and interrogations Mac never mentioned Laura. She was none of their business.

Woodman pronounced Mac fit for duty nine weeks after being rescued. Although his memory had completely returned that was also what concerned Mac the most. After the remaining hostages were freed he remembered landing behind Puerto Blanco and telling Toby of his decision to stay in the past—he would ditch the Apache at sea, where she would never be found. Toby was to send *Ringle* or *Seppings* to pick him up. After shaking hands for the last time he handed Toby a hastily written note for Laura that read 'Together my love, always.'

A black cloud dominated his conscious mind as he found himself increasingly thinking of Laura, wondering what had happened to her and knowing he would never see her again. First Belinda, now Laura—whoever he had loved had been taken away.

He decided it best not to tell Wilkins of the decision to ditch the Apache. That would remain a secret. He suspected the brass wouldn't take kindly to him intending to destroy the Apache or to desert, even if it had been two-hundred years ago and the Apache had been transported back to the present.

The more he tried to relax, the more he fretted about what had happened. The more he fretted, the more he thought about Laura—still unable to resolve the time discrepancy between his recollection of the months they had been together, and the few days he had been missing before his rescue. He considered returning to Canada to catch up with old friends but what could he tell them with the entire incident classified? Instead he sought distraction and isolation on Florida's keys.

Mac walked along the sand, his iPod set to select songs at random. Perhaps he could dispel the misery of his loneliness. If he couldn't be with Laura, he decided, he would discover what became of her. He still wasn't sure if it had been coincidence or fate that destined the iPod to play Beth Nielsen Chapman's Sand and Water at that particular time—it was beginning to feel like a million years. Then that damn schooner, carrying tourists on a sailing junket, rounded the breakwater. Its resemblance to *Ringle* was uncanny.

He wiped back tears and changed tracks on the iPod. Anything to end that song. Instead he got Blue Rodeo's *5 Days in May* for his efforts. In frustration, he poked the iPod again—which responded with The Beatles' *Yesterday*. "Fucking Hell," he exclaimed, tearing off his earphones, sure the bloody iPod was haunted. *Why else had it selected those songs out of the thousands he had randomly loaded?*

So, four days into his vacation, he muttered to himself, "Screw it," and checked out of his hotel within the hour. He had to find out what happened to Laura. He'd had enough of flying, and caught the afternoon train to D.C. from Miami.

Laura's fate dominated his thoughts; perhaps the National Archives would provide some answers about the Babbetts. He hoped that their name was prominent enough to have been preserved in documents—government records, newspapers, possibly 'The Saturday Evening Post'.

The next day Washington was cold, wet, and covered by a blanket of low cloud. The gloom mirrored his mood perfectly as he peered through rivulets of water streaking the train window and distorting the dreary cityscape.

At last, the train reached Washington Union Station where he disembarked and made his way to the taxi line. He had booked a boutique hotel in Georgetown—he didn't feel like being surrounded by lobbyists and politicians at the major hotels where there was a chance he would run into someone he knew.

By the time he checked in and cleaned up it was past six o'clock. He ate in the hotel's small dining room. Only three tables were occupied, one by a late middle-aged man and an attractive, younger woman who was clearly not his wife, for she appeared to hang on his every word. The woman bore a passing resemblance to Laura and Mac had trouble not staring at her. This is stupid, he thought and retreated to the hotel's deserted bar for a brandy.

He considered researching the Babbetts online, but there was something to be said for doing it in person. A knowledgeable archivist could direct him to specific sources far quicker than wading through the irrelevant hits generated by search engines. Even so, he had brought his trusty friend, a MacBook, to record any information he uncovered.

After another night of poor sleep, further disrupted by a dream of Laura reading his parting note, he arrived at the Smithsonian's archives in midmorning. Dennis Leigh, the senior archivist, appeared to be as old as the records Mac wanted to examine. A pair of half-glasses perched low on his nose accentuated his narrow face. Every time Leigh needed to look closely at something he pushed the glasses up, sliding them down the moment he was done.

Leigh directed Mac to the area dedicated to the Department of State, as it was known in 1804, and issued Mac a pair of thin white cotton gloves to protect the original documents. Mac marvelled at the pages written in a fluid copperplate hand—a long forgotten skill—and wondered how long it would have taken a clerk to produce each page.

He discovered the first useful information, after an hour of skimming, in an otherwise bland document dated April 1803. The pages had been censored, not with indelible ink, but by physically cutting out words. Babbett had accepted a new posting 'requiring him to travel to [removed] to pursue and develop the interests of these United States.' With the advantage of twenty-twenty hindsight Mac was certain Babbett had been sent to South America.

Late in the afternoon an internal memo chilled him to the bone. Dated January 16, 1805, it expressed concern that, with Babbett's untimely death, America's aspirations in [removed] might go unfulfilled. The memo did not give any details of Babbett's death, nor did it mention Laura.

He ate dinner at a little bistro two blocks from his hotel to avoid the possibility of seeing Laura's lookalike, then spent an unproductive hour on his room's internet connection before going to bed. When he returned to the archives in the morning, Leigh suggested trying the Maryland State Archives in Annapolis, particularly the periodicals held there.

Mac spent the morning in Annapolis searching microfilm records. Not knowing how long news would have taken to reach home in the early nineteenth century, he began with the November 15, 1804, 'Maryland Gazette and Political Intelligencer'. The search was a pain, figuratively and literally, because of the uncomfortable chair and the poor quality of many of the microfilm images. By noon he had a sore back and neck, stinging eyes, a headache, and nothing to show for it.

He grabbed a sandwich and a bottled water from the cafeteria, then ate outside where a weak sun dispelled some of his gloom and the chill air helped clear his mind. After a brisk walk he resumed his research; his heart raced when the December 30 issue contained a six paragraph story from a correspondent in Kingston, Jamaica reporting the rescue of the American diplomat, James Babbett, by the Royal Navy frigate *Lionheart* after being held hostage in South America. The story said Babbett was returning to the United States aboard the packet *Annie Jeanne* and was expected to arrive in Baltimore in early January. Babbett was not quoted directly in the story, nor was there any mention of Laura.

He wondered why the previous documents had been censored, while the news story had been published, and spent two more days searching records without finding any mention of Laura. Back at the hotel he remembered the extensive collection held at the National Maritime Museum and National Archives in London, England and wondered if it was foolish to go to England when he hadn't exhausted all sources in America. He couldn't identify it, but intuition—something—compelled him to look elsewhere. Perhaps the Royal Navy could help.

The next morning he contacted Wilkins, now a Lieutenant Colonel, and arranged to meet in Washington. Mac didn't mention Laura; instead he told Wilkins that he was still unclear on some of the details and wanted to clarify the sequence of events for his own peace of mind. Perhaps ship's log books, reports, dispatches and captain's journals might help. Wilkins, sceptical at first, was concerned that any enquiries might trigger alarms.

Mac reassured Wilkins that he would be discreet and said, "Anyway, I can always tell them I'm researching a historical fiction novel. Hell, even if I told them I was writing an autobiography about how I travelled back in time, do you think they'd believe me?"

Wilkins laughed and said, "Go."

THE HUMMING WHINE of the airliner's flaps extending brought a smile to Mac's face—largely from the anticipation of discovering what had happened to Laura, but also at a little boy's excited utterance from the seat in front, "Mummy, I can see a castle." Final approach into London's Heathrow was taking them over Windsor Castle. It was the first time in months that he remembered smiling.

With nothing to declare, he cleared Customs using the 'green queue' and followed the clearly marked route to the train station for the fifteen minute Heathrow-London Express to Paddington Station. At Paddington he caught a taxi to his hotel. The Seaforth, located two blocks from Hyde Park on Stanhope Terrace, appeared to be Georgian and stood out from its grungy neighbours because its stone facade had been recently cleaned. His room, small by North American standards, was adequate for his needs since he would be spending most of his time poring over records at Greenwich.

It was past four by the time he unpacked. Too early to go to bed, despite not having had a proper sleep for almost twenty-four hours, he decided to take a walk to fight the effects of jet-lag. Clutching a London tourist map, he navigated the narrow side streets to Bayswater Road then crossed to Hyde Park—alive with children running about on the grass while parents or nannies watched like geese guarding goslings and women pushed extravagant prams along the walkways.

The next morning, after consuming what the hotel claimed to be a continental breakfast, he caught the Central Line from Bayswater to Bank, then transferred to the HLR Line for Cutty Sark station. Resisting the temptation to tour the preserved clipper ship, he instead went straight to the National Maritime Museum, where he was immediately distracted by an exquisite glass-encased model of H.M.S. *Bellerophon* in the foyer. He recalled hearing some of the *Lionheart's* crew refer to their previous ship as the *Billy Ruffian*.

He spent the morning in the museum, enraptured by the models. All were exact scale models created by skilled hands hundreds of years ago. Some were presented by the ship's builders to the Admiralty; others were created to provide construction information before the age of blueprints to the mostly illiterate workmen who built the ships. Although he didn't find a model of Lionheart, he did see her sister H.M.S. Actaeon. The intricate model measured nearly three-feet in length and was so correct to the last detail that he could visualise the men on her decks and pictured himself in her top firing muskets. The scent of powder smoke and salt air seemed to emanate from the model's case.

For the first time since the crash he realised he was comfortable knowing he had travelled to the past. His memories of Laura were not figments of his imagination or the aftermath of a concussion. He checked his watch; it was past twelve thirty and he had consumed nearly half a day.

Archivist Basil Swainson placed *Lionheart's* logbooks on a massive mahogany table as Mac wondered if age was some part of an archivist's job description. Swainson, who moved with a slow shuffle that emphasised his stooped posture, appeared to be in his late seventies if not eighties. Perhaps it took that long to memorise the locations of all the books, maps and documents in the massive collection. When Mac mentioned that he was working on his first novel, Swainson first appeared sceptical if not cold, but brightened when he learned Mac was a Canadian and confided he had trained for bomber crew in Alberta during the war.

The log books covered *Lionheart's* last three voyages. Mac went straight to the third, which began in Portsmouth, England when H.M.S. *Lionheart*, under the command of Captain Ulysses James Cathcart, was ordered to join the West Indies Squadron. The log detailed the ship's movements through cryptic records of wind direction and strength, course steered, sails set, events such as 'did exercise great guns', and sightings of other ships.

Mac flipped through pages until he found the entry for 13 November, the day before *Lionheart* captured *La Señora de Noche*. His throat tightened as he read the dispassionate log entry of Cathcart's decision to check Quinta Ruban—a routine order that turned out to have profound consequences. While he was engrossed in skimming the entries, Swainson arrived with another mass of folios that included copies of Cathcart's dispatches, lists of all officers and sailors, and an accounting of the stores loaded aboard the frigate. Mac recognised Eames' handwriting—as Cathcart's clerk, Eames was responsible for transcribing the information into final form for the Captain's signature.

Mac pushed his chair back and moved to Cathcart's dispatches to the Admiralty in London piled on the far end of the ten-foot long table. Looking at the mound of documents, he wasn't sure if he should be thankful the Admiralty had been so diligent in their filing. He shuffled through the chronologically arranged reports until he found the one concerning *La Señora's* capture. He shuddered. It was one thing to read about history. Now, he was reading about events he had played a direct role in over two-hundred years ago.

It turned out that only six minutes had elapsed from the time *La Señora* fired until her surrender. Locked in the dank cell in the brig's hold, Mac couldn't see the battle. At the time, it had seemed much longer than six minutes. Cathcart's report also included a list of men captured, and noted that he replenished his personal supply of gunpowder from *La Señora's* magazine. Mac knew that Cathcart believed so strongly in effective training of his gun crews that he supplemented the Admiralty's meagre practice allowance at his own expense. The value of the Spanish powder, inferior quality from what Cathcart had later said, would have been deducted from Cathcart's share of the prize money.

Mac was surprised that he was an addendum. Cathcart reported that an American being held captive by the Spanish remained aboard *Lionheart*—he must have rushed to complete the dispatch so that it could be taken to Jamaica. Each time Mac confirmed more pieces of the puzzle, he felt a greater sense of relief that he had not imagined things. He wished typewriters had been invented sooner—'speed-reading' through the documents' flowery script was an oxymoron.

Cathcart's next dispatch followed the action against the Spanish frigates. According to the report, Mac had been designated a supernumerary. Unsure of what that meant, he asked Swainson who seemed to be checking on him on a regular basis.

"Why sir, that's someone who wasn't a member of the crew and carried separately on the ships books for victualing and slops. Why do you ask?"

Mac replied, as if it was of no consequence, "Just I'm not familiar with the term."

When he finished reading Cathcart's final report to the Admiralty, written upon *Lionheart's* return to Portsmouth, there was still nothing to help him discover Laura's fate. The last mention of her was her arrival in Jamaica before she seemingly vanished. He rested his head in his hands and stared blankly at the pile of documents, wondering where else he could search.

Swainson approached the table, "I do not mean to intrude, sir, but is there a problem?"

Mac smiled glumly, "I couldn't find what I was looking for. Is there anything covering the period after the logs?"

Swainson thought for a moment, then said, "I believe Captain Cathcart was Knighted and made Commodore. His family left us his personal journals some years back but no one has requested to see them. Let me see what I can find." True to his word, Swainson returned twenty minutes later with two leather-bound volumes. "Here, sir. These concern Commodore Cathcart's posting to Halifax, Canada and there are others, if need be."

Cathcart's antiquated hand writing was difficult to read. Mac began thumbing through the first book, looking for familiar names until one jumped from the middle of the volume. Toby had been promoted to Lieutenant Commander of H.M.S. Beaver, brig sloop, upon *Lionheart's* return to England. Beaver, the first rung on the ladder to Toby becoming a post captain, had been attached to Cathcart's new squadron.

Something on page twenty-six of the second volume caught Mac's eye—Cathcart had written of his upcoming role as father-of-the-bride in Laura's wedding. Laura had survived and had recently moved to Halifax where the ceremony was to take place on May 26, 1806.

Mac tensed, then felt a great weight being lifted as a sense of peace flooded over him knowing that she was all right. Mac skipped over several lines of the hard to read script, anxiously searching for the groom's name, until he spotted Toby's. Of course, it made sense that Laura and Toby would marry. Now, knowing of the wedding, he might be able to trace their family tree.

The image of Laura at the grotto clear in his mind, he returned to the start of the journal's passage disconcerted by feelings of jealousy despite the passage of more than two-hundred years.

Cathcart's flowing script became suddenly clear an instant before he let the journal fall to the terrazzo floor. Absorbed in thought and not realising that he had turned as white as a proverbial ghost, he hadn't noticed Swainson watching him. He guiltily met Swainson's angry glare and silently muttered "Holy shit."

I'm the one getting married and Toby is my best man.

EPILOGUE

OH DEAR, Mac has discovered, to quote the philosopher Yogi Berra, "It's déjà vu all over again." Unfortunately, with no memory of actually marrying Laura, he now realises he should have taken the time to finish reading Cathcart's journal—before allowing it to crash to the floor and get booted out of the archives by Swainson.

Perhaps, if he is to marry Laura, he'll have to travel back in time, again. Which might explain why he doesn't have any memory of a wedding—yet. Of course that possibility raises a number of questions. Will he be able to pick and choose when he goes back, or how he goes? If he marries Laura will he be stuck "back then" or is he destined to bounce back and forth between two realities.

Ooh! Wait a minute, maybe Laura gets zapped into her future and Mac's present?

Not to mention the complications that could arise if Toby contacts Sir William Congreve and offers tips on how to build rockets.

At the moment, the next book is tentatively titled "'Til Death Do Us..." Mac, grieving over Laura's absence and tired of his military career, accepts a buddy's invitation to get some R&R in Hawaii where he meets Erin. After all it's not like Laura will ever know about Erin since she's two-hundred years in the future. Besides, to paraphrase that well known jingle, "What happens in Hawaii stays in Hawaii." He should be so lucky!

To tell the truth, even I don't know what's going to happen... but it's going to be fun writing it and I'm pretty sure there are more bad things in Mac's future. Or are they in his past?

Boeing AH-64 Apache.
shown with FFAR/Hydra-70 rocket pods

"Posse", AV-8 Harriers on the hunt

U.S. Navy photo used in illustration.

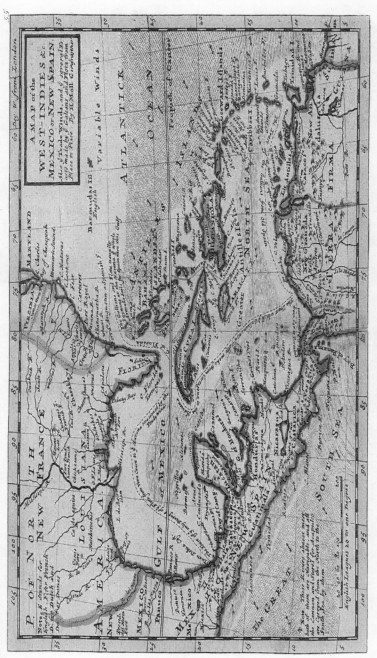

The Caribbean, as it was

HMS Lionheart under sail

Image courtesy: The Unicorn Preservation Society, HM Frigate Unicorn, Dundee, Scotland

HMS Ringle

Reefing a topsail

Reloading a gun aboard HMS Lionheart

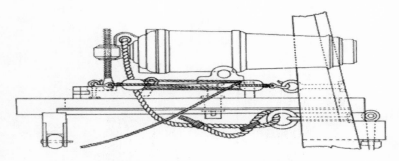

Twenty-four pounder carronade

From a drawing by Ch. Dupin in Wm. Laird Clowes, "The Royal Navy", vol. V, p. 540.

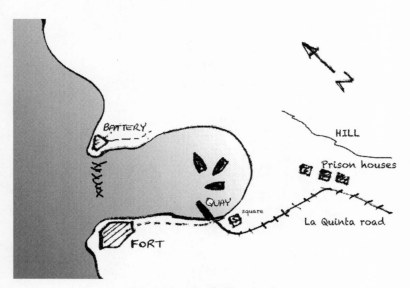

Mac's sketch of Puerto Blanco

HMS Lionheart sail diagram

Image courtesy: The Unicorn Preservation Society, HM Frigate Unicorn, Dundee, Scotland

A	Foremast	9	Inner jib & outer flying jib; fore topmast staysail (innermost) shown furled
B	Mainmast		
C	Mizzenmast		
D	Bowsprit	10	Fore Lower Studding Sail (Stun'sail)
1	Fore Course	11	Fure Upper Studding Sail
2	Fore Topsail	12	Fore Topgallant Studding Sail
3	Fore Topgallant (T'gan'sl)		
4	Fore Royal	13	Main Upper Studding Sail
5	Main Course (furled)	14	Main Topgalland Studding Sail
6	Main Topsail		
7	Main Topgallant (T'gan'sl)		
8	Main Royal	*N.B. Mizzen Course & Driver not set*	

HMS Lionheart vs Matilda

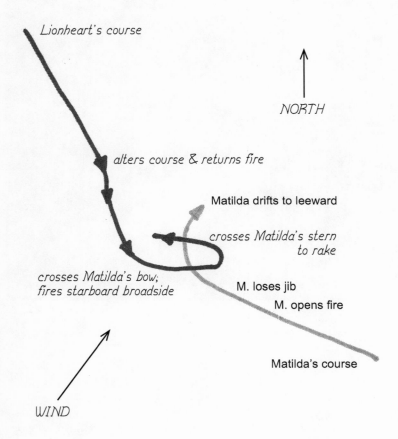

Lionheart's course

NORTH

alters course & returns fire

Matilda drifts to leeward

crosses Matilda's stern to rake

crosses Matilda's bow; fires starboard broadside

M. loses jib

M. opens fire

Matilda's course

WIND

HMS Lionheart vs Castellon de la Plana

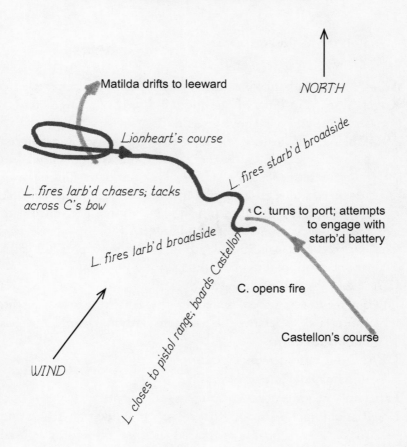

GLOSSARY

AK-47: Russian assault rifle, readily available on the black market.

Angel: altitude in units of one-thousand feet, i.e. "Angels ten" is ten-thousand feet above ground.

AWACS: Aerial Warning and Control System. An aircraft fitted with radar and other electronic monitoring equipment used to find and track enemy aircraft, provide advance warning of an air attack, and direct missions by friendly aircraft. In this instance the aircraft is a modified C-130 Hercules transport filled with really cool electronic gizmos and gadgets.

Cable: also *cable length;* the length of an anchor cable, 200 yards or one-tenth of a nautical mile

CIA: Central Intelligence Agency

CPG: Co-Pilot Gunner, seated in the Apache's forward seat, controls & operates the weapons although the pilot has duplicate controls.

DEA: Drug Enforcement Agency

ETA: Estimated Time of Arrival

Fathom: six foot unit for measuring water depth

FFAR: Folding Fin Aerial Rocket—an unguided air-to-ground rocket used against unarmoured targets or structures; housed in a pod of 19.

FUBAR: acronym for 'Fucked-up Beyond All Recognition'. An order of magnitude greater than SNAFU

Gatling Gun: 30 mm calibre cannon mounted in a turret beneath the Apache's nose; controlled by either the pilot or CPG, capable of firing 1,200 rounds per minute (usually a mix of armour piercing, shrapnel and incendiary rounds)

G-Force: The force of gravity measured in positive or negative g, one being Earth's normal gravity. A 3g force would make a person feel three times heavier than normal.

GPS: Ground Positioning System, calculates location by triangulating the positions of GPS satellites.

Halliard: a line used to raise or lower a yard arm; from *haul yard,* alternative spelling *halyard*

Head: toilets for the crew located at the bow; basically an open-air outhouse depositing into the water.

Hellfire: laser-guided missile used against tanks or protected structures

H.M.S.: His/Her Majesty's Ship (depending on the gender of the current occupier of the throne). Denotes a vessel belonging to the British Royal Navy

Hooker: sailors' irreverent term for a ship past her prime

Hydra-70: see FFAR

Intel: short for Military Intelligence (some would say your basic oxymoron)

Jakes: a toilet cabinet within the captain's quarters; enclosed for privacy but open to the water. Also known as a quarter gallery.

klicks: short for kilometers

Knot: measurement of speed used by ships and aircraft: 1 knot = 1.14 mph

LZ: Landing Zone

NATO: North Atlantic Treaty Organization

Nautical Mile: 6000 feet, as opposed to the *land mile* of 5280 feet

PNVS: Pilot Night Vision System, electronic imaging system working through goggles that allows user to see even in near total darkness. Sudden increases in light, such as gunfire or lightning can temporarily overpower the PNVS.

Pooched: a kinder form of FUBAR

Royal Navy ranks: Officers usually began their careers as midshipmen at the age of 12-14 years. Eventually (assuming they were smart enough, or possessed an influential patron, and didn't get themselves killed) they would take the Lieutenant's Examination after they were 18 years old. If they passed the exam, they became a commissioned officer and would begin advancement on the basis of ability, seniority, and patronage (although not necessarily in that order) by starting as the most junior lieutenant on a large ship. With luck, etc. they could be given command of a small ship and the rank of lieutenant-commander. The next step was to captain, designated by a single shoulder epaulet; then, after three years, to post captain and higher assuming the aforementioned ability, seniority patronage and good fortune.

SNAFU: Situation Normal, All Fucked-up.

Stone: English unit of weight, 14 pounds

USS: United States Ship. Denotes a vessel belonging to the United States Navy (USN)

Viceroyalty of New Granada: Spain's holdings in northern South America which included the current Colombia, Venezuela, Ecuador, northwestern Brazil and Panama.

Watches: Each day was divided into seven watches to prevent the same men working the same watch every day. If the crew was divided into two watches they were called the Larboard (port) and Starboard watches; if there were three watches they were referred to as Red, White and Blue watches. The watches were: Middle (graveyard), midnight to 0400 hours; Morning, 0400 to 0800 hours; Forenoon, 0800 to Noon; Afternoon, 1200 to 1600 hours; First dog, 1600 to 1800 hours; Second dog, 1800 to 2000 hours; First, 2000 hours to Midnight.

Z: denotes ZULU time (Greenwich Mean Time), a uniform military time system to avoid confusion with local time.

Made in the USA
Charleston, SC
11 June 2013